# Far Beyond Heaven

By Paul Moore

*Martin Sisters Publishing*

Published by

Martin Sisters Publishing, LLC

www.martinsisterspublishing.com

Copyright © 2016 Paul Moore

All rights reserved. Published in the United States by
Martin Sisters Publishing, LLC, Kentucky.
ISBN: 978-1-62553-094-3
Literary Fiction
Printed in the United States of America
Martin Sisters Publishing, LLC

FOR GAYLE

# Chapter 1

*Sex and Death*

The first naked woman Cody Palmeroy ever saw was a dead naked woman.

At two a.m. he rode the shiny freight elevator from the loading dock up to the embalming room on the second floor. Dispassionately, he looked down at the cotton blanket covering the lumpy, shriveled corpse on the stretcher beside him.

He had worked at the funeral home for only one month, but already death was routine. Nursing home patients, like the one on his stretcher, were especially easy to dismiss. Cody thought she must have welcomed death as an escape from what was surely a miserable existence. He could not imagine anyone really enjoying life after age eighty. At age nineteen, eighty was an eternity away.

As he rolled the corpse off the elevator, he saw the chief mortician putting makeup on a teenage girl laid out on an embalming table at the far end of the room. The man glanced up at Cody and waved. He was wearing a surgical gown smeared with blood. Around the funeral home, employees called him "Germ," a humorous, ironical reference to his obsession with cleanliness in the embalming room and throughout the funeral home complex.

As Germ turned back to the young cadaver to apply a few final strokes of blush, he called out, "Cody, you're just in time. Stash that body and help me move this young lady off the table."

"Yes sir. Be right there." Cody moved quickly, eager to please the venerable mortician.

The embalming room resembled a giant operating suite in a hospital. White tile on the floor and walls created an ambiance of sterility. The centerpiece of the room was a row of three porcelain embalming tables, each featuring a gutter around its perimeter to catch blood as it streamed out of the body. At the head of each table, numerous devices and supplies were neatly stacked in glass-front cabinets or on portable carts. The embalmers' armamentarium included surgical instruments, embalming fluids and cosmetics.

A heavy, stainless-steel door at the far end of the suite led to a walk-in refrigerator which could accommodate several bodies. It was a holding room for corpses awaiting the embalming procedure. Because it was a transitional area, funeral home employees called it "purgatory."

As Cody rolled the corpse into the room, he winced as the icy, acrid air assaulted his skin. The smell of death lay just beneath a predominant odor of strong disinfectant. He placed the corpse in a row with three others and turned to leave.

On the inside of the refrigerator door, the funeral home management had placed a neat plastic sign with a hopeful Bible verse.

*"Yea, though I walk through the valley of the shadow of Death, I will fear no evil; for thou art with me."*

Psalms 23

All around it, employees had scrawled mocking graffiti.
"Hell awaits."
"Wake not, want not."
"This is the first day of the rest of your death."
"In the middle of difficulty lies opportunity." Einstein
"It's all good."
"Do not arouse me until the second coming of Elvis."

Cody smiled as he glanced at the door. His own entry was the latest addition to the sardonic collection of wisdom.

"I am dead, therefore I am."

With a shiver, he exited the room, fetched an empty gurney and maneuvered it alongside the embalming table where Germ was working.

He looked down, but not too far down, the naked, embalmed body of an attractive teenage girl. He allowed himself a quick glance at her breasts, and then kept his eyes focused on her face. This was the first time Cody had witnessed a completely naked body in the embalming room. A towel usually covered the pubic areas of the corpses. This practice was established out of respect for the dead and for the sanity of the embalmers. Who could hope for a normal sex life at home after prolonged exposure to the pale, shrunken genitals of the dead?

Gazing at the girl's body, Germ announced, "I just finished her bath. She had blood, mud and algae all over her."

Cody continued to stare at the pretty face as a surgical light blazed harshly down from above the table. In spite of the cosmetics applied by Germ's talented hands, there was no mistaking that this face belonged to the dead. Cody had learned there was a subtle difference between living faces in a deep sleep or a coma and the faces of corpses. Some elusive energy radiated from living countenances. You knew there was a future in those faces. There was optimism and promise, even if it meant living only one more day.

The face on the table cast a spell on Cody's weary mind. To him, the expression was one of peace and serenity, but there was no hope in it, no hint of a tomorrow. Also, there was the stark and disturbing realization that this face was a reflection of his own. The only thing that separated him from this girl was time. This dead face would be his someday, as surely as it would be the face of every woman and man.

In Cody's trance, the sound of Germ's voice seemed far away.

"Makes you sick, doesn't it?" He did not wait for the novice to reply to his rhetorical question. "For me, it makes death a little too real. Old folks, I don't mind. They've had their lives and it's time for them to move on. It's part of the natural process." Emphatically, he pointed to the girl on the table. "But I've got grandkids about her age. One's a girl."

7

Sympathetically, Germ assessed Cody for a moment. He asked, "First time for you, isn't it?"

Cody was hesitant, "First time for what?"

The old embalmer's face morphed into a fatherly smile. "To see a young woman naked and dead."

Cody felt embarrassed, "Sorry. I really didn't mean to stare."

"Don't sweat it, kid. Everyone stares the first time. The reason I brought it up was to let you know that you never get used to the young ones. So you need to get used to the fact that you never get used to them."

Despondently, Germ again looked down on the dead teenager. "Her name is Pricilla, age sixteen. She drowned in a boating accident. When we move her off the table, we'll have to cover her with a sheet. There are no clothes for her yet. Her parents are bringing some in later."

Germ reached up to dim the surgical light, and then turned to the cabinet behind him in search of a sheet. "I'd be pissed if I was her father. There's no reason in the world for this kid to die, for this kind of shit to go down."

Cody looked at him thoughtfully. He doubted that Germ would have a good answer to the question on his mind, but he asked it anyway. "So, why did she die?"

Germ stared at the ceiling with an intense, penetrating gaze as though he were looking right through it, all the way to heaven. He glared back at Cody. His voice projected a disturbing element of haunted derision. "Every once in a while God likes to jump out and say 'Boo!' He gives us a little surprise just to let us know He's still in charge."

Germ paused and took a deep breath. "Anyway, I'm going to ask Him if I get the chance. He may send me to hell, but I want a few answers first."

Cody smiled, imagining the scene. "You want to go into a meeting with the Almighty and make demands? Somehow I don't think it works that way."

Germ nodded in resignation, "Yeah, probably not, but I'm damned tired of being one of God's laboratory rats. I want some answers." Then, with a dramatic movement of disgust, he stripped off his disposable surgical gown, wadded it up and tossed it in a nearby trashcan.

Respectfully, Cody had avoided looking at the girl's genitalia. However, when he took hold of her legs to help lift her to the gurney, his eyes moved inevitably to her crotch. While growing up, he had wondered about his first encounter with a completely naked woman. He knew boys often fantasized about that scenario, as he imagined girls dreamed of walking down the aisle. Never did Cody envision his first experience would be like this.

He had seen plenty of photos of naked women, but this was different. This was pathetic. It was overwhelmingly tragic. He thought of all that was lost in the abject morbidity and hopelessness of her lifeless vagina.

Cody observed Priscilla for a moment longer. There was no tattoo or body piercing that might contribute to defining some other contemporary young woman's identity or sexuality. She was just an ordinary sixteen-year-old who was much like other girls her age, except that she was dead.

They covered her with a crisp white sheet that smelled of lavender. The old embalmer folded back the top of it to expose her face and tenderly tucked in the sides as if he were putting a precious child to bed. He stretched out his long, gentle hand and briefly touched the side of her cold face with a soft caress.

Cody thought of a story about another dead girl, one who died in Galilee. Jesus came to examine the body, and although the girl was unquestionably deceased, He told her parents, "The maiden is not dead, she sleeps." So, the girl woke up and flung herself into her mother's arms, presumably to live a long, healthy life.

Cody looked around the embalming room. Where was Jesus when you needed Him?

He hoped that Priscilla would not sleep forever, but he did not know. How could he? How could anyone? He felt a dark, ominous cloud of despair begin to cover him. He pushed it aside.

If Priscilla was gazing down on him from somewhere like heaven, Cody wondered if she would mind very much that he looked at her nakedness. He hoped she would not be upset with him. Though his eyes lingered on her privates a moment longer than necessary, maybe she would understand that his intrusion on her privacy was not frivolous.

He thought about how every person who came into existence passed through a sacred portal like Priscilla's womb. Only through

9

women could new life come into the world. An image entered his mind of some great earth goddess smiling down upon him with radiant approval of his thought.

However, as he rolled Priscilla away from the table to place her in a nearby line of four other bodies morticians would display in caskets later that day, he felt an uneasy anxiety rise in his gut. He could not identify the cause but sensed it came from a deep, shadowy cavern in his unconscious mind. He wondered if he had violated some primeval taboo by looking at a dead girl's nakedness.

Germ sprayed the table with disinfectant and wiped it dry. Then he reached into a nearby cabinet and produced a bottle of decent Kentucky bourbon, two crystal glasses and a liter of Italian bottled water. Without comment, he pulled up a stool to the embalming table, set up the glasses, and poured a generous shot into each one. With a subtle, refined nod, he beckoned Cody to join him. He did not need to ask the young man if he wanted a drink. There seemed to be a tacit understanding between them that the moments they just shared and the death of a young woman in the prime of her youth called for a drink as much as anything in the world did.

Cody rolled another stool up to the table and sat down. He raised his glass to meet the one extended toward him by Germ's hand. When the glasses clinked, Germ offered a toast. "To Priscilla. May she rest in peace. And may God do something really good for her to make up for dying so young."

Cody felt flattered to be included in the ritual. With enthusiasm, he repeated, "To Priscilla. May she rest in peace." He thought, rather than spoke, the last part of his toast. *And may God, if there is a God, do something nice for her.*

Then he sipped slowly and thoughtfully. The whiskey burned his gullet all the way to his stomach and numbed his mind, mitigating the bleak reality of dead Priscilla, which, mercifully, faded with each sip he took.

After a moment, Germ broke the spell of silence. "Let me give you a little advice, son. Just because we are drinking tonight does not mean we should do it all the time. As you know, tonight is different."

Cody nodded.

"Keep your head clear in this business. Whiskey is okay in moderation. Tranquillizers are all right if you don't abuse them. Stay clear of pain medicine. It is too addictive. Antidepressants are almost a requirement to keep your sanity."

Cody was interested in antidepressants, which he heard were widely used by funeral home staff. He asked if the older man had taken them.

Germ looked up at the surgical light as if he were counting the time in his head. "Yeah, for about fifteen years, I guess. Without them I'd have blown my brains out a long time ago."

"How do they make you feel?"

Germ took another sip of whiskey before he replied. "Well, it's strange. You take them for a while and you think nothing has changed. Then one day you realize that things are different. You are still depressed, but you no longer care that you're depressed. That's the difference."

"What about the side effects?" Cody pushed for more information. "I hear they can cause sexual problems."

"Yeah, maybe for me, but probably not so much for a kid your age," said Germ. "The only thing I remember being a little strange was that I noticed my fly was open on a few occasions and I didn't know for how long. And I didn't care, either. I didn't much care about anything.

"One night I took some of the younger morticians down to this topless bar on Porter Street. It must have been someone's birthday. Anyway, there was this really hot girl who was dancing at our table. These guys were drooling all over themselves. Well, when she got everybody really worked up, she says 'I'll take off my panties for another twenty dollars.'

"And I said, 'I'll give you forty to keep them on.' That's what I mean. When you are on antidepressants, you sort of have this 'Get naked and see if I care' attitude."

Cody chuckled gently. Then he took another sip of whiskey.

A long, comfortable silence followed. It was the kind of mellow pause in conversation that usually transpired between two old friends who were so relaxed with each other that neither felt compelled to fill the silent void. Neither of them made superfluous comments for the purpose of polite conversation.

Morbidly, Cody's thoughts returned to Priscilla. Unbidden, pictures of Germ in the act of embalming her filled his mind. He winced at the disturbing images, reached for the bourbon and poured another shot.

Germ asked, "Why did you come to work here, Cody?" He smiled benevolently. "You seem pretty normal to me. Most average guys your age would run from a place like this."

Caught off guard, Cody took a moment to formulate his response. He really had not completely answered that question for himself. Against his parents' wishes, he was majoring in philosophy at the local liberal arts college. He was searching for answers to basic questions about human existence. Where did we come from? Was there an afterlife? Was there a God and, if so, why did He, or She, tolerate so much evil in the world? Why was sexual experience mysterious and transcendental?

Cody had noticed that while many people expressed a superficial interest in such questions, most lacked an enduring commitment to pursuing the answers. Mortgage payments, children with or without problems, cheating spouses, failing health, substance abuse, and office politics consumed people's lives. Fundamental questions to understanding the human experience did not often resurface until the Grim Reaper was just outside the door with a gnarly finger on the bell.

Cody was determined to keep these important issues in front of him. After college, he might train to be a professor or minister. For now, he thought working near death might provide some insights into his questions, so he signed up to work nights and weekends.

Cody met Germ's expectant stare. He decided to keep his answer simple, and perhaps add a twist of humor.

"You could say it's a personal quest of some kind," he said. "Sex and death are two great, mysterious experiences of our existence. I wasn't having much luck in the area of sex, so I thought I'd give death a try."

A hearty guffaw erupted from deep within Germ's belly and filled the room. "I heard that, my boy. I heard that."

After a moment, Germ continued, "I know this sounds crazy, but don't think that sex and death are mutually exclusive. Nowadays, some women have a crazy attraction to death. However, that's only a recent development.

"About twenty years ago I drove a hearse down to New Orleans to pick up a body. This old boy rode down with me. He was one of the newer embalmers at the time. I can't recall his name right off, but this guy thought he was a real ladies' man. He said there were a million ways to get laid in New Orleans and he knew them all. Well, we spent the night there and we were staying at this real nice hotel down in the French Quarter. I think it was the Monteleone. So we went down to the bar to have a drink and then we were going out to dinner and to find some bootleg Cuban cigars."

The excitement rose in Germ's voice as he recounted the experience. "But listen to this. There was a teachers' convention in the hotel, and we found ourselves sitting in the bar with about fifty women. We were the only men. And these teachers were buying us drinks and flirting with us. I was looking to score for sure. I mean there was absolutely no way we were not going to get laid that night. That is, until one of the women asked us what we did for a living, and why we were in New Orleans staying at the Monteleone. Before I could say we were accountants or something mundane like that, this fool I was with blurts out that we were undertakers and we were in town to pick up a corpse. Well, those women scattered as if we were living turds. Within five minutes, we were sitting there by ourselves. Don't you know I could have killed the bastard with my bare hands, right?"

"Yeah, you should have killed him," Cody said. He was staring intently at the whiskey bottle in front of him.

Germ continued, "But that was many years ago. Today, it's kinky out there. I hear from some of the younger guys that these wild girls they date want to come over here to get laid in a casket.

"Do you know the guy who works here with the hateful frown on his face all the time? I forget his real name but around here we call him 'Shine.'"

Cody sipped and nodded.

"Last month I came in about two in the morning to work on a man who was torn up in a car wreck. Well, wouldn't you know it? Shine was up here humping some coed on the middle table with a fresh cadaver on either side. That shows you how crazy these kids are nowadays."

The door to the embalming room opened and a sleek young man appeared, carrying a silver tray with a bottle of Irish whiskey and three glasses. He grinned when he saw Cody and Germ sitting around the embalming table. "I should have known you bastards

13

would be having a party up here while I've been slaving away downstairs, filling out paper work on that body we got from the nursing home."

Germ responded warmly. "Pete, I was just bringing your new trainee up to date on a few company secrets so he doesn't have to rely on your sorry ass for all the information about this place. Get over here and bring that bottle with you."

Pete was Cody's mentor and the young apprentice had observed him closely over their weeks together. He began his career as an undertaker at age seventeen. Now, ten years later, he was a well-regarded funeral director. His star had risen fast, and was still climbing.

Cody noticed Pete had an impressive charm about him that made him a good role model, so he often paired up with new employees for on-the-job training.

Pete's appearance was impeccable. Even now, in the early morning informality of the embalming room, his suit jacket remained buttoned. His black hair was combed straight back and slicked down with mousse for the wet look. He held his chin at that perfect angle of subtle aloofness that made one wonder if he came from an aristocratic lineage.

Cody tried hard to imitate the traits he saw in his mentor. Pete's charm was evident in everything he did. Every phone call, every encounter in the staff lounge, every interaction with a bereaved family was an opportunity to make a favorable impression. He glided across the room, carrying the silver tray as though he were serving sherry at the Queen of England's afternoon tea.

As he arrived at the embalming table, he noticed the girl on the gurney nearby. "Jesus, who is that?"

Germ cast a somber glance over at the body. "She's Priscilla. Boating accident."

Cody, reeling from the whiskey, broke in, "Yeah, and guess what, Pete?"

"What?"

"She's dead."

Germ was the first to break the awkward silence that followed. He tried to suppress his laughter, but the sound of air bursting out through tightly closed lips spilled out into the room. Then they all had a good hoot as Pete's face turned scarlet and Cody held his side.

It was the kind of laugh only possible in a situation so serious that humor was the best way to cope with it.

Meanwhile, pristine Priscilla lay there in beatific repose through all their hilarity, as though she understood and forgave them.

As the laughter subsided, Pete pulled up a stool to the table and cracked the seal on the Irish whiskey, then poured a shot into each glass. "So, what are you guys talking about up here?"

There was another round of laughter from Germ and Cody while Pete waited patiently for a reply.

Germ announced, "Well if you have to know, we were talking about how I caught Shine screwing that girl on the middle table."

Pete said, "I'm familiar with the story. It was front-page news on the funeral home grapevine for several days after the incident." He asked Germ, "Did you tell him that she screamed like a banshee when you turned on the lights and she saw your creaky carcass coming into the room?"

Germ corrected him. "She was screaming like a banshee *before* I turned on the lights. After I turned on the lights, she screamed like a she-devil-banshee-witch burning at the stake."

Pete chuckled. He enjoyed good-natured sparring with the senior man. "Yeah, if I saw you walking in the door, I guess I'd scream like that too." He turned to Cody, "You see, Germ here has another nickname. He's AKA 'Dead Man Walking.'"

Germ reached for his glass and stood up to stretch his legs, "Very funny, young Peter. Very funny."

As Germ looked out of a window onto the vacant side street below, Cody studied the older man's singular appearance. Part of Germ's mystique was his combination of gloominess and dignity. His beautifully streaked hair was a collage of grey and white lines. His face was pale and filled with wrinkles, each one an indelible imprint carved by a different crisis in his life. Cody had heard that Germ was sixty years old at most, but he had many more miles on him than that, and they showed. He wore heavily starched white shirts with solid-colored silk ties. Suspenders held the cuffs of his pants a little too high off the tops of his shiny cap-toe shoes.

Adding to the old mortician's mystery was his great sense of humor. Before he got to know him, Cody would never have guessed that he could crack a smile, much less tell a joke. Pete said humor was Germ's way of coping with the starkness and omnipresence of death in his job. In fact, Pete said joviality was a way they all coped, and if Cody did not have a sense of humor, he should develop one right away for the sake of self-preservation.

Though Germ was very dignified, a strikingly unnatural aura surrounded him. He had the classic look of a supporting character from a nineteen-thirties' horror film who dwelled in the catacombs under the castle only to emerge at night to bring a couple of cadavers up to the lab.

Because of his inherent eeriness, some funeral home employees avoided him, but Cody found him to be a benevolent and fatherly mentor. Even now, Germ's kindly face had turned from the window and was beaming at him. "Cody, it's really great to have you here. I have become very fond of you. However, I'm a little concerned about you, young man."

Germ looked over and winked at Pete. "Did you know your protégé has never been laid?"

Pete raised an eyebrow, "What a shame. We'll have to do something about that, for sure."

"I didn't say I'd never been laid," Cody protested. "I just commented that I was not extremely active in that area of life." He felt his face grow hot as the other men grinned.

"No problem," Pete said sympathetically, "It's not like Germ here is some graveyard Casanova. And me? I don't exactly score every time I go out either. But we know some girls who can come over one night and give you a real positive experience. It would be a good confidence booster for you."

Mischievously Germ added, "Yeah, Cody. We will set it up for you. Pete and I won't hassle you. We'll just stay out in the hall and peep in through the keyhole."

There was more laughter, as Cody wished he'd never confided in Germ about his sex life. However, the ribbing was not malicious. It was the kind of kidding you would get from your older brother.

Germ sat down and leaned across the table in anticipation. "Okay, Cody, let's get the picture here. Tell us what your sex life has been like up to now."

After a moment, Cody ventured, "All right, guys. I'll tell you, but none of this leaves this room, okay?"

"Of course. You can rely on our discretion in the matter," said Pete solemnly.

16

"The closest I've ever come to getting laid," Cody began, "was on my eighteenth birthday. Some friends from school arranged for a hooker to come over to my place while my parents were out of town. They paid for everything in advance, but they didn't tell me about it until an hour before she arrived. Immediately, I had a panic attack. I was so nervous that I had diarrhea and had to take a quick shower. Well, she showed up wearing this Mensa Society t-shirt and it just totally freaked me out."

Germ asked, "What's the Mensa Society?"

"It's this club for people who are geniuses. You must have a really high IQ just to get into the Mensa Society."

"So what happened?" Pete prodded.

"I was so messed up that I told her I was sick and she left."

Germ was amazed, "Damn, I can't believe that. What a waste."

Pete nodded his agreement.

"What you need is some self-confidence, son," Germ declared. "Don't you think girls find you attractive?"

Cody thought about it for a moment. He was a couple of inches above six feet and a little on the thin side. His body had not filled out very much since his late adolescent growing spurt. His brown hair had an auburn tint that he thought complemented his green eyes.

Although a certain dignity was beginning to replace his teenage awkwardness, he still did not have that confident glow that radiated naturally from those privileged types who had been born into affluence. Nor did he have the acquired self-assuredness of a football star or a top academic performer. In spite of these limitations, he was confident a number of women would find him acceptable, if he could meet them under ideal circumstances.

Cody's fragile confidence faded as his hand went involuntarily to his chin to feel an emerging pimple.

He looked up quickly to see if the others had noticed it. They were eyeing him expectantly, waiting for an answer.

Cautiously, Cody said, "When I look at myself in the mirror, I think I'm average looking. I tell myself that if I were an average looking girl, I wouldn't mind dating me."

"You are a good-looking kid," said Germ as he glanced at Pete for corroboration, "There's no reason you shouldn't be having sex at least twice a week."

Pete weighed in. "I agree. So, aside from genius whores and diarrhea, what's your problem?"

"I don't know what to say to girls," Cody complained. "All I can think to say to them is something like, 'Do you want to go on a picnic?' or, 'Tell me the story of your life.'"

"So what's wrong with that?" asked Pete.

"It's just not cool," protested Cody. "It's not what the beautiful people talk about. When you see these couples flirting and they are whispering in each other's ears and giggling, do you know what they are saying? Well, I don't. I don't have the slightest idea."

Germ said, "Okay. Just guess. What could they be talking about?"

"I really think they're saying something like, 'You smell so good.' Or, 'I have a condom in my pocket.' Or, 'I can't wait to go down on you'."

"That's not bad," Pete encouraged. "Why don't you say those things?"

Cody said, "I can't get up the nerve."

Kindheartedly, Germ counseled the young man, "You're not the only guy to come to work here as a virgin. As I recall, Pete came to us without any sexual experience except by his own hand. There was a towel following him around the funeral home dormitory with enough dried sperm on it to populate an entire continent."

Cody and Germ had a good laugh while Pete turned a light shade of pink and poured himself another shot.

Germ saw a grand opportunity to hassle Pete further. He continued, "Cody, you had to pass a psychological evaluation to get a job here. All of us did. We don't want any necrophiliacs or other perverts hanging around. So Pete went in to take the Rorschach test part of his psych assessment. But all he can see on the flash cards was a mysteriously recurring pair of crotch-less panties."

Ignoring the comment and the ensuing laughter, Pete ventured, "Do you know Susie who works in Accounting?"

"What kind of question is that?" asked Germ. "Of course, I know her. She should get a ten-thousand dollars a year raise just for having an ass like that."

Pete indulged the older man. "Not you. I know you know her. I'm asking Cody."

The young apprentice shrugged. "I don't really know her, but I know who she is. I've seen her around."

Energized by the thoughts of Susie's backside, Germ interrupted. "Look guys, I have a profound question for you. What's more important, big tits or a big ass?"

"I think more guys prefer big tits to a big ass," Cody answered.

Germ asked, "Why would you say that?"

Cody thought for a moment. "When God created Eve and brought her by and showed her to Adam, did Adam say, 'Gee, thanks, God, but could you make the tits a little smaller?'"

Germ replied, "Yes, but maybe Adam didn't say, 'Could you make the ass a little smaller?' either."

"Hey guys, let's stay focused here," said Pete impatiently, "we are trying to get Cody laid and, for the record, Susie has big tits and a big ass. More importantly, she is not dating anybody right now. She told me yesterday she had broken up with her boyfriend and was looking to hook up with someone new. So, it's settled. Cody can just go down to Accounting tomorrow on some pretense and chat her up."

Cody began to panic., his insecurity rising. "It's not that easy. I don't know what I'd say to her."

Pete winked at Germ. "Cody, I usually don't share my pickup lines but I'll give you one that's a sure score. Just walk over to her desk and say, 'Smells like a fart over here.'"

Germ was quick to pile on, "Or better yet, just say something like, 'I need to screw someone tonight and it might as well be you.'"

After their laughter subsided, Cody let out a dejected sigh. He said seriously, "Sex and death are the most real things you can experience. Don't take my word for it. It's all in this book I have about existential philosophy. I read this other book by the Dalai Lama. He is like the Pope of all the Buddhists in Tibet, except he is living in exile now because of the fucking Chinese. Anyway, the Dalai Lama says that just before you die you go into this special kind of consciousness called the 'state of clear light.' One psychologist says some people have a minor version of this state when they reach sexual climax. Orgasm and death are the most intense experiences we can have as human beings."

Pete appeared incredulous, "What does that have to do with anything?"

19

Germ shook his head. "How can you be more alive when you're dying?"

Cody replied, "Death is serious. Sex is serious. Both are sacred in a way. You can't just think of sex as some sort of conquest or something you can laugh at. You don't laugh at death, do you? Well, sex is a similar kind of phenomenon."

Pete was stunned into silence.

After a moment Germ commented, "This is worse than I thought, son. No wonder you've never scored. You've been reading philosophy when you should have been practicing your mojo. And if you found a girl who thought that shit was cool, she'd likely be some psychopath. She'd be the kind who would drop an iron on your head in the middle of the night."

"Yeah, girls want to have a good time," said Pete. "They don't want to sit around and talk about this philosophical shit. You'll freak them out with conversation like that. It's crazy talk. You'll come across as a serial killer or a pervert."

"Yeah, like getting laid by you morbid freaks is a big treat," said Cody defensively.

Germ reminded Cody about Shine. "There was a time when that was true. Nowadays though, at least some girls think it's a thrill to get laid in here or over in the showroom in a casket."

"Especially those Goth chicks," added Pete enthusiastically, "the ones that dress in black and wear sunscreen in the rain. They are sexy as hell, but they have a strong attraction to death. They seem to really feel some kind of connection."

Cody pounced on the opening. "That's what I'm trying to tell you. There's a relationship between sex and death that transcends all this crap about girls just wanting a good time."

Each man took another sip of whiskey as he contemplated Cody's comment for a moment.

Then Germ said, "You might just have something there. It reminds me of this death call I made many years ago. I am sitting in the staff lounge about the middle of the day when the boss comes in with this real serious expression on his face. He calls me down to his office. I think he is going to give me a pink slip, he's so somber. Well, he tells me the mayor called and he says that his brother just passed away and he wants us to go pick him up."

Pete complained, "Jesus, Germ. If I have to hear this story again, I'm going to fucking kill myself, but I'll kill you first!"

"I know you've heard it before," replied Germ tolerantly, "but it's not for your benefit I'm telling it. It's for Cody."

Germ turned back to the young apprentice and continued. "So I'm sitting there thinking that there has to be more to it. The boss is far too serious, and it couldn't be just because the mayor's brother died. And, sure enough, the next thing he tells me is that there's a little complication. Seems the guy died in a whorehouse down by the river.

"So the mayor has the cops and the coroner down at this establishment and they have it locked down. I have to get there fast and pick up the body. So I roar out of the garage in the first hearse I can find. When I get there, I pull around back, which is appropriate, because in a place like that the back door is really the front door. Everyone uses the back door because it's off the street. So I go in there and find no uniformed cops, just a detective and the coroner.

"I couldn't believe the mayor's brother went to a place like this. The carpet smells like vomit and beer. There is a menu up on the wall that gives the prices of the services they offer. You got a blowjob for seventy-five dollars, a straight lay for a hundred bucks, a half and half for a hundred twenty-five dollars, two girls for one-seventy-five, and so on."

Cody interrupted, "What's a half and half?"

Germ rolled his eyes. He said, "Pete, help me with the youngster."

Impatiently, Pete blurted out, "Half blow, half fuck."

Germ continued, "But the damndest thing is they have all these other services listed as side items. Like when you go into a fast food place to order a burger, they ask you what you want on it and if you want fries. Kind of like that."

"What were the side items?" asked Cody.

Germ thought momentarily, "Only thing I remember is that the sign said, 'Spankings: twenty dollars. With whip, five dollars extra.' Can you imagine the hapless fucks going in there to pay some girl to give them a spanking? Now, how pathetic is that?"

"Yeah. Did you get a look at the girls?" asked Cody.

"By the time I arrive at that fine establishment, all of them were sequestered in the staff lounge. They know some guy died there, but none of them knows he's the mayor's brother. Now, quit interrupting me with all these chicken shit questions, I'm trying to get a point across to you here."

Germ took another sip of the Irish and cleared his throat. "So the coroner takes me to this upstairs room where the body is stretched out naked on the bed. Everything else is just routine except as I'm leaving, the detective calls me aside and says, 'Did you hear about the mayor's brother dying at home in his sleep?'

"And I say, 'Yeah, I heard that. Too bad.'

"So the newspaper the next day says the mayor's brother died at home in his sleep. Seems he had a pacemaker. Can you believe that? A guy with a heart condition going to a bordello. What an idiot."

"Maybe not," Pete interjected, "Confucius says that 'Man who dies in brothel is happy man indeed.'"

"Did Confucius really say that?" asked Cody.

Impatiently, Pete blurted, "How the hell should I know? Probably not, but it's still true. I mean, that's the whole point of Germ's story. That's the whole sex and death thing. It's what you're talking about, isn't it? Sex and death. Well, if you die while having sex, you have the most intensely human experience possible."

"Yeah, it's got to be simultaneous to count as the definitive existential encounter," agreed Cody enthusiastically. "With AIDS you've got sex and death, but it's sex first, then death comes later. That's not as intense as sex and death at the same time."

"But you've got to die at the point of orgasm or shortly thereafter, not before," Germ stated. "If you don't get off, it would not be the ultimate experience."

The profundity of his comment took a moment to sink in.

"But what if you die during a hand job?" asked Cody, "does that count?"

After a minute of further reflection, Pete opined, "If you have a heart attack while masturbating, that shouldn't count. But if someone else is giving you a hand job when you die, that should qualify."

"I'm not so sure," said Germ, "I'd say a blow job definitely counts, but a hand job doesn't qualify. But I agree with you on the point that if a hand job did qualify, then it could not be self-administered."

"Since AIDS came along," said Pete, "you could argue that now people are more alive when they have sex, because you are risking much more than just herpes or the clap. Here you are screwing some hot-looking chick and all the time you're thinking, 'I could die because of this.' That's hardcore."

"That's what condoms are for," Germ declared.

Pete responded, "Yeah, but it's not one-hundred percent safe. Still, I always use protection, no matter who I'm screwing. I hate using a condom. It's like watching a beautiful sunset in a rearview mirror. It definitely compromises the experience, but it's not as bad as dying."

"Sex makes people crazy," Germ said, "they lose all reason. It's like this graffiti I saw above the urinal at this Red Ace gas station in Alabama. I usually don't read graffiti, but this was right in my face. It said,

'Here I stand trying to piss,
'Thinking about the girl who give me this.
*'If she were here and I was well,*
*'I'd catch it again.*
'Sure as hell.'"

"People are stupid when it comes to protecting themselves," Pete said.

"Or maybe," Cody ventured, "it means that anyone who does it without a condom has a secret death wish."

After a moment of contemplation, Germ glanced at his watch and exhaled a long, weary sigh. "Even if I had a death wish, I couldn't act on it tonight. I'm too tired to die. I'm going to bed. See you guys over at the dorm."

"Wait for me. I'll walk over with you," said Pete. He looked at Cody, "You going to catch some sleep?"

Cody could feel the attraction of his comfortable bed tugging at him. Employees who worked the night shift had small, permanent sleeping rooms in a remote wing of the funeral home complex. Cody was exhausted, however some vague but persuasive impulse called on him to stay up for a while. He said to Pete, "Go on over. I'll be along soon."

Germ shuffled out the door. "Turn out the lights and lock up the room, kid. See you later."

As the sounds of the others faded slowly down the hall, Cody looked over at Priscilla. Immediately, he felt a stunning blast of anxiety in his gut.

Her face had changed.

He jumped up quickly to her side, and then walked fretfully around her gurney, exploring her face from every angle. His hands tingled and he felt droplets of sweat break out on his forehead. He heard the rapid, hammering echoes of his heart pounding in his ears.

Unmistakably, Priscilla's countenance had altered profoundly. Her expression had transformed from one of peace and serenity to one of misgiving and infinite sorrow.

Cody was deeply troubled, even though the rational part of his brain told him authoritatively that the girl's apparent transformation was merely the result of the way the light stuck her face or the angle from which he viewed her. And if not this, then surely it was his imagination, because his rational mind knew that dead faces do not change.

Badly shaken, Cody could cope with the situation no longer. He had to escape. Quickly, he walked to the door and turned off the lights. As he took a step out into the refuge of the hall, he felt an overpowering impulse to look back at Priscilla one last time. With great apprehension, he turned slowly, just long enough for a farewell backward glance. Moonlight from the skylights filled the room. Priscilla's face was compelling, calling him to her side.

Mesmerized, he walked slowly over and stood above her. As he looked down, she called his name, "Cody, don't leave me. I have marvels to show you. Many and wonderful."

Cody reached under the sheet and found one of her cold, lifeless hands. He held it. He closed his eyes.

Somewhere in his childhood, a train whistle blew. He remembered listening for that whistle on summer evenings with his grandmother. Gently, he swayed in a swing on the big front porch while Granny rocked her chair in vague synchronicity with a chorus of frogs by the river. Lighting bugs glowed serenely on the lawn, and in the ancient oak trees Spanish moss stirred softly in whispers of wind.

Cody imagined sitting in the swing with Priscilla and talking to Granny about things that did not matter. The girl's countenance had changed again. Now her face was radiant with life. Her vibrant smile lit up the porch and her vivacious laughter spilled out onto the lawn. When Granny went upstairs to bed, Priscilla snuggled close to him and he felt her soft, sweet breath on his cheek.

24

If Priscilla would come back to life, he would marry her. He would devote himself to making her happy.

Cody opened his eyes and again contemplated the face that haunted him. This face would never look with affection into the tender gaze of a lover, or look with adoration to see beautiful children encircling her. This face was lost forever to the inscrutability of death and the mystery of human destiny.

As Cody stood there with Priscilla until dawn, he wept for her. And for himself. And for all the rest who died, or would die.

His soul, a flickering candle.

# Chapter 2

*Mrs. Montefigaro's Fingers and*
*the Graveside Breakfast*

It was hot; Mississippi hot. Humidity hung over the city like a clammy funeral shroud.

Cody opened the rider's side door of the black Cadillac and spun his legs around. He looked down and briefly contemplated the tar oozing out of the asphalt, and then felt a surge of nausea and regret as he recalled the debauchery of the previous night. Images of poker chips and whiskey bottles blasted into his consciousness. The tentacles of a dark foreboding wrapped around his soul.

Earlier, as they stumbled around the funeral home dormitory getting dressed, Germ said they would all feel better if they ate a good breakfast.

Now he heard the senior embalmer calling out to him from the back seat, "Don't look so glum, Cody. We can get the food to go and eat it by the graveside while we wait." He chuckled good-naturedly, "This is your day to shine, Cody. You da man."

Pete snickered. "I wouldn't want your assignment, not today."

Johnny said, "Yeah, Cody. Today, you the man."

Encouragingly, Germ offered, "Look at the positive side of this, son. No one at the funeral home has ever done this before, not that I can remember. If you pull this off, you will become a staff lounge legend."

As the grim foursome shuffled to the front door of the Waffle Shop, Cody felt the oppressive scorched air against his face, the waves of heat from the simmering sidewalk billowing up his pants legs. He thought about the unpleasant task awaiting him at the cemetery and gave a vague sigh of angst and resignation. The new employees at the funeral home always ended up with the worst assignments. Next time it would be some other hapless grunt. But today, he was the man.

They approached the restaurant's short-order counter and rattled off a litany of menu items, which included sausage, eggs, grits, hash browns and, of course, extra coffee. Cody thought they ordered too much, but maybe the extra food would help their hangovers. He knew they would have plenty of time to eat. It would take a while for the cemetery men to dig down to the bottom of the grave and bring up the heavy concrete vault. Then, they would use a small jackhammer to break through the side.

He thought what a shame it would be if the workers damaged Mrs. Montefigaro's exquisite casket. Last night around the poker table, Germ delighted in describing the seemingly endless virtues of the matriarch's final abode. The "Violet Rosary," he said, "was one of the finest coffins manufactured in modern times."

As the lecture began, Pete rolled his eyes and Johnny, a thirty-year funeral home veteran, left for the bathroom mumbling something about having heard it all before a hundred times.

Germ called after him, "Well, just go on, you old fart. You would get all the facts mixed up anyway in your grain alcohol brain. What's left of it."

Cody was genuinely interested. He wondered why anyone would spend so much money on a casket, or anything else that gravediggers would smother under six feet of dirt.

Germ continued, "Needless to say, only the most accomplished craftsmen participated in the construction. The unit was high gauge stainless steel in one of the most unusual colors I've ever seen, obsidian black with a hint of violent that rippled through it sort of like a hologram.

"Around the outside perimeter, artisans had painstakingly etched scenes from the rosary and the life of the Virgin Mary on an inlaid panel of silver. The centerpiece of this magnum opus was a medallion on the coffin lid engraved with a depiction of the victorious assumption of Mary into heaven."

As Germ enthusiastically described the coffin in greater detail, Cody thought it was more appropriate for a medieval emperor than a mere mortal of the twenty-first century.

Germ concluded, "Sadly, the Violet Rosary is no longer available. At seventy-five thousand dollars a unit, there was not much of a market for them. But the Montefigaro family was determined to have the finest casket in the country at the time. They were flagrantly pretentious in every way. And, until recently, they could afford it."

Back in the car, Cody sipped his coffee and leaned over toward the air conditioning vent to let the cool air caress his face. As they rode up near the gravesite, he saw three workers in coveralls setting up a jackhammer. Although the men had already lifted the vault out of the grave, they still had to penetrate its concrete hull and make an opening large enough for the casket.

"Let's just sit in the car. It'll be cooler," ventured Cody hopefully.

At the wheel, Pete said, "The motor will overheat." He smiled sympathetically as he turned off the engine, and then offered, "Hey, look over there. We can eat on the steps of that mausoleum. There's plenty of room to spread out."

The prospect of eating on the steps of the small family mausoleum did little to mitigate Cody's dark mood. Sure, there was room to spread out, but the site offered only a minimal amount of shade. The scrawny, parched hackberry tree leaning precariously over the structure was no match for the thermonuclear fusion of the sun which, courtesy of the speed of light, was only nine minutes away.

The funeral home entourage called out their greetings to the cemetery workers as they carried their Styrofoam boxes over to the steps. Germ smiled as he sat down and opened his breakfast eagerly, "Nothing like a little sausage and eggs to make us feel better. Then we can get down to business."

Suddenly, Cody did not feel at all hungry and was about to suggest that having a big meal in the heat just before opening a casket buried for eleven years was not such a good idea. But before he could collect his thoughts on the matter and attempt a protest, the others were diving in.

It was wretchedly hot for ten o'clock, and Cody thought, Lord, what we need here is a cool little breeze. Apparently, the Lord was not impressed. Maybe He did not approve of digging up the dead. Instead of a refreshing breeze, another rush of withering heat swelled up from the baked earth. Cody looked down at a link sausage and sensed a wave of nausea gathering in his belly. He quickly shut the lid of the take-out container and pushed it behind him. Unbidden, a memory crashed into his mind, then faded into the heat. It was a Bible story he had heard as a child, something about three men walking around in a fiery furnace. Cody slowly sipped his coffee as he glanced over at the others gulping down their food and recounting the rowdy events of the previous night. He looked around and studied some of the names on the tombstones. He thought how peaceful it must be down in the grave, just serenely lying there under the ground, out of the sun with no one to disturb you. Unless you were Mrs. Montefigaro and your family wanted to dig you up. For a moment, he amused himself with the idea that maybe she would put a curse on them like those Egyptian mummies that supposedly haunted the archaeologists who violated their tombs.

The cemetery men worked slowly, cautiously avoiding any damage to the treasure inside the vault. When they cleared a space large enough for the casket, they waved to the group of undertakers. It was their turn.

"Okay, boys, let's get this done," Germ said with enthusiasm. He wiped his mouth with a paper napkin, and then used another one to mop his brow, which was seeping sweat like a saturated sponge. "The sooner we get out of here, the sooner we can get back and have a few cold ones."

The four figures, miserable in their black suits under the scorching sun, trudged up the hill to the gravesite. Cody thought about taking off his coat, but the funeral home had a strict dress code. Even in this kind of weather, management would deem it unprofessional to strip off your jacket.

As they drew closer to the gravesite, Cody felt a burst of anxiety. He wondered if he would have the fortitude to carry out his assignment.

The group approached warily and peered in through the jagged, jack-hammered opening on the side of the vault. Nothing unexpected. No damage. Just a few crumbs of concrete on the casket lid.

Germ called out directions as they carefully pulled the Violet Rosary out into the sunshine, one man at each corner. The casket was indeed strikingly beautiful, as Germ had foretold, and Cody thought it was a shame to waste it on the bleak dungeon of the grave. However, early in his funeral home employment, he learned that the bereaved often went to great lengths to justify the purchase of an elegant coffin. Sometimes it was to honor the deceased, sometimes to assuage guilt, and other times for love.

The casket was extremely heavy, and the men struggled as they wobbled it to the ground in a bumpy landing. In the car, Germ had warned them that the massive casket would be overweight and unwieldy due to its heavy gauge components.

Johnny added that Mrs. Montefigaro was no delicate wisp of a woman. She weighed at least two-hundred-fifty pounds. At the time of her burial, he was one of the pallbearers who carried her coffin up the steep hill to the grave. "It was a hell of an effort," he said seriously. "I wrenched my back hauling the old bitch up there. The doctor put me on two weeks' bed rest."

Now, after setting the casket on the ground, Johnny reflected. "That wasn't as heavy as I remember." He grinned. "Wonder if she's lost some weight. Guess she's had to go on a diet in the grave."

Cody and Pete each let out a hearty chuckle, but Germ, who was becoming irritable in the heat, cut short further frivolity with a dark scowl.

He said, "Knock it off, you guys. Now let's get down to business." In the scorching sunlight, they huddled around him for last minute instructions. "Pete will open the casket and hold up the lid while Cody snags the ring. Johnny and I are the official witnesses. After Cody gets the ring, he hands it off to me, and then we can reseal the casket and get the hell out of here. Any questions?"

"Why do we need witnesses?" asked Cody.

Germ replied ominously, "In case the ring's not there."

Cody was curious about the diamond. It was reportedly worth two million dollars, a fiftieth anniversary present from the matriarch's husband. The children of the affluent couple insisted that she wear it to the grave. However, since then, financial disaster had descended upon the prominent family. They were desperate for money and, with great difficulty, secured a court order for the disinterment.

Cody sensed an odd odor hanging in the heavy air around the casket. Maybe it was Mrs. Montefigaro. Impossible. The casket was airtight.

Pete produced a casket key from his inside coat pocket. The "key" was just a fancy Allen wrench with a silver handle. One size fit all caskets.

A quick survey of the area revealed no people around except the cemetery workers. They were keeping their distance and had retreated to their flatbed truck where a new replacement vault sat strapped on the back.

Pete started turning the key, with difficulty at first, but then with greater speed. Suddenly, there was a hissing sound similar to the disturbing noise made by opening a spoiled can of food. It grew increasingly loud and ended with a definitive pop.

A second later it came: A tidal wave of horrific odor. Over the years, slowly rotting flesh and embalming fluid had produced a vile, putrid compressed gas inside the casket.

Later, as Cody was trying to describe the stench, someone asked him, "Did it smell like shit?" He replied, "No, shit would have been a blessing."

As the surge of released gas smashed into the undertakers, all four spun around and reached for their handkerchiefs in unison, as if they were performing a move in a choreographed dance. Then the vile wave came back, rebounding on a current of stifling air.

Germ turned and ran bent over down the hill toward the car. Johnny was close behind, irrationally trying to escape the stench by running a wild zigzag pattern, his handkerchief still pressed against his nose.

Cody watched them and started to follow, but his legs were unsteady. He sank to his knees and began to heave. Since he had wisely opted to skip breakfast, there was not much in his stomach for this offering to the gods of debauchery.

After a moment, he became aware that Pete was sitting under a nearby tree, holding his head in one hand while using the other to flick hastily masticated chunks of sausage off his pants.

The two men back at the car had puked all over themselves and the nearby area. Germ was walking around in circles taking deep breaths. Johnny lay on the hood of the car.

After a moment, the foul odor from within the coffin subsided somewhat. Cody again looked at Pete and then down the hill. Now, Germ was waving his arms and shouting, "The ring! Get the ring!"

Cody walked unsteadily over to Pete and knelt beside him. He whispered, "Let's get it."

Pathetically, Pete looked at him. He said softly, "I can't get up. And I'm too dizzy to walk."

Cody waited a moment, and then persisted. "All I need you to do is raise the lid long enough for me to snatch the ring. Then we'll get back to the car and sit in the air conditioning."

Apprehensively, Pete contemplated the casket for a moment. Germ was still calling out that they had to get the ring. "All right, Cody, but make it fast. I can't last very long."

They took three deep breaths, held the fourth one and staggered to the casket. Pete raised the heavy lid about halfway and then hesitated. He lowered it a little and then with a jerk pushed it up all the way.

Cody peered into the elegant interior of the coffin to behold Mrs. Montefigaro's shocking visage. Earlier that morning Germ had advised him what to expect. He said that the matriarch's face would likely be quite wrinkled and grey. The eyes would probably be somewhat sunken. However, overall there should be nothing drastically different from the face they buried eleven years earlier.

Germ was wrong. The putrefying flesh of Mrs. Montefigaro's face had hideously contorted into an asymmetrical expression of anguish. Decomposed tissue had pulled away from her cheekbone. The ample flesh that once covered her chin had oozed down into a vile pool of gore, which had collected at the base of her neck. One of her eyeballs had popped out of its socket and lay against her nose, still connected to strands of withered blood vessels.

The eye entranced Cody's traumatized mind. It seemed to be looking directly at him, glaring indignation and outrage at this violation of the grave.

Coming out from under the spell of Mrs. Montefigaro's shocking countenance, he could hear Pete making hurry-up grunting sounds while still holding his breath. Urgently, Cody looked down at the corpse's waist. There it was, a dazzling star on her withered hand. It was much larger than he had imagined and for a moment, the beauty of it immobilized him.

Finally, he reached for the ring and started to pull. It did not budge. More urgent sounds came from Pete. It was obvious he was out of air and desperate to drop the lid.

Cody pulled again on the ring. It moved a little. Then he felt Pete's presence melt behind him. He was alone with both hands in the casket, the heavy metal lid descending rapidly. He had time for only one last try. This time he pulled hard.

He could feel the firmness of the ring gripped solidly in his hand as he yanked his arms out just in time. The casket closed with a frighteningly heavy thud.

As he let out his breath and took his first steps of retreat, a feeling of exhilaration rushed over him. He had done it. He had retrieved the trophy from Mrs. Montefigaro's coffin.

Halfway down the hill, he looked toward the car where Germ's fatherly smile of approval was already spreading across his worn face.

Suddenly, Cody became aware that he held something else in his hand. Something mushy stuck inside the ring.

He stopped, looked down and, to his abject horror, saw them: Mrs. Montefigaro's fingers. He had stripped the rotten flesh right off the ring finger bone. And in his haste to snatch the diamond, he managed to snare the tissue from her middle finger, too.

He suppressed a violent surge of nausea, and then grunted with disgust as he reached down and pulled the flesh of the two putrid fingers away from the ring. It was messy, but he was able to keep most of the tissue intact.

He put the ring in his other hand and looked down with loathing at the fingers. He imagined he saw one them twitch just a little.

In revulsion, he flung the fingers under a giant oak tree nearby. Then, gasping for breath, he trotted quickly to the bottom of the hill and triumphantly deposited the ring in the fresh white linen handkerchief held by Germ's waiting hand.

They all gathered round to gaze at the marvelous diamond. Germ let them stare at it a bit longer and then produced a brown envelope from his inside pocket, deposited the treasure and sealed it.

The senior embalmer said to Cody, "Well done, son. Well done."

Johnny asked, "Hey Cody, what did you throw under that tree when you were running down the hill?"

Cody groaned, "Dammit I forgot about that. It's the flesh from her ring and middle fingers. I had to pull so hard to dislodge the diamond that I stripped the rotting tissue right off the bones."

Pete exclaimed, "Damn that's disgusting. I may puke again."

Germ said, "Well, looks like we have some unfinished business here. Someone's got to go back up there, replace the fingers and seal the casket."

Johnny said, "I'm not doing it, dammit."

Pete added, "Me neither. My legs are still shaky. I'd never make it."

In disgust, Cody surveyed their shamed, downturned faces. Finally, he shouted, "I'll do it. Give me the casket key. I'll be damned if I'm going to share the glory with any of you cowardly bastards."

# Chapter 3

*The Constipated Corpse*

The dust clouds trailing the hearse caught up with them as the young undertakers stopped at an intersection on a desolate country road outside Grundy. For a moment, the dust swirled around them.

At the wheel, Pete mumbled curses as he glared at the fine powder settling on the shiny hood. Any hearse Pete drove instantly became an extension of his ego. "Haven't these yokels ever heard of asphalt?"

Cody ignored him, consulting the county map in search of the right road. They had driven several miles since seeing a street sign. Everybody who lived in the area knew the names of the roads already, and no one else in the world cared about street signs here or the absence of them.

The rest of the world really did not care about anything in Grundy, a neglected, mediocre town in the middle of the Mississippi wasteland. It was best not to know anything about Grundy, and, if by accident you discovered something, it was prudent to forget it as quickly as possible, if you could. Otherwise, it might become one of those unwanted pieces of information that your brain kept sequestered in a dark, secret place only to emerge at a particularly inopportune time.

Cody's brain was like that. Bits of unsolicited data popped into his consciousness at the worst possible moments and distracted him from important matters. Once, when he was taking an oral exam in his psychology of religion class, one of the professors on the panel asked him to relate a personal religious experience. All that came to his mind was the time he threw a case of beer bottles at a "Jesus Loves You" billboard.

In Grundy for a moment, it seemed that time stopped and held them captive. Everything moved slowly, especially in the summer heat. It took too much energy to think or move. The heat made the locals move like zombies and think like zombies, if they took the trouble to think at all.

The sun-scorched misery of the landscape penetrated the womb of tinted windows and the luxurious air-conditioned interior of the hearse. Cody felt the heat on his leg where the sun's rays seemed to be burning a hole in his black suit. He looked down at the spot with a groan of resignation. Black was the dress code of his profession, no matter what the weather. And it didn't help that they were wearing so-called "tropical wool," an oxymoron, Cody claimed, of the highest order.

So Cody and Pete, mesmerized by the parched countryside in front of them, just sat for a moment, staring out at the intersection with no name. Meanwhile, the endless cotton and soybean fields, broken only by an occasional stand of corn, continued to wilt under the unrelenting Mississippi sunshine.

After a moment, Cody broke free from his trance. "Straight," he said to Pete. "I think it's straight down here a little farther." As the hearse started up again, most of the dust blew off, but a thin layer remained. "Look at this crap," Pete complained. "We should have brought an older hearse."

Cody did not bother to respond. They always drove the best and shiniest vehicles to impress the locals. When you died, men in expensive suits drove all the way from the big city to whisk you away in a sleek black hearse. You might not have been much in your life, but your last ride was something special. It was a statement that somehow you were important, even when everybody knew you were not. Really, you were just another local loser living on a few acres of land no one else wanted, and your death was your last chance to matter to no one in particular.

Judging from the neighborhood, Cody thought the deceased could probably be the poster child for the mundane, unremarkable life. Politely, the family and friends would not laugh at the lies his eulogy would certainly tell.

This was one of the peculiar practices surrounding death ordinary people did not feel comfortable discussing. Everyone played along, knowing that someday those who remained behind would do the same for them. Therefore, it was important to support the delusion. It was the business of death in rural Mississippi, and it was the reason Pete and Cody rode on into the heat and dust of an August afternoon inferno in the newest and shiniest hearse available. They were actors in the dead man's final scene. They were doing their part to make Mr. Fred Kimball special. Not that anyone had called him "Mister," either, not in a very long time.

As the hearse rolled on, Cody began searching for the signs of what he called the "death house." There would be cars parked along the road in front, mainly old people shuffling or standing about in the yard, staring down at their shoes or craning their necks to get the first glimpse of the hearse. In the face of death, easy conversation was difficult to come by. So if you were the first to exclaim, "Here come the undertakers," or, "There's the hearse," it gave you something to say instead of looking uncomfortably down at your shoes or someone else's shoes, struggling for your next sentence.

Often, there was a preacher in attendance, Bible in hand, wiping his brow with a white handkerchief, pacing back and forth, rummaging his mind and the scriptures for a consoling word.

Cody saw the death house coming up on the right side of the road. He said, "Slow down, Pete. There it is."

Even though they were late arriving, Pete pulled into the driveway at a crawl. To come roaring in would be undignified and perhaps precipitate thoughts among the bereaved that the undertakers were a little too eager to get their job done.

Fred Kimball's dilapidated home was like countless others Cody had seen in the region. The driveway consisted of two ruts of dirt with a strip of crabgrass running up the center. A broken-down pickup was set up on concrete blocks in the side yard, and next to it a rusty propane gas tank sat baking in the sun. A couple of discarded appliances peeked through a ragged hedge in the back yard.

As the hearse rolled to a stop, a weary looking woman came forward to greet them. Cody said, "That must be Gerty Potts, the sister of the deceased. She's the one who called us."

Cody had recently taken the leadership role in his partnership with Pete, who was experiencing some emotional problems. The older undertaker had gladly given up his responsibilities because the new arrangement proved less stressful for him.

The younger man opened his door slowly and rose from the hearse with all the solemnity of a bishop about to grant a lowly communicant an audience. As he extended a hand of greeting to Fred's sister, he felt a visceral tingle, a sign that his favorite part in this ritual was about to unfold. The death call had begun. He stood on the threshold of an existential moment.

"You must be Mr. Kimball's sister," he said. "I'm Cody Palmeroy, and this is my partner, Peter Russo. We're here for the remains of your brother."

"Remains" was a puzzling and sometimes amusing term to Cody. It implied the real Mr. Kimball, presumably in the form of his soul, had gone off somewhere leaving his body behind like a discarded garment. Cody thought the church doctrine of the human soul's invisibility was a convenient windfall for the stormy preachers of eternal damnation. Since the soul was undetectable, it was impossible to disprove its existence or the fiery fate evangelists claimed awaited the sinful spirit upon departure from this world.

Cody adamantly rejected the reality of any place like hell. And based on one night's harrowing experience, he also rejected the church doctrine of the imperceptible nature of the soul. He believed souls were at least sometimes visible. Very visible.

He and Pete had traveled to a rural nursing home to retrieve the remains of an elderly patient. However, when they arrived, the "deceased" was not yet dead. It seemed the aspiring corpse had surprised everyone and regained consciousness. When Cody entered the room, the nurse told him he would have to wait a while, but probably not for long. The patient was surely about to die at any minute.

In spite of the late hour, the place was busy with nurses and patients moving about the halls. Cody had observed on several occasions there was nothing like the presence of undertakers to enliven a nursing home population. Perhaps they were worried they would be mistaken for a corpse if they did not get up and show some signs of life.

Cody sat in the corner of the patient's room. The nurse was right. As if on cue, with the arrival of the undertakers, the shriveled-up woman emitted a gurgling exhalation in tandem with her head falling softly to her chest.

The nurse quickly checked the patient's pulse, then walked over to the wall-mounted intercom and summoned the intern from her nap in the staff lounge down the hall. The young doctor pulled a stethoscope from her white lab coat and listened for signs of life in the chest. Then she pried open the eyelids and checked the pupils with a small flashlight. She nodded to Cody and proclaimed, "She's gone. You can have her now."

Cody summoned Pete from the hallway and together they wrapped the frail, withered corpse in a sheet and loaded her onto their stretcher. Just as they turned to roll her out the door, Cody heard an eerie, unsettling sound, a soft flutter followed by a sigh. It seemed to come from the ceiling right above the bed. When Cody looked up, he was shocked to see a shimmering mist of blue-white light, and in the center of it a pregnant woman in a robe. The ephemeral mist lingered for a moment and then disappeared into the ceiling as though some cosmic vacuum cleaner had sucked it up. Stunned, he whispered to Pete, "Did you see that?"

Pete looked up at the ceiling. "No, what was it?"

Cody stared at the spot a moment longer. There was only empty space where the mist had briefly lingered. He wondered if the apparition was that of the dead woman as she appeared at an earlier time in her life.

He heard Pete's voice, disturbed and urgent. "What did you see, Cody? What the hell is going on?"

Cody asked again, "You didn't see it?"

"I didn't see shit. Now tell me what's going on. You're giving me the creeps."

Cody checked the spot again. There was only a bare incandescent bulb and a stained ceiling tile. He turned back to Pete and declared emphatically, "Nothing. It was nothing. Let's roll."

Later that night, Cody retreated to the funeral home library with a bottle of wine. As he paced the floor, he analyzed every aspect of the mysterious apparition. He reflected about the pregnant woman's face in the eerie, shimmering cloud. If you go to heaven, does your face resemble your earthly visage? If so, at what age? One thing stuck in his mind above all else: The woman in the mist was staring directly at him, and she was smiling.

Upon retiring for the evening, just before he lost consciousness to sleep, he remembered something else. At the time, he was barely aware of it. The woman spoke to him. Her lips did not move, but he heard her muffled whisper. "I see a tree by the river."

On the lawn of the broken farmhouse, Fred's sister declared, "I'm Gerty. Fred is my baby brother. I live next door. Thank you for coming. I'm so relieved you're finally here."

Even though Cody had spoken the words many times, he took pride in sounding sincere. "We are so sorry to hear about your loss. It must be very difficult for you. Unexpected deaths are always the worst."

With a bit too much eagerness, Gerty responded, "Fred suffered so many years from that awful accident. He endured so much. Finally, he is at peace."

Cody interpreted her comments as a tacit and perhaps unintentional signal that she felt Fred was better off dead than alive. His demise was fine with her, and the undertakers need not spend any more time consoling her.

Politely Cody asked about the nature of the accident.

"A freight train hit the car. His legs were smashed," she said. "But that's all passed now. He's gone off to a better place."

Cody cringed at the cliché. Any place at all would be better than a rundown farmhouse in rural Mississippi. He deemed it best not to make responses to religious statements by the bereaved. Many theological assumptions were inherent in her statement about a "better place" and Fred now residing there, so he let the comment pass.

Looking warily toward the house, Gerty announced, "He's still in the bathroom, I'm afraid. Been on the toilet since he died yesterday. That's what the sheriff said when he came out this morning. It looked to him like my brother died sometime late yesterday afternoon."

Standing on the other side of the hearse, Pete appeared worried. "Has the coroner been here? Because we can't take him if the coroner hasn't officially pronounced him."

Gerty's face drew up into a tight knot of concern. "Well, no, but the sheriff called him and explained the situation. The coroner said it was no use in him coming all the way out here. He said he would sign the death certificate based on what the sheriff told him."

Concerned that his partner was about to comment on the impropriety of this, Cody shot Pete a stern, preemptive frown, then smoothly turned back to Fred's sister to deliver a comforting word. "Well, that's all right, Mrs. Potts. Coroner or not, we will be proud to take your brother. And we'll take real good care of him, too."

Pete recovered quickly from his faux pas. "Yes, we will, ma'am. We surely will."

Cody glided forward and with one smooth motion put his arm around Gerty's shoulder and aimed her for the house. "Now what's that you said about your brother being on the toilet?"

Gerty moved with him, yielding comfortably to his charm. "That's right," she said. "He died right there on the toilet, doing his business, I guess. But I don't think he had time to flush. There's a terrible smell coming from in there.

"This is somewhat embarrassing to talk about, but Fred always had a problem with constipation. This latest bout had been extremely cruel to him. A few days ago, he sent me into town to buy him a good, strong laxative at Watson's Five and Dime. It smells like it worked. Fred had a history of strokes, so I figure he died from a clot that came loose while he was straining for his bowel movement.

"A couple of men from down the road tried to move him to his bed, but he wouldn't budge. It's a small bathroom and he's really wedged in tightly. And it smells so bad, no one can stand to stay in there for long."

Cody was interested in her description of the death scene, but not overly concerned. He and Pete had removed corpses from many awkward situations. There was the judge with a condom still clinging to his shriveled penis, as he lay handcuffed to a conference table in his chambers. From the cockpit of a downed airplane, they had extracted a pilot who had been flash-fried in his seat during the crash, the shoulder harness melted into his flesh. There was a gooey mess at the bottom of an elevator shaft after a construction worker had missed a step on the twenty-seventh floor. In addition, they had picked up numerous grotesquely bloated "floaters" gnawed by catfish during several days of swirling down the savage currents of the Mississippi River.

So, some guy sitting on a toilet in a decrepit farmhouse was not going to be any problem for him. However, he hoped it would make a good story to tell when he got back to the funeral home. News of any death with a different twist was always quite welcome in the lounge where bored undertakers took their breaks. Cody thought that if there was ever a group that needed a good laugh, it was this one. Most of the time death was mundane unless, of course, it was your own or someone's close to you.

When it came down to it, Cody thought death was pretty boring. Ho, Hum. Just another poor fucking soul passes on, probably without contemplating much about where he came from or where he was going.

As they mounted the creaky wooden steps of the front porch, Gerty seemed increasingly uncomfortable. Cody sensed that she did not care to see her dead brother on the toilet again. He spoke comfortingly, "Now don't you worry about a thing, ma'am. Toilet or no toilet, Pete and I will take care of everything."

Cody noticed that a preacher clutching a Bible had moved from the shade of a magnolia tree to a polite distance near the porch, close enough to offer assistance, but not so close as to seem intrusive. Cody nodded for him to come forward and take charge of Gerty. "Now you just go with the reverend for a few minutes. We'll take care of everything inside."

Gratefully, Gerty took the preacher's arm and headed for the shade. Pete brought up the stretcher from the hearse and they rolled it into the tattered living room of Fred's ramshackle home. A broken Naugahyde couch patched with duct tape stood in the center of the room and an ancient television with rabbit ears occupied a dusty corner. Across the floor, Fred had haphazardly stacked old newspapers and magazines.

On top of a scarred end table to the side of the sofa sat a glass containing Fred's dentures immersed in a few inches of cloudy water. Cody pointed to the glass and Pete nodded. They would need the dentures to preserve Fred's facial features during the embalming procedure. Without them, the face might not look quite natural, no matter how much cotton the embalmers stuffed inside the oral cavity. Fred's concave mouth could be unnaturally drawn up as if he had died drinking a thick milkshake through a straw. Pete walked over to the glass and fished the dentures out with a pen. He wrapped them in a towel, which he tucked snugly under the mattress of the stretcher.

As they made their way down the narrow hall leading to the rear of the house, a change in wind direction outside pulled a back draft of vile odor from the bathroom over them like a rogue wave of putrefaction.

Instinctively, Cody snatched a handkerchief out of the front pocket of his suit and covered his nose and mouth. Pete's eyes bulged as he tried to suppress a heave. Warily, Cody stepped down to the end of the hall and peered into the tiny bathroom.

Water dripped onto a large rust spot in the basin of a dingy sink. A nasty towel lay on the floor in front of it. Dark mildew grew in the corners of the grimy tub and a tattered shower curtain clung desperately to its rod, held up by two remaining hooks. A worn and bent pair of crutches stood against the wall by the sink.

Cody took in the entire scene with a single glance, and then looked apprehensively toward the end of the tiny room. Fred sat on a raunchy toilet by a small open window. He was grossly overweight and his fat, flabby buttocks, befouled with smudges of dried feces, spilled over the sides of the rickety toilet seat. His knees were wedged tightly against the side of the bathtub and his torso was slouched forward. One of his hands clutched a ragged copy of the Farmer's Almanac held open by a grungy rubber band; the other closed into a tight fist that came to rest under his cascading chin.

Cody whispered to Pete, who had followed him down the hall and was looking over his shoulder at the corpse, "Kind of looks like Rodin's 'The Thinker' taking a shit, doesn't he?" Pete grunted agreement through his handkerchief, which he held pressed tightly against his nose.

With an odd sense of reverence, Cody knelt beside the corpse. He pulled a pair of latex gloves out of his pocket and slipped them on. Then he addressed Fred, looking squarely into his vacant eyes, "Okay Freddie, let's see what you have for us."

Cody frequently talked to corpses in a familiar manner, as if they were old friends. He knew this eccentricity bothered Pete, in spite of his repeated explanation that it was more personal and respectful to include the deceased in his conversations than to ignore him as an inanimate object.

Besides, who was to say corpses could not still hear for a while after the official death event. There were many examples of people in a deep coma who would wake up after a few months in a hospital's intensive-care unit and accurately recount conversations that had taken place around them. Often, these occurrences had unpleasant outcomes, especially when the newly revived patient said something like, "I heard you bastards talking about taking me off my life support. Well, you can just count yourselves out of my estate. Send for my attorney!"

Cody stood up, peered out the window and saw that Fred's sister was sitting under the magnolia tree where someone from the church had set out folding chairs for the mourners. The preacher was fanning her with one hand and waving the other around for emphasis as he quoted Bible passages. Two deacons had taken up positions nearby. Their role was to stand in the background like the chorus in a Greek tragedy and occasionally to say something supportive as the preacher droned on.

"The Lord giveth and the Lord taketh away. Blessed be the name of the Lord," shouted the man of God.

The deacons responded, "Amen. Praise the Lord."

Cody gave his commentary on the scripture as he placed a familiar hand on Fred's shoulder. "I don't understand that, Freddie. Why should the Lord be blessed for taking away?" Cody lowered his voice to a whisper as he leaned in closer. "And look at you, Freddie. What a mess you're in. What do you think of the Lord now? Feel like blessing His name?

"Try to look at the positive side of your predicament, Freddie. You have been in the cheap seats of life since the day you were born. At last, it's your turn to come on down front and get on stage. Now is your time to shine."

From behind him, Pete hissed, "Shut the fuck up, Cody. You're going to get us in a shitload of trouble, if you don't shut the fuck up. Now, let's get on with it!"

Ignoring the admonishment, Cody looked at the open Farmer's Almanac in Fred's hand, and then placed the tattered book carefully on the side of the tub. "Looks like you were reading about planting some vegetables, Freddie. You could use some more starch in your diet. You're looking kind of poorly."

Pete's face turned a sickly gray color. "For God's sake, Cody, flush the pot before I puke all over both of you."

Cody looked through the tiny space between Fred's bulging legs and into the stinking toilet bowl. A wave of revulsion overcame him. Carefully, he reached around the blubbery corpse and found the handle. He flipped it and stepped back. For a brief moment, the toilet flushed normally, but then a choking, sickly gurgle emerged from its clogged throat. To the undertakers' horror, the toilet filled up and overflowed down the outside of the bowl and onto the floor, a putrid, brown waterfall of diarrhea mixed with chunks of feces.

Cody felt the contents of his stomach surge into his esophagus. He jumped up and rushed down the hall to the kitchen, opened the refrigerator and stuck his head inside. After a few deep gasps, he slammed the door. Pete had followed him down the hall. "Hey, let me have some of that." Cody opened the refrigerator door and Pete thrust his head in between a quart of buttermilk and a plastic container of moldy chicken wings. As he stepped back, Cody closed the door and noticed a thick, brown smear on his latex glove. "Look, I've got shit on my glove."

Pete looked down at his own hands and was relieved to see they were clean. "Where did it come from?"

"How the hell should I know?" Cody said irritably. "In case you didn't notice, there's shit in there. It's all over the place. God only knows what kind of contagion is festering in the place."

Pete was hastily putting on his own latex gloves. "This is taking too much time. Let's get on with it."

Casually, as if they were in no big hurry, Cody continued, "Do you realize that if some guy over in Africa hadn't fucked a monkey, I'd have shit on my hand right now instead of on this glove?"

Pete became increasingly annoyed. "What the hell are you jabbering about? Now quit that crazy talk!"

Cody was purposefully slow in his response, knowing every word added to his friend's agony. "What I'm talking about is this. We all know AIDS is a sexually transmitted disease, right? It's easy to see how humans transmit it to each other. But monkeys had the HIV virus before humans. So I want to meet that first guy who got it from screwing around with a monkey. I know the pervert is long dead, but I'd really like to ask him if he was so hard up for sex that he had to fuck a monkey."

Pete was about to have a stroke. "So what's your point?"

Cody responded professorially. "I'll tell you what my point is. If it were not for AIDs, we wouldn't be wearing latex gloves in situations like this, right? So that's why I say that if some guy hadn't fucked a monkey, I'd have shit on my hand right now."

Pete shook his head in displeasure as Cody sauntered over to the sink, washed off his gloved hand and then dried it with a dishtowel.

"You boys need any help in there?" The preacher was on the back porch peering in through the tattered screen door.

Surprised, Cody spun around. He replied hastily, "No thank you, Reverend. We were just assessing the situation in the bathroom and had a minor setback, but we will be bringing the body out soon."

The preacher was already on his way back to the shelter of the magnolia. He called back to them over his shoulder, "Well, just let me know if you need some help. Me and a couple of the boys out here will give you a hand."

Pete let the preacher get out of earshot then berated Cody. "I told you we were taking too damn long."

Cody stuck his head in the fridge for a few more deep breaths. "Okay then, let's do it. But first, let's get down on it like Jesse James."

Pete nodded his approval as they went to the sink, wet their handkerchiefs and wore them like outlaws, covering their noses and mouths and tying them at the backs of their heads. It looked ridiculous, but the simple procedure was actually quite helpful in reducing the effects of fetid odor.

At the entrance, the young undertakers peered into the tiny bathroom, reassessing the situation. After a moment, Cody declared, "Look at that fat ass, would you? Why don't skinny people ever die like this?"

Ignoring the question, Pete advised, "There's no way we can get the stretcher in this small space. We'll have to drag him out and load him in the hall."

Cody agreed, "Okay, but first we have to do something about this mess on the floor."

He fetched a broom from the kitchen and swept the stinking slime over behind the toilet. Then, before it could flow back into the center of the room, Pete threw down towels on top of it and stomped them. He brought in a mop to finish the job and though the floor was still a bit sticky with excrement, they could at least maneuver in the small room without soiling their clothes. Pete threw the mop into the tub and they turned their attention to Fred.

As they advanced toward their quarry, it became apparent that the two of them could not get hold of the corpse at the same time. The space between the tub and the toilet was too narrow.

Cody went in first, grabbed the dead man's shoulders and tried to pry him loose from the toilet. He would not budge.

Cody stepped over into the tub and motioned for Pete to come forward and try it. But Fred wasn't moving. Next, Pete got a sheet from the bedroom and they wrapped it around Fred's midsection. Each took an end of the sheet and gave a determined tug. With this maneuver, Fred rocked from side to side a little but would not give up his seat. Rigor mortis had set in hard, and his body was rigid and inflexible. To make matters worse, he was actually getting larger by the minute, a consequence of bloating brought on by the natural process of decay and accelerated by the heat.

Pete went out to a tool shed by the back door to look for something that might help, as Cody called after him. "Do you think you'll find a special tool out there made for prying a fat stiff from a toilet?"

Cody studied their quandary, breathing into his handkerchief. Both he and Pete were perspiring heavily and had taken the rare liberty of peeling off their suit jackets.

Pete returned with a crowbar and a can of WD-40, which they sprayed liberally onto appropriate areas of Fred's body. They applied the crowbar from different angles and sprayed more lubricant with special attention to the knees and buttocks. Still, Mr. Fred Kimball, in all his postmortem obstinacy, refused to relinquish his throne.

Pete cast another worried glance into the yard. The preacher was still holding forth, but his cadence had slowed considerably, and he was glancing anxiously toward the house. It was evident that his repertoire of scripture was almost exhausted.

Desperately, Pete begged, "Cody, please, let's ask the Reverend to help us. He said he'd give us a hand."

But Cody had an inspiration. "No, here's what we'll do. You stay in here and pull on the sheet. I'll go outside and push him your direction through the window."

Pete had serious doubts, "Are you sure? I don't think so."

But before he could state further objections, Cody was out the back door. His presence in the yard drew the attention of the mourners. Some of them followed Cody to the side of the house while the preacher and his deacons went inside.

Standing outside the bathroom window, Gerty, recently revived from a fainting spell, was distraught. Frantically, she asked Cody, "Can't you get Fred off the toilet? I am so embarrassed. All these people are seeing Fred on the commode." Unfortunately, the top of Fred's head was visible from the yard through the bathroom window.

The preacher called out to her from inside. "It's okay Gerty. The Lord will show us a way. He has never failed us before."

In the hall, Pete grabbed one end of the sheet and the preacher took the other. For added strength, a deacon clasped each of them around the waist.

Outside, Cody was confidently calling out instructions. He stood on a ragged pile of firewood stacked against the house, arms stretched inside the window, his hands on Fred's shoulder. "Okay guys, One … two … three … heave."

Their chorus of groans and snorts, sounding like a pigpen at feeding time, spilled out into the yard and elevated Gerty's anxiety even further. "This is so horrible. I'm so embarrassed."

The tug-of-war team ignored her as Cody called out encouragement. But in spite of their collective efforts, and though Fred rocked back and forth promisingly, the toilet refused to give up its hostage.

From inside, a desperate call came from Pete. "This is crazy, Cody. It's not working."

Cody was undaunted, "Wait. I'm climbing up higher to get my feet through the window. Stand by, I'm coming up."

Ignoring Pete's moans of protest, Cody pulled his body up to the level of the window. Like Spiderman, he clung to the side of the house, his hands grabbing the gutter above, his feet straddling the opening of the window frame. Every blood vessel in his head was bulging dangerously. In a strained, hoarse voice, he called out another command. "Heave!"

Cody hesitated a moment to give the inside crew a chance to pull the sheet tight. Then, like a trapeze artist, he swung his body up for an instant then came down with all his weight as he pushed his feet through the opening and delivered a powerful blow to the side of

Fred's body. Though awkward, the maneuver was enough to dislodge the corpse, which tumbled away from the toilet and spilled out into the hall landing on top of the preacher. Cody's forward momentum thrust him through the window. He lay sprawled in the narrow space between the toilet and the tub.

As he looked into the hall, he could see that Fred's posture was the same as on the toilet. The uncompromising grip of rigor mortis held him in the sitting position, except now he was lying face down on top of the preacher. The force of the blow had dislodged Fred from the toilet, but the toilet seat had refused to relinquish its grip on Fred's backside. What filthy adhesive was causing this, Cody did not want to imagine.

He jumped up quickly and pulled a sheet over Fred's posterior. The preacher had already come to his senses and was yelling hysterically, "Get him off me. For Christ's sake, get him off me!"

Pete snatched another sheet from the cot, and he and Cody, with the help of the quick-stepping deacons, pulled the body from atop the reverend. With considerable difficulty, they set Fred on the stretcher face down and hastily covered him.

An agitated Gerty now stood at the kitchen door looking into the hall. "Oh, this is terrible, just terrible."

The preacher stood and glided to her side. "It's okay, Gerty. It's all over now."

Cody could see that in spite of these assurances, it was not okay, and it was far from over , too. He had noticed a peculiar look come over Gerty's face, an expression he knew all too well. Freddie's sister was about to throw up.

She cupped both hands over her mouth and tried to suppress a gut-wrenching heave. But the force from below was too strong, and the contents of her stomach spewed through her fingers and sprayed the battle-weary group in the hall, with the main portion splattering onto the preacher's white shirt. As she ran to the kitchen sink to unload a second wave, Cody looked at the others and saw a situation developing that was quite similar to mass hysteria. Gerty's condition was contagious and could quickly lead to a phenomenon that he called "vomitus maximus populous."

The perfect conditions were present for communal, sympathetic regurgitation. The smell of vomit was strong, and they had all witnessed Gerty retching. Added to this was the horrific odor of putrefying flesh and human excrement, accompanied by extreme heat. So, when Cody saw one of the deacons begin to cover his mouth, he jumped up and shouted, "Everybody outside, now!"

A disorderly scramble dashed through the living room and out onto the front porch. For a moment, Cody and Pete stood there with the others, gasping like suffocating guppies, struggling to take in a few breaths of fresh air. When the afflicted deacon leaned over the porch rail and began to puke, Cody pulled on Pete's arm and they went back into the hall.

Compared to the previous farcical events, getting Fred to the hearse seemed mundane, except that he remained rigidly locked in the sitting position and had a toilet seat affixed to his abundant backside. The sheet they threw over him was woefully inadequate to disguise the ludicrous spectacle underneath it.

The unmistakable sounds of puking had attracted the bystanders to the front of the house. Now they stood in a sort of awkward semi-circle around the porch to witness a second wave of the deacon's violent regurgitation. Cody and Pete rolled their hard-fought trophy through the front door, past the crowd and out to the hearse.

Neither spoke until after Fred was properly loaded in the back compartment and they had washed their hands with a bottle of rubbing alcohol they kept in the glove compartment. In spite of their cleanup efforts, both men felt overwhelmingly polluted by the disgusting mess in the bathroom.

Pete said, "When we get back, I'll be in the shower for at least three days."

Cody looked down at his clothes in disgust. "I'm throwing this suit in the trash. I may even burn it." He grabbed a Bereaved Family Information Packet from the front seat of the hearse and headed for the house, calling back to Pete, "Crank up the AC. I'll be right back."

Cody found Gerty still in the kitchen, where one of the kindly neighbor women was sponging her face with a wet napkin.

He was concerned that the extraordinary nature of the preceding events would leave Gerty distraught and angry. He wanted to tell her, "You know the bumper sticker that says 'shit happens'? Well, it's referring to situations like this."

Instead, he ventured, "I'm sorry for all the mess and confusion, ma'am, but we have your brother all loaded up now. And we'll take real good care of him, just like I told you."

Gerty, drained and deflated by her episode of nausea, managed a weak smile as Cody handed her the packet.

He said, "Here's some information that may answer questions you have. We'll see you at the funeral home tomorrow to make the final arrangements, okay?"

Gerty looked down at the packet with a confused, embarrassed gaze.

It occurred to Cody she, like some others her age in these parts, might not be able to read. Intuitively he added, "You really don't have to read it. We'll answer any questions you might have tomorrow. The most important thing is to bring the suit, shirt and tie you want your brother to wear in the casket. Underwear and socks, too."

Gerty's neighbor asked whether there was a need for shoes.

Uneasily, Cody responded, "No, ma'am. The bodies, they don't wear shoes." He noticed Gerty seemed perplexed and added awkwardly, "They don't need them. They really don't go anywhere or anything."

Gerty was worried. "What about the second coming? Won't he need his shoes for the second coming of the Lord?"

Cody struggled to come up with an appropriate reply.

Then, like an answer to prayer, he heard the preacher's voice come from the doorway to the hall. "Now Gerty, on that glorious day when the Lord returns, He will provide Fred with everything he needs."

Relieved, Gerty replied. "We'll, I guess He will now."

The preacher added. "That's right, Sister. If He can feed the five thousand, He can surely provide Fred with some shoes. I wouldn't be surprised if the Lord doesn't put him in a brand new pair of shoes."

Cody walked back to the hearse, amused by the thought of new shoes for Fred, but vaguely troubled by the talk about the second coming.

As the hearse pulled out of Fred's driveway, Gerty's innocent reference to the apocalypse still held a grip on Cody's mind. It elicited a vivid memory of a childhood incident, which made a profoundly disturbing and indelible impression upon him.

While walking on the beach alone in front of his parents' cottage, a strange and marvelous light appeared in the night sky. At first, he thought it was nothing too unusual, perhaps a flare or an aircraft.

However, the eerie red light pulsated with increasing intensity. It looked as though some giant being above the earth had cut open the firmament with a sword and was peeling back the edges with its hands, allowing the mysterious light to spill in from heaven.

As the light grew, so did Cody's fear. The violent, thundering preaching he heard at church haunted him. Surely, this was the end of the world and the final judgment of the Lord. He wondered how a stern and unforgiving God would judge his flawed, nine-year-old life. A dark, horrific dread consumed him. Then, just as he was getting down on his trembling knees to ask for some serious, last minute forgiveness, the light started to fade and in just a few moments, the sky was dark again. The world had returned to normal.

In later years, he dismissed the incident as a combination of meteorological fluke and a massive overdose of psychopathological, toxic religion built on fear and manipulation. He reduced the cruel and delusional apocalyptic dogma he had been taught as a child to its simplest terms and entitled it the "Hell Fire Preachers' Creed."

*Hell is hot, very hot.*
*Everyone is a sinner, especially you.*
*God is pissed off.*
*He is coming back to earth to get you.*

To this, Cody added a sardonic tagline.

*And though it will do absolutely no good, run like hell*
*anyway.*

As if this was not enough to cause a major psychotic episode in a vulnerable, insecure kid, Cody's childhood pastor often added for good measure, "I think the Lord is coming back real soon, maybe tonight, or tomorrow at the latest." Though the Lord never came that night or any other, astoundingly, the preacher shamelessly repeated his prediction on a regular basis.

As a young adult, Cody had long since rejected the extreme dogmas he was force-fed as a child. Concerning conservative Christianity and its teachings, he was in full rebellion.

However, the memory of the mysterious light was often a catalyst that conjured up his deepest awareness of the cosmos. In a remote corner of his psyche dwelt a persistent inkling that the universe did not just happen without reason or cause.

As unsubstantiated as it was, this intuition was the basis for Cody's beleaguered faith in God.

Even though the rational side of Cody's brain told him to ignore such feelings, he could not. He knew that there were two kinds of knowledge and that each was valid in its own way. One was logical and demonstrable. The other was tacit, intuitive and personal. Through this second kind of cognizance, Cody felt the existence of a higher intelligence and perhaps some kind of afterlife. It was certainly more like a feeling than a knowing, but it was unfathomably deep, and he sensed the primal truth of it at the core of his being.

As the hearse passed the intersection with no name, Cody felt this haunting intuition stronger than ever.

In a remote corner of the universe, dwelt a supreme being which was infinitely beyond our imagination. And when we died, it would beckon us. Or, someday it might come.

As Pete accelerated the dusty black hearse onto the Interstate, Cody snapped out of his contemplative spell. He looked over at his riding partner and smiled. "Well, that was one hell of a death call, my friend."

Pete laughed, "It surely was. Oh, yes. It surely was."

As they sped toward the funeral home that scorching afternoon, the friends recounted with many guffaws and chuckles every detail that had transpired in the stifling, broken-down outskirts of Grundy. Later, Germ and other funeral home notables would designate "The Case of the Constipated Corpse" as one of the top ranked stories in the oral tradition of funeral home lore.

After a few miles, Cody peeked through the curtains into the solitude of the hearse's back compartment where the recently dethroned and liberated Mr. Fred Kimball rode serenely to his destiny.

Supremely gratified, the young undertaker hoped, not to be constipated and barefoot at the second coming of the Lord.

# Chapter 4

*Mater Nation*

The soft, mild breeze whispered a prophecy, a vague suggestion that the cruel drudgery of summer would at last be ending. Cody noticed it as soon as he stepped outside that morning. It was not so much a feeling of coolness as it was the absence of the oppressive heat and humidity that had plagued the Deep South for the past three months.

During periods of hot weather, a recurring nightmare of wretched discomfort invaded Cody's sleep. Chained to a fencepost in the middle of a withered, simmering cotton field, Cody wore a pair of rough wool pants that he could not remove. As he stood there in his misery, the sweat running down his legs became a frenetic swarm of chiggers and ants. No matter how he positioned his legs, the severe, maddening itch grew worse. Inevitably, he woke up drenched in sweat and grumbled curses at God as he stumbled into the bathroom for a cold midnight shower.

To Cody, many of the best experiences in life could turn sour if indulged in excessively. Too much fine wine could give you a miserable hangover. Even sex was subject to the law of diminishing returns. So were the seasons. He was sick of summer and before autumn was over, he would be tired of that, too. However, one of the benefits of this was that the next season was all that much more sublime when it finally arrived.

Each year about this time, a magical sensation returned to him on the soft breath of a late summer morning. Carried on that first hushed, delicate breeze of temperance was the promise of all that autumn would bring. There would be football games and the scent of burning leaves. He would find his favorite sweater in the attic's winter clothes box and wear it just a bit too soon. Friday night dates would overflow with potentiality and wonder. There would be icy windshields, firewood stacked neatly against the side of the house, and pumpkins foretelling jack-o'-lanterns and aromatic pies.

For Cody, this first hint of autumn was exhilarating, even sacred. Later that morning, as he rode with Pete in the dismal black hearse, even the morbid presence of their passenger, the late Mr. Thomas Goodman, could not diminish his cheerful mood.

"Did you feel it this morning, Pete?"

"Feel what?" Pete's bleak, hung-over eyes were on autopilot as he ploddingly steered the hearse on the incontrovertible course of Mr. Goodman's fate. An open grave awaited him at the Serenity Hill Cemetery in the rich farmland of west Alabama. Cody and Pete had already been on the road for an hour and had another good hour to go before reaching Mr. Goodman's final destination.

Cody continued, "The breeze this morning was a little cooler than usual. It carried a hint of autumn."

Grumpily, Pete said, "I didn't notice it. Whatever it was, it didn't last very long. It's plenty hot now."

Cody admitted that the magical breeze of the morning had long since dissipated into the harsh heat and dust of the day. "Yes," he said, "it's miserable now, that's true. But this morning, just for a little while, there was this delightful breeze. It made me think that fall is not too far away, that better days are coming."

Sourly, Pete argued, "Well, your little breeze is fucking gone now. I can tell you that." He checked the digital thermometer on the dashboard. "Goddammit Cody, it's ninety-four out there already and it's not even noon yet." He glowered at his riding partner as if he considered Cody personally responsible for the unpleasant weather. "I prefer a warm climate as much as any other Southerner, but this summer we've had excessive temperatures for several months, and I am so sick of the heat that I can't stand it anymore. I can't think straight. I can't sleep, either. And, I can't eat because I'm nauseated all the time. I swear to God, if I thought about food right now, I would puke all over the dashboard."

Cody was tempted to share more of his sentiments about the first hint of autumn, but observed his riding partner's stern, embattled face and decided against it. The company psychiatrist had changed Pete's medication again and when this happened, which seemed to be quite often lately, his personality underwent a decidedly turbulent period of adjustment.

When Cody came to the funeral home two years ago, Pete was his mentor, a bright, self-confident and polished young man who the company had designated as a promising future executive. However, since his meltdown, Pete had become a grumpy, scattered and disillusioned character. The public had begun to notice his erratic behavior, which included bouts of extreme anxiety and irrational outbursts. The company management sent him to the psychiatrist, who promptly hospitalized him for a month. His behavior had improved, but sometimes he assumed a zombie-like persona due to heavy medication and still had episodes of irritability.

When management was about to banish Pete to work only in the isolated obscurity of the embalming room, Cody stepped forward to help his friend by volunteering to watch over his permanent riding partner and accept responsibility for his actions. He would observe his friend closely, make sure he followed the medication regimen and intervene quickly to stop any inappropriate conduct. The company agreed that, as long as Pete's public behavior was acceptable and there were no other problems, then the pair could stay together. Now, instead of serving as a mentor for a young apprentice, management had reversed Pete's role and Cody had become his caretaker.

When the rant about the weather was over, they drove in silence while Cody reflected fondly about the morning's little breeze. He was determined that Pete would not spoil it for him.

After a few miles, Pete's irritability dissipated. He said, "I think we are about to go over into Alabama. I recognize that sign over there." He pointed to a faded Burma Shave sign overgrown with kudzu. "This might be a good place to pull over."

"Yeah, good idea," Cody agreed. We don't want to lose anyone when we go through this little town up ahead."

Pete led the small procession of cars onto the shoulder and stopped. Cody went back to talk to the Goodman family, which followed the hearse along with several other cars filled with mourners.

As he approached the first car, the driver rolled down the window, stuck out his head and asked, "Everything okay?"

Cody looked down at Mr. Goodman, Jr., son of the deceased. "Everything is fine. I just wanted everybody to stay tight as we go through this little town up here, so turn on your lights and stay close."

The middle-aged driver nodded his approval, and as he did so, a startling premonition that this Mr. Goodman would soon be following his father to the grave intruded, unbidden, into Cody's mind. He saw Mr. Goodman, Jr., in a casket dressed in a blue pinstripe suit with a white shirt and red tie. His face was slightly bloated. Then, his gray, metallic casket disappeared into the grave. He heard a woman sobbing uncontrollably and knew it was the woman who was now sitting calmly in the passenger seat of the car. Cody had experienced premonitions before but none so vivid and compelling. He stared, transfixed, at Mr. Goodman's face.

"Are you okay?" asked the man.

Cody jumped to attention. "Yes, sorry. I'll tell the others to stay close."

"And lights on," reminded the son.

"That's right, sir. And lights on."

As Cody went down the line of cars with his instructions, the image of Mr. Goodman, Jr., in his casket slowly faded. He hurried back to the hearse and with some urgency appealed to Pete. "Let's go, this place is giving me the creeps."

Pete turned on the headlights and pulled back onto the highway, carefully watching his side-view mirror to make sure everyone followed.

Around the next turn a giant "Alabama the Beautiful" sign nestled in a thick stand of pine trees. Beside it was a tattered wooden sign with a bleached paint job. It read, "Welcome to Haptown. Population 702."

Along the highway through the ragged little town, local farmers brought their produce to peddle to the passing motorists. Their pickup trucks were on the right of way, backed up so close to the edge of the road, you could almost reach out and snatch a couple of squash or cucumbers on the fly. More enterprising residents had constructed makeshift plywood stands along the road to display their produce. Signs read: "Lowry's Homegrown," "Freshest Vegetables in Alabama," "Maters and Melons."

The dress code in Haptown seemed to be coveralls for men and faded dresses, which retained only a faint hint of a pattern, for the women. Mixed breed dogs lazily lay in the dirt and rambunctious youngsters darted back and forth among the stands.

Cody observed, "I can't see who buys their produce. There's not that much traffic on this road."

Pete said, "Maybe they sell it to each other."

Cody replied, "I don't think so. Look at them. They're all selling the same stuff."

Every stand or truck seemed to feature similar produce. There was sweet corn, new potatoes, snap beans, collard greens, peaches and watermelons along with a variety of other homegrown fruits and vegetables.

Pete ventured, "Maybe it's sort of a social occasion. It's Saturday, right? They probably all come down here just to hobnob with each other. Selling their produce is of secondary importance."

Cody noticed the worn out trucks and the stands that were in disrepair. He doubted that money was unimportant to these people.

As the funeral procession crawled through town, many of the locals stopped talking and bowed respectfully to the passing hearse, striking a chord of sentimentality in Cody's heart. Some of the good folks removed their tired straw hats and held them over their hearts. Traffic in the opposite lane stopped in reverent deference to the deceased.

Cody found himself dreaming about the uncomplicated life in a small town. The zeitgeist of folksiness had some quiet appeal. He asked Pete, "Ever wonder what it would be like to live in a place like this?"

"I know what you're going to say, but I wouldn't like it."

Cody asked, "What was I going to say?"

"Something about how great life would be in the serene simplicity of this kind of town. You would know everyone and everything about them. And don't forget the fish fry at the church on Friday night and bingo on Saturday in the basement of the courthouse on the town square. Get the picture yet? Am I right?"

Cody conceded, "That's pretty close. I see you've thought about it before."

"You're right," said Pete with conviction. "Thought about it and rejected it."

"Why?"

"I don't want people to know that much about me, especially after my nervous breakdown. Can you imagine the gossip in a place like this? They would probably think I was some kind of serial killer just because I have to visit the shrink every week."

The funeral procession had cleared the town when they saw the flashing blue lights of a roadblock ahead. The patrol car was in the middle of the highway and cars were going around it on either side after a friendly wave from what appeared to be the local sheriff. As the convoy of mourners approached, the sheriff pointed to the hearse and motioned for them to pull over on the shoulder. Pete maneuvered to the side of the highway. He looked behind him to make sure all the cars in the procession had followed.

As the stereotypical southern sheriff meandered over to the hearse, Cody thought there must be a secret cloning factory that replicated these guys. The officer's belly hung over his low-riding belt and his intimidating sunglasses were at least three shades darker than normal, undoubtedly, Cody mused, to hide his disingenuous eyes. His quadruple chin cascaded down the front of his thick, short neck. He was vigorously chewing either gum or tobacco. Cody could not tell which one until the officer launched a sizable wad of brown spittle to the ground just before he spoke.

"Hello, my friends, and welcome to the municipality of Haptown. I am Sheriff Cletus Peavine, at your service." As he spoke, a wide, genuine smile grew wider across his pudgy face.

Pete said, "Nice to meet you, Sheriff Peavine. Very nice town you have here."

"Oh, indeed it is, my friends, indeed it is. I just wish you boys had time to visit some of the local folks. They're mighty fine people here. They surely are. Mighty fine." The sheriff stepped back from the hearse to check out the short funeral convoy. "I see you've got about eight cars of mourners here."

Pete said, "That's right. Those are the bereaved family and friends of the late Mr. Goodman, who is riding in the back with us." Pete used his thumb to motion to the rear of the hearse.

Sheriff Peavine peeked in through the curtains of the back compartment for a glimpse of the casket. "My, my, you just don't ever know when the good Lord is going to call you home, do you?"

Pete rolled his eyes at Cody and said, "No, you sure don't."

The sheriff continued, "That's why I always try to live at the foot of the cross. That's what my grand pappy taught me. He sure did. He said that if you live at the foot of the cross, you don't ever have to worry if Jesus is going to come back and find you in bed with another man's wife. The scriptures say that the Lord is coming as 'a thief in the night.'"

Pete said, "Yeah, I sure don't want to be caught in bed with another man's wife at the second coming of Jesus."

Cody interjected, "Yeah that definitely would not be cool."

The sheriff lowered his head for a better look at Cody in the passenger seat. His voice was hushed in reverence. "You boys know what a mater is, don't you?"

The question annoyed Cody. "Yes, we know what a mater is, Sheriff. It's a very good homegrown tomato. At least that's what it is in Mississippi."

The Sheriff grinned widely, relishing the inadequacy of Cody's reply. "That's not the half of it, son. Sure, it has to be homegrown, but a mater must be vine-ripened and extra juicy and have a flavor that is absolutely divine. In fact, I'll bet you didn't even know that Reverend Lonnie Moody from the Ephesus Baptist Church blesses all the vegetable crops in these parts. He makes the rounds to every garden, to the faithful and the heathen, to the gentile and the Jew. Or, he would go to the Jew, but we don't have any, at least that we know of. But if we did, Brother Moody would be there at their gardens, too, bringing down the spirit of the Lord to sanctify the vegetables. That's why our maters are special, like nowhere else in the world."

Cynically, Cody asked, "What about the livestock? Does he bless the animals as well?"

Sheriff Peavine examined Cody carefully as if he were trying to decide if the young undertaker was mocking him. Some of the smile evaporated from his round, chubby face. He answered Cody evenly. "No, Pastor Moody's specialty is vegetables. Brother Hosea Hill, from over at the Evangelical Chapel, does the animals. God gave him a gift for relating to critters of all kinds. He has a way with them.

Usually, he preaches with a couple of rattlesnakes in his arms. Never been bit either. Except his oldest boy, the one who used to play lead guitar in the choir, got bit one time handing his daddy a copperhead. He didn't quite die though. Not all the way. Now, he just sits on the front porch in his diapers and stares out at the road. Every once in a while he'll wave at you, but mostly he just sits and stares."

After a reverent pause, apparently to reflect upon the fate of the preacher's hapless boy, the sheriff continued, "So, we have maters here that are just not available in other parts of the world. Pastor Moody says that when you die and stand up there before the Pearly Gates, Saint Peter asks if you ever ate a mater from Haptown. And if you haven't, Saint Peter says, 'You have not lived the abundant life as the Lord intended until you have partaken of a mater from Haptown.' And he sends you back down here to eat one before he gives you a pass into heaven."

Cody was increasingly impatient. Mr. Goodman, Jr., had already made them late due to an untimely attack of diarrhea in the funeral home parking lot. Pete drove over to the drugstore for some Pepto Bismol, which Mr. Goodman urgently consumed, but still it was an hour before he felt comfortable enough to get on the road. Cody imagined the scene at the cemetery. Already, anxious gravediggers were kicking at dirt clods and glancing at their watches in macabre anticipation of the arrival of their newest tenant. Local friends of the deceased who had come to the cemetery for the graveside service were baking in the insufferable mid-day heat.

Urgently, he admonished Sheriff Peavine, "With all due respect to you and your maters here in Haptown, we are involved in a funeral here. These folks behind us are the bereaved. Don't you think it's little improper to ask these grieving family and friends to turn around and go buy tomatoes?"

The sheriff looked back at the cars lined up behind the hearse but was unmoved. "It won't take that long. Just go on back, would you? Just go buy some damn maters and be on your way."

Cody's anger was rising, "What are you going to do, arrest us if we don't buy tomatoes?"

The sheriff jerked up straight and looked back at the patrol car. He waved to his deputy to come join him. "Arrest you? No. Just show me your permit and be on your way."

Pete was incredulous, "We don't need a permit. What permit?"

The sheriff grinned with satisfaction, as if he had treed a fat 'possum. "That would be a Permit to Convey Human Remains through the Municipality of Haptown, Alabama. If you don't have such a document on your person, the fine is one hundred fifty dollars. That's about what two new helmets cost for the Haptown High Football Team. The coach called me last week and told me they were short a helmet or two."

Pete asked, "Well, we don't want to pay the fine, so where do we get one of those permits?"

With increasing delight, Sheriff Peavine proclaimed, "Can't get one today. Courthouse is closed on Saturday. Sunday, too. Come back the first of the week."

Cody was aghast. "We can't wait until Monday. We have a corpse in the back of our vehicle. We have a traumatized family and an open grave. We can't wait two days to bury this man."

Sheriff Peavine thought for a moment, "Well, I guess your situation is an emergency of sorts. You should have declared that sooner. In an emergency, I am authorized to issue permits as I see fit."

Pete said, "Okay, we want to apply for a permit."

"No problem. I can issue you one right here. The fee is one hundred fifty dollars."

Cody and Pete looked at each other in disbelief.

"Truth is, boys, just about anything you do is going to cost you a hundred and fifty dollars, except going back and buying some maters from the local folks. You can make a U-turn right here." He drew a wide u with his arm. "And take that caravan of mourners with you. Nothing will cheer them up better than a few recently sanctified Haptown maters."

The sheriff turned away for a moment to talk to a local woman with a car full of kids. Cody thought she looked good for rural Alabama until she smiled. Her teeth had turned a sickly gray. She was smiling real big at him now, brushing her hand across her breast and fiddling with her hair, a real redneck flirt. After she moved on, Sheriff Peavine turned back to the hearse. His mood had softened.

"It won't hurt any of you to spend a few dollars back there. Some of these folks are really struggling. Some may lose their homes to the bank. When you think of it, it's not much that I'm asking, boys."

He turned to watch the woman's car as it disappeared over the hill toward town.

"I'll tell you what. I'll leave it up to you. You can drive on through and ignore your fellow human beings who are suffering. Or you can put a star in your heavenly crown and buy a few items from the townsfolk. It's up to you."

"No permit?" asked Pete.

"No permit."

"No fine?" asked Cody.

"No fine."

Cody looked at Pete and at once knew they agreed on what to do next. He smiled as Pete put the hearse in gear and started his broad U-turn on the highway. Cody waved to the cars behind them to follow.

Twenty minutes later the caravan approached Sheriff Peavine's roadblock again. Pete pulled up and asked, "The family wants to know, when they come back through here this afternoon, will they have to buy maters again?"

"Why, hell no, they won't. Just tell them to put a mater on their dashboard. That way I'll know they done their part."

As the procession pulled past the flashing blue lights, Cody jumped out of the hearse to make sure all the cars got through. The sheriff, as each car passed, made a gesture in the air that looked disturbingly like the sign of the cross. With the biggest grin in Alabama, he proclaimed to the grieving in each vehicle, "God bless you, good friends. Haptown thanks you."

Two hours later at Serenity Hill Cemetery, the graveside service was over. Cody watched as the family and friends of the late Mr. Goodman retreated to the shade of a big sycamore tree in the middle of the cemetery. They spread tablecloths on the ground and began laying out covered dishes. Cody knew what likely was in them. It was usually the same fare. There would be fried chicken, potato salad and deviled eggs. There was usually pecan pie or boiled custard for desert and someone would bring a big five-gallon thermos of iced tea or lemonade. And he was certain that today there would be some of the best tomatoes in Alabama.

Cody had learned this postmortem picnic was part of a grieving ritual that country folk often followed. When the service was over, they retreated to a nearby area to eat while the cemetery workers came to fill in the grave and place flower arrangements over the freshly shoveled soil. After lunch, and perhaps a brief nap by some of the overfed men, the mourners would file by the grave for a final goodbye. There might be a few subdued sobs or a whimper here and there, but for the most part, the crying was over.

As the group under the sycamore tree spread out their lunch, Cody and Pete stood at the casket. In a few moments, they would lower it into the grave and call over the gravediggers to start filling in. But not yet. Nothing must seem too rushed.

Cody always had a few last words for the deceased. It was part of his private ritual at the grave. He had developed quite a talent for speaking through his clenched teeth so that no one out of earshot would know what was happening, like he was some ventriloquist from Village of the Damned.

But Pete was there, and he could hear, and it drove him absolutely crazy. He even reported it to Germ, who made Cody go to the company psychiatrist for three sessions. This did not faze the young undertaker, however, and he continued to relish his conversations with the dead.

After a few minutes, Cody turned to the casket and opened the lid, ostensibly for a final check of the corpse. Just a last look to make sure everything was in order. When he opened the coffin, the lid conveniently hid him from the view of the mourners under the tree and the gravediggers, too, who crouched nearby in the meager shade of a large granite monument.

As he ministered to the deceased, Cody recited the scriptures in a soft, reverent voice. "Though your sins be as scarlet, they shall be washed as white as snow. Though they be red as crimson, they shall become like wool."

Pete was uncomfortable. The gravediggers were close. Urgently, he whispered, "Get on with it, man. People are going to start wondering what's going on here. They'll think something is wrong."

Cody ignored him. "Now, you take care, Mr. Goodman. Hope it goes well for you on Judgment Day, whenever that comes." He straightened the corpse's tie and brushed a miniscule piece of lint from his lapel. "I'll be along to join you before too long. You never know, I might be right behind you."

Cody reached over, put his arm around Pete's shoulder, and drew him close. "And if you run into the Almighty, please put in a good word for Pete here, for he is sorely in need of forgiveness for his debauchery and wicked ways."

Pete got right up to Cody's ear and hissed, "Damn it, I told you to cut that crap out."

Oblivious to the protest, Cody continued his conversation with the corpse a moment longer. Then, with the ceremonial majesty of a high priest performing a sacred rite, he slowly pulled out from the inside pocket of his suit a particularly fine Haptown tomato, a sanctified mater of supreme quality.

Reverently, Cody placed it in the corpse's folded hands.

As he lowered the casket lid for the last time, he whispered, "Just in case, Mr. Goodman. Just in case."

The next morning coffee spilled everywhere. Cody dropped the full pot on the staff lounge floor. It exploded in a startling crash, sending hot coffee and shards of glass over the floor, the furniture and the pant legs of some unfortunate bystanders.

Cody was holding the coffee when Germ came in with the news. "You guys won't believe this, but you are headed back to Serenity Hill. You know that Thomas Goodman you buried over there yesterday? Well, his son got up this morning and dropped dead in his shower. Heart attack."

As Pete and a couple of other employees scurried to clean up the mess, Cody eased himself into a chair and stared blankly ahead. Then, a vision of Mr. Goodman sitting on the deck behind his house filled his consciousness. The man was chatting with his wife and drinking a cup of coffee. The Sunday newspaper lay folded on a small table beside him. Intuitively, Cody sensed the truth of his vision. He knew that somewhere, perhaps in another reality, Mr. Goodman was drinking his morning coffee, and at the same time, he was dead. The young undertaker felt he was living in two worlds simultaneously.

Germ waited for a moment for the confusion to subside and continued, "Guess I shouldn't have broken the news to a man with a full pot of coffee in his hand. Anyway, I figured you guys are the best team to send over there, since you are familiar with the situation and all. Maybe you can look in on your new friend, the sheriff, and pick up some more of those sanctified tomatoes. Doesn't look like they agreed with Mr. Goodman, though."

Pete asked, "When will we be going?"

"I don't know yet. The wife is coming by later today to make the arrangements." Germ looked down at Cody, who was still staring at the wall, "You okay, son?"

Pete interceded. "Yeah, he's fine. It's just a strange coincidence, that's all. Kind of spooky. We were with the guy yesterday and he looked fine."

Germ admitted, "At first, I had a weird feeling about it, too. When they called from the hospital emergency room for us to come pick up Thomas Goodman, I thought, how could this be? We just buried that rascal yesterday, and here he comes again."

Pete said, "He wasn't exactly the poster child for a fitness club, but he wasn't in that bad a shape. Wasn't that old, either. He looked to be about fifty or so."

Cheerfully, Germ proclaimed as he stepped into the hall, "Well, you never know when the good Lord is going to call you home, do you?"

All that day Cody desperately rationalized yesterday's premonition of Mr. Goodman, Jr.'s, burial in a hundred different ways. He knew the man would surely die someday, but not today, not so soon.

Late that afternoon, he was standing with Germ and Pete in the back foyer of the funeral home. They were surveying the parking lot when a familiar vehicle pulled up. It was the Goodman's family car, and inside sat the woman who had been sobbing hysterically in Cody's premonition. Only now, she was not crying. She had the blank, numb stare of abject devastation. In her bereaved trance, she stepped out of the passenger seat of the car and stood, gazing ahead at nothing in particular.

The driver of the car, one of the Goodman's teenage daughters, opened the trunk and retrieved a plastic garment bag. She unzipped it and reached in.

Cody turned away. He could not look. The awful pang of anxiety spewed up his spine like a geyser. Desperately, he whispered his mantra of the day, "Nothing but coincidence. Nothing but coincidence."

Oblivious to Cody's ordeal, Germ offered his commentary on the activity in the parking lot. "Well, it looks like the family is bringing in Mr. Goodman's funeral suit, something special so he will look spiffy in the casket. Because everyone knows, it is supremely important for a man to look suave in his coffin."

Silently, Cody pleaded, No. Don't say it. Don't!

Germ continued, "And it looks like he's going to be wearing a nice blue pinstripe suit with a white shirt and red tie." He smiled and nodded his approval. "Nice choice, Mrs. Goodman. Your husband will look debonair in that outfit, as debonair as a dead man can."

# Chapter 5

*The Recalcitrant Casket*

The winter storm came at a bad time for the burial.

Last night, Cody had retired to his room in the funeral home dormitory with the comfortable belief that the few inches of snow forecast for the area would present no great obstacle to the proper and dignified interment of the late Mrs. Lydia Dinwittie.

The streets would be almost clear of traffic because few drivers would dare risk the snow-covered roads. Folks in the South had great respect for winter weather. Because of their lack of experience navigating snowy roads, most people would just stay home. There was never a soul born in Mississippi who fought against the notion of a day off from work because of bad weather, or for any other reason, for that matter. While a good day's work never hurt anybody, neither did a good day's rest. And nothing created more angst in the gut of a sweat-loving Southerner than the weather forecaster's stern declaration, "Five inches in Texas and headed this way."

Now, as the young undertaker stood in the back foyer of the funeral home sipping his morning coffee and surveying the grounds, he saw the reflection of his scowling visage in the picture window. He stepped to the side for a better view of the lawn. The face with the frown followed him, so he turned at an angle to look out over the parking lot.

The cause of Cody's scowl was not snow. There was no snow. However, there was something worse, far worse. Outside, the sleet cascaded to the ground in shimmering waves of brittle white rain. It rattled down from the frozen rooftops and bounced off the icy asphalt as the scowl deepened on the young undertaker's freshly shaven face.

Snow was one thing. It was inconvenient but workable. Ice was quite another thing entirely. Ice was catastrophic. Since the streets would surely be deserted even more because of the ice, the ride out to Concord Cemetery would be manageable. However, the hills of the cemetery were steep and the road between the aged granite grave markers was narrow and winding. The snow tires Germ had ordered to be installed on funeral home vehicles would be almost worthless.

"Nobody said anything about sleet," said Germ irritably as he walked up beside Cody. The senior undertaker shivered as he placed his hand against the icy window. Then he stepped back into the warmth of the room and took a gratifying sip from his over-sized coffee mug.

"Have you ever driven a limo out into an ice storm?" Germ asked.

Cody shook his head and smiled. "I think you know the answer to that question, sir."

Germ nodded. "Don't worry about it. You'll do just fine. It's not as hard as you probably imagine. However, I'm plenty concerned about leading a procession with a lot of decrepit old people at the wheels of their Buick sedans. Trust me, there will be very few four-wheel drive vehicles in this motorcade. If the old coots don't fall on their asses in the parking lot, surely they will crash into something before we get out to the cemetery."

As if to validate Germ's fears, they watched as an elderly gentleman with a car packed full of old ladies, still looking spunky from the previous day's wash and set, spun into the parking lot and skidded into the wall of the garage. The old driver got out of the car, surveyed his dented fender, shook his fist at the sky, then got back in and proceeded to join the row of vehicles already lining up for the joyride to the cemetery.

Germ observed grimly, "See what I mean? Old people and ice just don't mix."

Cody asked, "How many cars are we expecting?"

"This is a prominent family. I would expect sixty cars under ordinary circumstances. But, given the weather, more than half of those will stay home or wreck before they get here. So, I'd say we should expect about twenty or so."

The two men stood and stared out the window, each contemplating the frightful consequences the icy weather could have for the orderly burial of the late erstwhile socialite, Mrs. Dinwittie.

After a few minutes, Pete hurried up the steps from the staff lounge in the basement. There was a compelling thrust in his step, the urgency that often comes with the pronouncement of ill fortune. He cleared his throat, paused a beat, and then proclaimed, "Now they're calling for sleet and freezing rain to go on all day. They say we could have two inches of ice on the ground before it's over."

Germ, whose sour mood was intensifying by the minute, did not receive the news gladly. "Who the hell are 'they'? I hate it when you say that, Pete. You say, 'They did this.' or, 'they said that.' But who are 'they,' really? These mysterious fucks you are always quoting. Do you have them locked up somewhere in a secret place? Just who the hell are 'they'?"

Germ's tirade caught Pete off guard, but he managed to eke out a subdued response. "The weatherman," he said hesitantly. "I was just watching the local weather down in the lounge." He looked over at Cody, who smiled sympathetically, an expression that let Pete know that he could count on his friend for support. Emboldened by this affirmation, he turned back to Germ. "Don't take it out on me because you don't like the weather forecast. Jesus, Germ. Lighten up, would you?"

Before Germ could launch another salvo, Cody quickly interjected, "To put a more positive spin on things, I guess we're lucky that the funeral is early in the day. Otherwise, we'd have to deal with a much bigger accumulation of ice." He then flattered the senior mortician. "And thanks to Germ's artful persuasion, the family canceled the funeral mass at the church. Now we only have to worry about driving out to the cemetery for the graveside service."

The room fell silent for a moment and Cody glanced down at his watch. It was seven-thirty. The family had scheduled the service at the cemetery to begin at nine o'clock. All other families had postponed the funerals scheduled for the day because of the prospect of bad weather, however, Mrs. Dinwittie's kinfolk were adamant about going forward with her service. Cody thought it was because most family members were from out of town and needed to get back to their jobs. Moreover, it would be unseemly to conduct the official reading of the grand old lady's Last Will and Testament before the burial.

The bereaved family and friends along with the priest and his entourage would gather at the funeral home and drive to the cemetery in a procession that would depart promptly at eight-thirty.

Cody said, "I guess I'll go over to the stateroom in a few minutes and check in with the family. We've got to leave here in about an hour."

Germ continued to glare out at the icy landscape.

Pete ventured optimistically, "Hey, Germ, don't look so glum. How bad could the streets get in just an hour?"

"Plenty bad," said Germ with resounding gloom. "Plenty bad."

There was no arguing with Germ's realistic assessment. Cody took another swig of coffee as he played out in his mind a scenario that included the hearse sliding into a telephone pole and Mrs. Dinwittie's casket crashing onto the ice-covered street.

Germ, who could well have been imagining a similar catastrophe, groaned and headed for the corridor with a quick, purposeful step.

Pete called out to him, "Where are you going, Germ?"

"To find my goddamned golf shoes."

Pete turned to Cody and said, "Now that is going to look real nice, isn't it? I know those shoes. Imagine, brown and white wingtip golf shoes with tassels sticking out from underneath the pants of a black funeral suit. It will look like shit. He can't be serious."

"I think he's serious. Besides, nobody will be paying attention to our shoes." Cody was wishing he had brought his old baseball cleats down to the funeral home dormitory when he moved in. They would be the perfect shoes for this occasion and would not look as out of place as golf shoes. He could even rub a little shine on them. However, he did have a good pair of snow boots that would provide decent traction.

Cody checked the thermometer just outside the back door. It read twenty-eight degrees, a drop of one degree in the last twenty minutes. Outside, a whirlwind howled and spun the sleet around in a crazy circular dance. Above him, ice pellets crackled and pinged as they ricocheted off the glass skylight.

For some mysterious reason, this was a catalyst for something deep in Cody's soul. He felt a familiar emptiness rise in him.

He wondered where Mrs. Dinwittie was now. Would she sleep forever, or had she already awakened in some magical promised land where the air shone like diamonds and angels whispered comforting words that made her forget the ugly experiences of her life? He could see her now, standing before a golden throne with a face of ecstasy, a visage much younger and very different from the one she wore in the casket down the hall.

Outside, the wind howled again as a chattering group of mourners came in the back door and broke the spell. Cody said to Pete as he turned up the hall, "I saw her. She's okay. She was smiling."

Spooked, Pete asked, "Who did you see?"

He called back over his shoulder, "Mrs. Dinwittie."

An hour and a half later, Cody felt the disquieting tentacles of anxiety spread through his midsection and up his spine as he guided his awkward limousine through the icy gates of Concord Cemetery. He was dreading the drive up to the hilly gravesite. Though sleet and freezing rain had continued unrelentingly, aside from a couple of old ladies who fell in the parking lot and the geezer who crashed into the garage, nothing untoward had occurred during the drama of Mrs. Dinwittie's funeral. The drive to the cemetery was painstakingly slow, and some of the cars dropped out, but none of the vehicles in the beleaguered procession had suffered anything more than a few awkward skids across the treacherous highway.

As expected, few other vehicles were on the road, and the motorcade was under the protection of a police escort, off-duty officers who moonlighted to provide safe passage for funeral processions navigating city traffic. Cody was particularly thankful for the escorts today, since they made it possible for the procession to avoid stopping at traffic lights. Before the funeral convoy started out, Germ strongly admonished the officers, "Whatever happens out there, don't let our cars get into a situation where we have to stop. If we stop, half these vehicles will not be able to start up again on these icy streets."

Now, as they came to the first of many sharp curves in the cemetery, Cody became increasingly apprehensive. Looking down on his pale, strained knuckles, he tried to bolster himself with a little humor. He thought, look, I have a death grip on the steering wheel. Ha ha. However, in the next instant, he briefly spun out of control on the perilous road, bringing his secret humor and ensuing smile to an abrupt end.

The bereaved family packed into the back of his limousine let out a collective gasp.

Involuntarily, Cody barked out harshly, "Damnation!" Whenever startled, he always used that expletive, regardless of the circumstances. So he was fairly certain that if he died in an accident of some kind, his last utterance on the earth would be "Damnation," hardly an endearing expression to have on his lips as he approached the Pearly Gates.

"Sorry," he called back to the passengers as he regained control of the unwieldy, stretched vehicle.

There were no complaints from the family. They were a polite, well-bred bunch. Up to this point, an occasional, subdued sob was all they had allowed themselves. The deceased was the matriarch of this prominent family, and though her death had been unexpected, her kinfolk were reserved and dignified in their grief.

Cody looked up at the hearse in front of him and saw the reflection of Germ's grinning face in the side mirror. Germ had seen the young undertaker's skid in the family car and was having a good laugh. For a moment, Cody was irritated at the old mortician but soon smiled as he imagined the picture of the extra-long limo swerving from side to side with the grim-faced family squeezed into the rear seats like slices of lunchmeat in a vacuum-sealed variety pack.

The wind blew the freezing rain and sleet sideways now, and Cody reached down to increase the speed of the windshield wipers which were making an irritating, grating sound as they scraped across the packed ice on the glass. He tried to spray the window with the car's windshield deicer, but the mechanism was hopelessly frozen. He glanced in his rearview mirror to see how the other cars were doing. To his surprise, everyone in the struggling procession seemed to be fine, but there was a marked decrease in the number of vehicles. Cody was not surprised that there had been some defections since they left the funeral home. Under the circumstances, this was quite understandable, but he hoped, for the family's sake, that a respectable number of mourners would make it to the gravesite.

On the next curve, Cody got a glimpse of the front of the caravan where Pete was at the wheel of the pallbearer's limousine. He was carefully leading the procession around the slippery curves, his head jerking from side to side, as he surveyed the road and surrounding landscape for trouble.

Johnny was sitting with Pete on the front seat. The fourth undertaker assigned to Mrs. Dinwittie's interment was an experienced funeral home veteran and knew every nuance of the winding roads of Concord Cemetery. He was giving Pete advice on how to negotiate the perilous curves. In the back of their limousine, eight aged and decrepit pallbearers gazed, grim and pale-faced, out the frosty windows.

Next in line was the monsignor's car, the back seat filled with acolytes. Riding in the passenger seat was the abbot of a local monastery, which the Dinwittie family had generously endowed. The priestly firepower was impressive. Germ told Cody that the family was taking no chances on the Grande Dame making it into heaven.

The convoy inched along the frigid lane flanked by gray, granite tombstones draped in ice. Finally, it advanced around a steep curve up toward the summit of the last hill. Cody thought it would have been better to approach the grave from below, but Germ had overruled the idea, saying the family, a generally portly group, would have a tough time climbing up the slippery hill with its coating of ice. He thought it would be easier to walk down from above the grave. Then, after the service, they could proceed to the bottom of the hill, and Cody could pick them up there. Besides, Mrs. Dinwittie was a rather large woman, and it would be hard on the pallbearers to haul her up the hill even without the wintry conditions.

Cody allowed himself another quick peek in his rearview mirror to see if the other cars were still keeping up. The caravan of mourners was in sight but keeping a comfortable distance. He sighed thankfully, as the motorcade pulled to a halt on a level area at the top of the hill.

He looked at the tent set up over the grave about halfway down the steep slope. The cemetery men were huddled underneath it. One of them waved and stepped forward to knock off a couple of icicles clinging to the side of the canvas.

Cody turned to speak to the family. "Please remain in the car until we get everything ready. We don't want you to wait out in this weather any longer than absolutely necessary. I'll come back for you in a few minutes and we can all walk down to the grave together with the pallbearers and the priests."

After a couple a grateful acknowledgments from the back, Cody opened his door and quickly stepped out into the storm. The wind had picked up and the sleet stung his face. Thankful for his snow boots with their thick rubber tread, he inched his way up to the other undertakers who had huddled under a leafless oak tree by the hearse.

Excitedly, Pete was pointing to Germ's feet, "Look at your shoes! Are those your golf shoes? What did you do to them?"

Germ replied, "I cut off the tassels and spray painted them black."

Pete said, "Well, the paint won't last in this weather. Look, it's already starting to peel. They look like shit."

"Don't you worry about it, young man," said the senior undertaker. "They just have to last about twenty more minutes. I've done this in the past, you know, probably before you were born, so just fuck off! These are the consummate funeral shoes for freezing rain."

"Let's get on with it, guys." Johnny's teeth were chattering. "We can talk about Germ's shoes some other time, goddamn it."

"There's trouble in the pallbearers' car." Pete, who held his hand over his face as a shield from incoming ice pellets, grimly reported this ominous development. "They don't even want to get out of the car, much less carry the casket."

Johnny looked back at the pallbearers' limo, and then weighed in on the matter. "Yeah, look at those geezers. If we ask them to help with the casket, it will be a windfall for the emergency room. Why don't we just call the hospital right now so they can send out a few ambulances?"

Germ was quick to add, "I see multiple lawsuits in the works here."

Johnny suggested, "Maybe we should ask for a couple of volunteers. There must be some able-bodied men among these mourners here." They all turned and surveyed the friends of the family as some of the reluctant group tentatively disembarked their cars pulled up behind the family limousine.

It was evident to Cody that some of the bereaved did not intend even exit their cars. And of those who did, there was not one man who appeared to be under the age of sixty.

He declared, "I see no one."

Germ agreed. "All I see there are more lawsuits." He pointed down the hill to the cemetery men who had moved from under the tent to the shelter of a nearby family mausoleum with a covered portico. "We could ask Henry, the cemetery manager over there, but he is always complaining about his back."

Cody inquired, "What about the gravediggers?" He pointed out the two men in coveralls who were with Henry.

Germ said, "They can't help us. Their union contract specifically prohibits it."

Cody was incredulous, "Surely, there isn't a union for gravediggers."

Germ cleared his throat and proclaimed, "The four of us will just have to take our chances. There's no other way. We can each grab a corner of the casket and ease it down the hill. The monsignor will be ahead of us. I'll ask him to take his time."

Cody was watching the mourners guardedly make their way down the icy slope to the gravesite. Some were taking tiny sideways steps. All of them looked worried. One had already fallen and two others, old ladies, astonishingly in high heels, just sat down on the ice-encrusted grass. The gusty wind wildly whipped their perm-curled hair which was the color of a Dallas Cowboys' football helmet.

It took a few minutes, but about a dozen mourners made it all the way down to the tent. They formed a shivering semicircle around the folding chairs reserved for the family in front of the grave. Cody thought that it was a respectable showing, given the circumstances. He felt good for the family that there would be a fair number of friends with them for the brief graveside service.

He looked back up toward the pallbearers' limousine. Mortified faces were gazing back at him. "What can we do with the pallbearers? We can't leave them sitting in the car."

Now the monsignor saw that everything was ready at the gravesite, so he and his passengers left the warmth of their car and began to take the crucifix and incense out of the trunk. The abbot, his robes billowing in the wind, was holding on to the side of the vehicle as he shuffled his way toward the hearse. There was no time left to debate the dilemma of the reluctant pallbearers.

Authoritatively, Germ spoke. "Here's the deal. Pete, you go up to the pallbearers' limo and have a Come to Jesus meeting with that group of soon-to-be-deceased gentlemen. We'll let them off the hook on carrying the casket, but surely they can hobble down to the grave. They can line up right behind the monsignor and his group. Then we can fall in behind them with the casket and the family can follow us. We'll just have to take it very slowly and deliberately. We can't let anyone hurry us."

The other men glanced at each other skeptically, but no one had a better idea. So they all murmured their assent as they broke the huddle and walked slowly on the ice to their respective duties. Cody looked down at his feet as he cautiously maneuvered an awkward, flat-footed gait for maximum traction, and tentatively tested his balance before each step. He waited outside the car for a couple of minutes to let Pete have some time to persuade the pallbearers. Then he opened the back door of the family limo and announced, "It's time."

While he assisted the portly family to struggle out of the car, Pete was lining up the priests and the pallbearers who, except for one, had agreed to walk down to the grave.

When the family arrived at the hearse, everyone was in position. With a nod from Germ, Cody and Pete walked up, opened the rear door and rolled out the casket. Each of the four men grabbed a corner.

The monsignor fired up the incense, sending up gray clouds of acrid smoke, which were blown chaotically by the wind. The crucifix bearer lined up in front of the priests, with the other altar boys behind.

Cody had a passing vision of the boy slipping and the crucifix falling to the ground. He wondered about the fate of such crucifixes. Was it an irreparable desecration or did folks just wipe it off and proceed? When he was a boy, the teachers were horrified one day when someone let the American flag touch the ground. No one knew what happened to the flag. A new one appeared shortly after the incident.

However, he did not have time to contemplate such issues as he felt the casket tugging hard on his arms. This was not going to be easy. To make matters worse, he was on the same side as sixty-year-old Johnny. This meant he would have to carry more than his share of the load. The weight of the casket was a substantial addition to Mrs. Dinwittie's generous frame. It was solid mahogany with an ornate crucifix carved into the lid. Nothing but the best for Mama.

The monsignor started his chant, nudged the crucifix bearer, and the beleaguered procession headed for the grave. The pallbearers fell in line, working their way down the hill in a sort of a guarded shuffle. One turned his ankle and fell over. Another dropped out of line and sat defiantly on top of a frost-caked tombstone. The ice had completely covered the ground and formed a thick crust over the top of the brown, dead grass. As the gloomy procession crunched its way down the hill, it sounded like a herd of elephants walking on a bed of seashells.

The undertakers struggled, bent over with the weight of their burden. Cody was thinking that Germ was right. They would never have made it hauling the casket up the hill from below. He glanced back to see if the family was falling in line. They were right there, holding on to one another as they half-shuffled, half-slid their way down the hill, their eyes fixed on the casket in front of them.

The monsignor's chant grew louder, and someone back in the family group let out a heart-rending wail. A mourner down at the tent answered with an emphatic response, an aggressive moan followed by a string of descending blubbers. Cody hoped this would not evolve into one of those dreadful crying contests in which various family members and friends tried to demonstrate who loved the deceased the most by a progression of sobs, moans and howls of bereavement. The contest usually culminated in someone playing the ultimate grief card, a dramatic faint.

Cody was now feeling the cumulative strain of carrying the dead woman and her coffin for several yards. His arms ached terribly and his legs bent painfully. He glanced across the casket. Germ's distorted face was bulging red in desperation. The blood vessels on this neck and forehead were alarmingly swollen and pulsating. Pete's eyes were about to explode under the strain.

Cody peered ahead of him to see how Johnny was doing. Though he could not see the older man's face, he heard his labored wheezing and the increasingly loud moans escaping through his clenched teeth.

Suddenly, Johnny caught his foot on the side of a low-standing tombstone. His other foot began slipping on the ice. The heavy wood coffin lunged forward as the older man's knees buckled. He let out a frantic yelp of pain followed by an anguished groan. As Johnny's corner of the casket dipped perilously, Cody instinctively began to work his way down the side rail toward the middle. But before he could inch his way very far, the old undertaker completely collapsed on the ground in a fetal position grabbing his groin.

To his horror, Cody was alone on his side of the casket. He looked over at Germ, whose face was a grim mask of anguish. Pete's eyes were bulging out of their sockets.

A state of equilibrium existed for a brief moment, as though the casket were trying to make up its mind what to do. Then, heeding the inevitable call of gravity, it thrust forward and downward in a wild, erratic plunge. The undertakers held on, digging in their heels as they tried to lower the casket to the ground. But both gravity and inertia were decidedly in favor of the coffin. Its momentum forced them to take another quick step, and then another. Now they were running with a falling casket. Pete stepped into a hole and Cody saw his agonized face disappear over the side. The casket hit the ground with such force that Germ and Cody lost their grip. Germ had the presence of mind to call out a quick alarm to those in front. "Look out! She's coming through!" It was too late. The runaway casket plowed through the remaining pallbearers, scattering them like bowling pins.

The forward motion of the casket slowed only briefly as it blasted through the elderly group and thundered on. Now it was in the open again and gaining speed. The monsignor heard the commotion and turned around, but the horror of what he saw immobilized him. The altar boys scattered and the abbot dove to the side as the casket roared down on the monsignor. In spite of a belated effort to jump out of the way, the priest was dealt a glancing blow at the kneecaps. The casket scraped the shine from the tops of his Gucci slippers and veered off toward a steeper part of the hill.

Some of the more agile members of the Dinwittie family had started to pursue the casket. Now they, too, were out of control and could not stop themselves from gaining more speed with each awkward, desperate step. One vainly shouted, "Mama, come back!" After a few more steps, the pursuing family members collapsed in an amorphous heap of sprawling flesh. The horrified mourners who had gathered under the tent by the grave gawked in disbelief as Mrs. Dinwittie, in her sepulchered sled, sped past them.

Cody had pursued the casket ever since it tore away from his grasp. He got close a few times only to see it pull away again. The icy hillside was treacherous, and he felt himself losing more control with each step. If he fell, there was no one else close enough to stop the casket before it hit the road below. In a final desperate attempt, he made a diving headlong lunge and was able to grab the back handle. He hung on, dragging his feet as he skidded on his stomach behind the runaway casket, which had become a toboggan from hell for a dead dowager in a Versace dress.

Back up the hill, Pete and Germ watched the spectacle in agony. Cody heard the older man yell, "Go on, Pete. Get down there and help Cody stop that casket!"

Pete retorted, "You're the one with the magic shoes. You go after it!"

Both men let out a simultaneous curse as they saw the casket hit a grave marker and flip over. The collision caused Cody to lose his grip on the rear handle. He watched helplessly as Mrs. Dinwittie's casket raced on upside down to the bottom of the hill.

The casket's momentum carried it across the road, where it jumped the small curb and traveled ten yards up the slope on the other side. Then it slid sideways down toward the road.

Cody was sending up a little prayer of thanksgiving that the horrid ordeal was over when he saw the casket again slide across the road and hit the curb with a forceful blow. The lid popped open and the ample, rigid frame of the deceased socialite ejected out onto the icy lane. She slid away on her back, still gripping a small bouquet of flowers in her folded hands.

Cody was, by far, the closest person to Mrs. Dinwittie, and he made another attempt to overtake the body. He slid down the hill on his backside awkwardly, using his hands as ski poles, but his efforts were in vain.

The corpse hesitated a moment as if to bid a final farewell to the aghast funeral party. Then the late Mrs. Dinwittie began to slide down the steep road, gaining momentum by the second, for a staggering, horrifying replay of her appalling coffin ride down the hill.

Her velocity quickly increased and she bounced back and forth off the curbs like an Olympic bobsled speeding for the finish line. As she rounded a sharp curve and disappeared around the bend, one of the youngsters called out from the hill, "Grandma! Don't leave us!"

Another shouted, "Awesome! Show us how you did that!"

# Chapter 6

Cody pulled up behind a line of cars at the security checkpoint in front of the Castle. A Led Zeppelin song, "Dazed and Confused," blared from the scratchy speakers of his ragged Volvo. As he waited for officers to process the vehicles in front of him, he looked through the drizzle on his windshield and pondered the massive Gothic edifice in front of him.

Built in the late nineteenth century, the structure was a formidable citadel of five forlorn stories. Its spires rose up to blend with the low, gray clouds that hung down from the sky. Lights from the turret rooms along the roof shined out into the bleak morning like eyes from glaring demons.

The main entrance to the building was a massive arched doorway. Those who walked through it disappeared into a foreboding darkness. Letters above the arch proclaimed the structure's ominous purpose: "Jericho State Prison."

Thick, stone walls stretched out on each side of the main complex into the stark countryside. High on the battlements, guards walked between barbed-wire barricades, the barrels of their carbines sticking out from under yellow rain slickers. Every thirty yards or so, other officers sitting in turret rooms used binoculars to scan the prison yard below for suspicious behavior. Within this desolate, gray penitentiary, two-thousand convicted felons lived, and sometimes died, in a state of harsh, unmitigated despair.

Cody recalled the new recruits' orientation of the day before.

"What we have here, ladies and gentlemen, is a timeshare situation. But it's not in some tropical paradise. No siree. It's a timeshare in hell." Johnny Mack Norton, better known as Warden Mack, surveyed his recruits with grim authority.

A cynical smirk, barely noticeable, flashed across his lips for an instant. "And if this is hell, then I guess that makes me the devil."

A standout on the state university's football team thirty years before, the erstwhile tight end displayed a once fearsome physique that had devolved into layers of flab, which spilled down his chest and accumulated around his waist in a massive paunch. Still, he was an intimidating presence as he stood gravely before the new employees who had gathered in the prison auditorium for orientation day.

The room was dark and musty, much like an old high school assembly hall. As Cody surveyed his surroundings, he sensed a malevolent energy in the place. The walls screamed out hate, misery, and abject hopelessness.

The young apprentice sat with a group of about a hundred men and a sprinkling of women clustered toward the front of the auditorium, near the stage. He looked around at the recently recruited corrections officers and thought they seemed proud to be wearing their new, starched uniforms. Cody was the only one dressed differently. He wore a black suit left over from his days at the funeral home and a clerical collar. Later, after prisoners and guards became familiar with his presence, he could wear a regular shirt and tie if he wished. But for now, his appearance in the yard shouldn't cause any confusion among the omnipresent lookouts and sharpshooters on the walls.

Up on the stage, Warden Mack wiped his brow with a white linen handkerchief. "Some people call this place 'the Castle' because it looks like some medieval fortress. But this is a hellhole, not a dreamy Disneyland palace in some never-never land. This castle is overflowing with misery. It's all around us. It's the collective hopelessness of two-thousand men with shattered dreams and broken lives."

Warden Mack paused to take a sip of coffee from his oversized mug imprinted with the Department of Corrections seal and then he set it down sternly on the wing of the podium. "As new employees, you have two big challenges ahead of you. First, you don't want to ingest the prisoners' despair. This despair is deadly. Of our last class of recruits, barely seventy percent made it through twelve months. And we had two suicides."

He waited to allow the mainly younger group to ponder that chilling bit of information. A somber apprehension smothered the room like a wet, steamy, mildewed blanket.

"When you're with the inmates, you must always put up a shield against their negativity. Don't let the poison of misery penetrate you, and, for God's sake, don't take it home with you. Go to the prison shrink if you feel trouble coming on. Or, if you prefer a more spiritual approach to your problems, go see a chaplain."

Warden Mack smiled proudly as he looked over at Cody. "In fact, we have a new chaplain with us in today's group—Reverend Cody Palmeroy. Cody, stand up so everyone can see you."

Amid scattered applause, Cody nervously stood and lamely waved his hand at the group.

The warden continued, "He's a fine young man. So, if you have any problems, you can go see Chaplain Palmeroy. He'll be glad to help you."

Cody slunk back into his chair, feeling small and inadequate. He wasn't yet officially a minister. His ordination would come when he finished his five-year program at his divinity school. He would become a real minister then, and a doctor of sorts, a Doctor of Theology. But now, he only had three years of training, a point he'd tried to emphasize to prison officials.

When Cody had met with Johnny Mack Norton two weeks previously, the warden insisted on calling him "reverend" and bestowing the title of "chaplain" upon him.

"I know this is rushing things a little, son, but we're sorely short on personnel in the chaplains' office. We have only two of them for two-thousand inmates. They're running around the institution like a couple of decapitated chickens. So, this is like a field promotion in a combat zone."

Warden Mack had propped his oversized feet confidently atop his giant mahogany desk. He unbuttoned the bottom half of the vest of his cheap three-piece suit, allowing part of his substantial midsection to bulge out like a strangulated hernia. Behind him, bookshelves stretched almost to the ceiling. Rows of manuals in binders and football memorabilia dominated this space, but a sprinkling of family photographs softened the hard edges of bureaucracy and masculinity. An arrangement of gold trophies gathered dust on the top shelf along with a lonely Bible.

The warden gazed at Cody with a winning smile. "Having another chaplain on board will make us look good. The public likes to think we have a lot of ministers here constantly preaching to our degenerate convicts about their sinful ways. It's comforting to them."

Cody objected, "But I've only had three years of training and I haven't even visited a prison before today."

Warden Mack blew past this protest as if he were galloping to the end zone through a pack of midgets. Persuasively, he told Cody, "I know, I know. You think you're just an intern. Don't worry about it. It's easier to see you as a full chaplain than to explain this internship business. No one around here even knows what that shit means." He grinned appealingly at Cody. "Hell, son, no one will notice, and if they do, they won't care. In this prison, you are what I say you are, and if I want to make you a fully sanctioned chaplain, no one here has the balls to say different."

The warden looked up at the ceiling, his hands folded behind his head.

"Credentials don't count for much here anyway. What matters is that you get the respect of these hard-ass convicts so you can be effective. One favor I ask of you. I don't want to violate inmates' privacy, and I totally respect the confidentiality of conversations between the prisoners and the chaplains, with one exception. I want to know if any trouble is brewing out there."

"Trouble?" asked Cody.

"Trouble as in violence, riots, that kind of thing. 'The needs of the many are more important than the needs of the few,' right?"

Cody looked admiringly at Warden Mack, who had just uttered an accurate paraphrase of the utilitarian principle. He said, "Yes, sir. You can count on me to let you know if I learn of anything like that."

The warden jumped up, quickly walked around the desk, and extended the hefty, gifted hand that had caught many a touchdown pass. "It's settled, then. Congratulations, son."

After they shook hands, Warden Mack ripped Cody's nametag from his jacket and glared at it disapprovingly. "This says, 'Cody Palmeroy, Chaplain Intern.' This is bullshit!" He walked behind his desk, and with dramatic flair, threw the offending ID into a trashcan, and then called out to his secretary in the adjoining room. "Hey, Peaches. Make Chaplain Palmeroy a new nametag. He just got a promotion."

On the stage during orientation, Warden Mack looked seriously at his audience of novices. "The second challenge you face is even harder. Almost every inmate you encounter will put you to the test. Especially at first, they will challenge you, try to see how they can put a mind-fuck on you. These outcasts of society, who are our happy responsibility to rehabilitate, will try to intimidate you with everything from mean stares to outright threats. They'll tell you that as soon as you let down your guard, you'll get a shank in your ribs or a prick up your ass. They have nothing better to occupy their warped, polluted minds than to think up ways they can scare you or bait you to fall for some bullshit story.

"Don't let me down." The warden pounded the podium with his fist like a thundering preacher in a revival tent. "Don't flinch. If you fall into one of their traps, they'll laugh at you, scorn you. If they lose respect for you, then you won't be effective in the cellblocks and in the yard. I'll have to take you out of daily interaction with the inmate population and put you up on the wall or at some checkpoint for visitors. That means they've won, and they know it.

"You've got to be tough, even brutal at first. You can ease up later, after they know you're a mean son-of-a-bitch and you won't put up with any of their garbage." He struck the podium again with his mighty hand. "So, get out there, and show the lowlife bastards who rules this place."

Now, as he moved forward in the line of cars outside the Castle, Cody felt a wave of anxiety ripple over him. Remembering the warden's speech left him feeling rattled and inadequate. He wondered how he could ever earn the respect of tough, street-savvy convicts. He pulled a small vial of Valium from his shirt pocket and stared at it. In resignation, he broke a blue, ten-milligram tablet in half, flicked it into his mouth, and chased it with a swig of Coke.

A few minutes later, after he crossed the threshold of the building and went through the metal detectors on the other side, he felt more relaxed, though a bit conspicuous in his clerical collar.

The foyer of the Castle resembled an old train station, with high ceilings, stone walls, and marble floors. Visitors crowded the area, waiting in one of four long lines for approval to pass through the checkpoint. The combined sounds of multiple conversations created a rumbling gibberish that echoed harshly around the room.

A guard standing at a desk near the front of the vestibule waved and called out to Cody. "Hey, Reverend, over here."

The young chaplain gratefully bypassed the lengthy lines and stood before the guard. Awkwardly, he explained, "This is my first day."

The officer, an ex-military type with a crew cut and excessively erect posture, checked out Cody's ID and consulted a computer monitor for a moment. "Okay, Chaplain Palmeroy. I'm Sergeant Fuller, watch officer for the Receiving Area, Checkpoint One. Welcome to Jericho. Pleased to have you here, sir."

Cody shook the outstretched hand and reflected on the irony of this friendly, middle-aged prison veteran calling him 'sir.' Humbly, he said, "Thank you, Sergeant."

No doubt wanting to help, Sergeant Fuller advised, "When you come to work, don't ever wait in one of these other lines. Always come over here first so we can get you processed quickly. This checkpoint is for employees only. Will you be going all the way today?"

Cody said, "I don't know. What do you mean by 'all the way'?"

Patiently, the sergeant spelled out, "It means all the way back into the prison population, into the cellblocks and the yard."

"Yes, all the way."

"I assume you know how to get to the command center."

"No." Cody explained, "On orientation day, they put the new employees on school buses and drove us through the back gate of the yard right up to the front door of the auditorium. Except for the warden's office, that's all I've seen of the prison."

"Okay, here's what you do. Go through this turnstile and the officers on the other side will shake you down for contraband. Then, walk straight down the long corridor that runs under the Castle to the command center or the 'Mountain.' We call it the Mountain because, even though it's on the ground-floor level, you can see most everything in the prison from there, courtesy of about a thousand closed-circuit video cameras. Sometimes the inmates call it the 'Screws' Nest.'"

Cody asked, "What's a screw?"

"That's what some of the inmates call the corrections officers. It's old prison slang. Anyway, the guards there will check you out one more time, and then let you out into the yard."

When Cody stepped through the turnstile, he saw officers thoroughly frisking the employee ahead of him, a roughneck guard with a greasy pompadour and a tattoo of a ship's anchor on his arm. Another officer was painstakingly examining the contents of the man's pockets, which he had laid out on a long table in front of him.

As Cody watched, he tried to remember what was in his own pockets. With a depressing wave of anguish, he remembered the Valium. He was sure prison officials would consider it contraband and cringed at the imminent and certain disgrace of its discovery. The guards would accuse him of smuggling a controlled substance on his first day at work. Dread clawing at his insides, he stepped up to the table with wobbling knees and a prominent mustache of sweat beads on his upper lip.

One of the officers sitting behind the table said, "Good morning, Reverend." The man reached down into a box to get a latex glove, which he donned ceremoniously. Then, he picked up a tube of personal lubricant and squeezed out a generous amount onto his raised finger. He looked up at the young chaplain and said sternly, "I'll have to check you for contraband. Step behind the curtain so I can give you the rectal exam."

Before Cody could respond, laughter erupted among the several guards gathered around. Sergeant Fuller popped in from the other side of the turnstile. "Don't you know the reverend has a big haul of crack cocaine in his anal cavity. You better check him out real good, Lester." Another round of laughter from the group.

Good-naturedly, Cody laughed, too, but the pills still concerned him. Awkwardly, he pulled the container from his pocket and held it up. "Actually, I have some Valium here."

His confession produced riotous laughter as the area filled with guards from other stations nearby.

Holding his side, Sergeant Fuller managed to stop his hearty guffawing for a moment. "Just don't perform a miracle like the feeding of the five thousand when you get into the yard." After more laughter all around the room, he continued, "I can see it now. The new reverend goes in with a bottle of Valium, prays over it, and produces enough for all two-thousand inmates to consume. Then, he has so much left over he can fill twelve baskets."

After the hilarity subsided, Lester ripped off the exam glove, threw it in the trash, and jovially shook Cody's hand. "Forgive us for having a little fun, Reverend. We don't get a laugh around here very often."

Relieved and embarrassed, Cody said meekly, "No problem at all. Glad I was able to provide a little amusement for you."

He began to unload his pockets onto the table, but Lester stopped him. "That won't be necessary, sir."

Then, Cody stepped forward and spread his arms and legs for the pat down, but another guard simply gave him a gentle tap on the shoulder. He explained, "We don't search the chaplains here, Reverend. If the world got so corrupt that chaplains started smuggling drugs in here, then, God help us, we all might as well just crawl into a hole and die."

As Cody walked down the long concourse under the Castle, he began to notice the large number of security cameras mounted on the walls and ceilings. Surely, the cameras weren't everywhere, but when he ducked into an officers' restroom about halfway down the tunnel, he saw a camera aimed right at the urinals. His curiosity led him to check out one of the stalls. He saw no visible camera. He chuckled to himself. At least the administration considered one activity private.

The underground corridor was much longer than he'd anticipated, and he contemplated the enormity of the structure above him. Finally, he approached the command center, a two-story facility that jutted out into the prison yard like an arrowhead.

As Cody walked into the middle of the room, he saw two men coming toward him. One was Head Chaplain Virgil Powers, with whom he'd talked before his meeting with Warden Mack. The other was Captain of the Guards Sonny Lagrange. Cody hadn't met Lagrange but had seen a picture of him in a slide show on orientation day. As he shook the officer's enormous hand, Cody impulsively looked down at the hefty, scarred paw that enveloped his own much smaller one. An image of the hand pounding a poor inmate's face burst into his mind and a memory flashed of another man with an enormous weapon at the end of his arm, Simon Legree, a fictional cruel slave owner from Uncle Tom's Cabin.

Cody shook hands with Chaplain Powers, who said, "No one is happier to see you here than me."

The captain was an immense presence in the room. Standing about six feet five inches and weighing close to three-hundred pounds, he dominated the area with his wide girth. His head was bald, and ragged scars, presumably the relics of battles with convicts over the years, littered his face, arms, and hands.

"Welcome to our castle," said the captain with a genuine smile. "And when you do that miracle of the Valium tablets, I could use a few of the extras for myself." His oversized stomach jiggled as he let out a vigorous hee-haw echoed by several other officers standing nearby.

Embarrassed, Cody said, "So you've heard about that already?"

"Why hell, yes, I have. I got a call on the radio from Sergeant Fuller before you even left Checkpoint One. I'll bet the boys in the front hall are still laughing their asses off. Fuller says to put him down for about one hundred of those ten-milligram tablets, if you don't mind."

Cody stammered, "I'm sorry to cause such a commotion on my first day."

The captain grinned. "Are you serious? You have nothing to be sorry about. You provided welcome entertainment for some very bored officers at the first checkpoint. See? You just got here a few minutes ago, and already you've given employee morale a boost."

Meekly, Cody said, "It was by accident, that's for sure."

Captain Sonny smiled cheerfully. "Well, we won't tell anyone that part." He winked at Cody and Reverend Powers, then said, "Let me explain what goes on here at our command center."

He pointed to the front of the large room where officers were watching the comings and goings of the inmates through large, reinforced windows. "As you can see, the prison architects designed this facility so no inmate can travel very far into the yard without our knowledge. From this bank of windows, we can see the entrances to the cellblocks, the dining hall, the hospital, the chapel and the processing building.

"This is real good as far as it goes, but obviously we can't see everything from here. That's why we have our video surveillance system. Over a thousand cameras have been installed, altogether, and we monitor most of them from here." He pointed to the back of the room where officers gazed at monitors stacked five high. "Here we have an inside view of the cellblocks, the prison industries, the dining hall, that kind of thing."

Cody said, "Wow. That's impressive."

Clearly encouraged by the young chaplain's interest, the captain enthusiastically pointed to the catwalks above them. "Now, the design of the second level was my idea. You see the officers up there? They have an even better view than we do down here, and they have a great tactical advantage in the event of a riot. Also, those guards have direct access to the armory." He pointed to a bank vault door at the back of the catwalk.

Finally, the captain directed their attention to a triple set of mechanized iron gates at the front of the first floor by the windows. "Now, that's the key to everything. If you control those gates, you control the prison. That's the entrance to the yard and the inmate population."

Cody noticed that on the side of the threshold someone had scratched the word "Rubicon" into the stone wall.

"And that's the quick explanation of what we do here in the command center," Captain Sonny said. "I'm sure Chaplain Powers will explain more to you as you go along." He directed a kind expression at the older man. "I'm a big supporter of the chaplains here."

In response to this statement, Chaplain Powers gave a vigorous nod of affirmation.

"But I can't honestly say I'm very religious. My wife pesters me so bad that I go to church sometimes with the family. I admit I like to hear a good sermon now and then, something real fiery that scares the hell out of people. Are you a good preacher?"

Cody said, "I don't know. I haven't preached but a couple of times and that was in front of my class. But when I give my sermons, I'll try to preach in the way that Andrew Jackson preferred."

Sonny looked interested in the comment. He asked, "And what did the president from the great state of Tennessee prefer?"

"He liked to hear a man who preached as if he had 'yellow jackets down his britches legs.'"

A chuckle among the eavesdropping guards ricocheted around the room.

The captain laughed heartily, then looked over at Chaplain Powers. "I think I approve of your new reverend here. We're going to get along just fine." He put his arm around Cody's shoulder and drew him tightly to his side with a crushing hug. "Yeah, we're going to get along just fine."

With a look of satisfaction and relief, Chaplain Powers smiled his approval at Cody. As the two chaplains crossed the Rubicon and strolled out into the gray prison yard, Powers said, "Well done, Cody. I hoped you would get along with the captain. It's important. If he likes you—and he doesn't like many people—then the guards will be a lot more helpful. The inmates, too. No one wants to get on the wrong side of Sonny, so if they think you might have his ear, then doors will open fast for you. I guarantee that news of the big hug he gave you back there is halfway down to the license plate shop by now."

# Chapter 7

*Beyond the Rubicon*

Chaplain Virgil Powers was a striking figure in his gray pinstripe suit with a starched white shirt and black tie. His tall, trim frame and soothing voice complemented his distinguished presence. Though his beautiful silver hair was rather long for that of a minister, he combed it straight back in a becoming manner. And while Cody thought the senior chaplain fit the mold of a typical minister in most ways, something about him seemed different than mainstream. Eccentric energy flowed just below the surface of his dignified decorum.

Powers said, "I've got a couple of hours to spend with you this morning before I have to cut you loose. I'm due over at the women's prison for a parole board hearing this afternoon. Anyway, I thought we could tour a cellblock or two, and then grab some lunch in the officers' dining hall before I take off. Sound okay to you?"

Cody was glad to have a tour of some of the more intimidating places. Enthusiastically, he replied, "Yes, sir. Sounds great."

As they walked over to the cellblocks, the senior chaplain called out greetings to the inmates and officers they passed. "It pays to be friendly. I speak to everyone. A few of the meaner inmates don't respond. They feel someone will think they're weak if they get friendly with the chaplains. To tell you the truth, I don't give a damn if they speak or not. They'll talk plenty if they get in trouble and think I might be able to help them."

"You mean help them through counseling?"

Powers laughed. "Oh, no. They seldom want that. It would be the ultimate sign of weakness. If word got out they came for counseling, they'd lose all respect. Other inmates would laugh at them. No, the kind of help they would want is for me to put in a good word for them at a disciplinary hearing. Or, maybe to ask the captain to let them out of solitary confinement—we call it the Hole—a couple of days early, to tell him I thought they'd suffered enough. Something like that."

"Do you do that?"

"Sometimes. It depends."

As they entered the building, Cody looked up at the five tiers of cages that comprised Cellblock A. Several dingy skylights covered with bars let in slivers of light, and bare bulbs hanging from the ceiling provided a bit more illumination. But, as Cody had expected, the building was a dreary, depressing place.

While they climbed the stairs to the third level, Powers said, "I thought we'd walk down one of the catwalks and check out some cells. No one should be home this time of day, and it will give you some insight into the prisoners' living conditions."

Each cell was about eight-by-twelve feet with a metal bunk bed, a toilet, and a sink. When they stepped into several cells to look around, Cody noticed the pathetic attempts to individualize the monotonous pattern of the dreary human cubbyholes. On many of the walls, inmates had taped pinup calendars, pages ripped from weight lifting and sex magazines, and pictures of sports heroes. In addition, some had composed desperate, pathetic graffiti.

"I gonna kihl dat bitch wit a baseball bat."

"Deez walls suck up my sole."

"Freedom day soon come."

"I found Jesus here. For true."

"I am just another of society's road kills."

"Wuz not borne to dye in some E-Z chair."

"I'm is a scarlet angel."

"For the love of Charlene, I die daily."

"Someday I get free. Same day I get even."

From the time they entered the first cell, Cody felt something was missing, something important that he had expected to find. After walking through the last cell on the tier, he asked the head chaplain, "Where are the pictures?"

"What pictures?"

"Pictures of their families. I don't see any photos of their loved ones."

Powers sighed in acknowledgment. "Yeah, you're right. It's sad. You rarely see such pictures. The tragic scenario goes something like this. I remember the circumstances well, even though it must have happened more than ten years ago." He sighed again.

"A new inmate comes in and proudly puts out a few pictures of his wife and kids in his cell, right? He sets up sort of shrine, a sacred area, something that he is going to come back to every day and draw strength from, and hope, the will to go on. Only, one day he comes back, and half the pictures are gone. One of his wife's pictures the thieving bastards leave behind has a big, hairy dick drawn into her mouth. Another has some gooey stuff on it, sperm. And it's not that old either, like it just happened a few minutes ago."

Cody interjected, "God, that's sickening."

Powers said, "It gets worse. The next day some of the stolen photos start to come back. One picture of his nine-year-old son has a penis drawn on it with a message on the back, something like, 'I'm out of here before you. I got this seven-inch rod with warts on it and three pimples at the base. When I squeeze them, puss comes out. I'm gonna find your son and stick it in his young, tight little ass until he bleeds. Sweet. P.S. I'll send you a picture.'"

With disgust, Cody exclaimed, "Jesus!"

Powers said, "Revolting, isn't it? But that's the reason for the absence of family photographs. In general, inmates who reveal too many facts about their personal lives set themselves up for abuse."

Cody said, "A piece of graffiti in one of the cells said, 'I found Jesus here.' Do you have many legitimate jailhouse conversions?"

"I guess we get a few," Powers replied. "It's a hard sell, riding Jesus's robe tails out of here. A man who claims to find Jesus in prison is immediately under suspicion. People think he's trying to gain favor with the parole board. Usually, a man gets extensive flak from other inmates when he converts. But, on the other hand, he's got a strong support group, too, a new set of friends. They look out for one another, and some mean, well-respected inmates are part of the Christian clique." He looked at Cody.

"My philosophy is this. I lay the gospel out there for them, and if they accept it, great. I'm pulling hard for them to have a genuine, life-changing experience, but I don't spend a lot of time worrying about who's sincere, and who isn't."

Powers and Cody walked up to the highest tier and stood for a while, gazing out over the guardrail onto the floor five stories below. Officers there were supervising distribution of clean linen for the cells.

The older chaplain surveyed his new apprentice for a moment. A hint of amusement spread across his dignified countenance. "By the way, do you really want to preach like you've got yellow jackets in your pants?"

Cody laughed. "No, I just said that as a joke. I don't have any kind of style. Like I said, I've only done it a couple of times."

"Well, you're going to get plenty of experience here."

"Really?"

"At least three times a week to start. We have to cover six services a week, four here and two at the women's prison."

Anxiety jolted Cody's body like a surge of electricity. The prospect of preaching to hardened convicts worried him. What would he say to them? Impulsively, he slipped his hand into his pocket for the Valium, but decided the drug had caused him enough problems for one day. Uneasily, he asked, "When's my first sermon? I need some time to prepare."

Powers replied, "Tomorrow night is your first assignment." The older chaplain saw the consternation on his apprentice's face, and in a kindly voice, he said, "Don't worry about the preparation. If you wish, I'll give you some of my sermons and outlines. You can just read from the notes, if you want to."

"Wow. Tomorrow night. That's soon."

"Don't worry, son. You'll do just fine." After a moment of silence, Powers continued, "I'll level with you, Cody. I'm tired, real tired. For twenty-two years, I was the only chaplain. Then, after I begged the warden, he let me have Reverend Malachi Hamm as my assistant three years ago, and the next year your divinity school sent me an intern. Naturally, this greatly relieved me, since I had someone to share the workload with. Unfortunately, the intern only lasted a couple of days. Some of the pretty boys in the boiler room took a shine to his backside and told him they were going to sodomize him out by the back wall of the yard. By the time Sonny found out, it was too late."

Aghast, Cody asked, "Did they rape him?"

Powers waved a dismissive hand. "Oh, hell, no. I don't think they ever intended to really do it. They were just trying to give the youngster a good scare. All in good fun, right? But it totally freaked out the kid. He ran all the way from the boiler room to the command center, looking back over his shoulder the whole way as though a pack of demons were on his heels. He fell three times." Powers barked out a laugh that held no amusement in it.

"The youngster was real naïve. You know the kind—a typical preacher boy. Anyway, by the time the captain rounded up the queens of the boiler room and sent them to the Hole, the kid had quit. I tried to persuade him to give it another chance, but he was too spooked. Secretly, I was glad about his decision. Everyone in the prison was laughing at him, even the warden. He'd lost all respect. Until you showed up, the divinity school wouldn't send me any more interns." Powers smiled.

"Anyway, as I was saying, I'm tired. Chaplain Hamm left for a two-week vacation this morning, so I'm going to put a lot on you. It'll be baptism by fire for sure, but in a few days you'll begin to feel confident in your role."

The two men strolled along the catwalk to the inmates' bathroom at the end of the cellblock. Cody looked around the big shower area apprehensively, imagining the horrible rapes and beatings that occurred in this ominous place. He saw the ghost of a young, new arrival held down by a gang of thugs while their leader penetrated the wretched victim from behind. Jeering comrades stood in line, awaiting their turns while occasionally stroking their erect penises in shameless anticipation.

Powers stated, "I'll bet you feel a lot of violence occurs here."

Grimly, Cody nodded his acknowledgment.

"Well, don't let your imagination run too wild. Let me demythologize this for you. Despite all you may have heard, few rapes actually occur in prison, at least in this facility. Now, consensual sex is another matter, but we don't have many rapes. Gang violence accounts for most all the sexual assaults here, but the incidence of rapes of new, defenseless inmates is rare. However, the convicts and the guards perpetuate the myth as a way of impressing outsiders." Powers paused before going on with a note of drama in his voice.

"Picture this scenario. A recently paroled inmate goes back to his hometown. Naturally, everyone is asking him what prison was like, were there really rapes every day in the shower. And the parolee says, 'Sure, it's everywhere. But if you're tough enough, the scum will leave you alone. As for me, I had to waste four of the fuckers one day when they tried to jump me. I sent two of them to the hospital. After that, the bastards let me be. They didn't know who they was fucking with.' So, do you see how that works? Inmates want to play up the insinuation that rapes occur every day to enhance their stature."

Cody acknowledged, "Yes. That makes sense."

In the crapper around the corner from the shower, stark rows of commodes lined the walls. Cody thought the toilets were so close together convicts couldn't help but rub shoulders and knees with their neighbors sitting next to them.

Powers gestured over the room. "Behold, the ultimate model of open seating."

Cody laughed. "Why don't they just use the toilets in their cells?"

"After the morning headcount, prisoners can't return to their cells until late afternoon except on the weekends."

"I guess putting in stalls for a little privacy wouldn't be practical."

Affably, Powers chuckled at the idea, "You're right. Can you imagine all the problems if the inmates could go into a closed stall? They would be masturbating and shooting up, and no telling what else. So, one of the privileges you give up upon incarceration is the right to take a dump in private." He smiled at his student. "Remember that next time you think about committing a felony."

Cody joked, "If potential criminals only knew about this, it would serve as a powerful deterrent."

Powers advised, "Try to avoid walking through here after breakfast. It's quite a spectacle with all the toilets occupied and a waiting line out the door. All these guys are sitting in here grunting, wiping their asses. In the past, fights often broke out over who was taking too long, who didn't flush, who used too much toilet paper, that kind of thing. The warden added a guard station so officers could supervise the place during the morning rush."

He pointed to an enclosed Plexiglas cubicle in the corner. "At first, they had no booth, just a chair for the guards to sit in. But they wouldn't stay in here because of the odor. Can you imagine having to sit in here for two hours every morning and smell that shit? Talk about an olfactory nightmare. So, the guards bitched about it until finally the warden gave them that little booth with an air-conditioning vent coming right into the top of it."

As the chaplains walked to the exit of the building, Cody looked back at the stacked rows of cells. They vaguely reminded him of a zoo, but with an important difference. The cages for zoo animals were typically much larger.

When they strolled back out into the yard, the outside light hurt Cody's eyes for a moment, despite the overcast skies. The drizzle of early morning had kept up, and now, tentacles of fog meandered through the yard as inmates filled the area on their morning break. As the chaplains made their way over to death row, Cody felt the harsh stares of some of the inmates follow them. He heard low whispers behind cupped hands, an occasional snicker.

"Why are they looking at us that way?" Cody asked.

Powers turned around to peruse the yard. Immediately, the inmates averted their unwelcome stares and turned their heads to pretend disinterest. "Don't worry about it, Cody. It's nothing serious. They're just checking you out. In a couple of days, they won't even notice you."

As they approached death row, a guard from inside opened the giant iron door that creaked and groaned on its massive hinges. The chaplains stepped inside into a large, brightly lit room, which served as the command center for the death row facility, a two-story concrete structure in need of a paint job.

Lieutenant Bragg, a short, sinewy man with a crooked, sadistic smile, introduced himself as the watch officer. After presenting his staff of five friendly guards, the lieutenant led Cody out into a long, wide hallway with cells on each side while Powers stayed behind to call his office for messages. Cody had read about the infamous corridor that led to an execution room at the end of the narrow building.

The lieutenant pointed out, "We're walking the 'last mile.' That's what this hallway is called at some prisons. Of course, it's only a short distance, but to a condemned man on his way to the chair it seems like a mile."

As the two men walked slowly down the corridor, some of the inmates awaiting execution stood at the bars to see who was coming, but most just lay on their beds staring at the ceiling or reading comic books and magazines.

Bragg commented on some of the inmates and the crimes they'd committed. "There's Johnny the Foot. The muddy tracks of his clubfoot at a murder scene led to his capture." Johnny raised his head from the dingy pillow on his bed and shot the lieutenant an obscene gesture.

Unfazed, Bragg pointed to the next cell. "And the delightful, upstanding citizen in here is Vinnie Hamiter. His specialty was dismemberment of his victims." The unshaven, spiteful-looking inmate walked up to the bars and glared out menacingly. Without acknowledging Vinnie, Bragg droned on as though he was a tour guide in a wax museum. "He mailed body parts of his unfortunate prey to the police, the TV stations, and the victims' families. Even the mayor got a severed head in a FedEx box on Christmas Eve."

As they passed his cell, Vinnie flashed a wicked grin and aimed a wad of spit at the lieutenant, who avoided it handily with a smooth sidestep. Cody thought the officer likely had plenty of experience at perfecting the evasive maneuver. Without looking back at the inmate, Bragg said, "That one will cost you, Vinnie."

As they came to the end of the hallway, Lieutenant Bragg pointed to the last cell. "And who do we have here, but our next in line to fry, none other than Kenny Masters, also known as Kenny the Ghoul. Seems he liked to rape teenage girls while wearing a Halloween mask of some type of goblin. Then, as a pleasant finish to his crime, he would suffocate them with one of those plastic trick-or-treat bags."

As Bragg spoke, Kenny came to the bars. His lonely, dim eyes peered out from sunken sockets, and his face radiated infinite sadness. "As you can see, Kenny is one ugly motherfucker—excuse my language, Reverend—so a goblin mask was definitely an improvement. He didn't want to scare his victims too badly."

Bragg let out a sick, twisted laugh.

"God willing, Kenny's going to ride the lightning in about six weeks." Mockingly, the lieutenant called into the cell, "How does it feel to have just a few weeks left to live, Kenny?"

The inmate stared at them, but said nothing in response. Cody felt a shudder shoot up his spine. Again, Lieutenant Bragg laughed at the man. "Trick or treat, Kenny. Trick or treat."

The harassment of the condemned man disturbed the new chaplain. He wanted to admonish the lieutenant but decided it wasn't his place to do so, at least not yet. Hopefully, he would soon feel more comfortable in taking a stand on behalf of beleaguered inmates, but for the moment satisfied himself with a stern glower at the officer, who sensed Cody's disapproval immediately.

In a somewhat apologetic tone, he appealed, "Don't judge us too harshly, Reverend. Without a little humor, we would all go bonkers in here."

Cody was about to say that he saw no humor in the lieutenant's remarks to Kenny, but Chaplain Powers joined them again, so he let the matter drop.

The threesome passed through an iron gate that led to an area designated by a small, hand-painted sign as the "Execution Suite." This part of death row contained a small conference room, a medical examiner's room, and a gallery for those who would sit or stand to witness the execution. The prison administration had also provided a rather large holding cell for the prisoner's use during his final twelve hours. Furnished with a television and conference table, it was sizable enough to accommodate several family members and a minister, if the prisoner so desired.

Overflowing with obvious delight, Lieutenant Bragg opened the last door of the suite and with a broad smile and sweeping gesture declared, "Here it is, gentlemen, the pride and joy of our great state, our very own electric chair."

As they stepped into the room, Cody felt a bitter chill. He stared transfixed at the crude device in front of him. Evil dripped from the killing machine like black, malignant sludge. Cody had expected something more sophisticated, more professional. Instead, the apparatus looked like a contraption some tinkering teenagers might throw together in a neighborhood garage on a Saturday afternoon. The oversized, wooden straight-back chair was outfitted with leather straps, dangling wires and hammered metal. A crude, misshapen alloy cap attached by a coil of heavy wire served as an inglorious crown. Cody supposed this was a "one size fits all" situation, but the asymmetrical headpiece was particularly crude, solidifying the amateurish appearance of the primitive machine. In the seat of the chair, someone had carved the forbidding admonition, "Fear This."

After a moment of silence, Bragg whispered reverently, "Ain't it a wonder? My favorite part is that metal cap we pull down on the inmate's shaved head. The official name for it is the 'helmet.' But, around here we call it 'the Easter bonnet.'" He laughed maniacally at the irony of the name, and then stepped over to the control panel, obviously preparing to give a lecture on the details of electrocution.

"At our facility we have these three switches." Smugly, he pointed to three large circuit breakers at the center of the panel. "The electricians wire only one of them into the chair. So, the way it goes down is that three officers volunteer to throw the switches at the same time. That way no one knows for sure who really zaps the prisoner. Some prisons have only one switch and a designated executioner, but I like our setup much better."

Mesmerized, Cody asked, "Do you have any trouble getting enough volunteers?"

Obviously somewhat annoyed, the death row jailer glared at Cody. "Why hell no, we don't. Why would we have a problem with that? We have a waiting list." Boastfully, he added, "My name is on it, too. Since we started electrocutions again, I've pulled a switch five times. Doesn't bother me at all, and you get a seventy-five-dollar bonus. I don't spend mine right away. I get the payroll department to add it to my Christmas Club account. Sure comes in handy, too, when you have three youngsters at home expecting Santa Claus."

Cody imagined Christmas morning at the Braggs' house where children played happily around the tree, enjoying toys purchased with their father's blood money.

Powers stepped forward to take charge of the conversation. "Thank you for showing us the chair, Lieutenant Bragg. And your personal observations are much appreciated, but could you give us a moment? I want to talk to Chaplain Palmeroy privately."

Bragg replied, "Sure, Reverend Powers. No problem. When you get ready to leave, call me on the intercom and I'll send someone to escort you back through."

Powers said, "Thank you, Lieutenant."

Bragg turned to Cody and offered a civil handshake. "Good to have you here, Reverend. Let me know if I can help you in any way."

Trying to muster some positive feelings for the lieutenant, Cody responded evenly, "Thank you. I learned a lot from my visit here today."

After Bragg left, Powers said, "Honestly, the chair has a mysterious attraction for me. It's a crude device, to be sure. But what haunts me is the singular purpose for which people made it. What other devices outside the military realm has our species designed exclusively to extinguish the life of one of our own kind?"

He touched the back of the chair cautiously, as though he were afraid it might spring to life and shock him.

"Consider handguns. Sure, they kill many people but you might also use a pistol to wound someone in self-defense or shoot a rabid dog. However, this contraption exists for one purpose only, to kill another human being. And for that reason it fascinates me. Sometimes, I come in here by myself just to sit and contemplate the device. I reflect on its significance for humanity. I'm amazed that such an apparatus exists in our modern culture, that we allow it to still perform its function. To me, it symbolizes everything that is deficient in humankind. It represents our failures as a race."

Cody looked at the chair again. This time he saw it wasn't empty. Kenny the Ghoul was sitting in it. Just before the volunteer officers threw the switches, Kenny looked up at Cody and smiled, his expression sublime. He said, "I forgive you, Cody. You didn't have the courage to speak up for me. But I forgive you. I forgive Lieutenant Bragg, too. I forgive everyone."

After a moment, Powers said, "I notice you seem entranced by the chair. Don't tell me you've already started seeing people in it."

Surprised, Cody asked, "Is that common?"

Powers replied, "It happens occasionally. People claim they see someone in the chair just before an execution. It sometimes happens in a dream, too."

As they turned to leave, Powers stopped, looked back at the apparatus and asked, "Would you like to sit in it before we go?"

Cody thought for a moment. "I admit it would be a unique experience, but I think it would be disrespectful in a way. Besides, I'd be afraid Lieutenant Bragg and his guards would rush in here, strap me down, and throw the switches."

They had a good laugh together, and Powers patted the young man on the shoulder. He said, "Let's get out of here before they bring out the straitjackets."

The officers dining hall was just a short walk across the yard. Chaplain Powers explained that although it was adjacent to the dining hall for prisoners, the food was vastly superior. "Not that the inmates' fare is all that bad. The prison runs a farm nearby, so all the produce is homegrown. Despite the bad reputation of prison food, the inmates here get three decent meals a day. Occasionally, I go over to the other side and eat with them."

As they walked into the crowded guards' eatery and picked up a tray to start through the buffet line, Cody noticed that all the other patrons were corrections officers. "Where are the other prison employees? Don't they eat here?"

"No, we have another employee cafeteria in the main building. In fact, it was the only dining hall for workers until Warden Mack opened this place on the inmate side of the Rubicon. It cuts down on the congestion in the control center, with guards having to go back and forth all the time for meals."

Cody noticed some guards pointing at them and whispering as the pair started through the line. The stares weren't mean, like in the yard, but curious with a few snickers here and there. Cody felt he had a sign on his back. "Place Your Valium Orders Here!"

The cafeteria had the look and smell of a cheap "meat and three" diner with plastic chairs around Formica-topped tables on which staff had placed napkins and condiments in wire baskets. The predominant smell was a mixture of hot grease and freshly cooked turnip greens. A few inmates dressed in white, instead of the standard gray pinstripe, walked around among the guards, serving iced tea and coffee or going back to the kitchen to fetch extra helpings of food. As the two chaplains went down the buffet line, Cody found the choices surprisingly appealing, and the variety of down-home comfort food on display overwhelmed him.

"I don't see the prices," he said to Powers. "How do you know what anything costs?"

"Everything is free to employees. It's one of the perks of the job. You can also get free haircuts in the prison barbershop, but I wouldn't recommend it unless you want a crew cut or a flattop."

Cody opted for a chicken-fried steak with mashed potatoes and butter beans. The helpings were large, and the gravy on his potatoes spilled over the side of the plate. A couple of sticks of cornbread and a generous slice of pecan pie rounded out his meal.

The two men headed for a small table in the corner as Powers pointed out that serving low cholesterol food wasn't a priority in the prison. And eating healthy meals wasn't popular with the guards, whose expanded bellies typically spilled over the tops of their belts.

After the two seated themselves, the older chaplain asked his apprentice about his first impressions of the prison.

Without hesitating, Cody responded, "Something disturbing happened on death row when I was alone with Bragg." He related how the lieutenant talked about the prisoners as though they weren't even present, as if they were some inanimate objects in a museum. He described Bragg's treatment of Kenny the Ghoul as especially offensive. "It was a demented, sick torment of a man who is next to die in the electric chair. If I were in Kenny's shoes, I'd have enough to think about without some crazy bastard like Bragg rubbing it in regarding how I was going to fry in a few weeks."

Powers commented, "Yeah, what you described sounds like Bragg all right. He's not one of my favorite guards—that's for sure."

Cody said passionately, "I just felt so helpless. I know I should have said something to point out that officers ought to treat everyone with some respect, even condemned murderers. That's what we're here for, right? Shouldn't we protect the prisoners from that kind of abuse?"

In a kind tone, the older chaplain said, "Yes, you're right. We should provide moral leadership and protect the inmates in such circumstances. Many times we're the only advocates they have."

Cody said, "I should have challenged Bragg, but I didn't want to come on that strong after just a couple of hours on the job."

Powers said, "Your instincts were correct. It's too soon for you to intervene in such situations, but you'll feel comfortable soon enough, probably in a matter of days. Unfortunately, what you witnessed was a mild case of verbal abuse. I have to ignore many of these, so when I speak up about especially bad incidents, the guards will take me seriously."

The comments disheartened Cody. "Wow, how unfortunate that it gets worse than that."

Powers said, "Death row presents a complicated and troublesome set of circumstances for many reasons. The guards take constant verbal abuse from the inmates, who typically feel they have nothing to lose. This isn't exactly true since the officers can always send them to the Hole for a couple of weeks, or take away their outside recreational privileges. But condemned inmates commonly have the attitude that 'Hey, I'm going to die, anyway, so I'll say and do what I damn well please. What else can they do to me?'"

Cody nodded. "I saw an example of that. This inmate, Vinnie, tried to spit on the lieutenant as we walked by his cell."

Powers turned more serious. "I'm sure someone will punish Vinnie for that. The guard who serves his dinner tray tonight will probably spill it all over the guy, or maybe they'll just forget to feed him for a couple of days. They'll blame it on a mix-up in the kitchen."

One of the inmates came to the table and asked if the chaplains wanted any more food. Powers ordered another slice of pie and some fresh coffee. Cody scanned his half-finished plate and remarked, "I guess I've been talking too much. I still have a lot here to eat."

The senior chaplain continued with their conversation. "Kenny the Ghoul is a sad case. Because he raped teenage girls, other inmates and the guards revile him. He's next to last on the prisoners' hierarchy of respect. Only a man who molests small children is lower than that. Other convicts call those perverts 'Short Eyes' because they're looking low down for kids. The life expectancy of a Short Eyes placed in the general inmate population is alarmingly brief. Now, there's a man who should never go to the shower alone."

Powers gulped a long drink of his iced tea and took a deep breath as if to prepare himself to address some unpleasant subject. "An incident occurred at Christmas a few years ago where I felt compelled to come to Kenny's defense. Kenny's family has deserted him. He gets no letters or presents from home at Christmas. He has no friends among the inmates. So, the guards pretended they took pity on him. They told Kenny they had taken up a collection to buy him a present so he would have a little something to open on Christmas morning. They all gathered round and presented him with a nicely wrapped package, but when he opened it, he found an old shoebox with a turd inside."

Cody shook his head. "That's disgusting. What did you do?"

"When I found out about it, I went over to death row and called all the guards together. I gave them a lecture on how their actions were a terrible insult to the spirit of Christmas. If they didn't like Kenny, they should just leave him alone, but don't drag down the birthday of baby Jesus with a turd in a shoebox."

"What did they do?"

"Well, they all listened respectfully and apologized for the prank. Then, they asked me if I was going to turn them in to Sonny. The prospect of facing his wrath scared them to death."

"How did you respond?"

"I said I wouldn't rat them out. Since they were remorseful and apologized, I considered the matter over. However, I wanted them to go out and buy Kenny a decent present and they agreed." Powers gave Cody a wry smile.

"Then, an amusing twist developed. Just as I finished my little sermon, Sonny came roaring into the room ready to kick some ass. Of course, he'd heard about the incident through his network of informers. News of a turd disguised as a Christmas present travels quickly. Well, those guards turned white as a bleached bed sheet, and just as Sonny was about to smash the ringleader's face, I said I'd already dealt with the matter and I felt he should let it go."

"What did he do?"

"To my surprise, and to the great relief of the guilty officers, he just said, 'Okay, Chaplain. If these scumbags satisfied you, that's good enough for me.' Then, he turned back to the guards and told them that if they did anything like that again, God himself couldn't save them from an ass beating like they'd never seen before."

Cody said, "Wow that surprises me."

"Frankly, it surprised me, too. For all his faults, Sonny is a big man. He's secure in his position. A small man would have considered my remarks an affront to his authority and my intervention as an infringement on his territory, but the captain took it all in stride. You know, those guards still remember how I stood up for them. I gained respect in their eyes, even though a part of me secretly wished Sonny had ignored me and beat the crap out of them. They deserved it."

Cody said, "You were saying that child molesters are at the bottom of the prisoner hierarchy. Who's at the top?"

Powers laughed. "Without question it's the armed robbers. It may seem logical to think the murderers should be at the top, but

111

many homicides are crimes of passion where a man just loses it and kills someone. And, in most cases, premeditated murder is considered a cowardly act. On the other hand, armed robbers are typically daring and mean. Most of the time, they're willing to kill if they have to. Sometimes, they kill when they don't have to. So, if another inmate crosses an armed robber, he may find himself looking at a casket lid from the inside."

Powers then received a call on his cell phone, so he left the table and stepped outside for a moment, giving Cody an opportunity to survey the dining room again. This time, he didn't notice any guards looking at him and smiling. Everyone seemed to be concentrating on what was happening at his own table.

When Powers returned, Cody said, "In the few hours I've been here today and in the orientation session last week, I've heard a great deal of talk about the importance of respect. Frankly, I'm scared that I'll screw up so the guards or even the inmates won't respect me."

Powers smiled. "It's true that respect is important. Inmates will try to test you, to see if they can rile you up or force you to lose your cool like that naïve divinity student who bolted for the command center when he thought his ass was in danger. But you're different. You'll be just fine. Use your instincts and be tough."

Powers then gave him a reassuring look. "Don't worry about fitting into the role of a traditional minister. If you have to be a little harsh, it's no problem. That's what they want from a chaplain here, both the inmates and the guards. When I was in Vietnam, the military chaplains sometimes acted in uncharacteristic ways. We picked up rifles and starting shooting when the unit was in danger, and by doing this, we garnered the esteem of our comrades." Cody was surprised to learn that Powers had served as a military chaplain.

"In my experience, respect comes naturally and easily for some people, and I think you're one of those. But you're not immune to trickery, so be ready for a challenge. As soon as I split after lunch, someone will probably come forward to test your resolve."

An inmate emerged from the kitchen and walked through the dining room as though purposefully searching for someone. When he spotted Powers, he walked quickly over to the table.

"Excuse me, Chaplain Powers, but we just got a call for you back in the kitchen. A courier from the women's prison is waiting in the

Screws' Nest with a confidential envelope for you. I would go over and pick it up, but you have to sign for it personally."

Powers rose from the table. "Thank you, Jimmy."

He said to Cody, "If you'll excuse me for a few minutes, I'd better go over and get the envelope now. It's probably something I need to see before that parole board meeting this afternoon."

As Powers made his way to the door, Jimmy, a scrawny, sickly looking man about age fifty, lingered, standing above the table. A threatening, ugly sneer hung on his lips like venom. As soon as Powers was out of sight, he said, "You're the new chaplain, aren't you?"

Cody said, "Yes, I just started today."

"I hope you're enjoying your lunch."

Cody said, "Yes, I am. Very much. The food is delicious." Something about Jimmy's sly demeanor made Cody suspicious. He thought, Well, here it comes. My first test.

"I'm glad you like the food, but I just wanted you to know that I pissed in the butter beans."

Incredulous, Cody exclaimed, "What?"

"You heard me right, Chaplain. I peed in the butter beans." He grinned cruelly. "And, that's not all. You see Ralph over there?" He pointed to a burly inmate with hairy arms replenishing items on the salad bar. He wore a wife-beater undershirt and a dirty white apron. Holding serving tongs in his hand, the nasty inmate smiled and waved at Cody, revealing long armpit hair, which he had braided and decorated with colored plastic beads. His sadistic smirk displayed crooked rows of yellow and brown teeth with several prominent gaps.

"Yes, I see him."

"Well, Ralph, he jerked off into the mashed potatoes. He does it every time. He can't help himself."

By now, Cody had recovered from the initial shock of Jimmy's revelations. Obviously, the inmate's intent was to test his toughness. The room fell silent as all the guards stopped talking so they could hear the new chaplain's response.

Cody knew Jimmy had designed his comments to shock him and even cause him to gag or throw up right there in the middle of the dining room in front of all the guards. Of course, this would be extremely humiliating, and Cody knew there was no quicker way of losing the respect of the entire prison population. For a moment, he felt decidedly nauseated, but recovered after a gulp of iced tea. Struggling against the image of the disgusting inmate spewing sperm over the cooking pot, he reached down, got a sizable bite of mashed potatoes from his plate, and shoved it into his mouth. He chewed thoughtfully as though he were a food critic sampling a gourmet dish at a renowned French restaurant.

The young chaplain eyeballed his challenger with determination. "Well, I don't know what Ralph did to these potatoes, but they're delicious."

This evoked a few chuckles and nods of approval from the guards. Though he tried to hide behind his wicked smile, Jimmy's face began to crack with frustration.

Cody continued, "Did anyone shit in the gravy?"

The astonished convict replied, "What?"

"I asked if anyone in the kitchen defecated in the gravy, because that's how I like my gravy, with the fresh taste of a real big pile of shit in it."

The guards broke out in riotous laughter. Embarrassed, Jimmy focused on the floor and said nothing.

Cody said, "Well, you tell them back in the kitchen that I'm not eating any more gravy here unless someone takes a crap in it. I knew something wasn't quite right about this gravy."

Humiliated, Jimmy hung his head and trudged back to the kitchen among catcalls and laughter from the guards.

To Cody's surprise, another inmate who had been serving coffee refills among the tables almost immediately approached him. Again, the room fell silent.

The man was a rugged young Hispanic with tattoos and scars on his arms and neck. His muscles rippled under a tightly stretched T-shirt and his face drew up into a stiff, malicious grin. He paused a moment to make sure he had everyone's full attention, and then announced, "I've had my eye on you, Reverend. I saw you in the yard this morning, and then again when you came through the line for lunch. I think you got a real fine ass."

Cody heard a few snickers from the crowd. The guards on the other side of the room had left their tables for a better view of the standoff. They stood in a wide semicircle around the chaplains' table.

Cody struggled for a suitable response. The bold statement flabbergasted him. Finally, he eked out a weak retort. "How could you possibly know anything about my ass? I've had this suit jacket on all-day. It covers my backside completely. You must have me confused with someone whose ass you've actually seen."

The inmate moved close to Cody, invading his space. Slyly, and with a sickening sneer, he said, "I can just tell you have a real sweet ass. It gives me a hard-on."

A few uncomfortable titters rippled through the onlookers. All eyes were glued to Cody.

The young chaplain struggled for a response. Suddenly, an inspiration flashed through his mind. He asked, "When is your next parole board hearing?"

Some of the smirk faded from the inmate's face. Hesitantly, he answered, "In a couple of months. What does that have to do with anything?"

Cody regained his composure and continued with some confidence. "How would you like it if I came to your hearing and explained to the board that you'd been telling me what a sweet ass I have? Do you think that might help you win your freedom?"

The comment staggered the veteran convict. This chaplain was playing by a new set of rules.

Cody went for the jugular. "Well you can count on my being there. And, you know, just the thought of it gives me a hard-on!"

The room erupted in laughter and applause as the defeated inmate turned and retreated quickly behind the kitchen door.

Gaining self-assurance, Cody waited for the noise to die down. He glared at the remaining prisoners around the room and declared, "Next."

Another round of hilarity rose up, but as it died down, surprisingly another inmate shouted the preamble to a new challenge from behind the buffet line. "Hey, Chaplain. Could you smuggle me in some K-Y Jelly?"

Cody didn't have time to answer, though. A booming voice from the doorway crashed through the room like an exploding hand grenade. "I'll bring some Texas hot sauce and personally cram it up your ass, you little pervert. Now, get back to work!"

Captain Sonny LaGrange's overpowering command sent the newest contender and all the other inmates who remained in the dining room scampering back to the refuge of the kitchen.

Sonny, who apparently had witnessed all the inmate provocations from the doorway, walked over to Cody and smiled down on him like a proud father admiring his newborn infant in a crib. Then, he surveyed the officers in the packed dining hall and asked, "Well, boys, what do you think of my new chaplain here?"

Cody blushed as the room erupted in robust applause.

Chaplain Powers walked back into the dining hall after picking up his envelope at the command center. He looked at the crowd that encircled his table, then at Sonny's' beaming face, and finally at his new chaplain. Anxiously, he asked, "Cody, what happened in here? What have you done?"

After lunch, the chaplains strolled out into the yard. Powers explained it was time for him to leave for the women's prison. He recommended Cody spend the afternoon in the refuge of the chaplains' office on the quiet second floor of the processing center. Apologetically, he stated they didn't have enough space to give Cody a private office, but offered him the use of a conference room with large windows that provided a good view of most of the yard.

Gratefully, Cody said, "That sounds fine. I appreciate any space you can give me."

"You can review the prison policy manuals or maybe look at some of my sermon outlines," Powers added. "Don't forget. Your first preaching assignment is tomorrow night."

"Sounds like a great idea. I could use some solitude to recover from the lunchtime drama, and I certainly need help with my sermon, too."

Powers smiled. "You won't find anyone up there except Frank, a prisoner trustee who acts as our clerk. You can learn a lot from him. During his thirty-two years here, he's developed a sophisticated information network. If you want to know what's going down on any particular day, consult Frank. He'll likely know everything before anyone else."

Cody asked, "What crime did he commit?"

"Capital murder. He wasted two guards and a bank vice president during a botched armed robbery. But don't worry, you're quite safe with Frank. In fact, I'd trust him with the lives of my own grandkids. After you spend some time with him, you'll see what I mean."

Powers went on, "He's AKA—also known as—Frankie Stovepipe, or Frankie the Finger. The governor commuted his death sentence on the recommendation of prison officials. Frank headed off a riot many years ago. He knew when it was going down and alerted the officers. I have no doubt that he saved lives on both sides. So, they rewarded him with a commuted sentence, from death to life without parole.

"As you probably have heard, the first of the Inmates' Ten Commandments is 'Thou shalt not snitch.' Frank snitched but came out in great shape, overall. He's a consummate politician. If he were free, he'd probably be a congressman or something." Powers smiled.

"The only prisoners who were extremely upset with him were the ten or so who planned to incite the riot by taking some guards hostage and attacking a rival gang, the Aryan Demons."

"Are they a white supremacy gang?" Cody asked.

"Not emphatically. They're all white guys, but they're not haters, just a bunch of mean biker-types. Sometimes you'll see one with a Rebel flag tattoo, but that's about as radical as they get. They're natural rivals to the black gangs, so sometimes we do have trouble."

Powers seemed to shrug as if that type of thing was inevitable. "The instigators of the failed riot were split up and sent to other prisons across the state, so they're no problem now. Any sympathizers left behind know that if they touch Frank, they'll suffer hellacious reprisals. He's safeguarded by the Aryan Demons, since he saved their asses from a deadly surprise attack. Also, the warden wouldn't take kindly to any violence against Frank. Undoubtedly, he would send the captain after the perpetrators. So, I'd say, in spite of his grand snitch, Frank is one of the safest inmates in this prison." Powers sneaked a glance at his watch.

"Anyway, if you spend some time with him, you'll learn a lot more about prison life than hanging out with me."

As Cody passed through the checkpoint at the entrance to the processing center, a cluster of guards gathered around him to shake his hand.

"Well done, Chaplain."

"You showed those lowlife scumbags. They won't be messing with you anymore."

"We never seen anything like this from a reverend before."

"Great to have you on our side, son."

Basking in the smiles of approval and pats on the back, Cody tried to shrug off the compliments. "Thank you, gentlemen, but it was no big deal."

The guards were having none of it. One of them said, "No big deal? Bullshit. You faced those fuckers out, man. You destroyed them."

An older officer with a corncob pipe steaming from his mouth excitedly called for the group's attention. He yelled out, "Hey, didn't anyone shit in the gravy?" The comment ignited a round of hilarity, and as the old guard guffawed, he spewed embers from his pipe onto his shirt and pants. He continued laughing as he brushed the fiery cinders from his clothes and stomped at them on the ground in front of him.

Another guard in the back of the group called out, "Hey, Chaplain. I need you to come over to Cellblock B and put some of the uppity fuckers over there in their place. Can I borrow you for about an hour tomorrow?"

As gracefully as he could, Cody slipped away from the smiling circle of admirers and made his way through the front door of the dingy processing center building where the chaplains kept offices on the second floor.

Powers had told him that upon their arrival at the prison, all new inmates spent two weeks at the center where a team of doctors, psychologists, and counselors tested and evaluated them. Based on these assessments, the warden assigned each inmate a cellblock, a cellmate, and a job. During the rest of their time in the unit, inmates learned prison rules and procedures, and trained for their work assignments.

Above the main entrance to the center, someone had placed a rustic sign obviously made in the prison woodshop. It said, "This is the First Day of the Rest of Your Life."

Of course, Cody had seen the popular, overused slogan many times over the years, but he mused about the mockery of its placement here. He wondered how he would feel if he were a convicted felon with a life sentence and no possibility of parole. He shuddered, and then shook off the disturbing sensation as he bolted up to the second floor, taking the steps two at a time.

An iron door separated the chaplains' office from the severity of the rest of the prison. An old, laminate sign with broken, jagged edges denoted the office hours and provided an emergency pager number. After Cody knocked, he could see someone peer through the peephole on the other side, and as the heavy door opened, the shining face of Frankie the Finger shot into view. Compellingly, the short, sinewy inmate drew Cody into the room with a friendly handshake and closed the door quickly, explaining, "Outside official office hours, I keep the door locked. If I didn't, inmates would swamp me with chicken-shit requests so I'd never get anything done for the chaplains."

Frankie's winning, boyish smile contrasted sharply with his wrinkled face, a visage creased so profoundly that only many years on death row could have chiseled it. Cody also guessed Frankie's Jimmy Dean hairstyle had been the rage at the time Frank came to the prison. He'd noticed many inmates with dated hairstyles and guessed they hadn't varied much from the first year or two of their incarceration. Time froze for the men when they came through the Castle portal. Not much inside the prison would have changed over time. Except for two hours of television a day, nothing really would reflect emerging trends on the outside.

The chaplains' office was large and bright, with fresh paint on the walls and neatly kept shelves containing various religious books. A faded, torn map of the Holy Land dominated one wall, and under it, some surprisingly nice leather chairs surrounded a polished conference table. This area reminded Cody of a reading room in a library. The other end of the long office space looked more like a traditional waiting room with rows of chairs and neatly stacked magazines on end tables. Cody liked the place, with its high ceilings and bright atmosphere. It was the first area he'd visited here that didn't feel like a prison.

Frank pointed to a large desk by the door. "Now, this is mine," he said with obvious pride. "I sit right here all day, seven days a week."

Cody asked, "You work every day?"

Frank shrugged his shoulders. "I got nothing else to do. May as well be here than out in the yard getting into trouble." He snickered.

Cody took another minute to survey the room and declared, "I like this place. Obviously, you take great care of it."

The compliment clearly delighted Frank. "Thank you, Chaplain. Not many people notice it, I guess, but I spend a lot of time keeping the office clean and organized." He looked at Cody admiringly, "I already heard about what you done in the lunchroom today. I would have given anything to see the look on Jimmy the Weasel's face when you told him to go shit in the gravy." Frank laughed. "I guess you heard what Sonny done to the bastards."

"No. What?"

"He rounded them up and took them to the Hole. Talk about humiliation. First, a new employee, a man of the cloth no less, faces them down. Then, they get a week in hell on top of it."

The comments worried Cody. He didn't want to see the inmates excessively punished and thought the public humiliation he'd given them was enough. Besides, the greater the punishment, the greater their anger toward him would rise. He said, "I don't like this. They'll really be looking for revenge now."

Frankie brushed it aside. "Don't worry about them. Sure, they'd like to get even, no doubt about it. But those bastards won't come within fifty yards of you again. If Sonny caught them trying to mess with you, he'd beat the shit out of them. And he told them that, too."

Cody said, "Well, I don't want them to get into a lot of trouble. I just want them to leave me alone in the future."

"No worries there. I'm sure of that. Besides, I wouldn't feel too sorry for them. The captain will probably let them out in a couple of days. But something else you might want to consider—keep your eye out for other guys who may try to challenge you. You'd think after today, that nobody would want to fuck with you, but a few always might want to try something foolish." Frankie gave Cody a grave expression.

"See, by totally wasting those assholes at lunch, you made sort of a reputation for yourself. Now, if someone can get the best of you, then he'll look all the better in the eyes of the other inmates. It's kind of like being Billy the Kid. Everyone was gunning for him because the guy who succeeded in killing him must surely be a mean motherfucker and the fastest gunslinger on earth, true?"

Cody acknowledged, "I see your point."

Frank continued. "So, you should always expect an attack. Of course, I doubt it'll happen because Sonny has put the word out that you're under his protection. That means anyone who tries to fuck you over will have to answer to him. Any rational man wouldn't mess with you at all, but that's the trouble. We have some crazy convicts in here. They do shit a normal person would never dream of doing. Usually, that's why they're in here in the first place." Frank seemed a little embarrassed and laughed.

"Despite the crazies, you have nothing much to worry about. If I hear anything, I'll let you know. The dumb bastards who would do something stupid like that usually brag about it first. They want to have a big audience to witness how tough they are. So likely, I'd hear something in plenty of time to warn you."

Cody felt deflated. Frank's sensible advice robbed him of some of the elation he'd felt after humbling the convicts in the cafeteria. Clearly, danger still lurked.

Frank read the young chaplain's face like front-page headlines. "As I said, don't worry about it. Just be aware. You'll be fine."

Cody said, "I can see why Captain LaGrange and Chaplain Powers depend on you to keep them informed. Thanks for looking out for me."

Sounding more like a maître d' than a convicted murderer, Frank said, "My pleasure." He motioned for Cody to follow him down a corridor off the reception area. "This way, Chaplain, to your accommodations."

Their footsteps rebounded on the brightly polished tile as they made their way down a long hallway illuminated by excessive rows of fluorescent lights. They passed the closed doors of the other chaplains' offices and walked into a large room at the end of the hall. As he stepped inside, Cody noticed a neat sign on the door that read "Conference Room." Beneath this, was another sign that made him feel proud. It said "Chaplain Cody Palmeroy."

Bookcases filled the walls of the rather large rectangular space, and several mismatched chairs encircled an embattled conference table. An old army cot dominated one corner, and in another, a comfortable-looking wingback chair sat invitingly alongside an end table and reading lamp. As Chaplain Powers had promised Cody, wide windows covered most of the outside wall. Eager to see what view they offered, Cody walked over and gazed down on the recreation yard. Though iron bars covered all of the opening, the vista was still a good one and provided a broad panorama of the area below, where inmates were playing basketball in the bleak drizzle of the chilly afternoon. Other prisoners lined the inside perimeter of the gray stone walls and chatted while bartering for cigarettes.

Frank proudly announced, "I had this phone installed for you today." He pointed to an old black phone in the middle of the conference table. "You can call anywhere in the prison, but not outside. We have no outside lines this side of the Rubicon. Otherwise, inmates would be trying to break in here all the time to call their girlfriends or arrange drug deals."

Cody said, "Hey, thanks for the phone and the sign, too. It makes me feel right at home."

Apologetically, Frank pointed to a stack of binders and file folders in the center of the table. "I hate to bring this up, but here are the manuals and sermons Chaplain Powers said you could review this afternoon. He called me from his car just before you arrived, so I pulled together the most important stuff for you. If I were you, I'd just read the summary at the beginning of each section in the manuals. Some helpful information is in there, but sifting through it will take a long time. To tell you the truth, I wouldn't be in a hurry to read any of that bureaucratic bullshit."

Cody looked gloomily at the stack of binders. "Believe me, I'm not. Besides, I don't think I can concentrate on it right now. That confrontation at lunch has me all churned up. I think I'll just look out the window for a while."

The comment pleased Frank. "Now here's a man who has his priorities straight. And a little nap might also be in order." With a conspiratorial smile, Frank added, "I'll shut the door so if anyone comes in up front, they won't disturb you. Sometimes guards will drop by in the afternoon just to chat."

As the trustee turned to leave, Cody said, "Chaplain Powers told me about your preventing that riot. That took a lot of guts, Frank. I respect you for what you did."

"Well, I didn't much consider the danger involved. I was too motivated."

"To avoid the electric chair?"

"Oh, for sure. But not for the reason you might think. It all had to do with my mother, God rest her soul. I was a hardened convict then. I didn't give much a damn about dying, I really didn't. But a few weeks before my execution date, when all my appeals ran dry, my momma came to see me. First time she'd been here since my incarceration. She rode the Greydog for six hours. When she saw me, of course she started crying. She said she couldn't bear to see her baby sizzling like a piece of bacon in an iron skillet." Frank looked at Cody as if to gauge his reaction.

"And that's what happens when they bring down the lightning. You sizzle. You hear the blood crackling and popping. Sometimes you even catch on fire. This was before they built glass walls between the chair and the gallery. You were right there in the same room, just a few feet away. You could see everything. You could hear it and smell it, too."

Frank leaned against the doorjamb and looked up at a large, stained ceiling tile as though it were a window into the past. "I begged her not to come to my execution, but she said that her baby wouldn't die alone in front of a pack of bloodthirsty strangers. She said, 'Just before they put the blindfold on you, I want you to look into my eyes and know that I love you. And that in spite of what you done, I'm glad I born you into the world. That's the last thing I want you to see, the face of someone who loves you.'"

Tears clouded Frank's eyes. His lips quivered. Cody regretted bringing up the subject, but before he could suggest that they discuss it another time, the death row refugee continued.

"Well, that torn me up so bad, I couldn't stand it no more. To think of Mama sitting there watching me while I'm frying like a piece of Sunday chicken, jerking around like some tortured animal, and shittin' in my pants, made me sorry for what I done for the first time."

Frank shook his head and looked forlornly at Cody. "So, I started plotting about how I could get out of my death sentence. Then, just like it was a blessing from heaven, this scuttlebutt came to me about the riot those rascals had planned and how they were going to kill some other inmates and some guards, too. Even the captain if they could get to him. So, I told on those fuckers, I surely did. I figured if they got to me and killed me later, it would still be better than frying in the chair in front of my mom. That way, she would just get a phone call and it would be over." He wiped at the corners of his eyes.

"Most prisoners would scoff at me for saying this, but I feel God gave me a second chance with that. So, I try to live the best I can every day."

Cody asked, "What happened after you moved from death row?

"For a while, I was a clerk in the warden's office. Then, I came to work for the chaplains. After a few years, they made me a trustee. Now, I can pretty much go anywhere in the prison I want this side of the Rubicon. Also, I go out to schools and churches to tell the youngsters my story and encourage them to stay out of trouble."

For a long moment, Cody didn't respond. He was studying Frank, trying to imagine the inmate's life compared with his own commonplace existence. Finally, he broke the silence. "That's a hell of a story, Frank."

The inmate laughed, "Ain't it though. Sometimes I can't believe it's me. I think it's a dream or I'm watching someone else's life in a movie or something."

Cody said, "I don't think I'd have the courage to stop that riot like you did, Frank. But I guess just getting up every day, knowing you have a life sentence ahead of you takes a lot of fortitude, too."

Frank said, "Inmates don't talk about this much, but waking up in the morning is the worst part of the day for most of us. Just as you come awake, only for a quick moment, you don't realize where you are or your circumstances. Then, like a load of shit bricks, it hits you. A flood comes over you and you remember it all, that you're a convict and you're here for life, and you have no hope for anything better. Sometimes you just want to die. After my momma passed, I prayed that I would die in my sleep. I studied about suicide a lot, even thought of paying someone to kill me. But somehow I kept on going. It wasn't just one day at a time. I lived by the hour, by the minute."

The phone on Frank's desk at the other end of the office began to ring, and as he closed the door to head up the hall, he looked back and winked, "Happy dreams, Chaplain."

Gloomily, Cody pondered the stack of reading material at the center of the conference table. While a nap was an appealing idea, his confrontations with the convicts at the dining room still had him so worked up sleep would be impossible, at least for a while.

He sat and selected a folder of Chaplain Power's sermon outlines and began to flip through them. The material was good, and he didn't need long to find something suitable for his first prison worship service the following night.

Next, he grabbed a couple of black binders containing institutional policies and procedures. The material was insufferably boring and within half an hour, he put his head down on a manual and fell into a deep, dreamless sleep.

Something awakened him, and he jerked up from the open notebook. By the time he was fully awake, he couldn't remember what had disturbed him. He glanced at his watch and was shocked to see he had been asleep almost an hour. He went to the restroom down the hall and splashed some water on his face, and then walked to the reception area. Frank had left him a note saying he had gone to pick up the chaplains' mail and run some other errands. Cody fetched a soda from the refrigerator in the small kitchen off the hall, and headed back to his office to tackle more policy and procedure manuals.

This time, Cody was more selective in his choice of reading material. Happily, he discovered a notebook filled with journal articles about understanding inmate behavior. After reading a couple of pieces about prison violence, he found an interesting article about inmates' tendencies to exaggerate their crimes and their experiences during incarceration. The piece said convicts imprisoned for long periods were particularly susceptible to aggrandizing their personal histories. Their embellishments and inventions often displaced reality to the point these inmates believed them to be true and could no longer distinguish between fantasy and reality. Although the author of the piece didn't explain the reasons for such exaggerations, Cody surmised the reality of prisoners' circumstances was so bleak they used make-believe as a coping mechanism.

He had no doubt that if he faced Frank's dismal fate, he would construct elaborate fantasies to deal with a lifetime of certain imprisonment. Perhaps, he would fashion himself as an Arabian sheik with several-hundred concubines. Maybe he would go for a superhero role, or life as a biblical personage. Moses might be a good choice. He could dream of using the holy man's magical staff—the one Moses transformed into a serpent to impress the Pharaoh—to part the prison walls as Moses did the Red Sea. Then, he would lead the entire inmate population to freedom as they chanted his name.

Cody found himself slipping deeper into the fantasy.

As he turned back to watch the exodus, the pursuing guards began to stumble over the rubble of the fallen wall, cursing Cody and waving their shotguns menacingly. While his followers cowered in doubt and fear, Cody raised his magical staff again and closed the wall.

Then, he began to hand out keys to each inmate for one of the two-thousand Ferraris he'd called down from heaven to expedite their getaway. Another wave of his staff produced a scantily clad Playboy model for each man. The convicts crowded around him, cheering and dancing.

A strange, fiery cloud appeared in the sky, and the face of a beautiful woman stared down from it. She told him to follow the cloud, which would lead them to the Promised Land, a refuge of ever-flowing wine and countless beautiful, naked women. Cody took the lead in the line of Ferraris and headed off toward the cloud. As the nubile young woman in his passenger seat leaned over and plunged her tongue into his ear, Cody's fantasy abruptly crashed due to the sound of a disturbing commotion out in the yard.

He hurried to the window and saw a dark spectacle unfolding on the basketball court right below his second-story refuge. In the bleak, gray light of the fading day, evil was gathering, and with it, hate and rage, too.

Hatred had etched vicious creases on the tightly drawn faces of two inmates who faced each other with crude shanks in their hands. It radiated from the growing mob of jeering prisoners who encircled the combatants, calling for blood. Or, death. Yes, death would be better. They chanted to the primal beat of aggression, each calling out the name of the contestant he favored. But this was quickly overcome with the unified mantra, "Kill! Kill!"

Cody felt a cold tremor course through his body. The cause wasn't fear for his own safety. No one could climb the wall to his office and penetrate the iron bars that protected him. His shaking was a primitive reaction to the vicious spite between the two men, the bloodlust of the crowd. He could feel the spirit of evil rushing to the scene, strengthened by the dark power of the inmates' malevolence.

Cody became aware of Frank's gentle presence at his side. It comforted him. Some of the chill dissipated.

Out on the asphalt, the chant abruptly stopped. As if choreographed, the inmates surrounding the two gladiators backed up and formed a wide, tight circle. Several-hundred spectators stood on their toes or craned their necks for a better view of the impending duel.

Cody thought the circle was a planned way to keep guards from reaching the conflict in time to stop it before some decisive conclusion. The dense ring of humanity made quickly moving to the front of the action impossible for the officers. Already, a wedge of about ten guards tried to penetrate the human barrier, but progressed only slightly in reaching the conflict.

Cody supposed the prison riot squad would soon arrive with rubber bullets and tear gas. They were probably already in the armory suiting up in their special gear.

Everyone knew the well-armed guards would eventually overcome the obstacle of the tightly formed crowd. They would pounce on the men with the crude, makeshift knives, stop the fight, and throw them in the Hole. But that was later. For now, the moment belonged to the prisoners. They were in control.

During the ritual of the chant and the formation of the circle, the fighters stood just inches apart, each glaring at his rival with a withering, toxic gaze. Now, the time had come for killing, and the inmates slowly backed away from each other to a distance of about ten feet. One removed his shirt and threw it to the ground. He was about fifty years old, but boasted a surprisingly muscular physique. Though much younger, his adversary, who had a tattoo on the back of his shaven head that said "Fuk U," was encumbered by considerable layers of fat.

With a vicious yell and surprising speed, the shirtless, older convict charged and plunged his shank deep into the fleshy, oversized upper arm of his opponent. Apparently, this was part of the younger man's plan, because as he offered up his arm in sacrifice, he gained an unchecked opening for a quick strike to his opponent's midsection. With his own version of a Rebel yell, the younger inmate stuck his shank into his victim's left side. Cody could see the potential for death. If the convict pressed downward, he could tear a deep gash all the way to the groin. Cody imagined intestines bubbling up through the wound like a pot of boiling snakes. Thankfully, the man kept the blade in place; however, he quickly began to turn the knife.

After enduring a twist or two, the shirtless convict used his fist to deliver a crunching blow to his opponent's throat. The fighters fell apart and landed on the asphalt, each taking a moment to assess his wounds. Neither seemed enthusiastic about jumping up to continue the contest.

The crowd was silent, waiting to see who would arise first to take advantage of his fallen opponent.

Since he'd walked to the window moments before, Cody had been trying to compose a command he might yell down to the inmates to stop the fight. He hadn't come up with anything yet he thought would penetrate the armor of hate or the lust for blood. Now was the opportune time for him to intervene, likely his only chance, in fact.

Not knowing what he would say to the fighters, he impulsively raised the window anyway and shouted, "Hey, you dumb fucks!"

Several-hundred heads followed the sound of his voice to the window of the chaplains' office. Cody thought he must have looked ridiculous to the hardened criminals below, but he had a single-minded determination to stop the fight. Through the bars, he shouted at the combatants, "Put away those shanks, and get over to the hospital!"

The shirtless man held his side as blood flowed around his closed fingers. He yelled at Cody, "Why should we?"

"Because if you don't, one of you will die, and the other will spend about a year in the Hole. That's real smart. That's just brilliant. Is that what you want?"

Someone in the crowd tried to rekindle the savage chant. "Kill! Kill!"

Cody cut him off. "That's real smart, too. Most of you can't even see the fight. All you can see is the back of the head of the guy in front of you, yet you still yell 'Kill!'"

Both convicts regained their composure and jumped up from the ground to face their new rival. The bald, heavy one yelled up in defiance, "We want to fight. Now leave us the hell alone."

The other shouted agreement, "Yeah, we want to fight, so what are you going to do about it, Reverend?"

Cody had no idea how to answer. He had no time to think. Unexplainably, he blurted out, "If you don't stop fighting right now, I'm going to come down there and whip both your asses."

Laughter broke out among the spectators.

The shirtless one took up the challenge, "What are you gonna whip us with? You got a shank?"

Cody quickly scanned the room. He spotted a large, heavy book on a table by the window. "I'm going to whip you with the Old Testament."

More laughter from the spectators.

Contemptuously, the bald inmate called up to the window, "So you are gonna whip us, are you? You and whose army?"

"I'll be by myself. Might bring God."

"That's bullshit. God don't go around whippin' people's asses. What kind of God would whip a man's ass?"

With confidence now replacing his awkward uncertainty, Cody yelled back, "My God. The God of the gravy."

The spectators whooped up a gigantic laugh that rippled around the encircled mob like a wave cheer at a football stadium. The two fighters looked at each other in disbelief. Bewildered and disarmed, they had lost control.

Cody took advantage of the moment. By chance, he had overheard two guards waiting in line at lunch discussing how inmates could resolve their differences in the prison's gymnasium with gloved fists, helmets, and supervision by the staff.

He shouted out from between the bars of his window, "Why don't you settle this in the boxing ring? I'll ask Captain LaGrange if he'll let this fight today go without punishment if you stop voluntarily now."

They were silent. They were listening.

Cody cried out to the crowd. "That way everyone can see. All of you will have a good seat."

A murmur of agreement pulsated through the spectators.

The two inmates looked at each other and shrugged their shoulders. The shirtless one said, "Who'll referee the fight?"

Cody said, "I don't know. One of the guards."

The other inmate said, "We don't trust them."

Impulsively, Cody countered, "I'll do it. I'll referee your fight."

The fighters eyed each other again and nodded. The shirtless one said, "Okay, we accept."

To Cody's surprise, applause broke out among the spectators.

The younger one asked, "When will we fight?"

Behind him, Cody heard Frank whisper advice. He grasped onto it like a life raft in a stormy ocean. He yelled down to the convicts, "If you heal enough from your wounds, the fight will be one month from today. Just before dinner. Now, shake on it."

The inmates begrudgingly shook hands, which precipitated another hearty round of applause. As the crowd scattered, some guards were finally able to break through to take away the crude, blood-soaked knives. Showing a degree of kindness that surprised Cody, they calmly escorted the injured combatants away, toward the prison hospital.

Frank shut the window as Cody unsteadily slumped down into a nearby chair. His experiences on death row and at the officers' cafeteria had been agonizing enough, but this was even more traumatic. Wearily, he asked Frank for some water.

A few minutes later, Cody's heart had slowed down a bit, though his hands were still shaking.

Frank said, "I can't believe you did that. I thought one of those guys was dead for sure."

The phone rang. It was Captain LaGrange. "Well, I'll be damned if my new chaplain isn't also a boxing referee." He laughed heartily into the phone as Cody held the handset away from himself for a moment. "I can't believe you faced those bastards down."

Cody asked, "Did I make a fool of myself?"

Sonny responded, "Hell no, you didn't. You did good, boy. You prevented a deadly encounter. Whipping their asses with the Old Testament. That has to be the damndest thing I ever heard." He laughed again, vibrating the handset. "I'm pleased with the way you handled it. It was an ugly dustup, that's for sure."

Cody said, "It scared the crap out of me. My hands are still shaking."

Sonny said, "You'll feel better soon. Maybe you should throw down one of those famous Valium tablets. This is the time to take one, for certain. By the way, do you know anything about boxing?"

Cody admitted, "Nothing. I just watch it sometimes on TV."

The captain of the guards laughed again. "Well, you'd better learn something about the rules before next month. Get with Nasty George Ledbetter. He's a guard on the third shift. He's pretty mean, George is. He was a state Golden Gloves champion in his day and usually referees bouts of this kind, but the inmates think he's dishonest. They've accused him of taking bribes. So really, it's good that you're going to referee this fight. The men will trust you. Nasty George won't like it much that you're replacing him, but don't worry. I'll have a talk with him and make him one of the judges. He'll teach you the rules and all the dirty moves to look for. Frank knows quite a bit about boxing, too, and he can help you."

Cody felt better. At least, he'd have some help in preparing to referee the fight, "Thanks, I'll get with them."

Sonny declared, "The boys up here on the Mountain have already started a pool. The bets are whether you'll wear a clerical collar or a referee's shirt when you step into the ring."

Wearily, Cody responded, "I don't know. I haven't even thought about it yet."

Sonny said seriously, "Okay, son. Good job. Now, go home and get some rest. I know it's been a hell of a day for you. They won't all be like this, I promise."

After the call, Cody leaned back in his chair to recover for a few minutes longer. The assurances from Sonny helped calm him down. He worried he had overstepped his authority by intervening in the fight. Gratefully, he accepted more water from Frank.

After a moment, the inmate advised, "What you did was good, real good, but you'll have to learn something about boxing before the match. You can make a fool of yourself if you don't do a first-rate job calling the fight."

Somewhat irritably, Cody said, "Okay, okay. That's what the captain said, too, and I know you're right, but I just can't think about it now. Tomorrow I'll get on it. But now, I'm exhausted."

After a few minutes, Frank announced it was time for him to go, since the prisoners' dining hall would soon close for the evening, and he didn't want to miss his dinner. He said, "When you leave, just be sure to lock the deadbolts." He handed Cody a ring with several keys and then shook his hand. "It's been an honor meeting you, Chaplain Palmeroy. You are something to see, man. You are really something to see."

A few minutes later, Cody heard Frank exit and lock the door behind him. The young chaplain felt the beginning stages of a migraine coming on, so he got up and turned off the lights. Still, the reflection of the powerful searchlights on the battlements bathed the room in an eerie, pulsating glow. He walked to the window and saw the yard was vacant now, except for a few officers taking a smoking break by the Rubicon. All the inmates were at dinner.

Watching the rhythmic sway of the spotlights, Cody began to wonder if he'd made the right choice in coming to the prison for his internship. What was he doing in this place, where venom spewed like malignant fountains from spiteful mouths and the hard rain of hate fell in torrents, where rogue waves of misery washed over the fallen? He wondered what good he could do here in this cesspool of human depravity, this bleak caldron of malevolence. Could he make any difference? Would anything he could accomplish in this prison really matter?

And what about God? Did He even care about this place, or had He forsaken it long ago as an incontrovertible and hopeless poisoned well of iniquity?

Then, some light began to creep in around the dark edges of his cynicism. As he reflected on the events of the day, he realized the intense, traumatic encounters had overshadowed some brighter moments, signs the prison was not the utterly godless place it seemed on the surface.

Cody had noticed an inmate use his lunch break to roll his friend in a wheelchair all the way from the hospital to the open yard so the patient could benefit from the therapy of being outdoors. He had seen Frank's eyes fill with tears of compassion as he'd talked about his mother. Cody had watched a prisoner by the back wall sharing cookies and cigarettes out of a care package from home. The man gave generously to his fellow inmates and the guards, too, until the package was empty. While sitting in his office, he had heard benign laughter in the yard and the friendly conversations of inmates passing the time with jokes and parting company with well wishes.

Compared with the relatively genteel world outside the prison walls, none of these acts was overly impressive. Nevertheless, they offered something positive in the face of the toxicity and despair that dominated Cody's first impressions of penitentiary life.

Although permeated with depravity, this prison could also be a place of hope and promise. Since it held potential for good, Cody concluded that God hadn't forsaken it. As wicked as it was, this human menagerie was God's place, too, just like every other place in the world that He had created. And, if God was within these prison walls, then Cody would be His man inside them.

As the harsh beams of the searchlights swayed haphazardly over the yard, and prisoners began to trickle back from the cafeteria to their cellblocks, Cody pondered the God of the whole world, of everything and everybody. The God of the beautiful, shiny places everyone loved as well as the ugly, desolate ones, which the world had abandoned. The God of the good people and the bad.

If He was the God of Reverend Powers, surely, He must also be the God of Kenny the Ghoul.

He was the God of Warden Mack and the Short Eyes, of Sonny LaGrange and the queens of the boiler room, of the south yard guards and the shower bitches of Cellblock B.

As Cody bolted the door of the chaplains' office and headed down the poorly lit hall, the images poured into his mind like floodwaters through a broken dam.

God of the innocent and the guilty, the watch commander and the rapist, of the prison doctor and the executioner, of the parole officers and the heroin zombies of the license plate shop, of the Gideon Bible and the revolver.

He felt a spotlight from the wall follow him for a moment as he made his way across the yard to the overhang that sheltered the shores of the Rubicon. He said goodnight to the cluster of deferential officers in the command center who gathered around him for handshakes and high-fives. He walked slowly, thoughtfully, down the long tunnel under the castle.

God of the infant and the inmate, of clemency and hard time, of the C Block cell warriors and the born-again bigots on the wall, of the prison pulpit and the electric chair, of the gold ankle bracelet and the leg iron, of the worn down shopkeeper and the sleazy shoplifter.

The glad-handing guards at Checkpoint One, still snickering about the miracle of the Valium, advised Cody to drive carefully. Already, news reports blaring from the small radio on Sergeant Fuller's desk described several serious accidents around the foggy city. Exhausted from the events of the day, Cody trudged slowly on the wet pavement of the parking lot to his car.

God of the gardenia and the steamroller, of the iron lung and the atom bomb, of the angels and the crack whores, of the preachers and the pimps, the cockroach and the rose.

He started his car and headed out into the misty night, driving on autopilot while the God of everything captivated his consciousness.

God of Mother Theresa and Jezebel, of the street cleaners and the streetwalkers, of the miracle and the mundane, of the supernova and the votive candle, of the rainbow and the crossbow, of the springbok and the hyena, of the lamb and the lion.

In a daze, he stopped at a light and waved off a beggar who approached his car. After a moment, he heard a horn blow impatiently behind him. Without looking back, he jerked forward into the wretched night.

God of sugarcane and the hurricane, of the beauty queen and the bar hag, the skyscraper and the slum hovel, the corner office and the sweatshop, the symphony orchestra and the Gook's trumpet, of the Good Samaritan and the pirate, the wedding vow and the broken heart.

He pulled into his driveway and sat for a while, staring at the dashboard lights.

God of redemption and discontent, of den mothers and Aryan brothers, of the White House and the whorehouse, of Camelot and the inner-city project, of the Senate orator and the car-lot hustler, of Tinker Bell and Frankenstein, of the convent and the coven.

As if in a trance, he slowly made his way up the wrought-iron stairs on the side of the house to the third story, pushed open the door and kicked away the letters beneath the mail slot. As he plodded down the narrow hall, he glanced into the kitchen, but the thought of food sickened him. In the bedroom, he nudged off his shoes, tossed his jacket and clerical collar on a chair, and crashed onto the bed. He lay there, staring at the stagnant ceiling fan, slipping under the spell of the gentle rain that began to fall on the metal roof of his garret apartment.

God of the lily and the landfill, of the goldfinch and the cobra, of the Stradivarius and the jukebox, of business class and the doublewide, of the quarterback and the hunchback, the celebrity and the hillbilly, of the holiday and Judgment Day.

His eyes closed, but the unstoppable, chaotic parade of images marched on.

God of the Promised Land and the Warsaw Ghetto, of the cathedral and the revival tent, of sunset's soft glow and napalm's fury, of genuine beauty and the face-lift lie, the schoolteacher and the psychopath, of forgiveness and unrequited rage.

He felt sleep began to creep into his bed. He fought it off, not knowing why. His thoughts became increasingly fragmented.

God of the comrade and the tycoon, of the daughters of the moon and the mall walkers of Zen, of regurgitation and fornication, of the dragonfly and the window unit, of dark matter and the nightmare, of Abraham and the Dali Lama, of the throw rug and the magic carpet, of the first kiss and the last farewell.

Even as sleep finally captured him, the images streamed on in a fractured, rambling dream.

God of the Haptown mater and the graveside breakfast, of the suffragette and the switchblade, of the microwave and the tidal wave, of the sexless spinster and the French tickler, of the Hittites and the Mennonites, the unicorn and the rooster, of Sitting Bull and Ramses, of Sappho and Caesar, of the handmaiden and the hand job, of Tampax and income tax, of the charmed particle and Angkor Wat, the limousine and the rickshaw, the black widow and the personal Jesus, the stock market and the fish market, the padded bra and the overdraft, the chicken bone and the asphalt road, the neurosurgeon and the shaman, of the crib and the coffin, of rapture and agony, of triumph and the stillborn dream.

Abruptly, the bewildering stream of images stopped, and for a moment, he floated blissfully in a dark void, a vast abyss of emptiness.

Then, as another dream enveloped him, Cody stood in a field of soft grass. A gentle breeze whispered through his hair. He looked up. The stars seemed infinite, immutable.

Suddenly, a golden staircase appeared in front of him. Wide and inviting, the steps rose in endless majesty far higher than Cody could see. Marvelous amber light radiated from within, and diamond-bright spangles glittered on the surface in an eerie dance. He sensed the staircase was always there, right before him, but only now, through a miraculous vision, was he able to see it.

Behind him, he heard menacing barks and wails from some pack of predators. Wolves perhaps, or jackals. Yes, jackals. He considered it strange that he would think of jackals when he had never seen one. He couldn't even remember how the animal appeared from a picture or movie he might have seen. But he was sure the baleful creatures were jackals, and he knew they were coming for him. Forbiddingly, they howled again. This time, much closer.

Now, carried on the wind, a whisper, a woman's gentle, enchanting voice. "Cody, climb. Come to me. I wait for you at the tree by the river. Come, drink the waters, and never thirst again."

The voice was familiar but he sensed that it didn't belong to anyone he knew or even a single woman. It was, rather, the collective expression of all women, the Greek chorus of the feminine universe.

Then for an elusive moment, he saw on the staircase the woman who whispered to him, a glorious, inscrutable figure with eyes that shinned like bright stars. She wore an open robe and from her belly a soft bronze light shined out in promise of some grand and unfathomable future.

Behind him, the howls grew louder, closer. He spun around to look, but could see nothing in the impenetrable darkness. Instinctively, he took a quick step toward the alluring safety of the staircase, but stopped.

The image of the mystical woman had disappeared.

He listened for her voice to return, but he heard nothing. Intuitively, he sensed she wouldn't repeat her mysterious plea.

Gazing up, he tried to see the end of the stairs, but couldn't. They rose to the farthest star and beyond. His head throbbed with questions. How long would it take to climb the steps? Where did they lead? Who was waiting for him at the top? What did whoever was waiting want?

Torn in the anguish of indecisiveness, he said, "I don't know what to do."

He evaluated the staircase again. Sensibly, he realized the journey was too far.

Finally, sadly, he called out, "I can't come now. I'm too tired to climb, and I'm afraid. Some other time, but not tonight. Forgive me, but please, not tonight."

Instantly, as though he had offended it, the majestic staircase melted into the darkness, and mercifully, just as the demon jackals were upon him, Cody's dream faded to black.

# Chapter 8

*Why Angels Puke*

The angels were vomiting. And God was, too.

The appalling image blasted into Cody's mind as he stood at the pulpit of the prison chapel.

He blinked his eyes to clear his head of the alarming scene that violated him, and then inhaled a deep breath, cleared his throat, and continued preaching.

The young chaplain was anxious about his first sermon to the convicts, and the size of the crowd added to his bothersome case of jitters.

Chaplain Powers had told him to expect about fifty inmates and a smattering of guards. As he surveyed the congregation, he reckoned he stood before at least two hundred inmates and about twenty or so officers. The group mainly gravitated to the front of the room with a few scattered about in the middle.

The back rows were empty at first, but two inmates came in late, during the spiritual hymn, "Joshua Fought the Battle of Jericho." Apprehensively, the pair glanced around, and then sat on the back pew.

Cody thought about inviting them to come down closer to the front so they could feel a part of the group, but he knew some people preferred the back seats of a church. So, he left them alone as the hymn marched on.

Joshua commanded the children to shout,
And the walls came tumbling down,
Joshua fought the battle of Jericho,
And the walls came tumbling down.

Cody thought the chapel was too big. The room had once served as the prison's main auditorium. Now, the space smothered the sense of intimacy the young chaplain hoped to cultivate with his congregation.

The pews were a dogged, mismatched collection donated by churches around town, and the gloomy, windowless room was dispiriting. To him, it looked more like a worn-out high school gymnasium than a church, despite pitiful attempts to hearten it with faded posters depicting Jesus and the apostles, crookedly affixed with masking tape to the dingy walls.

The young chaplain was about five minutes into his sermon, and so far, his presentation pleased him. At the last minute, he'd discarded his plan to use one of Chaplain Power's old sermons in favor of the familiar story of Jericho. It was a powerful account of how the Israelites put their trust in God, who obliged them by crumbling the walls of the ancient city, thus clearing another obstacle in their epic struggle for the Promised Land.

Cody hoped the story provided a meaningful analogy for the inmates. While God wouldn't raze the prison walls for them, their faith could set their spirits free from the oppression of confinement.

After a few minutes in the pulpit, Cody overcame his feelings of anxiety and settled into a relaxed rhythm. He surveyed the faces of the congregation. They seemed interested in his interpretation of the story. They were listening. They wanted more.

As he looked up from his notes, he noticed the pair of inmates who belatedly slipped into the back of the room had disappeared. Maybe they'd decided to leave, but he thought he would have noticed.

Then, he saw what was causing the angels to puke all over the twenty-four carat streets of heaven. A hairy, flabby-ass surfaced in the back pew. It rose and disappeared. Soon it rose again.

Cody stammered, then closed his eyes for a moment, and took a deep breath. He trusted the congregation would assume his confusion was the nervousness of a rookie preacher. As he glanced down at his Bible, he hoped that when he looked up again, the abomination might be gone. But as he unevenly continued preaching, he again surveyed the back of the room.

In the shadows of the dingy chapel, the disgusting ass of the inmate was rising and falling like a pump jack on an oil well.

Cody was not prudish about blasphemy. On many nights, he joined an elite coterie of his rebellious classmates to drink riotous quantities of sanctified wine in the balcony of his divinity school's massive, Gothic chapel. Often, their midnight revelry led to twisted worship parodies. He passionately entered into their drunken, off-key renditions of dark, sardonic anthems. Such hymns originated in crucibles of abstruse theology found mainly in seminaries and monasteries. They bellowed songs such as "Elijah Was a Titty Man," "Bathsheba's Ass Was the Kingdom of Heaven," and "Second Coming Circle Jerk."

Yet, none of his divinity school experiences had prepared him for this exact moment. The sacrilege was devastating, a withering jolt to the core of his sense of propriety. The two inmates were engaged in an unimaginable desecration. They were fucking in the house of God.

As Cody stumbled through his sermon, he lost his concentration and his rhythm. His own voice seemed far away. The audience was still politely listening, but he knew the emotional connection had dissipated.

However, the young chaplain had bigger problems. After overcoming his initial shock, he began to think about how to end the blasphemy in the back of the room.

As he glanced again toward the sodomizing convicts, one head popped up from the pew, and then another. After a quick looksee around, they disappeared and again the hairy ass that haunted him began to rise and fall like a relentless pile driver.

He tried to ignore the abomination, but sadly found it too spellbinding. His next peek toward the back lingered too long and several people turned to see what held the chaplain's attention. They could see nothing from their vantage points since they sat on the main floor while Cody stood behind the pulpit on a stage about five feet high. He couldn't count on any help from the inmates or guards unless he stopped preaching and called attention to the perverted pair hidden by the high backs of the pews.

As he continued his sermon, he noticed the inmates in the back had switched positions. Now, the previously subordinate lover was on top, giving it to his consort in a similar manner from behind. Cody saw the inmate's strained, muscular buttocks pumping like a locomotive wheel piston. He heard one of them emit a sigh. Hopefully, he surveyed the congregation, and though a couple of officers glanced toward the back, no one stood up to investigate the sound.

Just as he was about to stop his sermon and call down the guards on the pair, Sonny LaGrange, like some messianic hero, entered the chapel. Cody felt immense relief as the captain of the guards stood at the back door reverently listening, his hands folded in front of him.

Urgently, Cody eyeballed the captain who returned his gaze with a wide smile of approval that said, You're doing great, son. Even though you don't have yellow jackets in your britches, I like your preaching.

Disappointingly, Sonny hadn't noticed the sodomizing convicts nearby. So, the next time Cody caught the captain's eye, he titled his head slightly toward the inmates behind the pew. Sonny caught on immediately and followed the direction of Cody's nod. He took several steps toward the hidden convicts.

When the captain saw the bare ass rising and falling a few feet away, he exploded. "Goddamn perverts!"

Every head in the chapel snapped to the rear of the room as the captain of the guards jumped over the back of the pew and pounced on the shameless offenders.

As he recognized the inmate on top, he hollered, "Well, look here who's found himself another side boy. It's Lube Job!"

Cody had hoped that Sonny would quietly lead the inmates out of the chapel and render whatever punishment he'd cooked up for them outside. But this blessing was not to be. The captain erupted in savage rage.

"Fucking bitches. I'll castrate you both." He grabbed Lube Job's neck with his giant hand, jerked him straight up on his feet and spun around the fornicator—his trousers and underwear falling to his ankles. To Cody's horror, this maneuver exposed the prisoner's huge erection. Caught in the midst of sexual climax, the man ejaculated

140

wildly as his throbbing penis bobbed up and down. Catastrophically, some of his copious semen shot onto the tops of Sonny's brightly shined boots.

The captain's face changed from red to molten purple. A pulsating vein creased the middle of his forehead. He flipped out the telescoping baton on his belt and viciously whacked Lube Job's penis multiple times. Quickly, the proud phallus drooped to the size of a sweet pickle and spewed blood instead of sperm.

Then, Sonny delivered a devastating punch to the convict's stomach with the blunt end of the truncheon. As Lube Job doubled over and collapsed onto the floor, the captain hollered, "You bastard faggot. How dare you bring these vile acts into the church?"

Cody thought the violence and cursing just added to the sacrilege that had already occurred. Still, he couldn't find the courage to confront Sonny's fury.

The captain searched the floor for the other inmate, but the second convict had slithered away under the pews, toward the door. Moving with impressive speed for a large man, Sonny quickly pounced on him. "Well, let's see what ass-fucking pervert we have here."

The convict was face down on the grimy linoleum floor, covering his head with his hands. The captain kicked him in the leg and the man instinctively used his hands to grasp the site of his pain, revealing a face awash with anguish.

"Well what a surprise. It's Moonpie, chief faggot of C Block." Sonny put his boot on the convict's neck, and with the baton took aim at the back of his victim's head. "I'm going to spill your pansy-ass brains all over the goddamn floor!"

At last, Cody found his voice. "Captain, wait!"

From a faraway place, deep within his rage, Sonny vacantly looked up toward the front of the room and saw more than two hundred convicts and guards staring back at him, aghast. He seemed to be awakening from a trance as he let out a long, agonized sigh and removed his foot from the inmate's neck. The fire retreated from his furious eyes. He stood up straight, letting the baton clatter to the floor.

Several of the guards moved quickly to surround the fallen inmates. Cody came down from the pulpit and walked to Sonny's side, not knowing what to say. No one dared to address the volatile captain for fear of rekindling his terrible anger. So, the men stood there for an awkward moment while Sonny stared blankly at the inmate on the floor.

Finally, he raised his head toward the inmates of the congregation huddled at the front of the chapel and ordered, "I want all you men out of here. Half of you officers go with them into the bullpen." Yesterday, Cody noticed the bullpen, a large caged area on the side of the chapel where guards detained convicts temporarily.

Sonny added, "And no one goes back to the cellblocks for any reason. Church ain't over. We just have to clean up some shit on the floor."

For a moment, the staggered inmates just stood there, not disobedient, but immobilized by their astonishment at what had just occurred. Then, they started slowly moving toward the door. The captain bellowed, "I'm going to fucking kill the last convict left in this room." After a stampede for the exit, the room was suddenly empty of inmates except for the hapless perpetrators.

Sonny turned to Cody, "Allow me to introduce two of our finest Jericho citizens." He pointed to the inmate on the floor in front of him. "Moonpie here is a known pervert of the lowest kind and premier ass bandit of Cellblock C." The captain shook his head scornfully. "I can't think of a more vile and disgusting human being, if you want to call him that."

Moonpie squirmed awkwardly on the floor.

"When he was in jail down in Weakley County, they found him trying to sodomize a possum in his cell. How he ever got that poor creature in there, I don't know. But it was a living thing, so he was gonna butt fuck it."

He pointed to the other inmate a few yards away, still squirming in pain, clutching his groin and stomach where Sonny had struck him with the baton. "Lube Job over there, he's a real entrepreneur. He all but has the prison black market cornered on personal lubricant. As you can imagine, it's a real popular item here. It's a good rule never to turn your back on somebody who always carries lubricant, especially if it's a man in a men's prison."

He turned back to the inmate on the floor in front of him, "Your faggot lover over there jeezed his filthy, AIDS-ridden semen all over my boots. Now, lick it off you little whore."

Cody wanted to close his eyes. He wanted to get the enraged officer to stop, but something, some wisdom perhaps it was, prevented him.

Moonpie groveled over to Sonny's feet and licked off the gooey ejaculate.

The captain shouted, "Now, get up, you piece of shit, before I kick your brains out." He prodded him with his giant boot, and Moonpie slowly arose, trying to grab his trousers and underpants, which were still clinging to his knees.

Sonny commanded, "Just keep your pants down until you answer a few questions."

Moonpie looked nervously at the guards and then back to Sonny. Desperately, he said, "I swear to God, Captain, this isn't what you think."

Like a catapult, Sonny's huge left fist swept around the inmate's blind side in a raging arc. Then, a thunderclap as it slammed his jaw. Teeth skittered and rattled across the floor. As Moonpie fell hard onto the bare linoleum, Sonny screamed, "Fucking queer."

Cody's stomach clenched. What in the world should he do? He briefly prayed to God for guidance. Nothing came to him, so he did nothing.

Sonny walked over to Lube Job, who was lying on the floor where he had fallen between the pews, still groaning and writhing in pain.

Sonny kicked the convict, and then yelled to his officers, "Line these pieces of shit up against the back wall."

His men hauled the inmates to their feet and shoved them against the wall just under a poster of Jesus healing a group of lepers. Immediately, Lube Job collapsed onto the floor in a heap of groans and disturbing gurgling sounds while Moonpie, holding his jaw, began to cough violently and spit blood onto the floor.

This aroused the captain's rage. "Now, cut that shit out. It's making me mighty irritable. If you have blood in your mouth, swallow it. When you have sperm in your mouth, I'll bet you gulp it down. So, stop your fucked-up coughing and spitting you little bitch."

With grave contempt, the captain glared down on Lube Job and hollered, "Get up, pervert."

The man whimpered like a wounded animal but made no effort to stand.

Sonny spit on him. "I said get up, you disgusting faggot, or I'll stomp the life out of you where you lie." To emphasize his threat, the captain raised his boot and slammed it down on the inmate's arm.

Lube Job shouted in response to the pain, and then slowly, he began to stand. A couple of the guards came over and helped him to his feet.

Cody felt that he was trapped in a nightmare, too tense to even pray again.

Sonny said, "Now before I commence with more punishment for you revolting lowlife, I just want to know how long you've been coming here to Wednesday night prayer meetings and desecrating this holy place with your disgusting acts."

Lube Job stammered, "This is our first time, Captain. And that's the gospel truth, sir."

Sonny whipped a stun gun from its holster on his wide utility belt and spun the inmate around to face the wall. He shoved the weapon into the crack of the man's buttocks and fired.

With the howl of a tortured banshee, Lube Job shook violently as though he were having a grand mal seizure and collapsed to the floor.

Was this where God wanted Cody to be? Had He wanted Cody to witness such acts of brutality?

Sonny turned to a mortified Moonpie, held up the stun gun and asked, "Same answer as him or do you also want two-hundred-fifty-thousand volts shot up your ass, compliments of the Almighty?"

The man contemplated his lover on the floor and then the stun gun. He swallowed hard. "No, sir. I'll be giving a different answer."

The captain smiled, "Now, that's what I like to see, a convict who is cooperative with his caretakers." He held up the weapon to prompt the inmate to give his answer.

"We've been coming here for about a year, Captain."

"And you been butt surfing all that time?"

"Yes, sir. Most every Wednesday night."

Sonny's forehead wrinkled up in disbelief. "Well, that's a mighty long time. Why hasn't anyone caught you?"

Moonpie looked down at his shoes. "Well, I reckon because you never come to church before."

A few of the guards chuckled awkwardly. The captain spit in the man's face. "Don't get smart, you little queer. Now, I ask you again, why hasn't anyone seen you before?"

"Oh, people seen us all right, but just inmates, and they wouldn't squeal on us. It's the inmates' code of honor."

The captain snickered cynically. "Oh, I know all about the inmates' code of honor. It's bullshit. First, it doesn't make sense to use the word 'honor' in the same sentence as the word 'inmate.' Second, my office is full of assholes like you all the time, just dying to spill their guts to avoid going to the Hole for a few days. So, this code of honor don't mean shit to me."

He held up the stun gun and waved it in the convict's face. "I ask you one more time before I jam this up your ass and let it fly. It's going to feel like a streak of lightning about a mile long. Now, how come you never been caught?"

Speak up, man, Cody thought urgently.

Moonpie studied the weapon for a moment. "Well, sir. Most times, we wouldn't actually do nothing during the service. We'd come in late and slump down as low as we could on the seats. Then, just as church was getting over, we'd hide under them pews until everyone left and the lights were out. It was then that we'd come out and fool around awhile. When we were done, we'd sneak out into the yard and get back to our cells just before the final headcount. And that's how we did it, sir, for true."

The inmate squirmed and shuffled his feet, eyes darting across the floor.

Sonny stroked his chin as he considered the man's confession. "That's a good story, Moonpie, except for a couple of problems. If you waited for the church service to be over and the lights to go out, why tonight did you commence to butt fucking while my new chaplain was preaching his first sermon here?"

Nervously, Moonpie offered, "Well, Captain, like I said, we mostly would wait until everyone was gone, but sometimes, like tonight, the urge just come over us, and we couldn't hold back. We tried to keep low so as not to be noticed?"

Incredulously, Sonny demanded, "And you didn't think the preacher would notice a little inconsequential matter such your bare, pathetic ass rising up over the pew?"

"We tried to keep low, Captain, I swear we did. The itch was too strong tonight. We couldn't hold back."

"And another part of your little story puzzles me. After everybody left you here in the dark and you two perverts finished abusing each other, how did you get out of the building? The place is all locked down as soon as the last inmate leaves the room."

Moonpie looked around fretfully, then sputtered, "We'd crawl out the window behind the baptistery."

"You're full of crap. I had those windows barred years ago."

Awkwardly the convict said, "We found a set of keys someone lost. We let ourselves out through the front."

"Bullshit." The captain brandished the stun gun. "Don't fuck with me, boy."

Floundering now, the prisoner stuttered out, "I swear to God it's the truth, sir."

"Show me the keys."

Desperately the felon said, "We forgot them tonight. Someone stole them."

"Both lies, fucking lies."

Sonny spun Moonpie around and leaned on him, pressing him hard against the wall. He crackled the stun gun a couple of times then placed it against the inmate's bare buttocks. "Last chance!"

Dear Lord, Cody prayed.

In anguish, the hapless convict cried out, "It was Squirrel. We paid him for the use of the space. He let us out the side door after we finished. It's Squirrel that you want."

Sonny whirled around and glared at the guards. "Where is Squirrel? Now, bring me that rotten piece of shit."

As several guards hustled from the room, Cody quietly asked the captain, "Who is Squirrel?"

Sonny's face constricted into a tight knot of revulsion. "He's the so-called inmate caretaker of the chapel, like a church custodian. I never did like the little weasel, and now this happens. It'll be a miracle if I don't kill him."

Then, from near the front of the chapel, the ripping sound of tearing fabric pierced the room.

Cody looked up to see a wiry little man clinging to the baptistery curtains as they tore from their rods near the ceiling. Apparently, the man had been eavesdropping from some secret hideaway high above the baptistery. He rode the tearing curtains down to the choir section behind the pulpit with a protracted howl of trepidation.

Sonny screamed, "Squirrel! You bastard!"

Several guards rushed to the front to retrieve the wretched inmate from the folds of the curtains. Evidently, he was spooked from his hiding place when Moonpie called out his name. After a pathetic struggle by the scrawny, pallid convict, the guards threw him down in front of the captain.

Squirrel scanned around in fright like a trapped wild animal. Withering under the merciless scowl of the captain, he resembled an incorrigible sinner cast down in front of the throne of God on Judgment Day.

Without hesitation, the captain launched his assault. "You little queer scumbag. In all my years of prison work, I've never seen anything so vile. You've been pimping out the church where people come to worship. You've turned the house of the Lord into a whorehouse."

Squirrel was on his knees, pleading with the captain. "My wife has cancer. I was just trying to get some money for her medical care by renting out the chapel to some of my friends. I didn't mean no harm."

Sonny was utterly outraged. "No harm? What the fuck do you mean, 'no harm'? This is a holy place. Do you think people can worship here after they know about the ungodly acts that you allowed?"

Pointing an accusing finger at Moonpie and Lube Job, the captain said, "You filthy faggots are butt fucking and probably giving each other golden showers and the like. You're even heavy squatting for all I know. And it's a damn wonder how you clean up after yourselves, probably bringing in toilet paper to the house of God. It's so disgusting, I can't even think about it. You sick fucks make me want to throw up."

And throw up, he did. The captain forced one of his giant fingers down his throat, took a step toward Squirrel and vomited onto the convict's pleading, upturned face.

Overwhelmed by the absolute virulence of the attack on him, Squirrel fell onto the slimy floor.

As Cody stood by with mouth agape, Sonny circled the inmate like a mad tiger toying with its prey.

"I can't even imagine a punishment that would fit your sin. You are the lowest of the vermin and scum that crawl these prison corridors. I ought to snuff out your miserable life right now and do the Lord God and the rest of us a favor. But a worthless, vile roach like you ought to pay for his sins."

Back on his knees, Squirrel begged, "Please, Captain, I didn't know these men were going to get down on it with a church service going on. That part's not my fault."

"It's all your fault, faggot! Now, stand up and take your punishment like a man."

In evident dread, Squirrel rose to his feet.

The captain took an ominous step toward the inmate and raised his hand.

"Don't hurt me, Captain, I'm a sick man."

Sonny struck him across the mouth, and the inmate fell and then slid across the floor, which had become a foul causeway of vomit and the blood of the battered convicts. "You'll be a hell of a lot sicker when I finish with you, you slug. You don't deserve to live after what you've done."

Holding his mouth, Squirrel mumbled pitifully, "I've already repented to the Lord. I asked His forgiveness, now I ask yours."

His anger escalating, the captain said, "Yeah, God's going to have His hands full deciding how to deal with your sleazy ass. You've really thrown Him a curveball, haven't you? Probably no one's ever stooped as low as you."

Pathetically, Squirrel tried to crawl his way toward the door, but the captain stopped him by stomping on his back. "God's going to have to think up something real special for you. What you've done here is just so unimaginable that He hasn't had to deal with it before."

Cody tried to pray that no one would be killed in the chapel here today.

Mockingly perusing the room, the captain added, "But since God isn't on the premises at the moment, I'm sure He won't mind my standing in for Him."

To Cody's astonishment, Sonny began to recite Bible verses while walking in a menacing circle around his fallen prey.

"The Lord says, 'Vengeance is mine.'

"'The wages of sin is death.'"

148

Squirrel whimpered and squirmed. "Have mercy, Captain. Have mercy, Lord."

"'He who sows the wind shall reap the whirlwind.'"

Glaring down at his victim, with hate streaming from his eyes, the captain said, "Now, you, Squirrel, have sown the wind, so look here. Here comes the whirlwind."

Sonny let out a yell of vengeance, raised both arms above his head and slammed his fists down hard like blacksmith's hammers on Squirrel's back.

This elicited a terrible cry of torment from the suffering man.

The captain looked down with disdain and spit on Squirrel's crumpled body, which the inmate had now gathered in the fetal position, his arms pulled in tight over his head to protect himself.

Sonny reached down, pulled one of Squirrel's arms away from his body, and pinned it down to the floor with his size-fifteen boot. He focused on Lube Job and Moonpie, his anger remaining unabated. "Now, you see this? This is the evil hand that took your shameful money, which defiled this holy place." He raised his other boot and brought it down hard on Squirrel's hand.

A yelp of pain followed by another pleading, "Please, Captain! Have mercy!"

As he went on to crush each part of the man's offending anatomy, the Captain called out. "These are the legs that walked you to unlock the door to the yard." Sonny stomped on the back of Squirrel's scrawny, bird-like legs.

Cody dreaded the next assertion.

"This is the tongue that lied." A vicious kick to the mouth followed his declaration.

"This is the sick mind that thought up this slimy scheme." A boot to the back of the head punctuated the statement this time.

"And this is the perverted dick that got real hard while he watched from his hiding place." A stomp on the groin was the punishment for this.

Sonny turned to the wretched inmates against the wall. "I'll bet you didn't know, but Squirrel here, he likes to watch. He's been beating off while peeking from his hideout up in the baptistery. The little queer was spying on you."

This scenario amused the captain. He grinned. "Squirrel's been double-dipping on you faggots. He should have been paying you to watch."

Anxiously, Moonpie asked Sonny, "Captain since you have Squirrel now, can we go?"

"Go where?"

Moonpie shrugged helplessly. "Back to the cellblock, I guess."

Sonny yelled, "You can go to hell, you little faggot."

He turned back to his beaten victim, a broken bundle of flesh on the slimy linoleum. "The Bible says, 'If your eye offends, pluck it out, lest your whole body be cast into the lake of eternal fire.'"

The captain tried to poke Squirrel in the eye, but the inmate saw it coming and ducked his head under his arms.

This enraged Sonny. "Don't try to avoid your punishment, you little weasel."

Cody saw an even greater rage start to build in the captain. Cautiously, he ventured, "Captain LaGrange, I need to finish the worship service."

The captain paused and then looked thoughtfully at the new chaplain. "Of course you do, son." Then, he yelled to the guards, "Take these three soon-to-be-residents-of-the-Hole outside and bring in all the others from the bullpen."

Quickly, guards hustled Moonpie, Lube Job and Squirrel out, and soon the chapel was bustling with inmates speculating about the beating the Captain had surely given the ill-fated offenders. Everyone sat in much the same pews as before, but this time no one settled on the very back row. A few officers grimly stood at the exits while others walked up and down the center aisle giving the inmate congregation stern looks of disapproval as though they were somehow collectively guilty of the sacrilege that had occurred there.

Cody returned to the pulpit and tapped on the microphone. This stopped the chatter and everyone scrutinized him expectantly.

The young chaplain began, "Now before the interruption to our service…"

The inmates laughed knowingly, wickedly.

"…we were looking in the book of Exodus."

Cody cut his sermon short and quickly summarized the conclusion of the story of Jericho. He wanted to end the nightmarish experience of his first sermon to the convicts.

But to finish the service properly, he knew he must do an altar call. He particularly disliked this part of the worship ceremony because it reminded him of his childhood. At age seven, after a stormy revival sermon from an evangelistic preacher, his mother nudged him out into the aisle to surrender his soul to Jesus. To please his mother, he begrudgingly meandered down that seemingly endless path, but the concepts of sin, salvation, heaven and hell were far beyond the comprehension of his boyish mind.

Hesitantly, he gripped the waiting, wet, and sleazy hand of the evangelist who bent over to Cody's ear and whispered, "God bless you, boy. You're saved."

Now, in the prison pulpit he asked anyone to come forward who wanted to be baptized. Even though one needed to undergo this ritual only once in a lifetime, Chaplain Powers had warned him about the "regulars" who came forward at every service. And sure enough, several haggard prisoners came shuffling toward the front where trustee inmates, acting as chaplain assistants, greeted them with enthusiasm.

When the formality concluded, Cody started his benediction. "Almighty God…"

A thunderous commotion erupted at the back of the chapel as Captain Lagrange and several guards burst into the room, pushing Moonpie, Lube Job, and Squirrel. The officers hustled the trio to the altar where Sonny commanded them to kneel.

Then, the captain announced the inmates had a public confession in the form of a prayer to offer before the congregation.

Sonny instructed the kneeling convicts, "Now you lowlife scumbags repeat after me:

"Dear Lord, I present myself at your altar a miserable faggot."

The trio replicated the words in a weak, unconvincing mumble.

Sonny yelled, "Can't hear you. Louder."

The inmates complied with more commitment, and repeated the captain's litany with some enthusiasm.

Sonny continued, with the inmates following each new statement with an identical statement of their own. "I am the most despicable and vile among men."

"I am the lowest of the low."

"I have desecrated this holy place with loathsome, unspeakable acts."

"To pay for my sins, I promise to act as the custodian for the toilets in the cellblocks and hand out toilet paper and magazines to those on the commodes."

A derisive snicker rippled through the room. The captain angrily declared, "All you fucks in here, you better be praying to God right now that I don't catch you laughing, because, if I do, I'm going to give you a whipping worse than I gave these perverts."

Sonny concluded the confessional prayer, "And I will never come to this blessed place again because my wickedness is beyond even your grace, my God. Amen."

With obvious relief, the inmates finished with, "Amen."

The prisoners in the congregation grinned with scorn, obviously enjoying the suffering of their fellow inmates. The guards hustled the banished trio out the door, while Sonny remained and took a seat on the front row.

Cody didn't feel like giving a benediction after the sarcastic, mocking performance by the captain and the three inmates. With great relief, he announced, "This concludes our service for tonight, so you may adjourn to your individual study groups if you desire."

Chaplain Powers had advised Cody that after each worship service, he allowed the inmates twenty minutes to have separate meetings according to their individual religious inclinations. The four groups gathered in the corners of the chapel and arranged some folding chairs in circles. Most were harmless and spent their time in quiet meditation and prayer. But Powers had warned Cody about the evangelicals, who could become quite rowdy in their meetings. This group was in their corner only a short time when they began shouting and yammering in the name of the Lord. They prayed loudly for Jesus to bring down the walls of the prison.

Cody turned to the captain to see if he had taken offense at the supplications, but he only grinned at Cody and said, "Don't worry about those lunatics. I've heard they sometimes pray for lighting to strike me, but I guess God doesn't pay them any mind."

He stood up and a smile of respect and amusement crossed his weathered face. "You done good tonight, son. It was a hell of welcome for you."

Briefly, he put a caring arm around Cody's shoulder and led him toward the exit of the chapel. However, they stopped for moment to watch the evangelicals, whose leader began guiding his followers through a noisy chant.

The leader called out, "Who cast Satan down to hell?"

The group responded in enthusiastic unison, "Christ Jesus did!"

"Who is coming again to judge the living and the dead?"

"Christ Jesus!"

"Who brought down the walls of Jericho?"

Like a cheer at a Friday night football game, the men shouted out. "Christ Jesus!"

Cody advised the captain, "The fall of Jericho occurred fifteen-hundred years before Jesus. Should I tell them?"

Sonny said, "Why bother? Let them have their own version of the story."

The evangelicals then started to speak in tongues. Cody had witnessed the phenomenon once before at a rural church where the pastor, dangling copperhead snakes from each hand, went into a trance and started shouting nonsensical gibberish. Some of the inmates tore at their shirts as they fell jabbering to their knees. And though Cody didn't grasp the specifics of their rant, he felt the deep undercurrent of its meaning, a twisted cacophony of delirium, despair, and unrequited rage.

As the captain and his new chaplain headed out the door, the older man said, "Let's go over to the dining hall, I'm starving."

After dinner with Sonny, Cody drove straight home, wearily climbed the stairs to his garret hideaway and stopped by the kitchen for a shot of tequila. In his bathroom he stripped down to his underwear, brushed his teeth, and gulped down a sleeping pill.

Then, he crumbled into bed, stared vacantly at the ceiling and tried to calm himself. But the torment of the day kept playing over and over in his head like a horrendous, relentless video loop. His mind was aflame with haunting images of the inmates' bare asses rising and falling between the pews. After a few minutes, finally his mind settled enough for sleep.

But just before his consciousness faded, the memory of a recent, brisk and windy autumn afternoon erupted in his mind. He shot straight up in bed as he remembered that he and a nursing student from the university had finished a bottle of wine in the balcony of the deserted divinity school chapel. An innocent, friendly kiss transformed them into rutting wild animals. And as they thrashed and twisted on the slate floor between the pews, Cody remembered that alcohol and hormones almost always lead to shame. But it was too late. They were way past the point of stopping their actions.

Even in his euphoric intoxication, Cody had been strangely aware of his surroundings. Outside, the leaves were falling, swirling in the wind. The setting sun shining through the stained glass depictions of angels and saints in the chapel's Gothic windows cast magical colors over the floor and walls.

And on the nursing student's bare breasts through the labyrinth of falling leaves, the sun flung rainbows.

He looked up at the windows and saw that some of the angels seemed to be watching him, but strangely not in a judgmental manner. They all were smiling with affirmation.

Now, as he sat in his bed, sickened by his own hypocrisy, he reckoned angelic reaction was the acid test for the propriety of sex in a sacred place. If the angels smiled, it was okay. But, if it wasn't okay, they seized up and heaved all over the sanctified streets of heaven.

On that cool October afternoon, she took his phallus firmly and thrust it deep into her throat, so her mouth rested on his pubic area. And as she sucked her encircled lips up and down, Cody felt his ecstatic climax build. Considerately, he pulled out of the warm alimentary canal that enveloped him as his semen spewed on her face and neck, and then fell in hot globs onto her breasts.

After the moment of his release, Cody gazed high above at the immense stained glass depiction of the Last Supper that spanned the rear of the chapel. Among all the disciples at the table with Jesus was a single woman.

Then, in his bed as sweat poured from his body, dampening the sheets, he made a startling connection. Shockingly, he realized this was the same woman he had seen in a vivid dream, the one who beckoned to him from the golden staircase that rose up beyond the stars.

And in the chapel, like the angels, her stained glass visage was gazing down upon him.

She was staring straight at him.

And she was beaming.

A beatific smile.

# Chapter 9

*Trailer Trash*

Nervously, Chaplain Cody Palmeroy sat up straight in an uncomfortable, straight-backed chair in the warden's office. In the three months since his internship began, this was the first time the prison director had summoned him for a meeting. Cody had seen Warden Mack several times around the facility, and the warden always seemed encouraging and friendly, but according to prison gossip, a trip to his office often meant trouble.

Cody felt comforted by the presence of Captain LaGrange and Chaplain Powers, who were sitting beside him facing the warden across his massive mahogany desk.

Though they differed radically on the issue of inmate treatment, the young chaplain and the captain had become good friends. Cody found his job much easier because of his friendship with LaGrange. As he made his daily rounds through the cellblocks, inmates and guards treated him with respect. A mantle of authority rested on the shoulders of anyone the captain favored.

Sonny made it clear he held his young friend in high esteem. At the first monthly staff meeting after Cody's arrival, he'd introduced the new chaplain to the four-hundred assembled officers. The captain had briefly placed his anointing hand on Cody's shoulder. "I've taken a real shine to this young man. If he asks you to help him with something, do it quickly and do it well." Then, he vested Cody with the crowning emblem of authority. "Whatever he says, it's just like the words are coming straight out of my own mouth.

"Any questions?"

An officer raised his hand.

Impatiently, "What is it, Watson?"

"Well, I was just wondering what happens if he asks us to do something against prison policy."

Sonny thundered, "Don't trouble me with such chicken shit questions. He's not going to ask you to do that. I just told you, he's a fucking chaplain, you idiot. Ministers don't go around breaking rules. They uphold the rules."

With a scowl, the captain surveyed the room. "Any other of you geniuses have a question?"

Silence.

"Good." Further silence.

"And another thing, he's an educated gentleman and not inclined to barking out orders. He'll just politely ask if you would help him out. That's how he works. Unlike you fucks, he won't abuse his authority. He doesn't do that. That's why I trust him."

Now, Warden Mack was in his signature pose, which Cody had witnessed on his first trip to the prison. He leaned far back in his chair with feet propped up on the desk and hands folded behind his head. Every now and then, he looked up at the ceiling and then back at his subordinates. The former football hero remained a massive presence, though his once-chiseled physique had long ago morphed into rolls of flab. He spoke with the authority of a monarch endowed with the divine rights of kings.

"Okay, gentlemen, I've got a problem on my hands, and I need your help."

In ragged unison, the trio on the other side of the desk responded, "Yes, sir."

For a moment, the warden's gaze turned to the ceiling. "As some of you know, each year I attend the national meeting of prison wardens. Counting the travel days, I'm gone most of the week. This year, a special program will be offered for chaplains, and I'd like to take Chaplain Powers with me."

The captain spoke up, "Well, sir, you know you can count on me to be acting warden for the week."

Warden Mack quickly acknowledged his second-in-command. "I know that, Sonny. You've done a great job in that role in the past. So that part doesn't concern me.

"Here's the problem. The week of the conference, Jericho begins the conjugal visit program the governor approved. We can't postpone it or the inmates will be rightly pissed off. They've been counting on this for months. And I don't want hardened criminals running around here with stiff dicks and bad attitudes. It could cause a riot."

Sonny leaned forward assertively. "We can handle it, Warden Mack." Turning to Cody with a smile, he added, "I have complete confidence in our new chaplain."

"So do I," the warden responded. "That's why I'm going forward with the conjugal visits even though Powers and I will be gone. I think you two can cover any situation. All we need is Cody's agreement to act as the official chaplain for the program."

Cody squirmed uncomfortably in his chair. "I don't understand why you need a chaplain for this," he said.

Patiently, the warden explained, "We've modeled our program after the most successful such endeavors in the country. I've even made site visits. The role of the chaplain gives it a touch of legitimacy, so it won't seem like we're running some whorehouse."

"What about Assistant Chaplain Malachi Hamm?" Cody inquired.

Powers shook his head. "He won't participate on moral grounds. This initial program requires that a legal marriage exist between the participants. He feels some of the inmates will marry just so they can have sex. So, he reasons it's a mockery of the marriage sacrament. To him, it's really nothing but fornication, which the Bible condemns."

The warden said, "I assume you have no such objections."

Responding at once, Cody said, "No, sir. It doesn't bother me." Or anyway, he supposed it didn't.

Tentatively, Powers added, "And you'll need to perform a few brief wedding ceremonies. Since some of the convicts met these women on the Internet, you'll have to marry them before the conjugal visit."

"But I'm not ordained," Cody said with concern. "I can't legally marry anyone."

Warden Mack swiped his feet from the desk and leaned forward in his oversized chair, "The hell you can't," he said confidently. "The senior judge of the Superior Court is a friend of mine. He approved you to marry as many couples as you want." Sharply, he pointed to a stack of papers on his desk. "He even sent a letter of authorization with your name on it. The court has made you an officially ordained minister."

He called out to his secretary, "Peaches, find that letter from Judge Martin and make a copy for Chaplain Palmeroy."

The harried woman bustled into the office and flurried through the papers on the warden's desk. She found the document and said to Cody, "I'll have this for you when you leave."

In obvious relief, Cody said, "Okay, then. I'll do it, of course."

The warden stood, signaling the end of the meeting. As the others rose to leave, he walked around his desk to shake hands with Sonny and Cody. "I like the way you routed out those butt-fuckers in your prayer meeting, boys. This assignment will seem easy compared to that." Placing a heavy burden of expectation on their shoulders, he added, "I know everything will go smoothly while Powers and I are away."

As the two friends walked into the main corridor out of earshot of the warden and Chaplain Powers, Sonny confided, "This conjugal visit program is a fucking nightmare. It scares the hell out of me. Even if we don't screw up, the inmates may still riot."

Cody was puzzled by the statement. "Why would they riot if they can have sex?"

The troubled captain's heavy boots echoed along the wide terrazzo hallway. "It's not those two-hundred lucky bastards I'm worried about. It's the group of eighteen hundred who don't qualify and won't get any pussy. It's those motherfuckers who'll cause trouble."

The day before the first conjugal visits, the captain took Cody to a corner of the expansive recreational yard and gave his young friend a tour of the facilities, which the prison woodwork shop had recently finished.

"We started here with two doublewide trailers donated by the State Department of Education. They were temporary classrooms, so each unit was just one large area, which we converted to four bedrooms and private baths."

158

With pride, he opened one of the doors on a trailer and the men went inside. The room included a double bed, a pathetic bedside table and an oversized, rusty lamp.

Pointing to the tattered Venetian blinds that covered the single window, Sonny said, "We got these from the Salvation Army thrift store."

Cody peeked into the bathroom. It was small, but like the bedroom, it was clean and freshly painted.

With one of his giant hands, the captain knocked on the wall of an adjoining room. "Now this is a problem. With our limited budget, we had no way to soundproof the interior areas. So if there's moaning and screaming on the other side, the couple in this bedroom will be able to hear it."

Testing the wall with a couple of raps, Cody asked, "Why is it a problem?"

"Who the hell knows? It depends on who's moaning and who's listening. That's what troubles me about this program. Almost any scenario could be a flashpoint for violence."

Sonny pointed to a pull cord above the bed. "This is like a panic button. If any of the men get violent or inappropriate, the woman pulls the cord and officers come inside. The session is over. No second chances."

As the men stepped outside into the glare of the yard, Cody asked, "Okay, so how long do they have?"

The captain's slick, shaved head gleamed in the morning sunshine. "Each couple gets two condoms and has forty-five minutes of privacy. When the time's up, a warning bell rings. They have five minutes to come out and then the inmate cleanup crews have ten minutes to change the beds and clean the bathrooms. There's a two-man cleaning team for each space."

Impressed, Cody said, "Sounds like a well-planned program."

"Yes, but I foresee trouble out here in the yard."

In response to Cody's probing expression, the captain explained, "These trailers are just inside the back gate. Well, that means the prisoners who didn't qualify for the conjugal program can see the couples going into the trailers. They're sure to get catcalls and obscenities."

He swept his hand across the vista of the yard. "Do you see that crime scene tape about fifty yards from here? It's a barrier they can't cross."

Now disturbed by the arrangement too, Cody asked, "What if they charge the trailers and take the women hostage?"

The captain smirked. "The boys from the metal shop will put up a temporary chain-link fence this afternoon along the line of the tape. We'll rig it with high voltage. If the convicts touch it, they'll fry."

As though he were giving a tour of the Taj Mahal, the captain proudly pointed high above to the top of the back wall. "But the real deterrent is up there. Do you see those three gun barrels sticking out of the turret?"

Without waiting for a response, Sonny continued with growing enthusiasm, "Those are M-60s. We have a machine gun nest up there. Even if the fence malfunctions, the inmates won't charge."

"You sound confident about that," Cody observed.

"I know these men. They only riot when they're sure they'll have the advantage, at least initially. Most of their unruly behavior is just a bluff. We'll probably see some of that tomorrow. So, don't soil your pants if a rowdy crowd gathers at the fence throwing rocks at us and the trailers."

Checking out the back gate of the yard, Cody asked, "Why not put the trailers just outside the wall?"

"Warden Mack says we'd have a higher potential for escape attempts under that arrangement, and I agree with him on the matter. It's less risky to bring in the women and keep the inmates inside the walls. But this is the only space available. I can't deny most of the inmate population access to the yard for two-and-a-half days while their lucky friends are having sex. That could mean big trouble."

Unhappily, Cody snapped, "Two-and-a-half days?"

Sonny explained, "We have eight rooms, and we'll operate ten hours for the first two days which will take care of one-hundred-sixty inmates. Luckily, the third day is a short one, only five hours. Almost two-hundred men qualified for the program."

"Why just two hundred out of a population of two thousand?"

"It's partly because of the strict standards for this pilot project. To qualify, an inmate must be legally married and have a good record for at least three years. But that's not what hinders most of the convicts. After a judge sentences an individual to a prison term, most women file for divorce or just take up with another man. Many others won't come to have sex under these sleazy circumstances. I can't say that I blame them."

Sonny walked over to a nearby canvas canopy between the trailers and the back gate, and sat in one of the two high-backed swivel chairs in front of a large table. "This is our control station for the conjugal visits. I instructed the carpenters to put up this awning in case of rain. They built a two-foot platform to give us a good view. We'll sit up here to monitor the drama."

He pointed to several stacks of paper on the table. "The participants completed the signup sheets a month ago, so the couples know when to show up. If the spouses don't get here on time, then the inmate loses his turn."

Cody took his seat next to the captain. "Seems that these chairs vaguely resemble thrones."

"That's what I want. We should raise ourselves up higher than the scum we'll be dealing with."

"Everything looks good to me," Cody offered. "I hope we don't have any trouble."

Decisively, Sonny proclaimed, "Trouble, we can count on. We just don't know how it will surface." The older man smiled enigmatically as he observed his new friend. "So, come prepared for anything."

At six-thirty the next morning, Cody arrived with a hangover and a bad attitude. Feeling overall grouchy, he took his seat under the canopy next to Sonny. His hand wobbled as he raised a coffee cup to his lips.

"Looks like you partied last night," Captain LaGrange kidded him.

Cody thought about the nursing student who was still in his garret room bed. All night she had ridden him to exhaustion. The last time she crawled on top of him, he glanced at his bedside clock. It read two-fifteen.

Evading the captain's query about the night before, Cody said, "This is a bit early for me. Are we still on schedule to start at seven?"

Sonny glanced at his military wristwatch. "Count on it. We'll start on time."

An officer from outside the back gate approached them. "Excuse me, Chaplain, but a woman out here in the holding area for the wives says she and her inmate partner haven't married yet. In fact, they've never even met before. She's one of those Internet brides. Will you perform the ceremony for them now?"

In no better a mood than he'd been in before the first half of his cup of coffee, Cody groused, "Who marries before seven o'clock in the morning? This is bullshit."

With a grin, the captain said, "The chaplain will be happy to accommodate these lovebirds. Bring them forward."

Though he'd given up smoking years before, Cody helped himself to one of the captain's cigarettes. He fumbled through his copy of the Marriage Manual to find the shortest ceremony.

After a few minutes, the captain noticed the approaching couple. "You better decide on something. Here they come."

Cody snuffed out the cigarette, gulped his coffee, and stood up to face the betrothed.

The man was a sickly convict with a mean face that radiated the particular aura of crystal meth abuse that Cody noticed on some of the inmates. He appeared at least fifty years old.

The bride was a squatty young woman in her mid-twenties, poured into a cheap, used wedding dress with a noticeable stain near the crotch. She looked to the young chaplain like she carried a good two-hundred-fifty pounds.

As they stood before him, Cody asked to see the marriage license. Everything seemed in order so he began reading from the manual. "Do both of you come today with clear and firm intentions to become husband and wife?"

The captain interrupted, "Excuse me for a moment, Reverend, but I need to ask the bride a question." Sonny looked down on the fat girl. "Do you know who you are about to marry? The newspapers named him 'the Chainsaw Demon' because of the fact he slaughtered seven young women about your age. When he started chopping them up, they were still alive."

The inmate protested, "Come on, Captain, that was thirty years ago."

The girl said, "Yes, I know all about his past, and it doesn't matter. I still love him and I'm here today to marry him."

Cody eyed Chainsaw. "And do you want to marry this woman?"

The inmate looked over at the girl, "Well, she's at least a hundred pounds fatter than the pictures she sent to me over the Internet. But

I guess a hundred pounds here or there don't matter. So, yeah, I guess I'll marry her today."

Cody hurried through the ceremony. At the end, he declared, "I now pronounce you husband and wife. You may kiss the bride."

When Chainsaw leaned in to kiss the young woman, she turned away so he was only able to peck her cheek.

As the newlyweds walked off, Sonny said, "That's not what I'd call a 'match made in heaven.' Never tell a woman she looks a hundred pounds heavier than her pictures. Chainsaw is a stupid son of a bitch."

As Cody signed the marriage certificate, he said, "Well a hundred pounds fatter or not, I've officially married them, for better or worse."

Sonny said, "I've got a bad feeling about those two. There could be trouble in the bedroom."

A chime rang out. About twenty corrections officers surrounded the control station under the canopy, awaiting orders. The captain said, "That's the five-minute warning. Bring forward our first group of trailer harlots and their honorable consorts."

The participants, whom the guards had put together just moments before, trudged up to the tent.

Cody thought the procession was a grim one, with little eye contact between the couples. They could be going to a funeral.

The captain said to the group, "Okay, so you volunteered for this program and you've read and signed off on the rules. Do you have any questions?"

No one made a peep.

"The officers will walk you to your assigned rooms. You have to finish in forty-five minutes. No exceptions. So don't waste time on some pillow talk bullshit. Get on with it so we can start the next group on time."

As the guards led the group to their rooms, Cody laughed at the captain. "That was a great pep talk. It definitely set the mood for a romantic encounter."

"You may instruct the next group yourself, Reverend Romeo, if you think you can do better."

The two men began perusing the paperwork for the next wave of couples. Thankfully, Cody realized no marriage ceremony would be necessary.

After a few minutes, they heard shouts coming from one of the bedrooms.

Sonny asked a lieutenant standing under the canopy, "Who's in bedroom number four?"

Crisply, the officer replied, "That would be Chainsaw and his new bride, sir."

More shouts blasted forth from the unit, then the sound of a lamp crashing into a wall.

Captain LaGrange bellowed, "Send in the intervention team. Now!"

Three female officers ran to the unit's door and used their passkey to open the bedroom. But it was too late for Chainsaw.

Astounded, Sonny and Cody watched as the naked inmate came crashing out of the bedroom window in a collage of twisted Venetian blinds and broken glass.

Even as the officers subdued the woman, her enraged face dominated the window frame. Still wearing her pathetic wedding dress, she peered out contemptuously at the inmate sprawled on the ground and shouted, "So I look a hundred pounds heavier than in my picture, do I? Well, screw you, you little prick. I didn't get up at three in the morning to drive two-hundred miles so you could insult me."

Her furious face turned toward the chaplain and the captain. "Goddammit, I want this marriage annulled."

Sonny ordered the officers, "Make sure she's cuffed and bring her to me." To a sergeant standing next to him, "Get Chainsaw over to the hospital and see if the doctor will check him out. He looks like he's beat up bad."

A few guards covered Chainsaw with a sheet and tried to help him to his feet, but the man couldn't stand. An officer called the prison hospital for a stretcher.

The chubby, handcuffed newlywed, her face still red with rage, stood before the captain's scornful scowl of disapproval.

She started to restate her complaint about her new husband, but Sonny cut her off. "It's too bad your wedded bliss was so brief. But, that's not my problem."

Sternly, he added, "Now here's the way this will go down. First, I'm not arresting you for assault or the damage you caused. Second, you can petition the court for annulment. We can all testify you had no time to consummate your marriage."

The obese young woman, whose anger was rising before their eyes, answered, "What about the reverend there? He should be able to annul my marriage. Just tear up the goddamn certificate. The ink ain't even dry on it."

The captain said, "Sorry. The chaplain can marry you, but only a judge can revoke it. That's the law."

The woman protested, "That don't seem fair." She scowled at Cody in a rage. "Just tear up my papers you dick-less preacher and let me out of here."

Sonny's patience had ended. "Listen to me, you fat whore. I warned you about marrying a man whose name is 'Chainsaw.' But you did it anyway. So you can just quit your bitching. You shit in your own nest, now lie in it."

To the guards standing around her he added, "Take her outside and let her go."

As officers hustled the new bride out the back gate, she turned to the captain for a final salvo. "I hate that asshole."

Sonny shouted, "Tell it to a judge."

He called the maintenance shop on his radio. "Some fat slut just threw Chainsaw through the window in unit four. Get over here, now!"

He put down the radio and said to Cody, "We've got to get that window covered fast or we'll be behind schedule."

With Chainsaw dispensed and the window temporarily covered with a fragile veneer of garbage bags and duct tape, the next few rounds of visits went quietly. Cody performed eight more weddings, and the couples seemed content.

It was lunchtime, but Cody and Sonny couldn't leave their station except for brief restroom breaks. The ten-hour-a-day schedule left them no time for meals in the dining hall, so they called the staff for some burgers and fries.

Just as the kitchen inmate set the plates in front of them, a commotion erupted in the group next in line for the trailers.

Sonny yelled to his guards, "What is it now, damn it?"

A sergeant stepped forward. "We've got an issue between this inmate and his woman."

Sonny hollered, "Bring them over here."

165

The couple stood before the captain's throne. The inmate appeared hopeful, but the woman was decidedly unhappy.

Sonny asked, "What's the problem?"

The woman answered, "This isn't my husband. I don't know who he is, but somehow he feels entitled to have sex with me."

Sonny eyeballed the inmate. "Let me see your pass."

Guiltily, the man handed over his authorization.

Sonny looked at him in disbelief. "This pass belongs to Inmate Schrader. According to your shirt, your name is Matthews. Yeah, I know you. They call you Sunky. So why do you show up with another man's pass?"

Sunky looked over at the woman with obvious lust. "Captain, I need to talk with you and the chaplain privately. I can explain everything."

Sonny turned to the woman. "Just give us a moment and we'll clear up this mess. Go over by the gate with this female officer."

As the woman walked away, Sonny said, "Okay, make this fast. I can't hold up the entire group because of you. Now, tell us how come you show up here with a pass to have sex with another man's wife?"

Urgently, Sunky confided, "We'll, me and some of the boys from A Block were shooting craps and I was red hot." He went on excitedly, "You should have seen me, Captain. I was rolling nothing but sevens on the come out."

Not at all happy, Cody looked down at his untouched lunch. "Well, what the hell does that have to do with anything?"

The inmate whispered, "Well, Schrader didn't have enough money to cover his bets, so things started to get ugly. I was gonna have his ass." Appealing to the captain, he concluded, "Tell the chaplain what a serious problem that is here. You've got to cover your bets or it's your ass."

Knowingly, Sonny said, "Let me guess what happened next. Schrader put up his wife's ass to cover the bet and gave you his pass."

Sunky answered, a reborn hope shining in his eyes, "That's right, sir. You know how it goes around here."

Cody asked, "And you truly thought this woman would have sex with you today?"

166

The inmate replied with waning confidence, "Well, Schrader said he'd talked to her about it on the phone, and it was okay with her."

Sonny said, "Well, guess what, Sunky, you dumb fuck. He lied. Big surprise."

"I'll have his ass."

"Well maybe so, but you're not having his wife's ass. I can tell you that."

Snarling at his lieutenant, the captain said, "Get this motherfucker to his cellblock, and bring Schrader's wife back over here."

When the woman stood before them, Cody explained, "There's been a misunderstanding. That man somehow got your husband's pass. He shouldn't have been here today."

Urgently, the wife interrupted, "Well, can I see my husband? As you must know, he's serving a life sentence without the possibility of parole, so this visit means a lot to both of us."

Feeling sympathetic, Cody offered, "I'm sorry, but I don't think it's possible for you to visit him today."

The woman looked more than miffed. "I drove a long way this morning. I think I'm entitled to a better explanation than that," she said.

"Well you see, our chaplain is too kind to tell you what happened," Sonny interjected. "But I'm not that polite, and I'll tell you straight out. This is the true shit on the matter. Your husband lost a big craps game, so to pay his debt he offered up your ass. He gave his pass to Sunky, who thought you knew about this arrangement and were willing to comply."

Turning red, the woman told the captain, "I'll divorce the bastard."

"It doesn't matter how you feel about it. Your husband has lost his conjugal privileges by this nonsense."

She huffed away from the canopy. "I'll castrate him for this," she yelled back at them over her shoulder.

Sonny shouted, "You'll have to wait until he dies. The only way your husband will leave here is in a hearse."

"Why do I feel like a night clerk at a fleabag motel?" Cody asked.

Sonny laughed. "Because that's what we are, Chaplain, like it or not. In fact, we're more like pimps."

Cody finished his coffee in disgust. "That's extremely comforting, Captain. Thank you. In fact, this whole experience makes me feel like I'm the sleazy guy who rented out cabins on the outskirts of town when I was in college."

With interest, Sonny asked, "How so?"

"My high school sweetheart went to college out of town. I decided to attend a school close to home. So, until she came back for Christmas break, I was on my own."

Sonny responded knowingly, "And you couldn't wait that long without sex, so you went looking for some strange stuff."

Cody admitted, "I took up with this girl I met at a fraternity party at college. I'd take her out to Steve's Cabins. It was a clean place, and they rented rooms by the hour. Since I was still living at home, and she was staying in the dorm, I had nowhere else to take her."

"So what happened?" Sonny asked.

"The night before my sweetheart flew home, I took this girl out there, and the douchebag at the drive-in registration assigned us a unit. He always flashed this lewd smile like he was trying to imagine what you might be doing in the room."

Sonny said, "So what?"

Cody scanned the area to make sure no one else was within earshot. "I'll tell you 'so what.' I drove out to the airport to pick up my sweetheart the next night. She was hot to have sex. She said she was saving herself for me, and she hadn't hooked up with anyone else since classes had started in August."

A knowing smile spread over the captain's face.

Cody continued, "We couldn't go to her parents' house or my house, and Steve's Cabins was on the road from the airport."

Sonny's smile widened to a broad grin of anticipation.

"Okay, so we pulled up to the drive-through check-in and the creepy clerk recognized me from the previous night and just assumed, I guess, that I was with the same girl. So he says, 'Well, hello, son. You're getting to be a regular customer here. You want the same cabin you had last night?'"

Sonny laughed until his face started to sweat. "I knew there was a reason I liked you. You're sure not the typical clergyman."

Defensively, Cody explained, "Keep in mind all this happened before I went into the ministry."

"I can't wait to tell this story at the next officers' staff meeting."

Cody fired back, "If you tell anyone, I'll say you're a damn liar."

"You know, you're beginning to sound more like me every day," Sonny said with obvious satisfaction.

Throughout the afternoon, Sonny and Cody quelled several minor disturbances, but they met the schedule and finished the day on time.

Sonny said, "Let's go over to the mess hall."

Cody remembered the nursing student he'd left in his bed that morning and wondered if she was waiting for him. "I think I'll just go home. I'm exhausted."

The captain replied, "I'm worn out, too. See you in the morning about six-thirty?"

"I'll be here," Cody said. "I don't want to miss any of the fun."

He drove home and wearily climbed the stairs to his dark apartment. A note on the refrigerator told him the student had an exam the next day. She wanted to study in her dorm room then come to his place the next afternoon and stay over that night.

Dispassionately, Cody crumbled the note and tossed it in the garbage. He grabbed a frozen dinner and slid the tray into the microwave.

Thirty minutes later, he fell wasted into his bed. He was happy that the girl wasn't there. He needed sleep.

The next morning, Cody arrived at the prison a few minutes early. Captain LaGrange had already ordered them a pot of coffee from the kitchen.

Gratefully, Cody poured a cup and said, "Thanks for the coffee, Captain."

"You look a lot better this morning," the older man said. "You must have slept through the night."

They checked the paperwork for the day and everything was in order. Cody would perform sixteen wedding ceremonies. At six-fifty-five, the bell sounded, and Sonny called out to the guards. "Okay, bring us today's first group of stiff dicks and their trailer trash."

Throughout the morning, the conjugal program ran smoothly, but just after lunch, big trouble erupted in the prison yard.

With growing concern, the captain and the chaplain watched a group of several hundred inmates behind the electrified fence.

Sonny explained, "Here's the basic problem, Cody. It's Saturday, and the men have the afternoon off. They have nothing better to do than hang out at the fence and harass the inmates going into the trailers."

As the next group of couples approached the control station for final instructions from the captain, a convict at the fence yelled out.

"Is that your wife, Willie? She's ugly as shit. She ain't the same woman in those pictures you showed us."

Another shout came from the fence, "I see your wife, Jethro, and she's a looker. Fuck her good."

Other inmates joined in, "Yeah, ride that bitch hard."

"Give it to her in the ass, Jethro."

Sonny said to the waiting couples, "Let's get you to your rooms now. That will end this harassment."

After the officers shut the trailer doors, the men at the fence settled down for a while.

But toward the end of the session a few of the men started a crude chant.

"Fuck that bitch."

"Fuck that bitch."

This quickly spread throughout the group.

All in unison intoned, "Fuck that bitch."

The captain grabbed his bullhorn and shouted at the rowdy group along the fence. "Listen up, you miserable shits. No more of this crap. Just shut up and show some respect for these women."

For a while, the inmates were quiet, but when the session ended and the couples filed out of their rooms, spontaneous cheers broke out.

Then more comments were yelled down from the fence. "Jethro fucked his woman hard.

"Hooray for Jethro. He rode his bitch good."

The captain exploded into his bullhorn. "I told you sick bastards to stop yelling that shit down here. Now, get some hellfire, compliments of me and the reverend."

Sonny reached under the table and grabbed a flare gun. He fired a round at the middle of the fence and as it screeched up the hill, the inmates fled, falling over one another.

The flare hit a sign on a fencepost and exploded into dense smoke as a rain of sparks showered down on the fleeing convicts.

Grinning with satisfaction, Sonny said, "Some people don't respect a flare gun. But in a situation like this, it's invaluable."

As the smoke up the hill began to clear, he asked Cody, "Anyone ever shot at you with a flare gun?"

"No."

"It's like a combination of a shotgun and a flamethrower. It produces an instinctive reaction to run like hell."

A guard from atop the wall called out, "Warden Mack is on the phone. He wants to know how everything's going."

Sonny shouted, "Tell the warden all is well. I'll call him later. Can't come to the phone just now."

About a hundred men drifted slowly back to the fence to watch the trailers. Sonny glared up the hill occasionally, but no more flares were necessary.

Toward the end of the day, one of the inmates came out of his trailer bedroom twenty minutes early. Clearly troubled, he approached the table.

Sonny told Cody, "This one here we call 'Chicken Feed.'"

The inmate addressed the captain. "I don't mean to complain, but I got a problem with my wife."

The captain said, "The chaplain and I don't intervene in any domestic issues. But, go ahead. Tell us what's on your mind."

Chicken Feed lowered his voice and leaned forward, "I paid for my wife to fly up here from Miami. Her ticket cost almost three-hundred dollars."

Sonny, losing patience, said, "Get to the point, Chicken Feed. We don't have time to listen to this shit."

"Okay. Okay, Captain, here's the deal. I was one of the first inmates to qualify for a conjugal visit. After I waited three months to have sex with her, she comes here and she's on the rag, and she won't do it when it's her time of month."

Cody ventured, "Ever heard of oral sex."

Chicken Feed whispered, "She don't do that either, on account of her father forcing her to give him blowjobs ever since she turned eleven."

Impatiently, Sonny declared, "Well I guess you'll have to settle for a hand job."

"That's what she just give me, a hand job. I can give myself a fucking hand job."

Cody said, "We're sorry for your misfortune today, but what do you think we can do about it?"

Excitedly the inmate answered, "Go in there and tell her to have sex with me, whether she's on the rag or not."

Incredulous, Cody said, "I can't order your wife to do anything like that."

"Well, tell her she has to give me a blow job at least," the inmate pleaded in desperation.

"I won't do that either."

"Tell her she has to give me the money back for the ticket I bought her."

Sonny said, "Look, Chicken Feed, I like you. But as I already said, we can't intervene in your domestic squabbles. It don't concern us. It's none of our business."

Gloomily, with hate in his eyes, the inmate glared at them.

Sensing an imminent outburst, Sonny commanded his guards, "Chicken Feed's session has ended. Take him to the bullpen for a couple of hours and let him cool down."

As the officers led him away, the inmate shouted, "I won't forget this, Captain. And that goes for you, too, Chaplain. Don't either of you turn your back on me."

Unfazed by the inmate's threat, Sonny said, "Yeah, we're not turning our backs on any of you stupid fucks in here. I don't trust a single one of you."

The convict yelled back, "I'll get you someday, I swear I will."

Sonny said, "Go to the back of the line. They're about nineteen-hundred-ninety-nine inmates in front of you."

As Chicken Feed walked out of earshot, Sonny said to Cody, "He's got a point. If we only offer conjugal visits three days a month, some women are going to have their periods."

Cody suggested, "Maybe we could do the visits a couple of weekends a month, but on a smaller scale. That way the women could decide what's best for them."

Sonny said, "Make a note of that. We'll tell Warden Mack."

The final morning, Cody showed up with sore genitals and a migraine. He popped a couple of headache tablets and washed them down with a gulp of coffee.

Sonny smiled knowingly. "Looks like you had a long night."

"Yeah, I'm dating this nursing student at the university," Cody revealed. "She comes over a few nights a week."

Sonny said, "By the looks of you she must have kept you busy all night."

"I thought she was a normal girl when I started dating her," Cody confessed with a moan, "but now her kinky side is beginning to come out. She says she wants to experiment."

Sonny probed, "How so?"

"Last night she wanted to butt fuck me with a strap-on dildo. But I reminded her I'm studying to become a minister of the gospel, and clergymen generally are not disposed to be ass fucked by a woman with a dildo. It's not natural, not what men of God do."

Sonny laughed. "Looks like you got your hands full with that one, Reverend."

Cody felt good about confiding in the captain. Despite the man's joking, he believed Sonny would never betray his confidence.

He continued, "So the dildo was out of bounds, and I told her that, but next she wanted to tie me down to the bed and I reluctantly agreed. It wasn't so bad at first, but she rode me like a she-devil. Like a madwoman. And all the time I'm thinking about that movie where the woman has a man tied to the bed and she brings out an ice pick from under the sheets and stabs him about twenty times."

Commiserating, Sonny asked, "How long did you endure that pleasure?"

"Long enough so this morning my balls feel like ten pounds of throbbing concrete."

"Why are half the women prudes and the other half kinky?" Sonny asked. "It doesn't make sense to me."

"I like this girl a lot," Cody confessed. "This is just a phase she's going through. She'll settle down once she tires of experimenting. Most girls do."

A sergeant stood at attention at the back gate and called out, "Ready, Captain?"

Sonny said, "Yes. By all means. Bring the final day's first group of crack whores and their esteemed gigolos."

Just as the eight couples approached the desk, an alarming hum and then a loud bang erupted from an electrical transformer on top of the back wall.

Sonny said to the group, "Well there goes the electricity. Some drunken asshole out there must have hit a telephone pole. Unfortunately, the conjugal rooms aren't on the prison's back-up system. That means we have to wait until electrical workers can restore the main power grid to the area."

One of the eager inmates asked, "Why can't we go on? We don't need no electricity to get laid."

Sonny explained, "It's because all the air-conditioning and alarms and lights in the rooms don't work now. It's too big a risk to go forward."

Two hours later, workers restored electricity to the conjugal trailers. The inmates cheered, and the first group of couples eagerly walked to their rooms. By now the line of waiting inmates was long and, after a while, the men started complaining loudly.

Sonny asked, "Cody, would you mind going down the line and telling the inmates that we're processing everyone as fast as we can? We have a two-hour delay, but everyone gets his turn."

Cody said, "I'll take care of it." He began walking down the long row of disgruntled men. The first inmates were only moderately disturbed. But as Cody worked his way down the line, the situation turned ugly.

One inmate complained, "Chaplain, you got to do something. My dick has been hard since yesterday. If I don't get some pussy soon, I swear I'll have to kill somebody."

Another announced, "I got a bad case of the lover's nuts. I can't stand the pain anymore."

One obese convict, his face covered with tattoos, declared, "Hell, I just as well jerk off right here and be done with it. I'll tell you, I'm not waiting an extra two hours. Somebody is going to pay for this."

A young inmate with gold teeth yelled hatefully, "I'm going over there and rip down that fucking canopy and suffocate the captain with it."

Cody said to the group, "I sympathize with you men more than you know. Just hang in there. Everyone gets his turn today, no matter how long we have to stay here. It's fortunate we scheduled today for only five hours. We have plenty of extra time."

His comments met with a few mumbles of acknowledgment.

He asked the lieutenant who had accompanied him, "Would you please call the kitchen and ask them to send over water and sodas for these men? And some for their spouses, too."

This mitigated the convicts' mood. One of the men said, "Thank you, Chaplain."

Another declared, "Thanks, Chaplain Palmeroy. We won't forget this kindness. I know I speak for most of the men around here."

This comment elicited discordant, halfhearted grunts of gratitude from most of the inmates nearby.

When Cody returned to the canopy at the control station, the captain asked, "How did it go?"

"Near the back of the line some men complained of lovers' nuts, others threatened violence."

The captain asked, "What did you do?"

"I ordered some water and sodas from the kitchen. They liked that."

"Good job. That's exactly what I'd have done."

Cody doubted that. More likely, Sonny would have threatened them with an ass whipping.

Near the end of the next groups' time allotment, an inmate came out and approached the table. He said, "Have mercy on me, Captain."

Skeptically, Sonny prompted the convict. "What's your problem, Grifter?"

Urgently, the young man responded, "It's been so long since I had any pussy, that I came in about a minute. And then, I couldn't get it up again because of all the noise from the room next door. It's Bigfoot and his woman, the queen of his motorcycle gang. I never heard such screaming and moaning before. It's a terrible distraction."

Sonny asked, "Did you beat on the wall and ask them to be quiet."

"That was the worst part, Captain. I knocked on the wall a few times and shouted for them keep it down. Bigfoot smashed his huge fist through the wallboard. He stuck his head through the hole and laughed at us."

Surprisingly, the captain showed compassion for the man.

He said, "I'm sorry for your troubles, Grifter." He looked down at the schedule for the next session.

"If your wife is willing, just sit over there in the shade of the wall. I see some cancellations on this list. I'll let you have another turn."

"My wife said she'll give both of you a quick blow job if we could get more time."

Cody said, "That's a touching gesture, Grifter, but I think we're too busy out here to take you up on this generous offer. Let your wife know we're grateful."

After expressing appreciation, the convict returned to his room just as the bell sounded out the end of the session.

Cody grinned at Sonny. "You know, Captain, you're beginning to sound more like me all the time."

Sonny shot back, "Don't think I'm soft just because I showed sympathy for some unfortunate convict." With a wide smile, he added, "If you make any more such comments, I might just have to whip your sorry ass."

Then the captain growled at a sergeant, "Get the wood shop team over here to patch that hole."

Even though they were two hours behind schedule, the rest of the day ran smoothly until the final session when a terrible disturbance boomed through the makeshift window in room four.

A large woman with hairy armpits ripped down the patchwork of garbage bags that covered the widow opening. Her face was a dark portrait of rage.

Captain LaGrange signaled the intervention team to go into the room and then turned his attention to the naked woman.

"Please cover yourself and tell us your problem."

Cody saw female officers approach the woman from behind and cover her with a bed sheet.

She hollered at Sonny and Cody. "I drove all the way from Michigan to have sex with Rooster, and now I get here and he refuses to go down on me."

Rooster appeared in the window next to his wife. He pleaded, "I tried to eat her pussy but it stinks so bad I can't get near her. I can't even get a hard-on. She smells like roadkill sitting out in the sun on an asphalt highway."

The woman protested, "I might not be that fresh, but he doesn't smell that great either."

Sonny said, "Well, either way, your session is over. Put on your clothes and come out here. I want to talk with both of you."

The captain considered the woman a risk for violence and ordered the officers to handcuff her.

When she and her husband stood before the table, the woman blurted out, "I came all the way from Detroit. Somebody's going to eat my pussy."

She nodded at the captain and said, "What's the matter with you. Why can't you do it?"

A wave of laughter rippled through the officers standing nearby.

Cunningly, Sonny said. "I have to stay at this command station today." He pointed at Cody, "But this man might be up to the challenge."

The woman scrutinized Cody. "He's a little young for my taste, but I guess he'll do."

Cody grumbled, "As the captain well knows, I'm a minister. And clergymen don't have oral sex with women they don't even know."

Viciously, the woman snapped, "You people had plenty of sex with little boys. Is that what you like, going down on children?"

Flabbergasted, Cody couldn't respond.

The captain took charge. "Listen up, you fat bitch," he said angrily. "No one here is going to have any kind of sex with you today. Do you understand that?"

"I drove all the way from Michigan," she responded in defiance. "I won't leave until someone eats my pussy."

Sonny called out to the officers, "Take her outside the gate and let her go. Make sure she gets well away from the premises."

As the guards led the dissatisfied woman away, an inmate came running out of unit seven. He was holding his crotch and wore a bloodstained bed sheet around his waist.

He stumbled to the canopy and fell to the ground.

The captain asked, "What happened, Squirt?"

Through the groans of his pain, the inmate managed to tell his story. "Everything was going fine until my wife started giving me a blow job. She licked my dick a few times. But then she grabbed hold of my balls and put them in her mouth."

Cody noticed the bloodstain on the sheet expanding quickly, alarmingly.

Squirt continued, "She bit down and pulled hard. She wrenched her head from side to side like a pit bull with a death grip on a piece of beef jerky."

In sympathy, Cody told the man, "We'll get you over to the hospital right now."

A sergeant stepped forward. "I've already called for a stretcher, sir."

Squirt's wife came storming up to the canopy, her face smudged with blood. Caustically, she glared down at her husband. "That's to pay you back for all the times you cheated on me."

Sonny said to the woman, "You're lucky we don't arrest you for assault."

He looked at the inmate doubled up on the ground. "Do you want to press charges against her?"

Squirt shook his head decisively. "No, Captain."

Sonny advised the woman, "You best get out of here, before he changes his mind."

As she passed by her husband, she kicked him in the gut. "Fuck you, you miserable shit."

Sonny hollered, "Get out of my prison, bitch."

Two husky female officers quickly came to the woman's side and led her away.

Meanwhile, up at the fence, a crowd of several hundred inmates had gathered. Squirt's misfortune apparently amused them. As the officers helped him onto the stretcher, the convicts began to shout out vulgarities.

"What did she do? Bite off your dick?"

"That's one ugly bitch. She looks like a man."

"She looks more like a man than a man. She's a real bulldyke."

"Looks like Squirt lost his balls."

Ugly, derisive laughter retched up from the mocking crowd.

"Squirt didn't have no balls to begin with."

The captain grabbed his bullhorn. "All right you lowlife bastards. That's enough. Back off from that fence."

Defiantly, the convicts stood their ground, studying the captain, waiting for his next move. A few men in the rear tossed rocks over the fence. The missiles fell well short of any of the officers.

With grave resolve, Sonny grabbed his radio. He spoke loudly to his lieutenant on the wall, "Launch two canisters of teargas. If they don't disperse after that, hit them in the legs with rubber bullets."

Before the officers could launch the canisters, the inmates started to scatter.

Sonny shouted into his radio. "Hold the gas!" He hooted, "Look at those punk bitches scamper."

To Cody, he boasted, "These convicts know my ways. They realize what's coming to them. I usually start with gas and then go quickly to rubber bullets."

Cody asked, "What happens next?"

For a long, serious moment, Sonny seemed to picture that forbidding scene. Sternly, he spoke, "Beyond that, they've never tested me, and I hope to God they never do."

"Because what's next is death?"

Gravely, the captain nodded.

"What about the flare gun you used yesterday?"

Sonny smiled. "Now that was a wild card. I always like to have a few surprises when I face an ugly crowd."

Sonny reminisced as he leaned back in this chair, "About ten years ago, we had a nasty disturbance in the yard. Like today, but meaner, more dangerous. The convicts covered their heads with shirts. They thought we could never identify them. They threw rocks at us and any other shit they could find, even stones out of the goddamn buildings. We brought out this water cannon and they laughed at it. But I had a surprise for them. I put industrial orange dye in the water, so when we sprayed them they couldn't get it off their skin or clothes. We rounded up every orange convict."

The bell rang out, signaling the end of the final session. Sonny said, "Thank God that's over."

With his oversized hand, he gave Cody a pat on the back. "We done good, my friend. Of course, we had a couple of tense moments, but nothing that we couldn't handle. Our efforts will surely please Warden Mack."

Cody suggested, "Let's go out and grab some lunch and a couple of beers."

"Good idea."

Two hours later, Cody quietly stepped into his apartment. He thought his friend was probably napping, and he didn't wish to disturb her. He removed his shoes and crept down the hall to the bedroom.

Her name was Gail, and she sat in a meditative posture in the middle of Cody's bed, wearing only her bikini underwear, her eyes closed. Long, dark hair spilled over her shoulders and around her breasts.

Not wanting to disrupt her meditation, he retreated to the small living room and stretched out on the sofa. He closed his eyes.

Suddenly, he was off his couch and floating high above the city. He looked down at the receding rooftop of his attic apartment. His mind swept through a vast, shadowy cathedral, and then burst into a dreamlike mindscape of swirling mist and primordial light.

Not far away stood a small group of women dressed in robes. They seemed oblivious to his presence. They stared past him into the mist.

They were waiting for something.

Something unfathomable, immutable, vast, eternal.

What emerged from that shifting mist was the haunting image of a beautiful, gentle woman with eyes that shined like the stars.

At first, Cody thought she was a sophisticated hologram, but as she drew closer, she appeared more real. Then, her image changed again to something less tangible, almost transparent.

He didn't know what to think of her, but certainly she wasn't from the world he knew.

As the mysterious lady came near, a soft breeze parted her gown for a moment. She was pregnant, and Cody stared at the bulge of her exposed belly. From within her womb, marvelous amber light shined darkly. He realized he had seen her before in another dream where she stood on the staircase that stretched beyond the stars.

As he watched more closely, he sensed something was disturbingly amiss about her appearance; something deeply unsettling.

From afar, he heard Gail's tender, urgent plea, "Cody, wake up. Please, baby, you're scaring me."

He glanced at the ephemeral image one last time and then stepped toward the voice that called him home.

He awakened from his dream and felt his face held tightly against Gail's abundant breasts. She looked down with adoration. "You were sleeping so hard, I couldn't wake you. It was as if you were in a trance. I was really frightened."

Cody gazed up gratefully into her blue, caring eyes brimming with tears.

She leaned her upper body toward his face and cupped her breast with one hand, tenderly guiding her nipple into his mouth.

Instinctively, he suckled that consoling gift for a moment as a warm tear from above splattered on his cheek.

She pulled away for a moment, met his eyes, and gave him a deep, fervent kiss.

He could feel her rising passion, her labored breathing, her nipples hardening, her tongue now deep inside his mouth.

Cody gathered the young woman in his arms and carried her down the hallway to the bedroom.

Heavy rain began to fall loudly on the tin roof of their garret hideaway. The rumble of a storm rattled the windows and echoed through the room. As she helped him undress, Cody looked out the spattered skylight.

Through the gray clouds, he felt something watching them. It was the lady from his dream.

Suddenly, shockingly, he realized the flaw in her anatomy.

She had no navel.

She was made, not begotten.

# Chapter 10

*Kid Wicked's Christmas*

On the morning before Christmas Eve, Cody crunched through the crust of ice atop a couple of inches of snow in the prison yard.

Only minutes before, Frank, the trustee clerk in the chaplains' office, hustled down the hall to the conference room and interrupted the weekly staff meeting.

"Sorry for the intrusion, but the captain just called from the Screws Nest. He wants Chaplain Palmeroy to come right now. It sounded urgent."

Sitting at the head of the conference table, Chaplain Director Virgil Powers looked up from his notes. "Well, we're just about finished here. Chaplain Hamm and I are taking two weeks off. That means Cody will stand in for us until January sixth." Smiling gratefully at the rookie chaplain, Powers said, "This is the first Christmas in many years neither Chaplain Hamm nor I will have to worry about coming back to the prison. So our families thank you for covering for us."

He looked up at Frank, who was nervously standing in the doorway. Obviously, the inmate was eager for Cody to respond to Captain LaGrange's request promptly. No one liked to keep the volatile captain waiting.

Powers asked, "Any idea what's up, Frank?"

The convict said, "I'd wager it's about those fools from C Block torching their Christmas tree again."

Powers swore, "Dammit. That's the third tree they've burned up in a week." He looked seriously at Cody. "I'm sure Sonny is furious. Maybe you can calm him down."

In the chaplains' office reception area, Frank helped Cody with his overcoat and boots. "The captain seemed plenty pissed. Good luck."

As the young chaplain slipped and crunched his way toward another stormy meeting with the legendary captain of the guards, he felt uncomfortable that his friendship with Sonny often usurped the chain of command in the Jericho Prison hierarchy. If the captain wanted a chaplain for a crisis, he should call on Powers. But, instead, he tapped his new friend with whom he'd bonded strongly after the disastrous incident of sodomy in the prison chapel.

The two men had also grown even closer after supervising a difficult, but successful, start to the conjugal visit program in the absence of Powers and the warden. An unusual bond of friendship had arisen between the men that transcended all their differences in culture, education, and prison policy.

Cody peered ahead to the main gate into the Screws Nest. The Rubicon was the critical control point that separated the prison's two-thousand inmates from polite, civilized society outside the penitentiary's massive walls. Someone had hung a pathetic wreath on the barred gate.

For Cody, the Christmas season placed the prison in its sharpest possible contrast to the world outside. While most folks were celebrating the cheer and hope the holidays bring, this joyful spirit just deepened the bitter, utter anguish that suffocated the convicts' souls. Many of them had no hope, no promise of parole, no viable dream of celebrating the season with family, ever again.

As a maximum-security prison, Jericho housed the most contemptible rejects of society. Many of the convicts were serving life without parole, or long, consecutive sentences. Mass murderer Wizzy Jeevers held the indisputable record of six-hundred-fifty years. Cody imagined Christmas didn't mean shit to Wizzy, except a lukewarm turkey and dressing meal in the inmate cafeteria and a day off from work at the prison laundry.

As Cody approached the first entry at the Rubicon, the gate was already opening for him. He passed through two more control entrances before he stepped into the bright lights of the sophisticated command center.

Captain Lagrange was waiting for him. "Dammit, Cody, this is the third fucking Christmas tree those bastards in C Block have burned up. I wanted to just leave the charred trees in there and let them suffer. But you wanted to give them another chance. Well, they pissed all over your goodwill. And now comes the day of reckoning."

Sonny's rant didn't worry Cody. The captain carried on this way whenever he was upset, which was usually several times a day. The young chaplain tried to calm him by asking details. "Do we know who's responsible?"

"Goddamn straight. We got it on a video recording this time," Sonny blasted.

"Who was it?"

The captain calmed down a bit. "Come this way. I'll show you."

They walked over to the stacked rows of video surveillance monitors on the back wall. The replay revealed live cigarette butts and blazing socks thrown onto the tree from a second-tier cell at the end of the row. Those convicts were in a perfect position to ignite the tree.

"Look at those bastards," Sonny raged. "I'll whip their butts and throw them in the Hole for a year."

"Who's in there?" Cody asked.

"It's Kid Wicked and his cell bitch, Leg Iron. The Kid has been a pebble in my shoe ever since he came here. We'll need to mete out some serious punishment to these assholes. I've got the cellblock on lockdown, so it's time for us to go in there and confront them. And don't even talk to me about another fucking tree. It's not negotiable."

Cody had met the infamous Kid Wicked on his second day at Jericho. The convict was serving consecutive life sentences for a double homicide. At age fourteen, he'd kidnapped his former girlfriend and her new lover, tied them to a tennis court net, doused them with gasoline and set them ablaze. Because he was so young and his crime so cruel, he became known as "Kid Wicked."

Since he'd entered the prison, the convict had transformed himself from a middle school dropout into an articulate, educated prisoner advocate and jailhouse lawyer. He'd passed his GED exam and then earned two online degrees. Except for a couple of arson incidents early in his incarceration, he had a clean record. But since he was well spoken and better educated than many of the corrections officers, Kid was in constant conflict with the prison staff. So, the guards in the command center celebrated that they'd caught Kid in another arson crime, one that was quite serious because it put all the inmates in his cellblock at risk for potentially fatal smoke inhalation. The day of comeuppance for Kid Wicked had arrived.

Sonny and Cody along with about twenty officers with shotguns and automatic rifles made their way across the Rubicon and into the snow-covered yard. As they approached C Block, the captain said to Cody, "Look, I know we differ on the issue of inmate punishment. Even though I'm really pissed about this, I'm letting you decide their fate. So be thinking about a good payback for these lowlife motherfuckers."

When the heavily armed contingent arrived at the cellblock, Sonny ordered all the inmates to stand at attention in front of their cells.

Cody knew the armed guards were a show of force to the convicts and a statement that prison officials considered this a serious matter, not some juvenile prank.

Mixing with the inmates while armed was never a good idea, and in fact, was contrary to prison protocol. Prison history across the country abounded with incidents in which inmates subdued armed guards and turned the weapons against them. But Sonny was clever. He brought overwhelming firepower. The inmates would never dream of rebellion with such slim odds for survival.

So, the roughly three-hundred inmates in C Block stood expectantly outside their cells, awaiting the captain's verbal assault.

"You must be the most ungrateful cocksuckers on the face of the earth." He glared up at the five tiers of inmates outside their cells, his eyes filled with revulsion. "The chaplains arranged for you to have a tree in your cellblock. Then, you thankless pricks torched it."

He placed a hand on Cody's shoulder. "Then my chaplain says, 'Give them another chance.'" The captain's anger subsided. "So, I think, this is the holiday season, a time for giving and forgiving. I order another tree from the prison farm and ask Chaplain Palmeroy to buy more goddamn tree decorations for you bastards. And soon after it's put up and decorated, then some fuckers burned it."

The captain paced up and down in front of the inmates for a moment. He looked up and said, "Now here's where it really starts to piss me off. After you torch the second tree, the young gentleman comes to me again and says, 'It's Christmas. Let's give them one last chance.'"

Sonny continued, "And so I say 'Okay.' It's the birthday of Jesus, right? Maybe I've been too harsh in the past. Perhaps I should give a little. So against everything I stand for, I order yet another tree cut and let the chaplain buy another set of tree ornaments. There's no money left in the Christmas fund, thanks to you hateful fucks, so this time the chaplain pays for the decorations himself. Like all he wants to do on the way home after a long day trying to help you with your dog shit lives is to get off the interstate and go into Wal-Mart, which is packed this time of year with customers claiming their layaway and such." The captain paused and glared at the inmates.

"Last night some of you thankless bastards set fire to the third tree. So you've had not one, not two, but three goddamn Christmas trees in here, and you've shit on every one of them."

An inmate on the top tier of the cellblock protested, "We didn't all do it, Captain. It was just a couple of men. Don't punish all of us for what they done."

Sonny agreed, "Good point, Fester Head. Yes, I know it wasn't all three hundred of you scoundrels. It's only two of you." Pointing an accusatory finger at the cell on the end of tier two, he shouted, "It was those two punk bitches right there, Kid Wicked and his side boy, Leg Iron."

Feigning righteous indignation, Kid protested. "It wasn't us, Captain, I swear to God."

Sonny retorted, "Careful now, Kid. Don't ever swear to God in the presence of a man of the cloth, especially when you're lying." He pointed to Cody standing next to him. "He might just call down a lightning strike from the heavens to fry your deceitful ass."

Kid Wicked said, "I'm sorry, Chaplain. I meant no disrespect to you or the Lord. I just wanted to express my innocence to these ridiculous accusations in the strongest possible terms."

Sternly, the captain said, "Spare us your useless lies. We have it on a video recording. Clearly, you tossed the cigarette butts and flaming socks from your cell."

Still denying his culpability, Kid Wicked said, "There must be some mistake, Captain."

"The video evidence don't lie. We were recording this time."

Like a Marine drill instructor, Sonny delivered the telling blow. "What do you geniuses think all the cameras are here for, so we can watch you depraved bastards jerking off and butt fucking in the middle of the night?"

Again, pointing an accusatory finger at Kid Wicked, he said. "You fucks are guilty and it's you we'll punish."

General applause erupted from the inmates.

"Now, as you know, I hold our new chaplain in high esteem. I never met a minister like him before. He really understands the situation here. Unlike the other chaplains, he's not always whining and asking for mercy for you perpetrators. He knows there must be consequences for bad behavior. He gets it."

Sonny scanned the rows of cellblock tiers. The inmates were listening with rapt attention. He continued, "That doesn't mean we agree on everything. It's just that as a chaplain, he doesn't always take the side of the convict. I respect that, so when he makes a suggestion, I weigh it carefully.

"You can guess that one of the issues we disagree on is the severity of inmate disciplinary action. He thinks my punishment of sending men to the Hole becomes a badge of honor for the convicts. It just elevates their status in the inmate hierarchy."

Looking contemptuously over at Kid Wicked and Leg Iron, the captain said, "Normally, I'd send you motherfuckers to the Hole for thirty days, but today I'm letting my chaplain decide your fate. I want to see what he does with this. I have an open mind on the matter."

The cellblock was quiet as a graveyard at midnight.

"So, now we'll see what punishment Chaplain Palmeroy has in mind for Kid Wicked and Leg Iron."

Cody surveyed the crowd, trying to make eye contact with as many prisoners as possible. He was apprehensive. He hadn't realized Sonny would ask him to render his decision in such a daunting forum. Three-hundred inmates eyed him expectantly.

Without knowing exactly what punishment he would recommend, he began, "The captain and I reviewed the video and it clearly shows the cigarettes and burning socks coming from your cell." He pointed a dramatic finger at the culprits.

"I have a question for Kid Wicked and Leg Iron." He mustered an intimidating stare at the convicts. "Keep in mind that your answer will influence the severity of your punishment."

The accused inmates, who moments before had been arrogant, began to wither under the scowl of the chaplain.

"In light of the indisputable video evidence, do you still maintain your innocence?"

Leg Iron put his hands in his pockets and shuffled his feet in an awkward show of anxiety. Kid studied the disapproving scowl of the chaplain. After a long pause, he said, "It was me. I admit guilt, but my cellmate had nothing to do with it."

The admission shocked everyone in the cellblock. Seldom before had a convict admitted wrongdoing before a large group of peers.

Sonny muttered, "Well, I'll be damned."

Cody pursued the inmate. "You're admitting to torching all three trees?"

Kid responded, "Yeah, I did all of them."

"Well, you screwed up Christmas for everyone in this cellblock. So, I ask you another question. Do you have something you'd like to say to your fellow prisoners?"

Kid Wicked looked beaten and confused. Seemingly, he had no idea what the chaplain meant. He said, "I'm sorry, sir, but I don't know what you're asking."

Cody responded, "You just said those words to me, 'I'm sorry.'"

Bewildered, Kid asked, "You mean you want me to apologize to these bastards? It's a sign of weakness. I won't do it."

Confidently, Cody asserted, "Yes you will or I'll defer to Captain LaGrange's recommendation of thirty days in the Hole. Now repeat after me. 'I apologize to my cellblock for torching the Christmas trees.'"

Kid Wicked stuttered, "I ... I can't do it."

"I'll say it with you." Cody went on persuasively, "Come on. Let's do it together."

Cody began, "I apologize..."

Kid froze.

Tolerantly, the chaplain encouraged him. "Let's try it again. Here we go."

This time Kid said the words with him.

"I apologize ..."

Cody encouraged, "Good, a little louder."

"... to my cellblock for torching the Christmas trees."

To Cody's amazement, the inmates lining the tiers didn't scoff or ridicule Kid Wicked. They enthusiastically applauded. He heard the captain swear, "It's a fucking Christmas miracle."

Cody said to Kid, "It looks like your cellblock buddies appreciate your apology, and so do I, and the captain, too."

Sonny nodded in affirmation.

Cody continued, "So because of your admission of guilt and apology, your punishment is for one day, not thirty."

Happily, Kid Wicked said, "That's a good deal. So it's just one day in the Hole?"

Surprisingly, Cody replied, "You're not going to the Hole. That's not the punishment I have in mind."

Confused, the convict said, "If not the Hole, then what is it?"

"I like to study history." The chaplain surveyed the tiers of inmates, signifying he was addressing the whole group, not just Kid. "I particularly favor ancient times." Cody paused for dramatic effect.

"You know, they didn't always have prisons for those who broke the rules of society. Extended incarceration for rehabilitation is just a few-hundred years old. Before that, they had jails, but mainly for those people awaiting corporal punishment or execution."

Cody looked into the eyes of some of the inmates. His comments seemed to capture their interest. "The authorities converted some perpetrators to slaves, but usually they executed them or rendered harsh justice and let them go. The punishment was practical, so it wouldn't be a burden on the public. Frequently, societies banished criminals to outlying areas or handed out a severe penalty that fit the crime. If you were a thief, they'd cut off a hand. If you lied, they'd burn your tongue. That kind of thing."

Cody paused for a moment. The cellblock was eerily quiet.

"One punishment stood out to me above all others. Some early cultures dealt with murderers in a unique way. Instead of executing or banishing the perpetrator, they would tie the victim's body to his back. The guilty party would have to wear this rotting corpse around for a couple of months. As you can imagine, this severely limited his social interaction within the group. It meant no food, no sitting around the fire at night, no sleeping in the shelter, and of course, no sex."

The inmates howled. The image of a woman screwing some guy with a corpse on his back was hysterical.

Cody waited for the men to settle down.

He resumed, "So this brings us to the present moment. We don't have a homicide on our hands here. We have a dangerous, irresponsible act of arson. My punishment for Kid Wicked is this: If you burn it, you wear it. For one day, he must wear the burned Christmas tree on his back."

The crowd applauded while Kid appeared dazed, dumbfounded.

The captain was on his radio. "Get the wood shop boys over here with a saw and some chains."

Within minutes, the bewildered crew arrived. Cody directed the men and signaled for Kid Wicked to come down to the center of the cellblock. Quickly, the carpenters cut enough branches away from the tree truck to accommodate Kid's body. The guards backed the inmate into the carved-out space and used several feet of chain to secure a tight fit around his waist. The stump of the Christmas tree was about even with his ankles. The top dangled high above him and hung heavily over his head.

The woodshop crew chief fastened the ends of the chain with a padlock and handed one of the two keys to the captain and the other to Cody.

From within the charred branches, Kid's tormented voice called out in frustration. "This is fucked up. I can't even see where I'm going."

The captain stepped forward, "Well what do you think, men? Does he look like a fool?"

The prisoners cheered.

He turned to Cody. "Well done, Chaplain. I couldn't have thought of a punishment this good in a thousand years."

Kid Wicked managed to take a few steps. He complained, "I can't bend my knees. How am I supposed to sit down with this thing on me? Get if off me. It smells like shit."

The captain grinned, "A small tree on your back and you turn into a whiney little girl? I would've kicked your sorry ass from here to kingdom come."

Kid still protested, "I can't lie down to sleep. I can't sit to eat. I can't even take a shit with this tree on my back."

Roars of laughter from the crowd.

"You'll have to learn to shit standing up," Sonny needled him.

That image evoked snickers of scorn from the inmates.

Sonny continued, "Just think of all your friends making fun of you as you stroll around the yard with your new friend strapped on your back, ass fucking you from behind."

Kid said, "I'm not going to the yard. I'm staying in my cell for the whole goddamn twenty-four hours."

The captain said, "No, you won't. You'll keep up your regular routine and go to the cafeteria and yard just like usual."

The young chaplain interjected, "I also want you to sing some Christmas carols in the yard this afternoon."

"I'd rather have the thirty days in the Hole."

"Too late now," Sonny said with delight. "The man of God has spoken."

Cody said to a sergeant nearby, "Please parade this prisoner to the far end of the room so everyone can get a good look at him, and then take him back to his cell."

Among the hoots and jeers from the inmates, the guards led the erstwhile venerable Kid Wicked, now disgraced, in front of the group, and then tried to help him climb the stairs to the catwalk in front of his cell. With the tree on his back, he couldn't fit into the narrow stairwell.

Sonny said in delight, "Guess you'll be sleeping down here on the concrete tonight."

As Cody and the captain made their exit, cheers erupted from the gallery of prisoners.

The chaplain smiled and turned to wave at the men.

The two friends, surrounded by their armed guards, crunched proudly back to the Screws Nest.

The captain said, "I've got to hand it to you, son. That was brilliant."

Cody brushed off the compliment. "Not really. It's just different. That's why it seems somewhat impressive. But, as we've discussed on several occasions, I think public humiliation trumps isolation every time."

As they crossed the Rubicon, the officers in the command center stood and applauded. They had been watching the drama in Cellblock C on CCTV. By now, word that Kid Wicked would wear a charred Christmas tree to lunch had spread throughout the prison.

A red phone rang loudly. It was the warden's hot line.

An awkward silence filled the room.

The watch officer answered the phone and then handed it to Cody. "He asked to speak with you, Chaplain."

Cody said, "Yes sir, Warden Mack."

"I'm sitting up here in my office with the lieutenant governor. We patched into the video feed from Cellblock C. It was the funniest goddamn thing I've ever seen. We can't stop laughing our asses off."

Cody said, "Captain LaGrange deserves the credit, sir. It took a lot of faith on his part to trust me with that decision."

Excitedly, Warden Mack barked into the phone. "Stay where you are. The lieutenant governor wants to meet you. We're on our way."

Cody turned to the captain in the hushed room. "Warden Mack is coming down here right now with the lieutenant governor."

Urgently, the captain commanded his officers, "Get this place cleaned up and look sharp. We're about to get a visit from on high."

Later that day, Cody and Sonny ate a late lunch together in the officers' dining hall. They took a seat at a table by a window. It was early afternoon and the excitement of the morning's events had exhausted them.

It wasn't every day the lieutenant governor stopped by the command center. He was in a good mood and told his public relations man to take his picture with Cody and Sonny. Then he asked for a video copy of their visit to Cellblock C.

The state's second highest official had said, "This is the most hilarious event in State government in ten years. I can't wait to show it to the governor."

Turning to Cody, he added, "I might ask you to come down to the legislature to tell this story. I could even invite the media. I don't know how you thought this up, boy, but it could be a public relations knockout for state government."

Cody graciously thanked the political figurehead, but thought the story of Kid Wicked might stir up issues of "cruel and unusual punishment."

Now, the inmates' side of the cafeteria had shut down and the prisoners were out in the yard on their noon recess. During their lunch, prisoners howled over the clumsy way the Kid tried to eat his food.

The two friends reminisced about the comical events of the morning. Then, just as they finished dessert, the noise of a major commotion erupted in the yard. The sounds of laughter and taunts surged through the closed windows of the dining room.

Cody and the captain ran outside and saw Kid Wicked streaking from the yard desperately yelping for help. Apparently, some of the men had set fire to the remains of the charred Christmas tree strapped to his back. In a hopeless attempt to outrun the flames, the convict slid his way across the icy ground. The scene was farcical. It looked as if a burning tree with feet was frantically running through the prison yard.

Quickly, Sonny ordered his officers, "Get some fire extinguishers, fast."

As Kid ran past the dining hall with the tree ablaze, Sonny tackled him while a few guards opened up with a storm of white fog from the fire equipment.

Laughing heartily, the captain rose to his feet and stood alongside Cody to behold Kid's latest makeover. Soot and white residue from the fire extinguishers covered his face. A quick check of his shirt and pants revealed no scorch marks on the fabric. Luckily, the fire had burned only the tree.

The captain noticed a faint but familiar odor. He said, "It smells like some of the men in the yard doused the tree with lighter fluid before they set it ablaze."

Kid pleaded, "I can't wear this tree around for twenty-four hours. It's killing me."

Cody and Sonny exchanged glances.

The chaplain said, "I'm satisfied with your punishment. But Captain LaGrange should have the final word."

Sonny laughed and said, "I guess you've learned your lesson, Kid. But, don't forget, this is just the beginning of your troubles. You will certainly face formal charges of arson in court."

Sonny pitched his padlock key to one of guards and ordered, "Somebody get that tree off his back and take him to the showers."

As the two friends walked back toward the dining hall, the captain dusted the soot and white powder from his uniform.

He yelled at two inmate cooks near the door, "Stop loitering out here. The show is over. Go get the chaplain and me a fresh pot of coffee, and another slice of that hot apple pie. And put some fucking ice cream on it this time, goddammit."

194

Hearing the captain's rant, Cody smiled at the cooks and turned back to those tending Kid Wicked.

He said, "Merry Christmas, everyone."

The next day, after making his Christmas Eve morning rounds at the prison, Cody received a call from Warden Mack.

"Everything is quiet around here. I'm going home and you should do the same. I'll see you in a few days." And then he added earnestly, "You're a great asset to Jericho. I'm glad you're here. Merry Christmas, son."

Cody thanked the warden and wished him all the best for the holidays. He left the chaplains' office in Frank's capable hands. As he passed through the command center he checked to make sure the officers had his phone number. Cody was on call until well after New Year's Day, since the two regular chaplains were taking vacation time.

As he walked out of the prison's main entrance, an inmate trustee from the warden's office approached him. He pointed to some beautiful trees set up in the handicapped parking area. "Pardon me, Reverend, but Warden Mack had these cut from the prison farm just this morning. He wanted you to have one."

The inmate helped Cody strap the seven-foot spruce tree on top of his old Volvo. The chaplain said, "Thanks for the help, Ralph. And happy holidays."

When he pulled in his driveway, Gail was on her way out to the mall. In excitement, she said, "I wondered if we were having a tree. It's perfect. I'll get some decorations while I'm out."

She helped Cody haul the tree to the third floor apartment and gave him a passionate parting kiss before she left on her errands.

As Cody watched her drive away, he said aloud, "I think I'm falling in love with you."

Cody wasn't going home for Christmas because of his obligations at the prison. Two days before, Gail had canceled her plans to make the four-hour drive to her hometown in favor of spending the holidays with Cody. Last week, she'd moved in with him, although she kept her dorm room as a pretense of respectability at school and as a nod to the conservative values of her parents. Gail's father was a physician, so it was important in her family to keep up an appearance of propriety.

In just a few weeks, Cody's feelings for her had changed from friendship and affection to something much deeper. She had transformed from an energetic, serious student friend with a passing propensity for kinky sex to someone much different. Something strange and inexplicable had deepened his feelings for her. He felt a compelling, overwhelming force was drawing them closer—like magic. When she'd held him against her breasts as he awakened from his dream about the strange, pregnant specter, he'd experienced a brief but startling revelation. Just for a moment, her face resembled the vision from his dream. He wondered if he was losing his mind, or did these women share some kind of family resemblance deeply rooted in the psyche of the feminine universe?

Of course, this could be explained by coincidence, or more likely, the projection of his mind onto these experiences. Whatever the cause, the moment had forever changed his feelings toward Gail.

That Christmas Eve night with ice crystals and snowflakes dancing in the air outside, they happily decorated the tree.

With unbridled delight, Gail said she couldn't wait to give Cody a gift. Earlier in the evening, she'd opened a present from him, a glittering pendant of Roman glass set in a silver bezel.

Now, with enthusiasm, she said, "Close your eyes." She ran to the bedroom closet and from its hiding place among her clothes retrieved the gift. A moment later, she giggled with anticipation as Cody opened his eyes. Adorned with a red satin bow, a three-foot statue of an angel filled the room. Cody recognized it immediately as a rendition of the legendary image of the victorious Archangel Michael with a sword, his foot firmly placed on Satan's dreadful head.

Delighted, Cody said, "What a perfect gift. Thank you." He opened his arms and she came eagerly into his tender embrace. This time he spoke the words so she could hear them. "I'm falling in love with you."

She looked at him adoringly. "How long have you been keeping this secret?"

He smiled. "Just since this afternoon."

"I love you, Cody. I don't know for sure how it happened. I always considered you a close friend, but last week I woke up one morning and realized I'd fallen in love with you. That's when I asked if I could move in with you. I was afraid you wouldn't let me, and I was so grateful when you said 'Yes.' That's when I told you for the first time I loved you. And even though you didn't say you loved me, too, I knew it would happen for you just the way it did for me. You just took a little longer to say it."

Cody said, "I'm sorry you had to wait for me to catch up."

Playfully, Gail told him, "Don't worry. I won't hold it against you."

She gave him a sweet kiss, and then teased, "I have another Christmas surprise for you, but you'll have to come back to the bedroom to open it."

At two-o'clock Christmas morning, Cody gently extricated himself from Gail's enfolding arms. She had fallen asleep with her head on his shoulder. Carefully, he arose from bed and shuffled down the hall to the living room. Deeply needed sleep evaded him, so he picked up a book and stretched out on the sofa.

On a forgotten, dusty shelf of the divinity school library, he had found a ragged nineteenth-century, two-volume set on the subject of angels.

He alternatively read awhile and then dozed. The book fell from his hands onto the floor. When he retrieved it, he saw the volume had fallen open to an appendix on the esoteric subject of the anatomy of angels. It included a paragraph on navels.

The official position of the Catholic Church was that God made angels as separate, special acts of creation before the universe was born. These singular creatures didn't copulate and produced no offspring, thus the issue of umbilical cords was immaterial. Accurate depictions of angels should show no navel, although many famous artists sometimes ignored this obscure doctrine.

He jumped up from the sofa to examine his statue of the famous archangel. The stomach was smooth and without blemish.

Cody recalled his vivid vision of the spirit. Because she had no navel, assuming she was an angel was reasonable, except for one glaring inconsistency. She was decidedly, incontrovertibly several months pregnant.

But if she wasn't an angel, the mystery deepened dramatically.

What was she?

What was the uncanny amber light shining from her womb?

Why did she reveal herself to him?

Why did he feel she was watching him?

For the next four years, these questions would haunt him like a drug addiction. Then, suddenly, shockingly she intervened in his life again, in a most unusual and surprising manner.

# Chapter 11

*Pimping for Momma*

The Reverend Cody Palmeroy stood at the back door of the Mt. Sinai Church and surveyed the empty, icy parking lot with a scowl.

Around the hood, pimps weren't generally known for their punctuality, so Cody wasn't surprised Lester was late for their appointment.

Still, the young preacher was annoyed. He had other matters on his mind more compelling than counseling a known criminal on the morality of pimping for his own mother.

Unlike other churches, Cody's nine-hundred-member congregation welcomed everyone regardless of their personal iniquities. Many of his flock lived on the fringes of society and were ostracized from other area places of worship. Mt. Sinai's membership ranged from professionals living outside the neighborhood to pimps, prostitutes, drug dealers, and gang members with rap sheets as long as a roll of toilet paper.

Because of his prison chaplaincy experience, Cody felt these reprobates needed religion just as much as anyone else, maybe more. So when he became pastor of the congregation two years before, he declared that all souls were welcome, regardless of their moral or legal status. Of course, some members fled the church in righteous indignation, but many others came to fill their vacant pews.

Cody was drawn to the dark, back alleyways of life where the depravity of the human condition gave birth to a collage of existential meaning. He wanted to offer a ray of hope to the downtrodden, although he knew most of his efforts provided only temporary relief from the shadows of despair. How much could his feeble candle illuminate before it flickered out in the heartless storms of despondency? He dared not think of the hopelessness of his mission.

Mt. Sinai had once been a Roman Catholic institution. When the local bishop closed it a decade previously, the Episcopal Diocese sponsored the ministry for a few years before it, too, abandoned the parish due to frequent armed robberies in and around the sanctuary. However, the church had lived on in an independent status as sort of a patchwork of several faiths, though it still maintained a decidedly Catholic flavor.

Because of Cody's ecumenical leanings, communicants from a variety of religious subcultures also thrived here, including New Age advocates and even a few voodoo practitioners. He maintained that as long as members adhered to the church's basic core of beliefs, they could add their own personal religious twists.

Finally, Cody saw Lester's car appear from a side street of the housing project. The young man drove a shiny Cadillac with twenty-four-inch rims, the kind that kept spinning after the car stopped, creating a jarring optical illusion that the vehicle was still moving.

In what appeared to Cody as an agonizing slow-motion video, the black sedan crept into the church parking lot and crawled up to the back door.

Through the darkly tinted glass of the pimpmobile, Cody could see Lester yakking on his cell phone. He motioned for the pimp to roll down his window.

He shouted, "Dammit, Lester, get in here. You're an hour late already."

The pimp acknowledged his tardiness. "Sorry, Reverend. I just had to take care of some important business arrangements."

Pointing to the young woman in the seat beside him, Lester asked, "Can I bring Sweet Nutin? She's really strung out, and I have to watch her or she might hurt herself."

Impatiently, Cody agreed. "Bring her with you, if you must. Just get in here."

As he walked down the hallway to his office, the young clergyman questioned his decision to accept the pastorate at this unusual church. After his graduation from divinity school and subsequent ordination, he'd fantasized about leading a mega-church with ten-thousand members and a television following of countless others. But when he was offered a job initially as assistant pastor at such a church, he'd decided in favor of the unique opportunity at Mt. Sinai. He felt more comfortable with the outcasts of society than with the privileged.

Cody recalled his first pastoral counseling visit in the hood. Didler and his female companion needed some help with unresolved domestic issues. Nervously, Cody had rapped on the door, one of almost five hundred just like it in this compact cauldron of humanity.

Didler came and introduced himself. He was a garbage collector for the city, but Cody saw signs of other activity in the tiny living room including sheets of numbers-gaming cards, dollar bills rolled up as coke straws, and a modest mound of marijuana awaiting packaging in small plastic envelopes.

Didler asked his new pastor to have a seat on a sofa that was disgorging its foam-rubber innards through wide cracks in a cheap, faux leather covering.

After a few pleasantries, Didler declared, "The reason I asked you to stop by today is that me and my woman are having problems."

Cody nodded. "Describe the situation for me," he said.

Leaning forward, Didler confided, "She doesn't shower or keep herself clean anymore."

"Why, Didler?"

"You don't know this, being new to the hood, but that's how women here do when they don't like you no more. She smells so bad that I won't even sleep in the bed with her. I sleep on that sofa you're sitting on now."

Cody said, "I'll be frank with you, Mr. Didler. This isn't something my divinity school training addressed. But I'd like to start by talking to your female companion privately."

The kitchen screen door slammed hard.

The man said, "That was her leaving. She won't talk with you because she knows she's in the wrong." He cocked his ear, listening for her to return. "In a minute, she'll probably sneak back in the kitchen to listen to us."

He grabbed the remote control for his stereo unit and turned it on. The volume blared.

Didler picked up a chair from the dining table and came to sit face to face with his pastor. "This music will keep her from eavesdropping on us."

He increased the volume and got next to the minister's ear and started talking.

Cody yelled, "I can't hear you. The music is too loud."

Didler pointed to the floor and grinned. An army of roaches was pouring out of the subwoofer of his stereo system.

The man then lowered the volume for a moment as his new minister picked up his feet to keep the vermin from crawling up his legs.

"Ain't that the damnedest thing you ever seen. I charge the neighborhood kids a dime just to come see it."

Now, as Cody sat down behind his desk in the church office, he could hear Lester struggling with Sweet Nutin in the hall.

"Come on, you ho, just a few more steps."

As they entered the office, the girl stumbled and groaned.

Cody pointed to a seating area near the window. "Just put her on the couch, Lester, and let her sleep awhile."

The pimp said, "She shouldn't sleep. She's been at the heroin today. She's always this way on her day off."

Regardless of her occupation or appetite for heroin, Sweet Nutin was a faithful church member here. She and her sisters sang in the choir.

The minister said, "Okay, sit her up in that easy chair over there by the bookcase, and go down to the kitchen to get her some coffee. I'll watch her while you're gone."

As the pimp left the office, Cody approached Sweet Nutin. She was upright but sound asleep, softly snoring. One of her bra-less breasts had slipped out of her blouse. Cody walked over to the cabinet under the bookcase and found a light cotton blanket he sometimes used when he napped on the couch. He covered the girl and stepped back to admire the beauty of her face.

In spite of her gaping mouth and irregular snoring, she was still a stunningly beautiful young woman. Cody thought of all that was lost in her drug addiction and emotional dependence on a pimp. Her life could have been much different, much better had she been born into another type of environment. But that hadn't happened, so here she was, a might-have-been model or trophy wife snoring in the ghetto office of a might-have-been mega-church minister. As Cody gazed at her upturned visage, he saw a dim reflection of his own.

He imagined her strutting down the runway of some New York or Paris fashion show with the demeanor of a serial killer. A naughty little smile now and then would be nice. Why not throw a bone to the common man, the multitudes of hapless fucks drooling in front of their flat screens?

He wondered why those beautiful automatons always looked so pissed off. They possessed a visage that said, "I'm one of the most beautiful creatures on earth. Too bad you can't have me, because if you did, it would be the ultimate experience of a lifetime. Thereafter, you would think of nothing but me and the tragedy of not being able to have me again. Every time you screwed your wife, you wouldn't even be able to get off without thinking of me."

He heard Lester behind him. "We need to wake her up and give her some of this coffee."

Cody held the coffee cup as the pimp gently slapped the girl's face to awaken her. He coaxed, "Come on, baby. Come to papa. Wake up for me, you precious girl, and take some of this good, hot coffee."

No response from the could-have-been starlet.

Then Lester slapped her again, this time not so gently. She awoke gasping and coughing. Her wide eyes stared at them.

Lester pleaded, "Just take a little coffee and you'll feel better in no time at all."

She took a sip, and then another. Suddenly, light returned to her eyes. She sparkled.

The pimp pleaded, "Okay, baby, just hold this coffee and keep taking sips. You're getting better already."

Cody asked, "Are you sure it's heroin. I didn't see any needle marks on her arms."

Lester said, "She don't shoot up. She snorts it like coke. It doesn't soar you like when you take it in your vein, but it's still a good high and can last longer."

With Sweet Nutin propped up and drinking coffee, Cody returned to his desk and beckoned Lester to join him.

The pimp removed his faux fur coat and oversized hat and casually threw them across the sofa. He pulled up a chair opposite his minister. "I've never been asked to come in for a private audience before, Reverend. What's the occasion?"

Cody pointed to a picture behind him depicting Jesus preaching to the multitudes. He asked, "You see this picture of Jesus behind me? Now, why is Jesus not smiling?"

The pimp pointed to a crucifix on the wall nearby. "Well, Jesus is being crucified. Ain't nobody smiling when they being crucified."

Cody spun his chair around and pointed dramatically. "Not the crucifix, Lester. It's this painting of Jesus giving the Sermon on the Mount. Now, look at that picture and tell me why Jesus isn't smiling."

The pimp studied the scene for a moment. "I give up, Reverend. I guess He's pissed off at somebody."

Cody moved in for the kill. "That's right, Lester. He's pissed off at you."

"Why? I ain't any worse than the next person sitting in the pew."

"He's pissed at you, Lester, because he's sick of your sinful ways." Cody looked sternly across the desk. "Lester, I know a lot of our church members aren't of the highest moral standing, and that's okay with me."

"Yeah, that's good, Reverend. All of us, regardless of occupation, need to feel welcome at some church. Folks like what you've done in this place. It's talked about a lot in the hood. It's appreciated."

Cody continued, "And so the fact that you're a public relations man is no problem to me. I don't approve of it, but I'm not going to throw you out of the church."

Somewhat relieved, Lester asked, "So what's the problem?"

"I know your momma is a prostitute and has been for most of her life. That's not an issue with me, either. But here's the difficulty. I found out that now you're pimping out your own mother, and that's a line you cannot cross with me. That's going too far."

Lester jolted straight up in his chair. "Who told you that? It's a damn lie."

Cody shook his head, "About ten people told me about this, so don't deny it. Don't waste my time."

The pimp relaxed a bit and slouched back in his chair. "Okay, I admit it. I took over public relations for Momma a couple of months ago, but there's a good reason for it."

Skeptically, Cody said, "I can't imagine what it would be, but go ahead and tell me."

Lester leaned forward and lowered his voice almost to a whisper, as though someone were eavesdropping right outside the door.

"Do you know that pimp with little diamonds in his teeth, the one they call Snake Eyes? Well, he was Momma's pimp for almost ten years, and he was a cruel bastard, too."

Cody felt uneasy. He was certain Lester was about to tell him a story he really did not want to hear.

The pimp continued. "He treated Momma like trash. He beat her, took all her money from tricks and didn't give her shit to live on. He had her on crack and heroin at the same time. She was his slave. Every time I tried to intervene, Snake Eyes told Momma that he would kill me if I didn't back off. He had her so scared that she wouldn't even come to the door when I went to see her. In her own way, she thought she was protecting me."

Cody asked, "So how did you get Momma away from him?"

Lester's enthusiasm increased. "Well, that scoundrel Snake Eyes was shot in the face at the Get Down On It nightclub. Seems the scumbag was cheating in a craps game in the men's room. Three of them were rolling dice in the handicapped stall. Well, he survived the gunshot but had to go to the hospital ICU. He's still there in a coma and may not live. Anyway, even if he does, he'll go to prison. The medics on the ambulance found all kinds of contraband in his suit— coke, crack, and a couple of loaded guns. They gave it to the police, who came up to ICU and arrested him. They read him his rights and he wasn't even awake."

Lester laughed. "They cuffed him to his bed. Can you believe that shit? The man is barely alive and they cuff him. Even if he lives, I knew Snake Eyes wouldn't be back out on the streets for a while. So that's when I stepped in and snatched up Momma. I got her in rehab, and now she's living at my place so I can keep an eye on her. You should see her, Reverend. She looks ten years younger. She's even started cooking again and keeping up the place."

Cody said, "Well, that's a mighty good story, Lester, but it still doesn't explain why you started pimping her out."

Lester paused for a moment of thought. "Momma's been a ho for thirty years," he said. "It's the only way she can get by—the only world she knows. I realized if I didn't do something, she'd go with some other pimp. So, I decided that I'd represent her. And she's done well. She has her regular clients, plus I picked up some new business for her. And I treat her good. I let her keep all the money. I give her a ride over to the clinic every morning, making sure she gets her methadone."

Lester appeared pleased with himself, but he wasn't done. "I tell all her clients to show proper respect, or they'll have to answer to me. Snake Eyes would let some slime abuse her if they paid for it. He even let some dog fuck her one night for an extra fifty dollars while the client and his friends stood around and laughed."

Cody observed the pimp as he considered the young man's story.

Lester concluded his appeal, "So now that you know the facts, Reverend, what do you think? Am I not a good son?"

Cody said, "Well, the case you present here is impressive, even touching. So in the context of the circumstances, you did the right thing. I'd be happier, though, if you'd told her she didn't have to work anymore, that you'd take care of her. But you didn't do that, and the big picture is still a problem. Most church members don't know the details. All they know is that you're pimping out your mother, which unfortunately is still the truth no matter how you spin it."

Lester suggested hopefully, "Maybe I can stand up before the church Sunday morning and tell my story. That would stop all the gossip. What do you think, Reverend?"

"I can't let you do that," Cody said emphatically. "It's too public. You'd be admitting in front of hundreds of people that you're engaged in criminal activity."

"Ain't no big deal. Everybody already knows I'm a pimp."

Cody said, "Here's how it works, Lester. Sometimes it's called the clergy-penitent privilege. If you tell me, as your minister, that you're committing certain crimes, I have no legal responsibility to tell the police, although I might have a moral duty if someone was in danger of being hurt. I always report child abuse cases."

"That's cool," Lester told his minister enthusiastically. "I didn't know that."

Cody continued, "But if you stand up in front of the congregation and say you're a pimp, you have no protection. Anyone could go to the police and tell what you confessed."

"Yeah, but who would do that?" The young, admitted pimp seemed perplexed.

"Maybe someone who'd move in on your territory if you ended up in prison."

This sobering comment snuffed out the light of hope in Lester's eyes.

Cody said, "Here's what I'll do. We have a vestry meeting in a few days. With your permission I'll tell them of the rumors I've heard about this situation. I won't reveal my sources, but I'll emphasize I heard from a very reliable individual that you have temporarily taken your mother into your own network because Snake Eyes abused her, and to keep her away from other pimps."

Lester said excitedly, "That's great, Reverend."

Cody continued, "That way they'll hopefully see that what you've done is a humanitarian act, just the way you explained it to me. My story will get the word out that you're a good son who rescued his momma from an abusive environment. It will have almost the same effect as you standing in front of them. This will work, Lester, I'm sure, but I must have your permission." Cody scanned his parishioner, seeking his approval.

Lester grinned his acceptance. "Sounds good to me, Reverend Palmeroy."

Hearing a gurgling sound, the two men turned to Sweet Nutin.

Alarmingly, the young woman had fallen asleep, spilled her coffee on the floor, and slumped down in her chair.

Quickly, Lester hoisted the girl and laid her flat out on the carpet where she emitted more disturbing sounds. The pimp turned her on her side and slapped her back with his hand. Coffee mixed with mucous slime spilled out onto the floor from her open mouth.

Cody thought Lester must have done this before.

After an endless moment, she coughed her way back to consciousness.

Cody said, "We need to take her to the emergency room."

Lester shook his head. "Ain't no need for that, Reverend. She'll be good as new in just a minute."

As though responding to his prediction, the girl suddenly sat upright and beamed a smile at them.

With the pimp's help, she arose and wobbled to her chair.

"This girl needs medical attention, Lester," Cody countered at once.

Sweet Nutin protested, "I ain't no girl. I'm nineteen."

"You're right," Cody acknowledged. "I apologize for calling you a girl, but you still need medical help."

The young woman declared, "What I need is the bathroom."

Lester was at her side. "Come on, you precious thing, it's down the hall. I'll take you."

After a moment, Lester returned to Cody's office. "Well, I pointed her to the door. I guess she'll be all right."

Sternly, Cody reiterated, "Lester, I'm instructing you to take Sweet Nutin to the hospital. She should be seen by a doctor."

"She'll be okay, Reverend." Lester blew it off. "I've been pimping this girl since she was…"

"Stop." Cody interrupted him. "Don't tell me anymore, Lester. If you say you pimped her out before age eighteen, that's child abuse. I'd have to report it. So spare me the disgusting details of your relationship with this young woman. Just do as I say, or you might be driving around in your fancy car with a corpse in the passenger's seat."

Unconcerned, Lester answered an incoming call on his cell phone. He checked his calendar and made an appointment for his client. After the call, he continued to view the calendar. With a mischievous smile, he said, "I see Momma has an opening tonight. Could I put you down for half an hour? My treat, Reverend."

Before the young minister could protest, the pimp broke out in a good-natured laugh. "I'm just messing with ya."

Cody said, "Dammit, Lester, quit talking that crap. This is how rumors get started."

Lester smiled. "Okay, Reverend. I was just trying to have a little fun with you. Lighten up."

Sweet Nutin's spiked heels echoed in the hallway. From the office, the two men listened to the sporadic, uncertain steps followed by a protracted sigh, and then the morbid thud of a fall.

Lester ran out to tend to her.

Cody thought she'd probably snorted some coke in the restroom or even took another hit of heroin. Either way, he'd had enough. He picked up the phone and called 911.

"This is Reverend Palmeroy at Mt. Sinai Church in the JFK Housing Project. I've got a medical emergency here. A nineteen-year-old female. Probable heroin overdose."

"Well, hello, Reverend. This is Kate."

"Hi, Kate, sorry I didn't recognize your voice. I'm traumatized at the moment. I have this young woman here and she's looking bad. Can you send help?"

Confidently, the 911 operator said, "Help's already on the way, sir. An EMT unit down the street from you at the fire hall is available. I just dispatched them via my computer. Since the situation is drug related, a police unit will automatically come along too. You should be hearing the sirens any moment."

Gratefully, Cody said, "Thank you, Kate. You're an angel."

He ran into the hall and saw Sweet Nutin stretched out on the floor. Lester was kneeling over her.

Frightened, the young minister asked, "Is she still breathing?"

Lester, too, looked worried this time. "She's breathing, but I can't wake her up. I've never seen her this bad off before."

"I called 911," Cody declared. "An ambulance is on the way."

Upset, Lester yelled, "What the hell did you do that for?"

Somewhere in the depraved, frigid wasteland of the ghetto afternoon, sirens wailed.

With the authority that comes with moral correctness, Cody answered, "Because it was the right thing to do."

The scream of approaching sirens grew louder.

"Lester, leave now. Get out of here before the ambulance arrives. The police are coming, too. I told 911 it was a probable heroin overdose."

The pimp hesitated. "But how will you explain?"

"I'll take care of it. Just go!"

As Lester ran out the back door, EMTs rushed in the front to tend to Sweet Nutin in the hall. Quickly, they began their diagnostic assessment.

After a moment, the senior EMT looked up at Cody and said, "I think we have her in time. I'm glad you called when you did."

Two police officers rushed into the hallway. One had his hand on his holstered 9mm. He said, "You must be the minister here."

"That's right," said Cody. "Thank you for coming."

The officer seemed more relaxed. "We heard it was a drug overdose. Mind if we ask you a few questions?"

"No problem. Just give me a minute."

The young officer replied, "Sure thing, Reverend. No hurry."

Cody walked back to his office and picked up the phone. He called the police precinct station next to the fire hall. A familiar voice answered his call.

"Southeast Precinct, Sergeant Nelson."

"Hey, Jimmy, it's Cody. How are you?"

"Well if it's not Reverend Palmeroy."

"I've got a situation here with Sweet Nutin and Lester Ayala."

The sergeant said, "Yeah, I hear the rascal started pimping for his own mother. Can you believe that?"

Cody said, "Get the word out. It's not as bad as it seems. His mother was represented by that bastard Snake Eyes, and he was cruel. He had her on several drugs. She was like a slave to him."

"Yeah, Snake Eyes was a heartless pimp," the sergeant sympathized. "Finally, street justice caught up with his slimy ass."

"Now, Lester brought in Sweet Nutin and dumped her on me," Cody said. "But he's trying to be a good son. He's representing his mother so some unscrupulous pimp can't get to her."

Jimmy said, "I think I see where you are going with this, sir."

The young minister explained, "A couple of officers are here who answered the 911 call with the ambulance. I don't know either of them. They want to question me on where Sweet Nutin got her drugs. And you know, if they ask me about the source of the heroin, I can't lie about it. I could decline to answer but I don't like that option either, not when I'm trying to build positive relationships with the police."

Cody paused a minute to gather his thoughts, and then went on. "If I talk to them about the heroin, the trail will lead straight back to Lester. He'll be arrested and maybe held without bail, since he's a borderline habitual criminal. Then, some rough, ambitious pimp will move in on his mother, get her on drugs, and she'll become a wretched sex slave again."

Cody paused a beat and then added, "I can't see how it would be in the best interest of all those concerned to pursue the source of the heroin right now."

Without hesitation, the sergeant replied, "I see your point, sir. I agree. I'll call those officers on the radio. I'll tell them you'll give all the details directly to me and the gang unit here at the precinct. That should do it."

The young preacher said, "Thanks, Sergeant. I owe you a beer."

"I'll hold you to that, sir," Jimmy replied.

Cody waited a moment and then returned to the hallway. The police were gone. He followed the EMTs as they rolled Sweet Nutin's stretcher to the ambulance waiting on the street.

The police officers were just getting back into their squad car. The officer who'd asked him about the heroin gave a friendly wave and said, "We're all clear here, Reverend. See you around."

The young minister returned the gesture with a vague sign of the cross and said, "Thanks for coming by to help. God bless you."

Just before the medics picked up the stretcher to lift Sweet Nutin into the ambulance, Cody took her hand. "Now don't you worry, Sweet Nutin, dear. We're going to get you some help so you won't be dependent on drugs. I'll come to see you in the hospital."

In response, the young woman gave his hand a squeeze and said, "Thanks, Reverend. And call my mother to let her know what happened, and that I'm okay."

Cody said, "Of course. Just as soon as I get back to my office."

He bummed a cigarette from one of the EMTs, took a couple of long, comforting drags and then snuffed the rest out in the ashtray outside the front door. He headed inside toward his office, stopping by the kitchen to grab some coffee.

Back in the hallway, he experienced a disturbing premonition that something wasn't right. The disquieting presence of evil filled the air. And it was close, very close.

His cell phone vibrated. It was the Southeast Precinct. Just as he pushed the answer button, he turned the corner into his office. He was shocked to see seven armed men standing in the room. Some of them aimed their weapons at him, but most targeted the known drug dealer and Mt. Sinai vestryman, King Tut. Cody put the cell phone and coffee down on his desk and then sat slowly in his chair.

The leader of the group spoke.

"My name is Elijah Coffin. I regularly transact business with your friend King Tut."

Cody said, "I've heard of you. I'm Reverend Palmeroy."

The intruder continued, "We hate to trouble you, Reverend, but we have a big problem, and I'm afraid you're the only one who can save King Tut's life."

Cody said, "I don't like this, Mr. Coffin. You can't just come busting into my church with weapons drawn and expect me to help you. What you've done here already is a major sign of disrespect to me and my religion."

Elijah Coffin seemed unmoved by Cody's protest. He said, "Okay, Reverend. Here's the deal. King Tut owes me twenty-five-thousand dollars for some blow I sold him at a big discount. But when he comes over to deliver the cash, he's short two thousand. Every time he counts, it's twenty-five. When I count, I get just twenty-three. So we agreed to let you count it, and we'll go with your decision, either way. Everyone in the hood trusts you, including me."

Shakily, Cody protested. "I'd like to help you, Mr. Coffin. I really would, but I can't be a part of a drug transaction. A minister should never be put in that situation. I hope you understand."

Elijah smiled, revealing a grill of gold teeth. "I know what you're saying, Reverend Palmeroy, and I respect it. But we've got a problem here, and you're the only one who can help. Otherwise, we default to the theory that King Tut is a lying, scheming bastard who must die."

Cody looked over at the vestryman. Elijah's men had covered his mouth with duct tape. From the neck down to the crotch he was bound by plastic wrap. A waterfall of sweat washed over his forehead into his wide, frightened eyes, which desperately begged Cody for help.

The Reverend Palmeroy stared evenly at Elijah Coffin. "Okay, I'll do it. To save King Tut's life, or any life, I'll cooperate. But I don't like this, Mr. Coffin. I don't like it at all."

He paused then continued with a stern expression, "Let's get on with it. Where's the cash?"

Elijah hoisted a bag and poured the contents on top of Cody's desk, producing an avalanche of small bills, mostly fives and tens.

And then Elijah dumped out another bag, bigger than the first, and emptied it on the mound of money already on the desk. Some of the bills fell to the floor while others fluttered around in the air for a moment before settling on nearby furniture.

Cody said, "Look at this mess. No wonder you can't make any sense of it."

He glanced annoyingly over at King Tut. "Couldn't you go to the bank and get some stacks of fifties, or even twenties?"

He spoke emphatically to Elijah's henchmen. "Sorting and stacking this, gentleman, will take a long time. I suggest you make yourselves comfortable. You'll find some coffee in the kitchen down the hall."

He said to Elijah, "I need you or someone you trust to assist me in arranging these bills."

Elijah said, "I'll do it. Half of my guerillas can't count past a hundred."

Cody gestured for him to sit in the chair on the opposite side of the desk.

"Now, the first thing we have to do is sort this money by denomination. You take the ones, fives and fifties. I'll take the tens and twenties, agreed?"

Elijah Coffin said, "That's a good plan. I like it."

Cody said, "And we also need one of your men to stand over the desk as a referee to make sure there's no sleight of hand. Okay?"

Elijah directed, "You, Chucky, stand over here and watch us separate the bills."

With obvious disappointment, the henchman known as Chucky, acknowledged, "Okay boss." He hesitated, then asked, "Now what exactly do you want me to do?"

Impatiently, Elijah Coffin explained, "Just look over the desk and make sure none of the money goes into the wrong stack or in somebody's shoe. I'm not sure how the Reverend here knows but this is how professionals count."

The henchman was flustered. "You mean if I see you sneak one of the bills in your pocket, you want me to tell on you?"

Coffin shouted, "Just stand over the desk, goddammit, you fucking moron."

The three-hundred-pound Chucky said, "Okay, boss. But if this is going to take a while, I need the bathroom and maybe some of that coffee the reverend was talking about."

Elijah Coffin said impatiently, "Go on then. Take Ruination and Cruel Shoes with you. And bring me some of that coffee, too."

In a surprising display of decorum, he asked Cody, "Do you want anything, Reverend?"

"No, thanks. I've got my coffee right here."

He searched for his coffee cup but realized that he had put it down beside his cell phone when he'd walked into the room. It sat on the far side of his desk, next to Elijah Coffin.

He said, "Would you kindly pass me my coffee, Mr. Coffin?"

The drug dealer handed the cup over to Cody. Casually, he looked down at the pastor's cell phone and asked, "What about your phone?"

Calmly, Cody looked out a window at the fading daylight. "Leave it. This time of day, it would just be my ball and chain calling. I don't have time for that shit right now."

The group in his office laughed in sympathetic unison at the clergyman's comment. All of them could relate to that situation.

Three of the six men in Coffin's group left the room for the facilities down the hall.

Meanwhile Cody said to Elijah, "Let's go ahead and start. We can't wait until all your men come back from the restroom."

Elijah said, "Okay, you're right. Chucky would probably just get in our way. Let's start separating the bills."

As the two men began to sort the money, Coffin talked about his life. "I'm not such a bad person the way you might think, Reverend. My name's really not Coffin. It just sounds cool and it's intimidating. It's like if you fuck with me, you'll end up in a coffin. I didn't have a very good situation growing up. My most vivid childhood memory is hearing my mother being fucked for money through the thin walls of our trailer. Then, when I tried to make it on my own, there were too many scrules in my way. You know what 'scrules' are don't you? They are rules that are meant to screw you."

In about ten minutes, the two had arranged all the bills in stacks by denomination. A few wayward hundreds they put off to the side.

But Elijah became concerned about his absent men. He yelled out the doorway, "Hey, Chucky, Ruination, Cruel Shoes, where'd you go? We need you here, so come on back. This ain't no party."

Nothing but Elijah Coffin's hollow echoes came from the long hallway to the kitchen.

Quickly, Cody interjected, "They probably went out on the loading dock for a cigarette."

Elijah Coffin pointed a nervous, wobbly finger at one of his men. "You, Felonious, go out and round them up. They need to get the hell back in here. They're about to piss me off real good."

214

As the thug walked out, Cody evaluated the situation. Only two hoodlums plus Coffin remained in the room. He was hopeful that the police were capturing these henchmen as they arrived in the kitchen. He tried to distract Elijah. "They'll be back soon enough. Now that we've sorted these bills, let's start counting."

The drug dealer wasn't dissuaded. He walked to the door and called out. "Felonious, where the hell did you go?" When his man didn't answer, he said, "Something isn't right here. I came to the church with six men. Now, four are unaccounted for."

He reached into his suit and slid out a high caliber, nickel-plated revolver, which he held at his side.

The drug kingpin said, "I don't know what you're up to here, Reverend, but if you've fucked me over, it'll cost you your life."

At the worst possible moment, Cody's cell phone beeped a warning that the battery was low. Suddenly, Elijah made the connection. He picked up Cody's phone. "This line is open. The caller ID says Southeast Precinct." With hatred in his eyes, he glared at Cody. "You've known this all the time. The cops have been eavesdropping on us." He began to raise his weapon toward Cody.

The minister heard the ping of broken glass in a nearby window and watched Elijah Coffin's head explode on the side of the bullet exit.

Simultaneously, SWAT team members ran into the room to cover the two remaining men of Elijah's entourage. One of them raised his weapon. The police quickly put an end to his miserable life in a hail of bullets. The other thug wisely discarded his gun and dove for the floor. The officers cuffed him and hustled him out of the room.

Cody reached over and wrenched the duct tape from King Tut's mouth. The man pleaded, "Reverend, you've got to get me out of this."

The young clergyman watched the SWAT team milling around the room, taking photos, and placing evidence in plastic bags. Then, he surveyed the cash stacked neatly on his desk, now bespeckled with Elijah's blood along with bits of skull and brain scattered about the scene.

Cody looked at King Tut sympathetically. "Sorry, but this is too big for me to contain. I'm afraid you'll have to take this hit by yourself. You should never have brought that trash in here."

As Cody watched the police haul King Tut away, Sergeant Jimmy Nelson rushed into the room. "Are you okay, Reverend? Are you hit?"

Cody laughed. "Thanks to you, Jimmy, I'm fine."

The sergeant grinned. "I almost hung up when I realized you weren't responding to me. I thought you might be in the middle of some confidential confession with one of the church members. But then I heard Elijah Coffin introduce himself. That's when I called in the SWAT. Their dormitory is in the building just behind the precinct office so the team arrived at your place in less than five minutes. They had you covered almost the whole time, Reverend Cody."

The minister slumped in his chair and took in some deep breaths. "It was serendipity you called at exactly the right time. No, it was a miracle."

The sergeant laughed. "You know why I was calling? A few of the dayshift boys and I were going out for some beers after work. We wanted you to join us."

Cody laughed at that. "You just wanted me to buy you that beer I owe you, you dog."

A cadre of smiling officers from the Southeast Precinct filed into the room. Sergeant Nelson said, "Yes, that's right, Reverend. In fact, you could buy all of us a round or two." The officers laughed.

Cody said, "It'll be my pleasure, I assure you."

He rose from his chair and shook hands with each officer in the room. "Thank you, gentlemen. I owe you my life."

A splattering of blood and bits of Elijah's brain still clung to Cody's shirt. He used a handkerchief to brush away the grey matter fragments, thinking that blood was okay in public but to wear someone's brain on your shirt was decidedly in poor taste. He went outside to express gratitude to as many officers as possible. He asked the men from the precinct to follow him.

On the loading dock, he found most of the SWAT team. Respectfully, the area fell quiet when Cody appeared. Along with the men from the precinct station, the officers formed a tight circle around him.

"Thank you, gentlemen," he began, and then spotted two females suited up in SWAT gear. "And you, too, ladies. I'd be dead without you right now. So I owe you my deepest gratitude. Thank you for what you did here today."

Silence fell heavily on the loading dock area, broken only by some chatter on the police radios in nearby vehicles.

A young woman's frantic shout came from the back hallway of the church. A desperate cry, "Cody, where are you? Please! I need to see that you're not hurt."

Eagerly, Cody called out, "Gail, out here."

The tight circle of officers opened like the Red Sea as Gail ran into Cody's arms.

Tears cascaded down her cheeks like rain.

In response to this touching reunion, the officers began to applaud and cheer.

This broke the spell of the couple's embrace.

As the clapping faded, Cody put his arm around Gail's shoulder and pulled her close.

Proudly, he announced, "This is my wife, Gail."

She said, "Thank you a million times for saving Cody today. I am so grateful to all of you. You're the best." Her comments elicited more applause from the cluster of officers.

Cody said, "Just one more thing, before we go."

He raised his hand as the group bowed their heads.

Blessed be the tie that binds us,

Blessed be the light that guides us.

Blessed be the sword that slays the demon.

Blessed are you, Archangel Michael, the prince of heavenly hosts.

May you bless and defend these venerable warriors standing here with me, and bring victory to them in the face of peril.

Arise, Invincible Prince, and avenge the fallen, as you protect us in battle against the forces of darkness.

As Amos, the prophet of God, proclaimed, 'Let justice roll down like mighty waters and righteousness like a never-ending stream.' Amen.

Cody and Gail walked down to a large conference room in the church, where a group of police officials had gathered to take his statement concerning the incident. After an hour of talking about the details of his ordeal, Cody desperately needed a break. He said, "I'm spent. I feel as though I've had a frontal lobotomy. I can't think of anything else to tell you. I feel a migraine coming on, my hands are still trembling, and Sergeant Nelson just handed me a note that the media wants to interview me. It seems they've set up in front of the church and won't leave until I make a statement."

One of the officers from police Internal Affairs said, "You don't have to talk with them, sir. You don't even have to go out there. We'll handle the media."

Nelson chimed in. "Yes, we can just put you in the back of a squad car and drive you home." He nodded toward Gail, who sat in the corner with her head in her hands.

Cody protested, "But I want to make a statement. The community should know how these brave men and women saved my life."

"The best plan is for us to adjourn this meeting now," Nelson said in a kind voice. "Cody can go out front to give a brief statement if he desires. Meanwhile, I'll help Gail get her car to the back door, so they can make a quick getaway."

Cody glanced over at his wife. She looked up and with her eyes pleaded for relief from the meeting, which had seemed as if it would never end.

Cody said, "Thank you, Sergeant. That's a great plan."

Everyone stood to leave. In the midst of the handshake ritual to end the meeting, with the police media relations man all over him, Cody lost sight of Gail. "I'll introduce you to the reporters just before your statement," said the public information officer. "If they ask follow-up questions, you don't have to respond. When you're finished, just nod to me, and I'll step in to tell them the interview is over, but that I'll have a press release for them in time for the ten o'clock news."

As they walked out the front door of the church, Cody was stunned by the bright lights of the television cameras. He moved across the line of reporters and cameramen. He shook each hand and thanked them for coming and then stood behind the portable podium.

Cody praised the police department effusively. "I can assure you that without the professionalism and incredible competence and bravery of the SWAT team and my friends at the Southeast Precinct, I would not be alive to give you my comments here tonight. To the bright and brave men and women of our police department, I offer my highest praise and deepest gratitude."

Of course, the reporters asked penetrating questions about the incident, which happily Cody could deflect on the grounds that it was under ongoing police investigation.

When one reporter asked how the event had affected him, Cody quipped, "I'm not really sure just yet, but I do know I'll be going home right after this to change my boxers." A sympathetic ripple of laughter ran through the group of journalists, who Cody could barely see through the bright lights shining in his eyes.

He thanked the members of the media and nodded to the police spokesman. But just as he stepped from the podium, a reporter fired off another question. "Will this incident cause you to resign from the church due to safety concerns?"

Briefly, the young minister returned to the cluster of microphones. "There is an old spiritual hymn based on a verse from Jeremiah that comes to mind right now. It says, 'Like a tree planted by a river, I shall not be moved.'"

Without looking back, Cody briskly walked into the church and down the long corridor to the loading dock at the back door. He smiled when he saw that Nelson had made good on his promise. Gail was standing by at the wheel of her car, engine running.

The sergeant held the door open for Cody and patted him on the back as he slid into the passenger seat. "Good job today, my friend," said the policeman. Then he waved to the young couple as they drove away.

After a few minutes of silence, Gail said, "I love you so much, Cody. But I can't live knowing when you go to work you might be murdered by some thugs." Her voice quivered as she tightly gripped the steering wheel. "Just going into that neighborhood puts you in so much danger. I wish I were stronger but I'm not."

After a moment, Cody said, "Something will happen to change your mind."

"Like what?" she challenged.

"Perhaps something strange, something beautiful."

She pleaded, "Don't talk that way, Cody. It gives me the creeps when you start talking that nonsense."

After a long silence, he continued. "You'll see. But in the meantime I plan to go to the vestry for help."

"What can they do?" Gail asked distrustfully.

Cody replied, "I'll get them to install a security system at the church."

"That won't help. Not in a situation like today."

"It would prevent anyone entering the building without my knowledge."

"Cody, that's a great plan, but it doesn't comfort me," Gail said. "You're still in the most violent part of the city. The police won't go in there after dark. Instead, they call on you to deliver messages for them, since they think that even hoodlums respect the clergy. But today proved that was wrong. Dead wrong."

A grim and icy silence enveloped them.

After a moment, Cody said, "And I'm going to ask the vestry for some weapons for my personal use."

Skeptically, Gail said, "Oh, that's really great. Is that supposed to make me feel better, knowing that you might get into a gunfight with some of the local thugs? That's bullshit, Cody. I can't live like this anymore. If you won't move from that church, I'm leaving you."

"I can't believe what you're saying. Listen to what you're saying," Cody answered, deeply shocked.

Gail pulled the car to the side of the road and parked. With tears streaming down her face, she reached across the seat to embrace him. She whispered, "I'm pregnant, Cody. That changes everything."

The next morning, Cody waited for Gail to wake up just to make sure she was okay after the prior night's argument. She stumbled into the kitchen late, at almost nine. She had the day off, but Cody didn't.

He offered her a cup of coffee, and as she sat at the kitchen table in silence, he sensed a difference in her. Something had changed.

"Did you sleep well?" he probed.

She said, "I had the strangest dreams. They were the kind where you're aware that it's a dream. I think it's called lucid dreaming."

Tentatively, Cody asked her to tell him what she'd dreamed.

"It doesn't make any sense."

He pressed her, "Tell me anyway."

"I dreamed I actually saw God."

Cody enjoyed the answer, which excited him. "That's awesome," he said. "What did He look like?"

"Not He, Cody. She. God is a she. She was this woman who looked like some Greek goddess. She was pregnant, and when I looked down at her open robe, I saw a beautiful light shining from her belly, the light of a new world about to be born."

Cody felt even more excited now because he knew the dream must have at least some element of truth. He himself had seen this women in more than one vision of his own. "How do you know that? Did she tell you?"

"It's not as if she moved her lips or anything like that, but she discerned that I wondered about the light. And then, I just knew."

Urgently, Cody encouraged his wife. "What happened next?"

"She spoke to me and then smiled, and at that moment I knew that everything would be okay, no matter what happened. Even if you died. Even if I died with our baby inside me, that we would all be okay."

Cody wondered at the statement. "But how could it be okay if all of us died? How could that be good?"

"She said something strange and beautiful. 'I forged your souls in the furnace of eternity. Now, take comfort, and fear not for I am always with you.' And, Cody, her eyes were a kaleidoscope of the universe. You could see all the past and future if you gazed into her eyes. It's as if she could view it all in a single moment."

"Did you notice anything else different about her?" Cody asked,

"She had no belly button like a regular person."

Shaken, Cody whispered, "I know, Gail. I know."

# Chapter 12

*The Visit*

Cody left Gail at the kitchen table of the same garret apartment they'd shared for the past few years as she pondered her dream about the Goddess of the cosmos and Her mission to give birth to a new world.

He drove his old Mercedes into the minister's parking area at the city hospital, thankful for a spot close to the door. As he walked briskly from his car to the facility's entrance, icy winds mixing with sleet stung his face and hands.

In the lobby, he made a quick visit to the gift shop and glanced at the bold headline of the morning newspaper that read "SWAT Saves Life of Local Pastor." He promised himself that he would return to buy a copy on the way out.

Once on the elevator, he remembered too late his intention to take the stairs at his next visit. The old elevator jerked and grinded its way to the third floor while occasionally bouncing noisily against the shaft. When the doors finally opened, Cody escaped into the hallway and made his way down to an eight-bed ward designated for hopeless patients at the end of life. He thought it was really more like a nursing home or hospice. The nursing staff had named the ward Curmudgeon Row.

He found his church member in the familiar bed next to the ward's only window, her home for the last six months. Every bed in the packed room was occupied, and family members and friends sat on stools or hovered around their loved ones.

Only at Rennie Bowers bedside was there no one. She had no family who would visit her. Friends, too, had long ago abandoned the elderly patient because of her perpetual and depressingly morbid state. All the members of her Sunday school class had died off, leaving Rennie with no visitors, nothing to look forward to, nothing to live for. But still she clung to life by her raunchy, gnarled fingernails.

At age ninety-six, she had long ago been branded an invalid by the world, meaning a person who wasn't a valid individual and was of no use to society. Rennie was just one of the masses of the withered and disdained, waiting for a welcome visit from the angel of death. And even he seemed not to care.

Rennie suffered from a multitude of medical problems, including Alzheimer's.

As Cody approached the sickbed of his forlorn church member, he steeled himself for her assault.

Rennie exclaimed, "Well look who's finally here. My pastor. How many months have you let me lie here in pain and suffering without a single visit?"

The minister regarded Alzheimer's as a major enigma. His mother had suffered from the disease for ten years before she'd died. She'd always complained he hadn't visited her for months, even though he sat faithfully at her bedside several times a week. Why did she never say, "What are you doing back here so soon? You just left ten minutes ago."

Cody took the patient's shriveled hand and said, "Now, Rennie, you know I visit you every week."

"That's what you say, but I know better. You haven't been to see me in years."

Cody offered, "Let's just forget about all that and enjoy the moment." From behind his back, he produced a bouquet of flowers.

Rennie's wrinkled and worn face glowed like the springtime sunshine. "Oh, they are beautiful. Thank you."

A nurse walked over to the bedside. "Rennie, I'm so happy you have those flowers. Maybe you can look at those instead of gazing out of the window all day at this miserable weather. Let me get you a vase."

The young woman winked at Cody as she turned to leave the room. It was the kind of conspiratorial gesture that people sometimes exchanged when humoring an elderly person or a child.

Meanwhile Rennie held her flowers close to her face, occasionally bringing them to her nose for a whiff of their fresh aroma, which inspired optimism.

The nurse returned with a nice vase half full of water. She wrestled the flowers from Rennie's vigorous grip, arranged them, and placed the bouquet on the nearby windowsill.

"There you go, Miss Rennie. You can look at these beautiful flowers all the time."

As she turned to leave the ward, she slipped Cody a note written on a hospital prescription pad and brushed her breasts against his arm.

He didn't acknowledge the message but held it uncertainly in his hand.

Cody's head was spinning. Since Rennie seemed mesmerized by the flowers, he held the note below the edge of the mattress. The prescription form shouted out a compelling message. Call me at 227-8124. It's important. Kathy.

Cody read the note slowly and then shoved it into a pocket of his wool suit as Rennie turned to him from her enthralled gaze at the flowers.

She said, "I saw that nurse hand you a note. What did it say?"

Cody responded nervously. "It's just a personal note."

Knowingly, Rennie eyed Cody. Never had he felt so transparent.

"Well she's a good nurse. You should give her a chance. You would make a nice couple."

Apparently, Rennie had forgotten for the moment his marital status. He protested, "I have a wife. I can't be involved with a nurse here at the hospital."

Rennie didn't acknowledge his objections. Her fragmented mind moved randomly in different directions.

Their conversation turned into a collage of comments about the church. Facts about its history eluded Cody, but he conversed well about the recent changes at Mt. Sinai.

Most of the people Rennie asked about were long dead or imaginary. Her conversation reminded him of a bird flitting around in a tree from branch to branch, never content in one place.

Abruptly, Cody's cell phone vibrated in his pocket. He checked the caller ID. The identity of the caller and number were blocked. He decided to answer.

Sergeant Nelson's voice conveyed a sense of urgency. "Sorry to bother you, Reverend, but I need you to come to your office right away. I'm with the sheriff and some of his men. We sort of let ourselves in. You don't have much security here. One of the deputies picked the back door lock in under ten seconds."

Nervously, Cody asked, "What's going on, Sergeant?"

"Everything's fine. Don't worry. Just come on as soon as you can."

"Okay, I'm only a few blocks away at the hospital. I'll be there soon."

Cody advised Rennie, "Sorry, but I have to go now. That was the police. They're at the church."

A mischievous light sparkled through Rennie's eyes. "Did they come to arrest you?"

Laughing, Cody said, "I certainly hope not. It's probably something about one of our church members."

Feeling some dread, he began the worn-out ritual of his departure. It was the same every time he visited Miss Bowers. Her hearing seemed just fine during their chats, but when he was ready to leave, she feigned deafness, an obvious ruse to delay his exit.

Purposely, he raised his voice a bit. "So, I'll see you in a few days, Rennie. I enjoyed our visit."

She pleaded, "Aren't you going to pray with me before you leave?"

"Yes, of course." He reached down to find her withered hand. "Dear Lord…"

Loudly, she declared, "I can't hear you. Speak up."

Trying to be considerate of others in the crowded ward, Cody bent over closely to Rennie's ear. "Dear Lord, today we pray for…"

The elderly patient interrupted, "I can't hear a word you're saying, Reverend. I'm ninety-six and I don't hear very well. Talk louder."

Normally, Cody would humor the woman and stay a few more minutes, but he was concerned about the phone call from Sergeant Nelson. He really wanted to leave.

"Rennie, everybody else here in this ward can hear me, and God can too, so that's going to have to be good enough."

He began to shout out a prayer right in Rennie's ear. He had no doubt she could hear him this time. "Dear Lord, we pray today for your servant Rennie Bowers." His voice thundered through the room and out into the hall. The other patients in the ward and their visitors hushed in silence out of respect for the young minister.

Cody prayed on for a moment and then asked a blessing for Rennie and all the other patients in the room. He concluded with a hardy "Amen."

He squeezed her hand and leaned over to gently kiss her forehead. "Good-bye, Rennie. I'll see you in a few days."

When Cody stepped out into the hallway, he heard the panicked voice of Miss Bowers call out, "Reverend Palmeroy. Come back! When are you going to pray for me?"

Cody drove through the housing project in a shortcut to the church. He slowed his car to a crawl as he approached a pickup football game on the icy streets. He waved to some of the youngsters who were members of his congregation and watched as a long pass spiraled its way into the hands of a receiver about a half a block away. The boy spiked the ball and danced around in celebration. Cody knew that in the boy's imagination he had just scored the winning touchdown in a Super Bowl.

The dream of becoming a professional sports star was all too common among the ghetto boys. The young minister thought it distracted them from preparing themselves for life in the real world. While some minuscule percentage of such teenagers would become professional athletes, the overwhelming majority would not. And the promise that if you stayed in school and out of trouble and tried your hardest, you had a decent chance at becoming a star, in time became a lie, a lie that lasted a lifetime, the bogeyman of the American Dream.

How many missed rent payments, bounced checks, broken-down cars, dead-end job interviews, food stamps, and diaper changes would it take until the brutal realization that you would never be a star eclipsed the dreams of youth? And in that cruel crucible of disillusionment, the broken, betrayed spirit forged despair and desperation—and sometimes the acid rain of hate.

Minutes later, Cody pulled into the church parking lot. He saw a police squad car, several deputy sheriff vehicles, and a black SUV he assumed belonged to the sheriff.

He was just turning his key in the back door, when it sprang open to reveal the smiling visage of Sergeant Nelson.

"We heard a car drive up. I was hoping it would be you. The sheriff is sort of in a hurry."

As they walked together down to the church office, Nelson said, "Hope you don't mind us coming in like this, but after last night's scare, I wanted to make sure you were okay. Your office is back to normal, though. The crime scene boys worked through the night. Everything's cleaned up now, though I'm afraid your church secretary wasn't too pleased to find us here. She just looked around and then sulked off to her home. Said she would be back tomorrow."

As they turned into Cody's office, the sergeant introduced the group, and the sheriff wasted no time stating his mission. "Sorry to be in a hurry," he said, "but I'm due in court in half an hour. I hear from the mayor you're doing a hell of a job in this neighborhood, boy. We want to support you in any way possible."

The man stepped forward and laid one of his big hands on the minister's shoulder. "Reverend Cody Palmeroy, I hereby declare you to be a deputy sheriff in the county of Wainwright and upon you bestow all the privileges of the office from this day forward."

One of the deputies handed Cody a packet. The sheriff said, "This will tell you about all the rights and responsibilities of being a deputy. It's great to have you on our side, son. Good luck."

Instinctively, Cody said, "Thank you, sheriff, but I really…" His voice trailed off as he realized he was addressing the backs of the sheriff and his entourage as they quickly exited the room.

The young minister asked his friend Nelson, "What was that all about? I can't be a deputy sheriff and a minister at the same time. I'll lose all credibility in the neighborhood."

Nelson said, "We'll keep it a secret. Outside law enforcement circles, no one will know."

Perplexed, Cody pressed, "But why do I need to be a deputy sheriff? What possible good does it do?"

The sergeant took his young friend by the shoulders and turned him around to face his desk. "I think you missed this on the way in here."

Two pistols, a shotgun, and a military rifle along with boxes of ammunition had become the centerpiece of the room.

Nelson said, "The quickest, simplest way for you to legitimately have these weapons in your possession and carry them wherever you want is to become a deputy sheriff. No permit, no waiting period, no problem. Of course, the deputies nowadays go through a rigid training program, but an old law still on the books allows the sheriff to deputize ordinary citizens in special circumstances."

Cody pointed to the weapons. "But where did these guns come from?"

Jimmy Nelson said, "From the evidence room downtown at the central office, all of them set to be destroyed."

The young clergyman felt troubled.

"Don't worry. We got authorization from the chief himself." The policeman smiled. "Although I'll have to say, we all had a good laugh when I put on the requisition form that these four weapons were donated to the Mount Sinai Church."

Cody was speechless as he surveyed the cache.

Sergeant Nelson filled in the void. "Even the mayor gave his approval. We all were at a breakfast meeting this morning to review yesterday's SWAT kills. It's standard protocol. Since he's the former police chief, the mayor sometimes comes to such hearings, and he knew of this Coffin character. He started asking questions about you and how come we let you remain isolated in the projects with no protection, even though the precinct headquarters is just down the road.

"So the mayor got pissed off and yelled at the chief and said to put in a silent alarm in the church office that rings at the precinct just like it does if there's a bank robbery in progress. He said, 'Meanwhile, at least get that minister something to defend himself.' Then, he said, 'I'm going to call the sheriff right now and instruct him to go out there this morning and deputize that boy.' He started storming out of the room." Nelson smiled.

"But just as he got to the door, he shouted back over his shoulder, 'The last thing we need in this city is a dead clergyman on our hands. And I'm up for reelection this year, goddammit.'"

Cody objected, "I don't know how to use these weapons."

The sergeant said, "No worries there, either. I'm going to teach you myself. We'll have to go over to the training center to use the firing range, but we can do that in the morning. In the meantime, let me give you a quick look at this gun." He picked up a small automatic pistol. "This is a twenty-five caliber Berretta. It's small enough to take with you anywhere, and that's what I strongly recommend you do."

Cody was astounded at the idea. "I can't go around carrying a gun. But I have to admit I've thought of keeping something like this in the top drawer of my desk or under the seat of my car."

"What good would it do you there? That's where dead men kept their weapons," Nelson responded vigorously. He waited a moment for that thought to impress Cody, and continued, "I recommend you keep this in the right pocket of your jacket. When you're in a vulnerable situation, keep your hand on it until you feel safe."

"What do you consider a vulnerable scenario?" Cody asked uncertainly.

"When you go out back to get in your car, how do you know some street zombie, desperate for a fix, won't jump out and hit you in the head just for what's in your wallet?"

"I don't carry much cash," Cody answered weakly.

"The zombie doesn't know that. What are you going to do? Wear a sign on your back that says, 'I don't carry much cash.' And since he's probably an elementary school dropout, he can't even read. Besides, we've seen people killed for five dollars. Three years ago, right here in this vicinity, two teen punks killed a ten-year-old boy for the shoes he was wearing. And the shoes didn't even fit the perpetrators. The assholes threw them over the wall onto the interstate."

The sergeant surveyed his new apprentice. "Now do you get it? Always have that gun in your jacket, and keep your hand on it if you feel danger."

Cody put the weapon in the pocket of his black suit. He walked a few steps to get the feel of it. "It doesn't seem too awkward, but I'll put everything else, like my cell phone and keys on the other side to balance it out." The young minister walked to the window of his office and then returned to Nelson. "I think I've got the hang of it. It feels okay."

Nelson said, "After a while, you'll develop instincts that will help you discern dangerous situations. The key is constant awareness."

"You know, yesterday afternoon just before I walked into my office to find Coffin and his henchmen, a sense of evil enveloped me. It was just a feeling, but a distinct and powerful one," Cody said.

"Then, you already know what I'm talking about," the sergeant encouraged him. "Just stay focused. Don't ever let your guard down. You know, this degenerate Elijah Coffin had friends and family who are likely to want revenge. Even though we kept the details from the media, sooner or later the bastard who saw it all, the one who ditched his gun to save his miserable life, will squeal. He's probably singing in his jail cell right now." Hearing that, Cody touched the Beretta in his pocket. He now understood.

"Word will sooner or later get back to Coffin's friends about how you tricked him with your phone. Eventually, they may come for you." Nelson gave Cody a serious look. "Although it's unlikely," he then added. "Killing a minister would stir up community outrage, and anyone associated with Coffin would be a prime suspect. Really, they should be praying that nothing bad ever happens to you, but you never know. People out there are crazy."

Cody confided, "I argued with Gail last night about the dangers in this part of the city. She threatened to leave me unless I moved away from here."

"Well, that's for you to decide," Nelson said. "No one could blame you for going to a safer area. But you have a big advantage over Coffin's friends right now."

"What's that?"

Sergeant Nelson swept his hand across the desk to emphasize the deadly potential of the weapons laid out before them. "We'll be ready for them this time. We'll be waiting. And you'll have the Berretta twenty-five handy everywhere you go. The bastards won't be expecting it. And we have some other surprises for them."

"Like what?" Cody asked apprehensively.

Sergeant Nelson lifted his radio out of its holster on his belt. He called the precinct headquarters. "This is Nelson. Are Johnny and Uther ready to roll?"

The radio crackled, "Yes. All set to go."

The sergeant responded, "Okay, send them down."

He smiled at Cody. "I think you'll like this next part."

Nelson's cell phone rang. He looked at the caller ID. "It's my wife. I'll take it in the kitchen. Maybe start some coffee."

When the sergeant left the room, Cody examined the mesmerizing weapons on his desk. Even though they were manufactured primarily to kill or hurt people, his emotional response to them wasn't revulsion, but infatuation. He sensed a strange, twisted kind of elegance in each weapon, carefully lifting each one from the desk. Vaguely, they reminded him of the electric chair at the prison.

After a few minutes, Nelson reappeared to find the young minister pointing the military rifle out the window.

"Don't point that thing unless you intend to use it," the policeman admonished him. "It's a dangerous practice, but truthfully, all of us do it. It's a natural inclination."

Cody gently set down the rifle on his desk. "This deputy sheriff status has probably enticed me into some kind of fantasy," he admitted. "Right now I don't know if I'm a clergyman pretending to be a lawman, or a lawman pretending to be a clergyman." He laughed at the idea. "Don't worry, Sergeant. I know who I am. I'm a minister who is trying to survive. In a few months, I'll also be a father. Gail told me last night she's pregnant. Now I have to try to stay alive to take care of my family."

Sharply, he pointed to the weapons on his desk. "Twenty-four hours ago, I don't think I would have tolerated any of this."

From the doorway, a man's voice called out. "Reverend Palmeroy, come meet the newest member of your family."

Cody and the sergeant spun around to find a policeman with a large German shepherd at his feet.

The startled sergeant exclaimed, "Dammit, Johnny, you shouldn't creep up on people around here, especially after yesterday's bloody mess."

Johnny laughed. "Well, you shouldn't leave the back door unlocked."

Nelson smiled. "We are going to fix the security problems around here in the morning. That is, if Reverend Palmeroy approves."

The K-9 officer stepped into the room with the dog. "Reverend, this is Uther. He's a well-trained police officer who's looking for a home."

Cody kneeled down on the floor to greet the dog.

Johnny said, "Come on, Uther, and meet your new friend."

The dog sat before the minister and offered his right foot for a handshake greeting.

Cody shook the outstretched paw enthusiastically. "Hello, Uther. My name is Cody. Nice to meet you."

The police dog lay at Cody's feet. Then as Cody stroked the dog's head, he asked, "So what's his story?"

Johnny said, "Uther has been my riding partner for four years, but he's developed joint problems. It wouldn't be that big of a deal for a family pet, but when I put him through the training course at K-9 headquarters, I can see it really hurts him. I'll have to give him up, but it breaks my heart."

He sat on the floor next to Uther and affectionately caressed the dog. "My captain attended that SWAT meeting this morning with the mayor. He called me afterward to tell me to loan the dog to you as a foster parent so I could train a new canine partner."

Sergeant Nelson said, "You don't have to commit to this for the long term. Just let him stay at your home tonight and see how things go. Do you think Gail will like Uther?"

"Of course she will."

Nelson said, "Good. Now, here's what I suggest. I still have matters to discuss with you, but I think Johnny should go over to your place right now and start getting the dog acclimated to that environment. He'll teach Gail the basic commands. That way, when you go home tonight, Uther will be settled in. Okay?"

"That's a good plan. Gail is off today. I'll call her."

Five minutes later Cody and Nelson stood on the loading dock and waved goodbye to Johnny and Uther.

When they returned to the office, the sergeant said, "With your permission, of course, we'd like to put in some surveillance cameras and motion detectors at the church, inside and out. All of the cameras can be observed from the monitor that's already on your desk. We're setting it up so we can see a couple of images from the precinct office, too."

"I understand the cameras, but what's with the motion detectors?" Cody questioned.

"Cameras are great if you want to look back to get information about a crime that's already been committed. But aside from the deterrent factor, they don't do much to preserve your safety, not unless you want to just sit here all day and watch the monitor." Nelson laughed.

"The motion detectors tell you if someone is coming for you. When one of them sounds an alert, the system automatically brings up the corresponding camera image on the monitor so you can see where intruders may be in the building. If a real threat is present, you hit the silent alarm that signals the precinct, arm yourself with the shotgun, and brace for the worst-case scenario, which, of course, would be Coffin's friends and family coming for revenge."

Cody felt uncomfortable. "Don't I need to pay for all this equipment?"

Reassuringly, the sergeant said, "The equipment is free since it's all stolen property, and no one has come in to claim it for at least five years. The police department will pay some of our technicians to install the entire system."

Cody felt grateful but amazed. "How do you justify that cost?"

"We're trying to capture hoodlums in this neighborhood. You're an enticement. And while I hope they never come, if they do, we'll be ready. It's all part of our plan to get bad characters off the street. I assure you, these are public funds well spent. Besides, as the mayor said, he doesn't want you to be harmed. It might cause troubles for his campaign." Nelson seemed amused by this last rationale for protecting the church and its minister.

Cody laughed outright. "It's comforting to know I'm live bait for the mayor's reelection."

The expression on the sergeant's face softened. "We want you to be safe because we like you. I'm speaking now for all of us at the precinct headquarters and many others in the department, too. We're all pulling for you. Among the officers, you're sort of a hero now. Yesterday's entrapment of Coffin and his thugs took a lot of balls. You were cool and confident to the very end."

"I can't take any credit for what happened," Cody responded in genuine humility. "I was petrified. It all simply fell into place the way it was meant to be, and I was just a clueless, unwitting participant in some bigger drama."

Sergeant Nelson said, "You can spin it any way you want. But the police interpretation is that you're a brave, sophisticated ally. You deserve our admiration and support."

That night when Cody ascended the steps to his apartment, aggressive barks rushed down to meet him. As he stood on the third story landing, Gail opened the door guardedly. Once Uther saw him, his aggressive bark changed into yelps of friendly greetings. Cody stepped into the room and sat on the floor to acknowledge the German shepherd. Gail also sat down and the three of them hugged each other like long lost relatives at a family reunion.

Cody looked at his wife. Obviously she was infatuated with the dog.

She said, "Cody, I can't believe how much better I feel having Uther around the place. I've never felt this much affection and protection in my entire life. And knowing that he'll be going to work with you sometimes really makes me feel better about the entire situation."

Cody was a little jealous of Uther.

Gail smiled, "I know what you're thinking, but it goes without saying that you're my number one." She leaned over and gave him a kiss. "You know, all this drama and danger we've been through these past two days has made me love you more than ever, more than I ever thought possible."

She hugged him as the dog nuzzled his way into their embrace.

Cody asked, "Has he eaten his dinner?"

"Yes, about half an hour ago. Johnny, the K-9 officer, said it was important to keep him on schedule. He eats two cups of kibble in the morning and two cups at about six at night with treats in between to reward him for good behavior."

"Shouldn't we go to the grocery store to buy his food?"

"That won't be necessary. Johnny left off a huge bag of food and some treats as well."

"Let's give him a treat," Cody said eagerly.

"Johnny said we can give him random treats occasionally, but the overall concept should be a reward for doing something we want him to do."

She hopped up, went to the kitchen and returned with a couple of small dog biscuits. She ran down the hall to the bedroom and called out, "Hide and seek. Uther, come find me."

As the dog charged down the hallway, Gail ran into the bathroom and hid behind the shower curtain.

Uther scampered into the room, sat down in front of the shower, and barked.

Gail squealed with delight as she gave the dog a treat. "This is too easy for him. Let's try something else."

Cody walked into the kitchen pantry and shut the door. He called out, "Uther, bet you can't find me."

Within seconds, he heard the dog's paw scratching on the door. Cody tried to open it, but the canine shoved it back.

Laughing, Cody yelled, "He's already nailed me. Bring another treat. He won't let me out without his reward."

Later, eating dinner in their dining nook, the young couple swapped stories of the day's events. After Cody left that morning for the hospital, Gail had gone back to bed. She was unable to fall asleep again but just lay there staring at the ceiling, trying to make sense of her series of disturbing dreams. Finally, she went to the kitchen for more coffee, and it was then that Cody called with the news that Uther and Johnny were coming over. The rest of the day was spent with the delightful experience of welcoming the dog into their home.

Cody told her about the sheriff coming to the church to deputize him and the weapons Sergeant Nelson had requisitioned. To Cody's surprise, Gail seemed to take comfort in these developments, despite the fact that guns were involved.

He said, "Last night, when I told you that I would try to acquire weapons, you were horrified. Yet, tonight you seem okay with it."

She said, "It's totally different to me. Yesterday, you intended to ask that worthless vestry for approval to buy weapons. But today, the police chief, even the mayor, are on your side. They're providing you with guns and training, and the fact that you're now a deputy sheriff makes it all seem more official and legitimate."

Then she added, "When Uther came over, I immediately fell in love with him and the whole idea of the police department's commitment to help you."

"Last night you wanted nothing to do with guns," Cody reminded her.

"A lot has changed since then." She reached under a cushion on the sofa and pulled out a sizeable revolver. "I'll bet you didn't know that the police chief ordered the K-9 officer to bring me one of these. He even gave me some training this afternoon on how to use it."

Cody was shocked but after a moment, somewhat relieved.

Gail teased, "Now let me see the gun Nelson gave you to carry in your suit."

Cody approached a chair where he had hung his coat and retrieved his Berretta. After making sure the safety was on, he handed it over to Gail.

She stood before him and held up the two weapons side by side. Irresistibly, she smiled, "Looks like my gun is bigger than your gun."

As they kissed fervently, she opened her blouse and casually let it fall to the floor. As usual, she wore no bra. She pressed her turgid breasts hard against him, and then took his hand, and together they walked down the long hallway to the bedroom. Cody heard her heavy breathing and sensed her almost desperate yearning.

After their quarrel last night, he felt they needed to reaffirm their love for one another. And that could be done most effectively in bed. Suddenly, Cody realized he hadn't seen the dog for a while. He asked, "Where is Uther and where will he be sleeping? Did Johnny offer any suggestions?"

At the end of the hall, they saw the police dog lying in the middle of their bed. He sat up and wagged his tail.

Gail laughed, "I guess that answers your question." She bantered, "Now, where will you be sleeping? I think the living room couch is still available."

After a moment spent discussing their dilemma, Gail suggested, "Let's just call him out to the living room and get him settled on the sofa. We'll throw him a couple of treats and then slip back to the bedroom for a few minutes."

An hour later, they guiltily crept back down the hall to check on Uther. The faithful canine lay stretched in front of the threshold just on the other side of the door to the living room. He looked up at them happily and then walked back to the bedroom and lay down on the floor at the foot of the couple's bed.

Cody said, "I'm going to check the outside door, turn out the lights, and go by the kitchen for a bottle of water. Do want anything?"

She smiled seductively. "No thanks. I've had everything I need tonight."

A few minutes later, as Cody turned off the lights in the kitchen, he noticed the phone's blinking message light. He checked out the time indicator. The call had come through about a half-hour before. He looked at the wall clock. Ten o'clock. He hit the play button.

A well-spoken, dignified gentleman's voice projected from the wall-mounted speaker. "This is Jared Dettwiller calling. I'm a neurosurgeon at St. Francis Hospital. This isn't a medical emergency, but a personal matter I urgently need to discuss with you. Please return my call at any time, day or night."

Cody turned to call out to Gail, but she was standing in the doorway.

"Did you hear all that?" he asked.

"Yes."

Since Gail worked at St. Francis Emergency Room, he questioned her about the doctor. "Do you know Dr. Dettwiller?"

"Oh, yes. However, I doubt he remembers me."

"Why do you say that?"

"Fifteen-hundred R.N.s work at that hospital."

"Well, please tell me what you know."

Dressed only in her pajama bottoms, Gail pulled a stool up to the counter and said, "Well, he's the chief of the Neuroscience Department and very highly regarded by the nursing staff and other physicians. He hardly comes into the ER though. He usually sends one of the residents to do the initial assessment. If the case warrants, he catches up with the patient in the Imaging Department or Surgery."

"Do you think I should call him tonight?"

"I would."

"You say that without hesitation."

"Nurses are trained to make quick decisions," she teased. "Unlike the clergy, we don't have the luxury of contemplation or extended discussions, not when someone's life hangs in the balance."

"Okay, I conceded that to you several years ago." He stepped into the living room and grabbed her blouse from the floor. Tenderly, he draped it around her.

"Thanks. I was feeling cold. How did you know?"

Cody said, "I didn't know that. The reason I put it around you is that if I look at your breasts for very much longer, then it'll be a long time before we get any sleep."

She laughed. "Well that's a truthful answer, given quickly and decisively. Looks like you're picking up some of my better traits."

"Why would you call the doctor back tonight?"

"He's a very busy man. Just as most physicians, he values his time away from work. Dr. Dettwiller isn't likely to say to call him day or night. For some reason, he feels talking with you is very important."

Cody sighed. "Okay. Here we go." He pressed the return call button on the phone.

After a couple of rings, the doctor answered. "Thank you for calling me back tonight, Reverend Palmeroy. By the way, I know your wife from the hospital. She's an excellent nurse."

Cody smiled over at Gail. "That's kind of you to mention, sir. I'll be sure and let her know what you said."

The physician hesitated as if to gather his thoughts. "My wife and I have been discussing all day whether or not to call you. I told her that we needed to respect your privacy and that what transpired was just a coincidence. It wasn't until an hour ago that she convinced me I owed it to our daughter to contact you."

Cody said, "Please, sir, tell me about your daughter."

"Malia is sixteen. A year ago she was hit by a drunk driver and has been in a coma ever since then."

"I'm so sorry, Dr. Dettwiller. It must be a very difficult time for you and your family."

"Indeed it is," the father admitted sadly. "After the accident, she spent six months in the hospital ICU before we decided to bring her home. I knew death would likely come for her, and I didn't want my baby girl to die in an institution. We set up her room with a hospital bed and all the equipment needed to care for her. She's had nurses around the clock since then. For all this time, she's shown no change. She's never moved or opened her eyes or said anything for almost twelve months. That is, until last night."

"What happened?"

"I go through a ritual with Malia to let her know I still love her and that I haven't given up hope. Unless I have an emergency at the hospital, I sit in her room for an hour or so before going to bed. My wife usually joins me for this vigil. Some comatose patients can hear you and feel your presence even though they can't respond. But after several months with no positive feedback, we started turning on the ten o'clock news to pass the time. In fact, we just started that a few nights ago." The doctor paused a minute before going on.

"Last evening, we were watching the news, and the story came on about what happened down at your church with the SWAT team. At the end of your interview, a reporter asked if the incident would cause you to resign. I believe you gave your answer based on a passage from Nehemiah."

"Jeremiah."

"Yes, what was it you said?"

"Like a tree planted by a river, I shall not be moved."

"Yes, that was it. When you spoke those words, Malia sat straight up in her bed and pointed at the television. She spoke her first words in a year. She said, 'I know you, magic man. I see you there by the tree drinking the waters of life. Come to me for I have marvels to show you. Many and wonderful.'"

# Chapter 13

*Last Days' Diary*

The young minister was exhausted, already having spent the morning at the Police Training Academy with Sergeant Jimmy Nelson and his boss Captain Hooper, commander of the Southeast Precinct. The policemen took turns teaching Cody how to safely handle and fire his weapons. After a couple of hours of target practice, they went to the gym to work on basic self-defense moves and the use of stun guns and pepper spray. Later, they drove to the church to instruct the waiting technicians on the placement of over a dozen security cameras and an even larger number of motion detectors in and around the property.

As they parked at the back door of Mt. Sinai, Miss Alma, part-time church secretary for more than thirty years, met them with a tongue-lashing.

"How do you expect me to keep up with things around here if nobody tells me where they are? I called the precinct headquarters because I guessed that my pastor was hanging out with his new best friends. But the officer who answered the phone had no notion where the three of you were hiding." She looked sternly at the policemen. "Somebody there just guessed you might be at the firing range, but nobody knew for sure. What kind of police department do we have in our city anyway? With such inefficiency, no wonder the crime rate is so high."

During this rant, Cody smiled at his friends, who were taking their punishment from the elderly lady with down-turned expressions of shame.

Miss Alma looked over at him and snapped, "You wipe that smirk off your face right now, young man, because you're in even worse trouble."

The men walked down the hall to the church office with Miss Alma pecking at them from behind, jabbering about Cody's transgressions.

"I took a couple of days off. I was resting at my apartment, about to retire for the evening. I turned on the news to see my pastor had let some riffraff into this holy place. And what did they do? Shot up the church like a bunch of godless mobsters."

As they sought the refuge of Cody's office, the men felt the assault of her tirade continue from her small office next door.

"So I came to work the next morning, only to be greeted with crime-scene tape and broken glass."

"I know, Miss Alma, I should have called you," Cody apologized. "I was just so traumatized, I could hardly remember my own name."

Unimpressed by his apology, the well-meaning mother hen continued. "The place was swarming with deputies. The sheriff was here, too. They were all asking where you were. But, of course, I knew nothing. So I turned around and went home. And today these nice police department workers came to install their equipment. But do I know where the cameras go? How would I know that?"

Cody said, "I'm sorry, Miss Alma. I truly am, but now we have to discuss some matters. Excuse us for a while, please."

Before the elderly secretary could respond, he gently shut the door.

Sergeant Nelson declared, "I know Miss Alma talks a lot, but you should be grateful to have someone like her to look after you."

"Believe me, I am. She's priceless."

Captain Hooper added, "The woman has a big heart, and not much goes on in the hood she doesn't know about. Plenty of times she's helped us identify victims, and suspects, too."

From the top shelf of his bookcase, Cody grabbed the architect's floor plan for the old church and rolled it out on the conference table. Although the drawing was more than sixty years old, it provided an excellent overhead view of the sanctuary and surrounding rooms.

After discussing the most sensible locations around the property for cameras and motion detectors, Cody surrendered the drawing to Sergeant Nelson, who would instruct the waiting technicians on the placement of the security equipment. He let the police officers out by the side door to avoid more scolding from Miss Alma.

A few minutes later, she called Cody on the intercom. "I saw your buddies leaving your office by the side door. Have you had your lunch?"

"No, ma'am. I haven't had time." Cody responded.

"Did you eat your breakfast?"

Somewhat irritably, Cody confessed, "I had to be at the police academy at eight."

"You're going to shrivel up and blow away, young man. You better start taking better care of yourself."

"Okay. I promise I'll do better if you'll leave me in peace for a while."

Unmoved by his promise, Miss Alma retorted, "I'm not fooled by that kind of talk. That's what you say every time."

Cody didn't respond. He hoped his well-meaning secretary would leave him alone.

After a moment, she said, "I'm going down the street to the diner to get you a decent, hot meal. Oh, and a lady from a Dr. Dettwiller's office called about your meeting with him at eight o'clock tonight at his home. Is it okay to confirm that with her?"

Cody said, "Yes, thank you."

"Okay, Reverend. I'll be back shortly."

Quickly, Cody rose from his desk and intercepted his loyal secretary in the hall where workers from the police department were noisily hammering and drilling all around, harshly interrupting the usual quiet solemnity of the church building. As he handed her his wallet, he said, "Please get some lunch for both of us. I'm sorry if I seem a bit grumpy today."

Miss Alma gave Cody a sympathetic smile. "No need to apologize, sir. I know the past few days were really an ordeal for you."

Cody walked through a nearby door into the sanctuary and strolled up behind the pulpit. He often did this to practice his sermons or just gaze out at an imaginary congregation for inspiration. Now, he looked out at all the sad, hopeful faces. They wanted to believe what he preached was true. Not that they cared about every little Bible story down to the last detail. No. They could live with some uncertainty and even some fallibility, but what they needed on the most basic level of human existence was for something to be true and unchangeable.

Without this truth, many couldn't get out of bed on Monday morning. They could hardly shave or put on makeup as though it mattered. Desperately, they needed to know that something was waiting for them at the end of the tunnel. Something that could explain it all, that could wipe away the tears of despair, that could make sense out of their hardships, that could somehow whisper the answers to their most important questions; something that could still love them in spite of their unworthiness.

He returned to his office and stood before the formidable collection of volumes in the tall bookcases. Miss Alma's reminder about the meeting at Dr. Dettwiller's prompted Cody to recall a journal he'd kept over the years. He thought that tonight's meeting with the doctor's daughter might produce additional material for his unusual records.

Cody scrutinized the books with the diligence of a devoted librarian searching for a precious masterpiece among a miasma of mediocrity.

Textbooks and book club offerings on the subjects of theology, philosophy, and history dominated the disorganized shelves. When Cody had accepted the pastorate at Mt. Sinai Church, he'd hastily placed his book collection in no particular order. He told himself he would find time someday to neatly catalogue and arrange the volumes, but that respite never came, and now, he conducted a haphazard, hurried look on every shelf for the treasure he hoped wasn't lost. His pulse accelerated with each unfulfilled moment.

Some of the dark titles that he faced reached out to grip him with their messages of hopelessness. Fear and Trembling, The Sickness Unto Death, Heart of Darkness, Nausea, No Exit, Radical Theology and the Death of God.

At last, Cody spotted a seemingly empty space between two big volumes of the History of Western Civilization. He saw a tall, thin book with red leather binding pushed to the back of the shelf.

As he retrieved the work from its obscure resting place, he smiled in satisfaction and relief. The volume had a sturdy cover like an accountant's ledger. The front of it was entitled in bold, black letters: Last Days' Diary. He set it reverently on his desk.

Opening the journal, he reflected on its content. It contained his handwritten entries describing the thoughts and ravings of people who were about to die. Most of the accounts were based on personal interviews and questionnaires he'd collected during his last two years in divinity school, when he'd volunteered to visit patients and hold worship services at area nursing homes, hospitals, and hospices.

Cody had used a small digital recorder so taking notes wouldn't be a distraction for his subjects. He was giving these patients a death bed exam, what he considered the definitive test for the meaning of life. He even included some material he'd gathered from his work at the funeral home. The sudden death of a loved one often thrust the bereaved into reflections on their own mortality. Also, death row inmates and hospitalized convicts at Jericho State Prison had made their own twisted contributions to the compilation.

As a divinity student, Cody occasionally stood at the bedside with family members, or every now and then, alone at the time of a patient's death. Sometimes he held a feeble, dying hand and felt life slip away into a stark wasteland of emptiness.

More often, he fantasized a glimpse of a grey tunnel with a light at the end. He skeptically thought his mind was mimicking the many, well-documented cases of near death experiences of people whose souls or spiritual essence had traveled the length of the tunnel and stood in the presence of the light. Then, often to the astonishment of the attending medical personnel, they inexplicably returned to their bodies to resurrect flat lines on heart monitors. Most of these patients went back serenely to normal life, albeit with vague talk about seeing the world differently and facing death without fear.

The fact that he hadn't made additional entries in the diary for the last two years discouraged the young minister until he remembered a file in his desk where he'd stuffed notes to be inserted into the journal. Since becoming pastor at Mt. Sinai, he'd had no time to bring the diary up to date because his congregation was an unrequited black hole of human need. He now placed the folder with the scribbled accounts in the front of the book, vowing to add them to his handwritten journal at the earliest opportunity.

Curious about the notes he'd made over a number of years, he flipped through the diary to take a sampling of its entries. He remembered a few of the people whose musings he'd recorded, but mostly he couldn't recall the face or name of the contributors. They left behind only thoughts about their lives and impending deaths.

As he thumbed through the volume and his folder of recent notes, he randomly stopped to reflect on some of the particular accounts.

Funeral Home. "I know they say Daddy lived a long, full life and we should be grateful. But that doesn't mean squat. All that really matters is being able to live just one more day."

Funeral Home. "I'm afraid Uncle Chester isn't too happy now that he's dead. He's going to find himself in a long line of people waiting to be judged. Too bad, since he never liked to wait in line or be judged either."

Funeral Home. "My Daddy must be in heaven now. He was a faithful member of the Great Harvest Church of Jesus. I went there a couple of times with him until I saw what they aimed to harvest. They aimed to harvest me."

Jericho Prison Death Row. "What you talkin' about, Chaplain? Me and the Grim Reaper? I seen him coming through here to visit. He don't look like such a bad guy. I admit he don't smile much, but who can blame him? It's a big responsibility. He probably has a lot on his mind. He mostly comes late at night, wandering up and down the mile, looking into our cages, sizing us up, trying to decide who will be the next to fry in the chair or die of a heart attack or something. And when I see him comin', I always smile and wave. It's true, he's not too friendly, but you never know when you might need him to do a favor for you."

State Prison for the Criminally Insane. "Hey, are you a minister? They say I have lung cancer. Just two months to live. I'll bet you didn't know this, but I fucked your mother. She was in a wheelbarrow at the time and I wore cowboy boots. I told her, 'I know you hate cowboy boots, so I'm going to fuck you while wearing these boots.' I rolled her out onto the pasture. That's when I put it to her. She squealed like a piglet. And when you go by the warden's office on the way out, tell him this fucking straightjacket is driving me crazy."

State Prison for the Criminally Insane. "God is going to send us all to hell. I'll tell you why He's so pissed off. I call it the anatomy of humankind. The brain hatches sinister plots, the tongue lies, the hands hold knives, and the feet run from responsibility. And here's something else, Chaplain. Never trust women or God. Women are the consummate bait-and-switch artists and God likes to play hide-and-seek."

State Prison for the Criminally Insane. "The doctors say I've got this brain tumor. I guess that's why they called you here to see me. They can't do anything about it but try to keep me comfortable while I'm dying. Now, you may be a preacher but I'm a prophet. God lets me see things."

"What kind of prophet are you?"

"A prophet of doom. What other kind is there? What do you think God tells the prophets? 'I've given everything a look-see and you're all looking good? Everybody is happy, got a good spouse, a good life and all that. Maybe there could be a little more fornication. That would be nice.'

"One day He showed me the earth being swallowed up by a black hole and an army of fat girls dancing with Jesus in the rain. He hasn't shown me much lately, though. To tell the truth, I was a lot happier before they put me in here. I was night manager at a fast food drive-through and part-time serial killer. And get this. Several years ago, I got a hearing at the Parole Board. They asked me if I got out of here would I kill again. Ha. I told those fuckers that you never know what might happen when the boogeyman come a-callin'."

Jericho State Prison Hospital Psychiatric Ward. "I know I have little time left to live, but God sent a vision to comfort me.

"I saw Jesus walk down from heaven on a golden stairway. Wu...Wu. He was wearing a lime-green suit. Wu...Wu. Lightning was shooting out of his fingertips. Wu...Wu. He was zapping the unrighteous. Wu...Wu. Better get your shit together, Chaplain, or He could be zapping you. Wu...Wu."

Saint Joseph's Hospital Cardiac ICU. "I'm not worried at all about dying, Reverend. I've led a faithful life. Even when we traveled, we always went to church. I remember one time in San Juan I found this church where a service was in progress. A statue of Jesus stood right outside the door flanked by vending machines. You could kneel before Jesus while eating some chips or drinking a soda. I went inside. The priest spoke in Spanish, so I understood none of it. And yet, somehow I understood all of it."

Ravenscroft Nursing Home. "Reverend Palmeroy, I sure appreciate you stopping by, but I'm not worried about what will happen to me when I die. I read the whole Bible several times. But I have one issue I don't understand at all. Why does God want us to worship Him?"

Gentle Winds Hospice. "Some ministers claim that when you get to heaven you can look down and see what others are doing. I don't mind facing God's judgment, but I am scared as hell about my born-again grandmother. If she's been watching me since she died twenty-five years ago, then things won't be very pleasant when I'm reunited with my family. I can picture her now, spying on me with a scowl of disapproval, in her high-button shoes, Bible in hand, as my throbbing penis spewed sperm over some cheap whore's tits."

Rosedale Nursing Home. "I think of all I'll miss after my death... Sweet young things wearing halter tops in the summer, Monday night football, babysitting for the grandkids, sitting down to a good plate of ribs. I guess this is the time you start thinking more about life after death. Things you haven't thought much about for fifty years, now become very important. And the hell of it is, nobody really knows for sure. The ones who think they know it all, know least of all. I think we're going to be in for a big surprise. It's going to be very radical. Something no one has ever imagined before, because visualizing such things is impossible. The human mind isn't capable of it.

"And as far as this reincarnation thing goes, it doesn't much matter if I'm a rapper, or NFL star, or owner of a diamond mine, just as long as I can have sex any time I want it. In the end, that's the only thing that really matters."

Gentle Winds Hospice. "I've been attending church all my life. I strongly believe in God and the Holy Scriptures, so I have a good chance of making it into heaven. However, my three precious children are mature adults and not one of them believes in God. I don't know what I did wrong, but I ended up with three atheist children. My question for you is, 'How can I enjoy heaven while knowing my kids are tortured for eternity in the depths of hell?' That doesn't seem like heaven to me."

Langford Nursing Home. "I would take a lethal dose of pills, if I could get my hands on them. But they're always watching me here.

Why should they care if I want to take my own life? It's none of their business anyway. They should rejoice that they wouldn't have to change my diapers anymore. "There's this woman here who changes people's diapers. When she gets to the end of the hall, do you think she can forget about it? No, she goes right back to the first of the hall and starts all over again. That's all she does, all day long. Can you imagine a worse job? Looking at peoples' bum holes and shriveled up genitals all day. And constantly cleaning up feces and most of it messy, smelly diarrhea because these old farts take too many laxatives. They're deathly frightened of constipation. I even asked my roommate one time what was the worst thing that could happen to her, and she says, 'Being stranded on a desert island without any prune juice.'"

Grandville Heights Nursing Home. "There was this kid at work who thought you were going to have sex in heaven and that all you do up there is screw all day long. If God is going to let us fool around in heaven, He should take care of a few issues first. One is erectile dysfunction. Others include body odor, menstruation, premature ejaculation, and, as Gore Vidal says, 'the tyranny of the female orgasm.' These are just a few of the things I want straightened out before I start screwing around up there."

Evergreen Nursing Home. "I don't much care what happens in heaven. I just want the pain to end. They say when you get to heaven, the angels come and make you forget all memory of your earthy pain. I know a few things I'd like to forget about, that's for sure. One of them is how much my first husband cheated on me, the bastard. Another one is the time I went to the casino and lost my mortgage payment. Sure don't want to think about that again. Another thing was when the kids came into the bedroom at two o'clock in the morning. One of them had an earache or something. I was screwing my second husband. I don't know how long they'd been there, but we had been doing the sixty-nine. I don't want to think about that anymore."

Gentle Winds Hospice. "Like a lot of people around here, I figure I pretty much wasted my life. Always living for tomorrow, never living in the present moment, trying to accumulate things. Always at the mall, laying up for myself treasures on earth. They say life is short, but that's not true. It's long. I just didn't spend my time wisely."

Langford Nursing Home. "I had this little dog once. I loved that little puppy more than I did my own husband. A lot more. Well, it killed me when that little thing got run over. I hope I get to see my dog again. What do you think, Reverend? Will I get to see my little dog in heaven?"

A gentle knock at the door revealed that Miss Alma had returned. Her faced beamed with delight as she brought the take-out box to his desk. "I hope this will taste good to you," she clucked as she opened the container. Enthusiastically, she pointed to each item. "I brought you meatloaf with mashed potatoes, turnip greens, and white beans." She opened a small brown paper bag with grease stains showing through. "And here are some corn muffins and a piece of chess pie. I hope you enjoy."

"I'm sure I will, Miss Alma. This is exactly what I would have chosen for myself. Thank you." Cody smiled, hoping to make up for his grouchiness earlier.

She handed him his wallet. "Thank you for paying for mine, too. You're always so good to me. Oh, down at the diner they were talking about the big snowstorm that's supposed to hit us this afternoon. The forecast is for seven inches or more."

Cody looked out the window. Already, light snow was falling on the parking lot, and the clouds appeared heavy with potential. Snow was always a major issue in the South because residents were relatively inexperienced in driving under bad conditions and municipalities lacked much of the heavy snow-removal equipment of their Northern neighbors.

After finishing his meal, Cody returned to his journal, perusing random entries.

Ravenscroft Nursing Home. "As sure as I'm sitting here right now, judgment of the sinners is coming. Those people who slept in on Sunday morning all those years are going to get their comeuppance. Sweet."

Rosedale Nursing Home. "I'm dying in this place. I wish I would hurry up and die, because I'm coming back as a demon ghost. I'm going to find my wife in bed with that bastard, and I'll haunt them until the day they die. Then, I'm going to escort them both to hell and personally turn them over to the devil."

Gentle Winds Hospice. "When I think of dying, I remember my grandmother. One of the saddest parts about growing old for her was that no one read her letters anymore and she knew it. At one time her letters meant something. Compliments and encouragement from the matriarch of the family could fill a grandchild's heart with pride. Sometimes we found wisdom in those letters and sometimes money. But both had stopped years before. So when we opened the letters and saw they had no money inside, and the wisdom had just turned to the gibberish of a confused mind, we would read a couple of lines and put the letter aside. No one cared what she said anymore. It didn't matter. She didn't matter. Now, the same thing has happened to me."

Evergreen Nursing Home. "Something is bothering me about the Resurrection. According to St. Paul, when Jesus came out of his tomb, he had a different kind of body, a new body, a 'soma pneumatikon' which in the Greek of the New Testament means 'spiritual body.' It was fundamentally different from our earthly bodies. So different in fact, the disciples didn't recognize Him right away. Jesus, being firstborn of the dead, will give all believers a spiritual body like His, good to last an eternity in heaven.

"Now, the spiritual body has nothing to do with your earthly flesh so that a person who was lost at sea five-hundred years ago, and whose molecules and DNA spread throughout the oceans will get a spiritual body just like someone who was buried in the ground yesterday. The same happens to someone who is cremated and their molecules are scattered in the wind. The spiritual body is a completely new act of creation that isn't dependent on our earthly remains. So if we follow the doctrine of St. Paul, Jesus' dead, earthly body should be in the tomb, since He appeared post-resurrection in His spiritual essence. The tomb should not have been empty. Isn't that right, Reverend Palmeroy?"

"I, too, have struggled with this dilemma. Technically, maybe the body should be in the tomb, but this might have caused confusion if we consider the historical context. The Pharisees believed in the resurrection of the body. The Jewish version of resurrection wasn't a new act of creation but revitalization of human remains. Thus, if Jesus appeared in the spirit only, he might have been seen as a ghost or otherwise be misunderstood. So the most practical way to get across the resurrection idea was to imply that his earthly body was transformed into a spiritual one."

251

County Nursing Home. "I haven't had sex since Lottie died. She went to heaven and took her vagina with her."

Saint Jude Hospice. "It's so strange, Reverend. I keep hearing these voices, whispers really, mainly female. When I was a teenager, I had this mole on my chest, just above my bra. In biology class one day, our teacher showed us a picture of a melanoma to encourage us to use sunscreen. Well, I thought my mole was surely a melanoma. It seemed to grow and change color every day. I obsessed about it and convinced myself I would soon be dead.

"So, my mother caught me crying one evening, and I told her about the mole. She took me to a doctor who cut it out and sent it to a lab for analysis. A few days later, he called and told my mother that it was nothing. He said, 'It's just a harmless freckle, nothing but a freckle.' Now, as I lie here dying, these voices—I like to think of them as angels' voices—keep whispering, 'It's just a freckle. Fear not, for death is just a freckle.'"

County Nursing Home. "They say that when we get our fancy new bodies in heaven that we won't get hungry anymore. We won't need to eat. Something's not right about that, Reverend. How could it be heaven if we don't get to eat some fried chicken every now and then?"

Evergreen Nursing Home. "I can't get over why God allows so much evil in the world. He's supposed to be all powerful, right? Well, why doesn't He intervene? Natural evil like tornadoes and hurricanes take many lives every year. Moral evil like the Nazis has claimed millions throughout human history. If God is indeed omnipotent, why does He tolerate so much human misery? The only conclusion I can come to is that if there is indeed a God, He must not have the power to correct the evil of this world. And if he is incapable, then He really is not the ultimate God deserving of our worship and respect. What do you think, Reverend?"

"I understand what you're saying and I've had some of those same feelings. I think maybe God permits evil in the world as a challenge for humankind. If it weren't for evil, we would have far fewer opportunities to show compassion and help those affected by it. It also helps us grow ethically when we choose good over evil. Our problem in understanding why an all-powerful God tolerates evil in the world is that we might not have the big picture.

252

"Here's a little story that may help us with this dilemma. A newspaper reporter based on the East Coast was assigned to cover a story out West. During a major winter storm, he traveled by stagecoach for the last leg of the trip because the trains had stopped running. An obviously pregnant woman was the only other passenger. As the stagecoach strained and churned through the deep snow, the High Plains weather became even colder. Icy winds surged around the flimsy coach curtains. The stagecoach stopped and the driver jumped down to check on the passengers. The reporter hadn't noticed, but the woman had fallen asleep. Rather roughly, the driver slapped her until she awoke with a scream. He explained that she had to stay awake.

"She nodded her head in compliance but during the time the driver was checking on the reporter, she fell asleep again. The driver hurried her out of the coach and into the deep snow. He got back in his seat and drove off, leaving the startled woman behind. And then panic consumed her and she began running wildly after the coach. After about a quarter mile, he stopped and waited for the pregnant lady to catch up. He greeted her courteously and assisted her to her seat as if nothing odd had happened at all.

"At the end of the trip, the reporter told the driver, 'That was one of the worst examples of cruelty I've ever seen. I'm going to write a story about it for my newspaper.'

"The driver said, 'Fine, but be sure to include the reason I made her run.'

"The reporter said, 'What reason could there be for such intolerable cruelty?'

"The driver replied, 'I had no choice. If I let her fall asleep for a long time she could have frozen to death, and I wasn't about to arrive here with a corpse in my stagecoach. By running after us, she got her blood circulating strongly. It probably saved her life.' The reporter was shocked. How could he have been so rash as to draw conclusions before he knew the full picture?

"That little anecdote sometimes helps people cope with the problem of evil. There is so much about our world and God we don't know. We shouldn't judge Him. The Bible teaches us that Satan will eventually be contained, and God will demonstrate His omnipotence. But until that time comes, evil and confusion will be manifested in our world, and Satan is the cause of it. But I believe God is omnipotent and He will eradicate evil in the future."

Evergreen Nursing Home. "I heard you talking with my roommate over there about the problem of God allowing a universe that still has evil in it. I'm scared of evil and Satan all right, but let me tell you what equally scares me. God Himself. When he helped Joshua take down the city of Jericho by causing the walls to crumble, He ordered genocide of the residents of that unfortunate place. He told Joshua to put them all to the sword, including the women and children. Now, that's scary.

"I don't feel good about going before the judgment throne of a god who would order the slaughter of innocent children. Also, God describes Himself as sometimes being jealous and the Bible says He gets angry. You would think that a being as sophisticated and powerful as God would have overcome such base emotions. Looks to me like He could use a little cognitive therapy and anger management, too."

Saint Joseph Hospital. "As I lie here dying, I've been reading my Bible. A story in there is about God sending a chariot of fire, and that right after it appeared, a whirlwind carried Elijah up to heaven. Now, ponder that for a little while, Reverend. It will put a mind fuck on you."

County Nursing Home. "I'm really not worried about going to hell, Preacher. It's already overcrowded with a waiting list as long as you can imagine. Most of the people I know will be in line ahead of me, half of them born in a laundromat, while their father was screwing the sister in a potato chip truck out back by the dryer vents."

Hillcrest Hospital ICU. "I'm dying and I feel I've lived a good life, so I hope to go to heaven. But I can't get this memory out of my mind. I was a little girl and I was scared I'd go to hell. According to the way our minister preached the gospel, almost every one of us was going to hell. So, I told my mother about this, and she said, 'As long as you're good, you won't go to hell, but keep in mind that all bad girls go to hell when they die. And if you're just awful, the devil may come get you while you're still alive. Don't you remember that time when you and your sister were really bad, and you wouldn't obey me? I picked up the phone and called the devil to come get you. But then

254

you started to cry and promised never to be naughty again so I called the devil back and told him not to come.'"

Saint Jude Hospice. "I'm so tired of all the pain I've had. I watched two of my children die. I can't wait to die. I want out of this place fast. I need for someone to buy me a gift certificate for Dr. Kevorkian."

Pegasus Nursing Home. "Chaplain, don't let my first wife attend my funeral. She'll spoil it for everyone. Don't be fooled. She can act sweet, but she's really a bitch from hell and a has-been trailer park princess with a terminal case of penis envy."

County Nursing Home. "Reverend, I know this is sinful to say, but I really want to die. The nurses here don't even feed me anymore, and they keep my pain medicine for themselves so that I'm in a constant state of torture. Please, please just turn off my oxygen and put a pillow over my face. It will only take a minute to free me from this hell. I know we talked about this before, and you support euthanasia. You said I have a right to die, but the court would need to appoint a guardian ad litem. My case would need approval from a judge. I can't wait for all that. I want to die today. Right now. Please, help me. Please, in the name of God, set me free from this hell and give my soul some peace. I have no one else to turn to. I asked one of the nightshift nurses to do it, but she wanted five-hundred dollars."

Baptist Hospital. "I pray to God every day to forgive my sins. He can do that since He's all powerful. But in one of your visits, you mentioned a few things that God cannot do—like forget, lie, hate, and change the past. That really shocked me at the time, but now I see the wisdom in it. And I know even though He can't change the past, He can forgive it, and for that I'm extremely grateful."

Saint Francis Hospital. "I hear the angels calling my name. See you in heaven, Reverend Cody. I really like you. I hope you make it."

Dillard Nursing Home. "I don't consider myself a spiritual man. I've never had any kind of religious experience. The closest I came to it was when we went to the beach for summer vacation. I held up a seashell to my ear and thought I heard some angels singing, but my brother gave me an empty beer can and I heard the same thing."

Saint Jude Hospice. "When you get to heaven, one of the first things that's supposed to happen is you meet up with your dead relatives. I hate my family, and if I see any of them, I'll tell them to kiss my ass. My mother-in-law again? I don't think so. Also, in heaven you are supposed to meet all these people in life that you helped. I don't want to see any of those either. All they did was take advantage of me."

Saint Francis Hospital. "You know, Preacher, even as I lie here dying, they keep calling me from work to ask me about the business. When the undertakers are closing my casket for the last time, someone will slip a cell phone in there with me. Even though I started that business, I hated it. In every meeting, I was thinking about something else, something that mattered. So I hope at my funeral you'll tell everyone that I was never there. I was never totally present—anywhere."

Evergreen Nursing Home. "I can't even get a good night's sleep in here. There's too much noise. I learned a long time ago that insomnia is a wakeup call from the Almighty. So, if you can't sleep, you best get up and see what He wants. If you ignore Him, it could be big trouble for you later on."

County Nursing Home. "I sold my soul and the best years of my life to the diner down the street from the church. Sometimes I'd work there seventy hours a week just to put food on the table for the kids. The hardest part was knowing I used my best energy on endless trips to the kitchen, looking under dirty dessert plates for tips, and constantly pouring extra coffee for overweight middle-aged men who unashamedly twisted their fat necks around for a good look at my ass as I left the table.

"I remember one customer in particular who was especially sleazy. He was some bootleg evangelist with a bad dye job. He offered me twenty dollars for oral sex back in the men's room. I desperately needed the money so I did it, and then he left the diner without paying me. But what could I do? Call the police and tell them this guy stiffed me for a twenty-dollar blow job?

"Christmas was the worst time of year for me. I hated Christmas because I had five children and very little money. But I always somehow bought them a few toys to share. One year I was sick and couldn't work for two months, so when the holidays came around, I had no money at all. Well, I played this little game with myself so I would feel better. I made out a list of presents for each of my children and caught the bus from the projects out to one of those fancy malls in the suburbs. I went in the store and pretended I had money.

"I worked through my list and put all the toys, sweaters and other presents in my basket. I stood in the checkout line just like the other customers. Then I pretended I forgot something and stepped out of line. After a trip to the restroom, I snuck out the front door. I walked out to the bus stop in the rain and cried all the way home. When I opened the door, I saw the faces of my children when they realized I didn't have any packages with me. I never will forget those faces. It broke my heart, Reverend Palmeroy. It was the worst day of my life.

"The doctor said when I'm about to die, there's no point going back to the hospital. They've done all they can for me. So, this is it. Look around the room, Pastor. This is where I'll die."

Saint Jude Hospice. "My sister Hootie comes to visit me every day. She's been dead eleven years. Someday soon she'll get tired of coming here and take me home with her."

Saint Jude Hospice. "When the doctor said I had pancreatic cancer and could expect to live less than three months, I called my family and friends together. The room was full of people, but I told them I had a slight chance of making it. I said, 'I can beat this. I know I'll survive.' Everyone in the room knew it was a lie. But proper etiquette prohibits you from honestly declaring, 'Looks like I'm a dead man.' The cheap veneer of polite society would crumble under the utter reality of that brutal comment. So, you have to play the game, even until the very end."

Gentle Winds Nursing Home. "Yes, Preacher, I do believe in angels. Not because of what the Bible says but on account of my Uncle Elmo. He was on his farm one day, sitting in his favorite easy chair in the gazebo. He looked up and saw three angels. One was sitting in a rocker on the front porch. Another was swinging on a rope tied to a branch of an old oak tree. The third was driving my uncle's tractor in the front yard. He was doing figure eights and stirring up clouds of dust. All of them were laughing and cutting up, having a great time. He went over to chat with them, but they disappeared."

Saint Jude Hospice. "Some folks tell you they are going to live life to the utmost, even until the day they die. It really doesn't work that way. It's hard to sprint to the finish line when you're doubled up in the fetal position in a hospice bed begging for your next pain medication."

University Hospital. "Since I hope to be meeting God sometime soon, I've been lying here trying to figure out what He's like. I know you said one day that we have to get away from the notion that God is some angry old white man with a scraggly beard stomping around heaven, scaring the shit out of people by dropping atom bombs on Sodom and Gomorrah. But you have to admit He allows a lot of weird stuff to happen in His universe. Eternal punishment in hell's Lake of Fire is a real crowd pleaser. And then you have dead men like Lazarus rising from the grave only to die later on, after all.

"But what is He really like? Why does He exist? Why did He create the universe? I don't know and I don't think you do either, or you would have told me."

Deathbed at Posey Reynolds Residence. "They're here."

"Who?"

"The angels."

"Do you see them?"

"No, I hear them."

"What do they say?"

"They call to me."

"What do they call you?"

"They call me Posey. What the hell do you think they would call me? What kind of question is that?

"They told me about my place, my house in paradise. Then, they took me there. The house had ivy and big white columns, and nothing had a roof, and I asked them why, and it was because it never rains. And come to think of it, the house had no doors and no walls because the neighbors don't spy on you. Everyone knows everything about you anyway.

"Getting to heaven was very complicated. I felt myself lying on this deathbed but I started to grow younger. I was a healthy adult, then a teenager, then a child. Time flowed in reverse. As an infant, I went back up into my mother's womb who, like me, grew younger as she traveled back to her mother's womb, and then through all the wombs of every living creature that preceded us. And you could see these fish-like creatures walking on their fins out of the water. And you knew this was where we came from because some of them had human faces.

258

"A great ball of fire fell from the heavens and made a wall of black water that went around the earth covering everything. Then we went back further still and saw the earth as this mass of thick gases and rock, and then back to that big explosion that started it all. But even before that, there were other astonishing blasts and it was all such a marvel that I asked if I could stop and watch, and they let me."

From the bedside, one of Posey's cousins said, "Don't mind her. She talks this way all the time. She's obviously out of her head. You'll have to pardon her. She's been suffering most of her life from a bad case of Jesus."

Posey continued. "I died three days ago. But I keep coming back. I don't know why. I'm confused. I don't know what I'm supposed to do."

Ravenscroft Nursing Home. "I've had this recurring dream that aliens came down to earth and said, 'Hate to break it to you, but this guy you call God, the one that created your world, died many eons ago. He was a problem child of a super race with a universe erector set. And he wasn't very nice, either.'"

Baptist Hospital. "On a frigid Christmas eve, we stopped outside of Birmingham at this famous barbeque place to buy some sandwiches for the road. I had my wife and two small kids with me at the time. As we were waiting for our order at the takeout window, I saw this man with a small boy standing across the parking lot. The hood to his beat-up pickup truck was up. It looked like a dead battery scenario. The man stood there holding his kid's hand. He wasn't asking for anything or calling attention to himself. He just looked at us.

"Part of me wanted to go over and give him a jumpstart, but dark thoughts came unbidden into my mind. 'What if he robs me? What if his dead battery brings mine down?' It seemed to take an eternity to get our food. And then we left and got back on the interstate in our warm car, eating our warm sandwiches. Even though that happened thirty years ago, I still think about it. I should have helped him, but I was too selfish. I still feel guilty about it. Sometimes I even think he was an angel sent to give me a chance to do something good for a man less fortunate. As I get closer to death, I'm more confident than ever that I'll somehow see the man and his boy in heaven and he'll be asking why I didn't help him."

Hillcrest Hospital. "Well, as you know, Reverend, I've been a politician most of my life. When I first got sick, this bitch from my district called me to say I would surely go to hell because of all my falsehoods. I admit I stretched the truth every now and then, but it's no worse than a woman wearing falsies or a pushup bra. At least I'm not wearing my lies. I'm just telling them."

County Nursing Home. "Reverend Palmeroy, I'm having real difficulty understanding the concept of sin. I regret some of my decisions in life and I've lost my temper a few times, but nothing so egregious that I deserve to spend eternity in hell where truly evil people will be tortured for eternity. I'm not perfect but I'm a good person, so it's hard for me take seriously the concept of sin. What do you think?"

"Heaven is a perfectly pure place. No person with unforgiven sins will be allowed to enter. Even if the sin is a small one, it still would represent an unclean presence in heaven. But God makes it easy for sins to be forgiven. Just sincerely ask, and forgiveness follows instantly. The Bible says, 'Though your sins be as scarlet, they shall be made as white as snow and though they be red like crimson, they shall become like wool.'"

Hillcrest Hospital. "I don't want to talk about this because I'm really mad at God right now. He took two children from me. One was killed by Reyes Syndrome, the other on his bicycle in front of my house. Now, what kind of God would allow that to happen? I missed out on so much—seeing my babies grow up, playing with grandchildren, and helping them find a home for their families, which of course they never had. What possible reason could God have for letting my children die so young?"

"I have no idea, ma'am."

"You're a minister. You're supposed to have the answers to questions like this."

"I know this is the impression, but it's not always true. I do know this, though. Both your sons are in heaven right now, and when you arrive there, you'll have a joyful reunion, and you'll spend eternity with them."

"I wanted both the time here on earth and eternity, too, like most folks have. But God cheated me."

"Don't underestimate the importance of eternity. Sometimes I think we really don't appreciate the concept of infinite time, and I don't think God is always mindful of how long earthly time can seem to us. To a being who lives outside of time or in infinite time, forty or fifty years is very, very short. The Bible says in heaven 'a thousand years is like a day.'"

"Well, let me ask you this. If I believe in God, but I'm mad at him, will he let me into heaven?"

"If you hate Him, you won't be a resident of heaven. Hate has no place in heaven. You must forgive God, just as He has forgiven you. Only then will you get to spend eternity with your children."

University Hospital. "At the end of the tunnel, I saw this shimmering blue-white light, and it was sort of like a human figure but not like a human at all. And maybe it was Jesus. I don't know, but it made me feel totally loved in spite of my sins. And I saw some other people there, and they were crying with joy because it was all over, and everything had been forgiven."

Evergreen Nursing Home. "If I have to live another day on this planet, I'm going to kill myself. I wish the Death Angel would walk the halls of this dump, do us all a big favor and 'clean house.' The way I see it, ain't nobody having an especially great time."

Hillcrest Hospital. "Get as much sex as you can, Reverend, because where you're going, you aren't getting any. For sure you won't be getting any in heaven, and I don't think the devil will hand out any weekend passes for R and R, either."

Mallory Assisted Living. "As you know, Reverend, I was a major in the army. I fought those commie bastards in Korea. That war defined my entire life. I was never the same afterward, and every day I still think about it. The biggest mistake the United States ever made was not using nuclear weapons on those chinks. We should have nuked them when we had the chance. Yeah, we should have nuked them for morbid, every one of them."

Evergreen Nursing Home. "Preacher, could you go out and get me a carton of cigarettes? What difference could it possibly make now that the doctor has officially given me the death sentence? I want cigarettes so I can at least die happy. All they offer me here is a nicotine patch. Just you wait. They'll send me to the grave with one of those damn patches. By the way, do you think heaven is a non-smoking facility?"

St. Jude Hospice. "Last night I dreamed I saw my mother in heaven. She was sitting at a card table with one of her friends. They were playing canasta, cackling and carrying on. I yelled up to Mom, 'Save me a place at the table. I'll be coming up to join you before long. And could I get a big plate of that chicken and dumplings you used to make?'"

Baptist Hospital Cancer Ward. "We were in Ecuador, taking a city tour of Quito which included some stops at these beautiful, early colonial-era churches. I recall one church in particular having these remarkably detailed murals depicting various tortures sinners would endure in hell. One of them showed the torture for adultery where a naked man was tied to a post. Some demon was breathing fire right onto this hapless guy's genitals. Our guide reminded us that this torture wasn't a one-time occurrence. Satan, or one of his henchmen, would keep his fiery breath on his balls for eternity.

"And then, this stanza from 'Amazing Grace' popped into my mind. 'When we've been there ten-thousand years, bright shining as the sun, we've no less days to sing God's praise than when we first begun.'

"The way I see it, the devil has to keep the same kind of time in hell as God does in heaven. That means after the guy has his nuts roasted for ten-thousand years, he is still no closer to relief than when he started, because eternity is infinite time, like it says in the hymn.

"As I confessed to you before, I've had my share of strange in my lifetime. I probably had relations with twenty different women, since I was married. And that's not even counting the whores. These women I fooled around with were other men's wives. So I'm a bona fide adulterer. Now, I'm willing to step up like a man and take some reasonable punishment for my sins, but I don't care to have my nuts flash-fried for eternity. That seems a bit excessive.

"I admit I didn't seriously consider my predicament until my doctors told me I have just a few weeks to live. Now it's all I think about. That image from the church in Quito has taken over my mind.

"So, Reverend Palmeroy, what can I do to get out of this mess? I'll say or believe anything at this point. Just show me where to sign."

Lowry Residence. "I was brought up in this small independent Presbyterian church over in Louisiana, where the preacher taught the doctrine of predestination. According to him, it really didn't matter what you did in life—God has already preordained certain people to go to heaven and others to go to hell.

"You really helped clear up this dilemma for me, Reverend Cody. You taught us God stands outside of time, and to Him the past, present, and future are all experienced as one. Thus, He knows the future. He already sees if you'll believe in Him or not, and whether you end up in heaven or hell. But you still get to decide for yourself. You still have free will."

University Hospital. "Here I am at the end of my life, and I'm still confused about whether there is a God. But I think I'll do the wager recommended by that French philosopher. What's his name, Reverend?"

"Blaise Pascal."

"And tell me again about the wager. It sounded like a really good deal to me, and it's important that I get this right."

"If you're not sure about the existence of God and the truth of the Bible, it's better to place a safe bet and believe. Because if all of it turns out to be true, you've got everything to gain and nothing to lose, except your intellectual integrity."

"What was that last part? I don't remember anything about integrity from our previous discussion regarding this."

"Forgive me. That was just a little sarcastic humor I inserted at the end. It's really not a part of Pascal's Wager."

"Well, okay then. I hereby declare my belief in the Almighty and the truth of the Holy Scriptures. Am I now safe from the Lake of Fire and all the other tortures of hell?"

"It's not quite that simple. God knows what's in your heart. It won't work out if you're just saying the words, and you're not sincere. I doubt He would like it much if you try to use Pascal's Wager as some 'Get out of Jail Free Card' to avoid hell."

"Dammit. I knew there would be a catch to this somehow. It's just a cheap parlor trick."

Baptist Hospital. "People took advantage of me all my life because I never found my voice. Even my own family abused me. It didn't help being the youngest, but also I can't stand conflict. So my siblings would get me to do their chores. If I refused, they would pretend to get angry. They knew I would do anything to keep the peace. Even my mother called me a gutless wonder. When I finally moved out and got a job, those horrible co-workers quickly figured me out. I always ended up doing other people's work. They all said,

'Lyla will do it. She can't say no.' 'Lyla will do it.' That should be my epitaph.

"When I married, it was the same with the added torture of regular beatings from my husband even though I did everything he demanded. So, here I lie on my deathbed, and finally I've found my voice, and do you know what it's saying to almost everybody in my life? 'Go to hell, every damn one of you. Don't come visit me. Don't come to my funeral. Just go to hell.'"

Rosedale Nursing Home. "My life is spilt milk."

Hillcrest Hospital. "Once my doctor told me I had a terminal case of cancer, I felt an immense relief that shortly the struggle would be over."

Baptist Cardiac ICU. (Dictated by patient, recorded by wife on back of hospital menu.) "Dying didn't turn out the way I expected. I thought I'd have more time to say goodbye to my family and friends. Now, I'm out of time and energy, too. I can hardly lift my head up off this pillow. If it weren't for this balloon pump machine that keeps my heart beating, I'd be dead right now.

"In a couple of days, the doctors will disconnect the machine and see what happens. That's when I'll die. I know it. I have severe congestive heart failure, and my heart isn't strong enough to pump on its own. But they can't leave the machine hooked up forever. It's strictly a temporary solution.

"Most of my family made it here so I could say goodbye to them, but I have some close friends I'd like to talk with just one last time. I wish I'd stayed in closer touch with them over the years, but I was simply too busy with my job and family. When I think back over my life, this is one of the biggest regrets I have.

"Anyway, I suppose it's not too practical to call them now. Even if I had the strength to talk, what would I say? Would I tell them I'll be dead in a couple of days, but wanted to have a final chat to remember the good times we had in our youth? No one wants to get a call like that. No one wants to chat with a nearly dead man, a soon-to-be-cadaver. It would be too awkward, too depressing."

Broadmoor Nursing Home. "You asked me if I'd live my life again without any changes. That's a good question, Reverend. It's the acid test for the meaning of life.

"I worked in advertising. We had to wear a three-piece suit every day. We called it the executive straightjacket. I worked long hours under incredible pressure and hardly knew my children. I often had to miss my kids' happiest moments, their birthdays and recitals, or their games when they scored a goal or a basket. The company fired me when I was fifty-eight and hired a twenty-six-year-old to take my place. I became too expensive, and my creativity was sluggish. My wife divorced me the next year because she couldn't adjust to a downgrade in lifestyle. So the answer to your question is no. I wouldn't live my life again if I couldn't make changes. It wasn't worth it."

Broadmoor Nursing Home. "Live my life again? Yes, of course I would, even with the same mistakes as before. The reason is my three children. I brought new life into the world. I helped the Creator pass life along. Nothing is more noble than that. I made plenty of mistakes, that's for sure. But I would make them again for the sake of my precious children's lives. If you take away the children though, I'd have to say no. Life is too hard and filled with great suffering. Ironically, some of the suffering is caused by your children."

Hillcrest Hospital. "Preacher, they told me yesterday I don't have much time left. I got something on my mind that is really bothering me. Remember when you baptized me not long after my first stroke? Most people just get a sprinkle of water but I asked for baptism by total immersion because that is how I was brought up. You were really nice to accommodate my request. I was kind of in a hurry so you baptized me in the whirlpool over in the rehab department of this hospital.

"My problem is that because I was hooked to an I.V. and oxygen monitor, you were unable to immerse my left arm. Now, does that mean when I get to heaven I'll just have one arm? I really don't want to go through eternity as some one-handed freak."

Pegasus Nursing Home. "I'm afraid I overplayed my hand with my family by engaging them in what I call the Last Will and Testament Game. A lot of senior citizens make this mistake. As I was getting older, I noticed the kids paid far less attention to me. But when I dangled my will in front of them, they always became instantly respectful and solicitous. It was kind of fun for me. If I mentioned I was thinking of changing my will and maybe leaving a good chunk of my estate to charity, I immediately became the center of the universe for them. Unfortunately, over the years I've lost almost all my assets through bad investments. Also, I've had to pay plenty to stay in this luxury nursing home these past twelve years.

"My kids know I'm almost broke, and now they hardly ever come to visit. Oh, they might bring the grandkids by to see me on a holiday once or twice a year, but nothing on a regular basis even though they both live right here in town.

"Now, keep in mind I have a real nice pair of genuine alligator hide loafers still in the box, so my will might read something like this. 'I leave all my worldly assets to charity with the exception of my alligator loafers. I hereby bequeath the right loafer to my eldest son, John, in case he's in an accident and loses his left leg, which I fervently pray will happen. Likewise, I leave the left loafer to my other child, Henry, in the event he's in an accident and loses his right leg which I also pray will occur soon. These loafers aren't interchangeable and under no circumstances are both to be worn by the same person.'

"Reverend Palmeroy, you see how tragic life becomes when you run out of money. As far as my family is concerned, when no money remains, no love remains either."

Methodist Hospital Cancer Ward. "If I have one blessing with my horrible disease, it's the fact that you don't go quickly. It can take a few weeks, but seldom does it end your life instantly like a heart attack. Now the good part of this is you have time to sort out your affairs and think about things. Lately, I've been thinking about heaven. It's mostly good except for my dilemma. I had three husbands in my long life. Which will I choose to live with in heaven?

"Wait! I just thought of something. None of those bastards will probably make it to heaven anyway. So, what am I worried about?"

Hillcrest Hospital. "You've got a lot of nerve, Mister Reverend, coming in my room with this shit, asking me how I feel now that I know for sure I'm going to die soon. Actually, I'd feel okay about it if people like you from organized religion would leave me alone to die in peace without all these stupid questions. No, I won't be part of your asinine survey. Now, get the hell out of here and leave me in peace. Existential cannibal, get your own goddamned food."

Rosedale Nursing Home. "The way I look at life is that when you're born, God gives you a blank canvas. You paint your life as you go along and when you die, you present your finished self-portrait to the Lord so he can see what you did with the life He gave you.

"Now, let me give you a little advice. Don't paint your high salary or other professional accomplishments because that is not what the Lord is looking for. I've even heard it said that when you show your portrait in heaven, all that kind of thing disappears. Paint the things that show your compassion and how you helped people or loved God. Otherwise, you may arrive before the Judgment Throne with what you think is a beautiful picture, but when the Lord looks at it, all He'll see is a blank canvass. It will be as though you never even lived at all."

Dillard Nursing Home. "I'm an atheist and proud of it. I know what happens after you die. Nothing. It's just like going to sleep and not waking up. There's no heaven or hell.

"I'll tell you what pisses me off, Reverend. You know all these Christians who reside here are always talking about the bliss and beauty of heaven and how they simply can't wait to get there? Well, if heaven is so sweet, why don't they just kill themselves? This place is bad. The food sucks. All up and down the hallways you smell shit and urine. Half the people don't know where they are. So, if this nursing home is so awful and heaven is so awesome, why don't the Christians kill themselves and get on to their eternal bliss? I'll tell you why. They really aren't sure, are they? They say they believe in heaven, but their faith's not strong enough for the ultimate test. I'm surrounded by cowardly hypocrites."

Rosedale Nursing Home. "I worry about my children. What will they do when I'm gone? They can't get along, so I'm their referee. They can't manage their fiscal affairs, so I'm their banker. They make poor decisions choosing spouses, so I'm their psychologist. I'm the matriarch. My children depend on me for everything. I'm afraid when I'm gone, the whole family will fall apart. Well, I guess you could say there will be no more family."

Gentle Winds Hospice. "I've got a mess on my hands in regard to the women in my life. I have a current wife, two previous wives, and a former girlfriend. They all hate me, and each other. I'm like a lightning rod for female trouble. One of my ex-wives says she'll come to my funeral and slap me violently while I lie defenseless in the coffin. The other threatens to put a turd in my casket when the family comes up before the funeral service to say their last goodbyes. She says she'll hide it in a white handkerchief and when she leans over to kiss my forehead, she'll drop it in there with me.

"However, I have a plan to thwart them. I'll simply write in my will to have a closed-casket service. I can hear my first wife beating on the lid, trying futilely to get to me. And the other will be sitting through the whole funeral service with a fresh turd in her hands. But I'll be grinning in my sealed casket. I'll have the last laugh."

Evergreen Nursing Home. "Hello, Reverend Palmeroy. How kind of you to come. I requested to see a minister because even though my Ouija board and Tarot cards tell me I'm going to heaven, verification by a true man of God would be comforting to me. I think the devil is putting doubts in my poor, ancient mind."

"Okay, I think I can help you with this. Have your Tarot cards or Ouija board ever been wrong before?"

"Seldom, but yes."

"Do you believe in God the Father, the Son, and the Holy Spirit? Do you believe Christ died for you, and that He resurrected Himself and ascended into heaven? And have you genuinely asked forgiveness for your sins?"

"Yes. I can say 'yes' to all that."

"Then you can tell the devil to go back to hell and leave you alone. And tell him to take your Ouija board and Tarot cards with him."

University Hospital. "Pastor, I'm somewhat concerned about my future status in heaven. I believe in all the basics. Take the Nicene and Apostles' Creeds, for example. I have no problem with those statements of faith and sincerely repeat either one of them during worship services. Where I get tripped up is on some of the miracles. Take the raising of Lazarus. His sister told Jesus he had been dead three days and his body stank from decomposition.

"I worked in a pathology lab. I know the state of degeneration the cells of a human body undergo after three days. It's impossible to reverse. If it had been three hours, I could believe it. The Virgin Birth is another miracle that's hard for me to accept. So my question is whether I have to believe all the miracles in order to get into heaven."

"My answer is no. I don't believe it is necessary, although many ministers would disagree with me. Here's the way I look at it. The raising of Lazarus is a stretch for me, too. But, when I consider the immensity and complexity of the universe, raising a dead man, even one who has been deceased three days, is really nothing that special.

"The cosmos contains as many as two-hundred-billion galaxies. The number of stars in these combined galaxies roughly equals the grains of sand on all Earth's beaches. In the first second after the Big Bang, many complex events took place in perfect sequence so that the result was the universe as we know it today. If even one of those events didn't occur when it did, we'd be living in a very different world than we know today, if indeed we'd be alive at all.

"Please understand that this isn't a strictly logical proof as to why we should believe in miracles. Saying the universe is big and complicated, therefore, Jesus raised a man who'd been dead three days isn't logical. It's just an emotional response for me, though I don't see anything wrong with that. Such belief is still a matter of faith.

"If you and I can believe in a God who created something as vast and complex as the universe, raising an occasional dead man shouldn't test our faith—yet it does. Maybe Jesus knew a way to reverse time for Lazarus. If He could do that, it would help with the dilemma of cell decomposition.

"Still, if this miracle is giving you trouble, I think it's best for you to suspend judgment on it. Instead of disbelieving the Bible, simply say that this is a matter about which God has not enlightened you yet. That's the way I would handle it."

"Thank you, Reverend. I think you helped me. But, I have another question. Parts of religion are logically demonstrable. Shouldn't we accept those based on logical truth, and what we can't prove take on faith?"

"Did you have something particular in mind?"

"The existence of God is proved by the cosmological argument of Saint Thomas Aquinas. He used principles of causation found in the logic of Aristotle. Nothing exists or occurs without a cause. So if we trace the things we experience back through a regression of causality, we finally come to the Primal Cause or Unmoved Mover, which, of course, is God. He set everything in the universe in motion. I think this is a valid proof of God, don't you?"

"No. Werner Heisenberg, the father of quantum physics, came up with the theories of non-locality and non-causality relative to the subatomic world. In this very small part of our universe, some particles seem to come into existence without any apparent cause.

Therefore, the existence of God can't stand on logic alone. It, too, becomes a matter of faith.

"The issue about the relationship between science and religion is interesting in that we have seen a change in this during the past fifty years. Scientific discoveries used to chip away at the foundations of religion. The discovery of dinosaurs and ancient human remains exploded the misguided theory of Bishop Usher that the world was created in October, 4004 BC. Evidence of evolution has compromised the biblical notion that humankind was a special act by God to create a being that reflected His own image.

"However, some recent discoveries have strengthened religion. We talked about the scale and complexity of the universe. Many people reason that the more complex the universe, the more unlikely its creation occurred randomly or just by itself. Every year, important new findings point to increases in the size and intricacy of the cosmos. These discoveries are often accompanied by the idiom, 'textbooks will have to be rewritten.'

"Science has shocked itself by declaring that we see or know only about ten percent of the universe. The other ninety percent is relegated to the vague and sometimes disturbing categories of dark energy and dark matter. For many people, this kind of news has eroded some of their confidence in science, which had bedazzled them in the past with its remarkable certainty. For me, the odds that a super-intelligent being is responsible for the Big Bang outweigh the probability of a purely scientific explanation.

"It's ironic that, for some people, it's now more of a leap of faith to believe in science than to believe in God. If we apply Ockham's razor—the principle that all things being equal, the simplest explanation tends to be the truth, then we have even more reason to believe in a single divine cause for the universe."

Hospice Floor Hillcrest Hospital. "When you stand on the cliff of eternity, everything in this life looks cheap."

Cody remembered the man and was impressed with the concept that dying people often see the world's transitory nature and the things in it as mere shadows of the reality that lies ahead. Following the entry, he had written a poem that reflected his own feelings on the matter.

Through the cheap, ragged lampshade, the judgment rays of a sixty-watt incandescent bulb illuminate our shame.

Through the cheap, thin-cotton glove, I feel the clammy hand of disingenuous friendship reach out, bejeweled, fat fingers bulging in osmosis with the air.

Through the cheap validation of looking up my own name in the phonebook, I can make sure I truly do exist.

Through the cheap restroom walls, I hear bathroom sounds from the women's side.

Unspeakable horrors await the sewer pipes, then the rivers. The sea also waits.

Through the cheap green glass of dime store sunglasses, I glare at her blond hair and shiny, oiled skin in the beach bar.

And through the cheap plastic straw immersed in the icy sludge of a Margarita with green dye number five, I suck numbness, despair, and delusions of grandeur, visions of the Kingdom of Cum.

Through the cheap housing project walls, made thin by kickbacks and shoddy labor, I hear it all. Intolerable cruelty, child abuse, orgies with handcuffs and midgets, broke-down drug deals, and plans for a homicide.

Through the cheap revival tent promises of everlasting life, I watch as people weeping and shouting heed the altar call from a child evangelist in a shiny, polyester suit.

Through the cheap material of the girl's skirt the headlights of passing cars show the outline of her legs as she stands as a living silhouette by the road, waiting for her sordid destiny to give her a ride.

Through the cheap latex condom, I feel a slight shift in the cosmic ether, and then it's gone.

Lawrence Assisted Living. "They say John died in the bathtub, Ella choked on a piece of beef, and someone else—I can't remember who it was right now—died of something else. Oh, I'm getting married next month. I forgot to tell you."

"That's great. Who is the lucky lady?"

"I don't remember that. You're just too full of questions."

"Well, is she going to be moving in with you, or are you moving in with her?"

"Who?"

Pegasus Nursing Home. "Jesus is coming soon so you better look sharp every day. You won't have time to go home and change clothes. It's the universe's biggest come-as-you-re- party."

Chesterfield Hospice. "When I talk to you about the good old days, I mean the ones with bowel movements."

Broadmoor Nursing Home. "Every cloud has a silver lining, Preacher. When they told me I had terminal cancer, I just laughed and said, 'Good. Bring on the morphine.'"

Gentle Winds Hospice. "When I was young, I saw this sign on the side of a bus. It said, 'Sin No More, Jesus Now.' But I said, 'Sin Now, Jesus Later.' Now, here it is almost too late. I'm dying and I can't find Jesus. He must be hiding from me."

Cody's eyes grew heavy and he began to yawn. The combination of the big meal and sitting at his desk in the warm office had produced in him the overwhelming urge for a nap. He looked longingly at the couch over by the radiator. Since the police technicians had gone for the day, the building was quiet.

He perused his desk for signs of any pressing matter that needed his immediate attention. "Oh, no," he groaned as he saw a note scribbled on a prescription form. It was the message that Kathy, the hospital nurse, had shoved urgently in his hand when he'd visited Rennie Bower. He felt bad that he hadn't responded to her plea, but Rennie was probably correct in her prediction that it involved a romantic motive.

Nevertheless, he felt obligated to respond.

The nurse answered after the first ring. "Hello, Reverend. I saw on the caller I.D. that it was you. Thank you for contacting me."

Cody responded, "I'm sorry I didn't call sooner, but it's been a hectic two days."

"The reason for my note is to get your advice on something. You probably don't know this but after my seven-to-three shift at the hospital I go over to help look after Dr. Dettwiller's comatose daughter three evenings a week until midnight."

Surprised, Cody said, "Dr. Dettwiller mentioned that he provided round-the-clock nursing care for Malia, but I didn't know you were part of that effort. He chose an excellent nurse."

272

"Thank you, Reverend," she said. "Lately, strange things have been happening at night in Malia's room. I need your advice about whether or not to tell Dr. and Mrs. Dettwiller."

"Describe the strange occurrences."

She fell silent, leaving an awkward pause.

Finally, the nurse said, "Maybe contacting you wasn't such a good idea. I know what I experienced, but when I start to talk about it, I lose my nerve. It sounds so bizarre. I'm afraid you might laugh at me or worse, think I'm a little nuts."

"I can relate to what you're feeling," Cody reassured her. "I've experienced some uncanny circumstances myself lately. Please, go ahead. I promise to keep an open mind about whatever you tell me, and, of course, this conversation is absolutely confidential."

"Angels come to Malia's room late at night," Kathy blurted out.

"What do they do there?"

"They walk, or more like float, around the bed. Sometimes they hold her hand and whisper in her ear. But it's bizarre because they lean forward so that they're close to her ear but their lips don't move, yet I feel strongly they are communicating."

"Why?"

"Sometimes Malia responds by squeezing the angel's hand. At least I think that's what happening but the image of the angels is fuzzy. You can see through them."

"They're translucent?"

"Yes, that's the word."

"Do they acknowledge you in any way?"

"No, but I feel they undoubtedly know I'm there, and then several nights ago someone new came with the angels. She wasn't an angel because she had no wings. And another odd thing about her, she was pregnant..."

Cody interrupted, "And beautiful amber light shone from her belly."

Shocked, Kathy exclaimed, "How did you know that?"

"Because I, also, have seen this mysterious woman of whom you speak."

She pressed, "Who is she?"

"I believe she is the Creator of our universe."

Incredulously the nurse replied, "You mean God is a woman?"

273

Cody ignored the question. He didn't want to be diverted by a side discussion on the gender of the Almighty. To him, it made no difference. "Did She say anything?"

"Yes. She said it to Malia, but I swear She knew I could hear her. She said, 'Do not be discouraged, my dearest, for magic man soon come.'"

"And I was there a couple of nights ago when Malia sat up in bed and called you magic man. The next morning, I gave you the note."

Cody gazed out the window of his office. The snow and the wind had picked up considerably. He asked, "Are you on duty at Dr. Dettwiller's tonight?"

"Yes," she answered. "Four until midnight."

"The doctor has invited me to visit Malia at eight. I'll see you then. After I assess the situation, perhaps I'll have a better idea of whether you should tell the doctor and his wife what you've seen."

"Thank you, Reverend Palmeroy. I'm so grateful that you'll help me with my dilemma."

Cody said, "I'm glad you contacted me. We'll work through this together. See you tonight."

Cody rose from his desk and walked to the door of Miss Alma's office. Inside, the secretary was busy at the computer keyboard, slowly but meticulously typing the sermon notes he'd given her for next Sunday.

"Miss Alma, it's snowing hard. I want you to go on home right away."

Miss Alma continued typing.

Firmly, Cody said "The sermon can wait. You must get out of here now, or you might be stranded for the night."

"Don't fret so much over me. You know I have my hooded jacket and snow boots. Since I only live three blocks away, I can walk home anytime."

"You're not walking anywhere on these icy sidewalks. Now get your things. I'll run you home. I'm driving Gail's Jeep today."

Sheepishly, she revealed, "One of my daughters who lives with me is on the way to pick me up right now."

"How did you know I would let you off because of the snow?" Cody teased.

"Like most men, your mind is an open book. I knew that after you saw the snow pick up, you'd break your neck to come tell me to take off."

Cody smiled. "I have precious few secrets around this place. Since you know so much, tell me my plans for the afternoon."

"You're going to stretch out on that couch by the radiator in your office and take a nap."

Cody replied, "You are correct. But that's what I do every time the weather is bad."

With a motherly smile, Miss Alma replied, "Just like an open book."

They laughed and said their goodbyes, and then Cody went into his office, stretched out on the couch and closed his eyes.

After a few minutes, he heard the door to Miss Alma's office creak open, and her soft footsteps across the room. He feigned sleep. He was tired and didn't want to engage in another conversation with the well-meaning woman.

He heard her tiptoe over to the cabinet beneath the bookshelves. After a moment, he felt a blanket spread over his body and gently tucked under his chin.

Without opening his eyes, he whispered, "Thanks, Miss Alma. You're an angel." He drifted into a deep, peaceful sleep just as she gently closed the door on her way home.

# Chapter 14

*Here Be Angels*

At eight p.m., Cody stood in front of the Dettwiller mansion. A golden hue glowed from the frosty windows of every room as heavy snow drifted silently down. He thought a picture of the house would make a good Christmas card from Bella Lugosi because of the decidedly gothic tilt of its architecture. Stained and leaded glass covered the windows; turret rooms on each end of the mansion rose above the snow-covered rooftops; and gargoyles perched at the head of each copper downspout. Two stone dragons guarded either side of the massive front door.

Cody hurried up the recently shoveled slate walkway. As he reached for the massive brass knocker, the wide door opened to reveal an imposing staircase and a huge foyer that opened into a parlor with a roaring fire in the hearth.

A refined gentleman smiled pleasantly from inside and made a sweeping gesture for Cody to enter. He quickly closed the door after the young minister walked across the threshold.

Cody gratefully took a few steps into the warmth of the grand vestibule and shook the snowflakes off his black cashmere overcoat. He spoke to the older man, "Thanks, Dr. Dettwiller. What a beautiful home you have."

The distinguished older man chuckled softly while taking Cody's coat. "I'm Richard. I'm on the staff here, but I do agree with you, it's a magnificent home."

Somewhat embarrassed, Cody said, "I'm sorry. I've never met Dr. Dettwiller. I just assumed…"

Richard patted Cody on the shoulder. "Think nothing of it, Reverend. It's a common misunderstanding for many of our guests on their first visit here. Dr. and Mrs. Dettwiller are upstairs in Malia's room. I'll escort you."

"No need for that, Richard. I'll take Reverend Palmeroy upstairs."

Both men looked up to see Kathy smiling in her spotless, white scrubs cheerfully descending the wide stairs. She had pulled her blond hair back into a tight ponytail that bobbed in synchronicity with each energetic step she took down the Oriental rug runner that spilled over the center of the marble staircase like an elegant waterfall.

"As you wish, Miss Kathy." Turning back to Cody, the manservant said, "I'll hang your overcoat in the closet by the front door." He stroked the garment, looking somewhat impressed. "What a fine coat," he observed. "Undoubtedly, pure cashmere."

"Yes," replied the young clergyman. "It was a gift from my mother."

Happily, Kathy approached Cody and gave him an enthusiastic hug. A ripple of sexual tension ran through him as she pushed her ample, firm breasts against his chest. Her embrace lasted a bit long and almost exceeded the bounds of propriety. Could there be some truth to Rennie Bower's observation of a physical attraction? Cody put it out of his mind as they ascended the stairs.

Kathy declared, "I can't thank you enough for listening to my problems this afternoon and promising to help me. Now that I've shared my dilemma with you, I feel a great burden lifted from my shoulders."

Cody responded, "It is my pleasure and also my duty to help you. I hope tonight will offer some opportunity for me to bring up the subject of your quandary."

As they arrived at Malia's room, which was located at the back of the west wing, Kathy paused outside the door. She said, "Dr. Dettwiller thought it best to meet you out here in the corridor before you go in to see Malia. Is that okay with you?"

"Of course, I'll just wait on this bench."

Cody hardly had time to sit before a distinguished gentleman emerged from Malia's room and gave him a genuinely grateful handshake. "Thanks so much for coming to see us, Reverend Palmeroy, especially in this dreadful weather."

He was followed by Kathy, walking arm in arm with an attractive lady, whose eyes were wet with recent tears. In spite of this, the doctor's wife managed to give Cody a weak smile. She said, "We're so appreciative that you would come to help us tonight. This last year with Malia has been such a difficult, heart-breaking time that we're inclined to look for hope anywhere. When Malia responded to seeing you on television, we were shocked."

She looked tenderly at Dr. Dettwiller. "Of course, my husband, being a man of science, is naturally skeptical. He thinks that it was nothing but a coincidence. But I persuaded him that we have to consider every possibility."

"Has Malia demonstrated any more movement or activity since the television news program?" Cody asked.

"No, nothing," Dr. Dettwiller replied. "She resumed her usual comatose state."

"Is there any possibility she might have seen me before or attended worship services at Mt. Sinai?" Cody continued.

Apologetically, Mrs. Dettwiller said, "It's highly unlikely, Reverend. We're not church people. We all sleep late on Sunday mornings, and then have, or I should say we had before the accident, brunch together."

"Okay, one last question. Do you believe in any kind of paranormal phenomenon and if so, could such forces be manifest in this situation?"

"Not a chance," the doctor answered defensively. "And if you're going to try to introduce such nonsense into these profoundly tragic circumstances, I'm afraid we made a mistake asking you to visit our daughter."

"Take no offense, doctor," Cody responded. "It was just a question. But, if at any time you feel uncomfortable with my presence, I'll gladly leave. To tell you the truth, I'd really rather not be here myself. I drove to your house in a snowstorm so that I could honor your request."

Under the withering scowl of his wife, Dr. Dettwiller quickly regained his composure. "Forgive me, Reverend. My nerves are quite frazzled over all of this. I hope you understand."

"Of course, sir," Cody answered diplomatically. "I can't even begin to imagine the emotional trauma you must be suffering. "

He spread his arms to include the group. "I have no more questions, so let's go in to see Malia, shall we?"

Mrs. Dettwiller led the way as they filed into the dimly lit room.

Cody thought that despite all the medical equipment and paraphernalia, the Dettwillers had done a remarkable job keeping the oversized room just like a sixteen-year-old girl's retreat. They'd pulled the bed into the center of the space so that the medical supplies and monitors were stored behind the headboard, out of Malia's field of view. In front of her, class pictures shared the wall with a plasma TV. A dresser stood nearby with fashionable jewelry along with a picture of Malia in a ball gown standing beside a handsome young man in a tuxedo. Framed posters of rock bands and movie stars dominated the wall by the windows.

The Dettwillers stood hand in hand at the foot of the bed, while Kathy went over to the monitors to check some of the readings. She shook her head at the doctor, indicating that nothing had changed.

In what Cody felt was slow motion, he approached the patient. Briefly, he glanced at her almost lifeless face, then reached down and took one of her folded hands into his own. When he looked back at her face, an icy chill ran through his body.

He recognized her. He had held her hand before in the embalming room of the funeral home. The face he gazed on now was the exact visage of Priscilla, the drowned teenager whose death had so deeply moved him eight years before. Involuntarily, a gasp escaped his open mouth.

Urgently, the doctor asked, "What is it, Reverend?"

Cody's mind reeled. He felt unsteady, lightheaded. Finally, he was able to stammer, "I've held her hand before. Her name was Priscilla then. Eight years ago. She was naked underneath a sheet. And she was dead."

The girl's mother whimpered. "Priscilla is Malia's middle name. It's after my sister, who tragically died in her teens."

Dr. Dettwillers growing agitation overflowed. He glowered at Cody. "It looks as if the Reverend has been doing research into our family obituaries."

"I can assure you, sir, that nothing could interest me less than reading about your deceased relatives," Cody snapped.

"Daddy, it's true. He did hold my hand until the sun came up that morning."

Every head in the room turned to the front of the bed where Malia, propped up on her elbows, smiled radiantly.

The girl continued, "And we sat in a big swing on his grandmother's porch by the river. We laughed and talked the entire night. It was marvelous, fantastic."

Her parents rushed to hug and kiss her in a joyful reunion.

She asked about matters typically discussed at a family gathering. "How are Uncle Robert and Aunt Lois? Has Daddy been busy at the hospital? Does Jimmy call to check on me?"

Occasionally, she stole a quick look at Cody, who was now standing at the foot of the bed. He didn't like the message her poignant glances conveyed. He was certain that something worried her deeply, something that concerned the two of them.

After about thirty minutes, she said, "I must go now. I'm very tired, and I hear the angels coming. But I'll return tomorrow." Her smiling face transformed into a deep frown of concern. She reached for Cody's hand, and when he took it, she said to him, "Tomorrow will be a horrible day, but there is hope. In the end, you must come to me so that I may guide you. Without my help, you might lose your way. You must find me before it's finished."

Flustered, Cody asked, "Guide me? Where are we going?"

Malia looked surprised by the question. "To the tree by the river, of course."

Cody said, "Okay, until tomorrow." He squeezed her hand and stepped away from the bed to allow her parents to embrace her again.

After a moment, Malia laid her head on the pillow, closed her eyes, and returned to a comatose state.

To no avail, her mother called after her, "Malia, come back. We want to talk to you some more and show you how much we love you."

Malia lay there in sublime repose.

Mrs. Dettwiller began to cry. Her husband came from the other side of the bed and put a reassuring arm around her. "Don't cry, my dear. She'll talk to us again tomorrow." Looking hopefully at Cody, he said, "You will come back tomorrow, won't you, Reverend Palmeroy?"

"Yes, of course, that is, if I'm able. Remember Malia saying that tomorrow will be a horrible day for me?"

"I am somewhat of an authority on comas and I can tell you that anyone who comes out of that state, for even a brief episode, will likely be very confused, likely talk nonsense for a while," the doctor said kindly. "So, I wouldn't be too concerned about that remark."

Cody knew the doctor was right, but the comment still haunted him.

He looked over at Kathy. She was staring rigidly at the corner of the room. Cody followed the direction of her gaze and saw two shadowy figures whispering to each other. As he continued to observe, the image of the angels brightened to the most intense white color he had ever seen. Their robes shined with brilliance. Beatific smiles adorned their faces. One angel carried a sword and the other a bouquet of rainbows, flowers from heaven to comfort sweet Malia.

As Cody and Kathy stared at the marvel in the corner, Mrs. Dettwiller asked, "Why are the two of you looking so intently over there. Do you see something?"

"Angels," stated Cody. "I see angels. Kathy sees them, too."

"No such thing as angels exist," the doctor scoffed. "They belong to the long-dead mythology of the Bible."

Mrs. Dettwiller said, "I don't see any angels either."

"It's because you've closed your minds to the possibility that they could exist," said Cody. "The Bible says, 'Eyes have they, but they cannot see. Ears have they, but they cannot hear.' Therefore, it's really a matter of faith. If Pontius Pilate had been present at the resurrection of Christ, he wouldn't have seen it."

He stared at the heavenly creatures as they conversed. Apparently, they decided to return later because the brilliance of their images faded and gradually disappeared.

"They're gone now," Cody told them.

Mrs. Dettwiller said, "But I want to see them."

"I'm sure they'll be back," Kathy bravely declared. "Perhaps later on I can show you what to look for, ma'am."

Cody said, "I feel my work here is finished for now. I'll see you all tomorrow night."

After the Dettwillers expressed their deep gratitude for his visit, Kathy escorted Cody to the front door and helped him put on his overcoat. She gave him a hug and said, "Thank you for introducing the subject of angels to the parents. When I get back to Malia's room, Mrs. Dettwiller especially will have a thousand questions, but I'll feel comfortable now discussing it with her."

She looked closely at him. "You're sweating," she said. "Do you feel ill?"

As Cody brushed past her for the door he said, "I'm having one of my panic attacks, and this is a bad one."

Kathy was concerned. "What triggered it?"

"Malia's comment to me about tomorrow."

"But you heard the doctor say confusion is common in coma patients."

"Nevertheless, she said it," he stated emphatically. "And now I must go. Goodnight."

Back in his car, Cody sweated even more profusely. His hands shook as he fished out of his pocket a small plastic container that held his emergency medicines, some for panic attacks, and others for migraine.

He popped a Xanax tablet, started his car, and trembling with dread of Malia's ominous prophesy, headed out into the snowy night.

# Chapter 15

*Blood Red, Snow White*

Cody sat behind the antique desk at his church office, staring at the clock, mentally urging the second hand to move more quickly. Seemingly, the more he willed it forward, the more slowly it went. Already, the day felt like an eternity though the clock showed only one-twenty-one.

Last night had been a total, sleepless nightmare. By the time he'd arrived home from his visit to the Dettwillers, the tranquilizer had calmed him somewhat, but Malia's comments about a horrible day haunted him relentlessly.

Gail patiently, supportively, listened to her husband's ravings, and when she had an opportunity, broke into his monologue of doom. "I've seen several of these recovering comatose patients, and they're likely to blurt out things that have no basis in reality. And Malia's case is severe. It's as though she's been under anesthesia for almost a year. She's out of her mind."

But Cody refused to be consoled. "Everything Malia said up until that time was rational," he insisted.

"Like hearing angels coming is rational?" Gail retorted.

"I saw angels. Kathy saw them, too."

Gail bristled. "Kathy is a promiscuous bitch who's looking for her next score and has you in her sights."

"You've never even met her."

"With her reputation, I don't have to. Everybody at my hospital says the administration fired her because she had affairs with two doctors and then bragged about it to the staff. The same thing happened at several other places. That's why she ended up at that dump, the county hospital. It's the only facility left that would take her."

Cody wouldn't listen to rational persuasion and refused to be comforted, so at one-thirty Gail gave up on him and headed for bed. "Cody, I wish I could find a way to help you with this, but if you continue to be so stubbornly disconsolate, I'm going to sleep and suggest you try the same."

Astonished, Cody retorted, "Sleep? How can you even think of it under the circumstances? This could be the worst day of our lives."

After some serious coaxing, Gail was able to get him into bed. Despite taking a sleeping pill, within thirty minutes, he was back up and pacing the living room floor like a caged animal.

When Gail came out to check on him at five o'clock, he was still awake, although not walking aimlessly around. He was sitting wide eyed on the sofa.

"Did you ever get to sleep?" she asked.

"No, but I feel okay, thanks. How about you?"

She sat on the couch next to Cody and put a comforting arm around him. "It wasn't the best night's sleep I ever had but I'm off again today so it really doesn't matter about me. I can take a nap later. What about you? Why can't you just take the day off, too?"

Cody stood up and began to pace the room again. "I'll take the morning off, but I have a few counseling appointments this afternoon that I should keep."

"Reschedule them," Gail pleaded. "No one could possibly want to come out in this weather."

Cody walked over to the window. "Looks as though the snow stopped falling but there's a good eight inches on the ground."

He went to the kitchen table to consult his pocket calendar. Walking back into the living room, he said, "I have a noon appointment with Mrs. Kilibrew. I don't see any way out of that because she lives just a block from the church. She usually asks for money and she has a genuine need. I can't let her down, so I'll have to go in for that one, but the next two appointments I can definitely reschedule."

"Good," Gail said cheerfully. "We can spend the afternoon together and snuggle in. I see a nap, popcorn, a movie, and maybe even some wild sex in our future. See? Little Miss Malia isn't the only prophetess in your life." She laughed.

Cody's mood brightened. He said, "I know I'm over-thinking this whole matter, and a lot of things just don't add up. For example, Malia was eight years old when Priscilla died. It would make a lot more sense if Malia were eight right now. Then, at least we could make an argument that upon Priscilla's death, she was reborn as Malia. The only way the years fit correctly is that when Priscilla died, her spirit inhabited Malia's eight-year-old body. I don't believe that kind of crap. I don't even believe in reincarnation.

"Definitely, the time sequence erodes the credibility of this whole situation, but on the other side of the ledger is the content of Malia's remarks. How could she know that eight years ago I held a dead girl's hand? The part of this that creeps me out the most is her knowing the fantasy I had that night about sitting with Priscilla on my grandmother's porch. I didn't even speak those words. How could Malia possibly know what I was thinking or that the whole thing even happened?"

Gail came over to give him a long, warm hug. "Now, don't get yourself agitated again. I'm sure the answer to all these questions will be revealed in future meetings with Malia."

Cody rambled on. "And then there's the matter of Malia's middle name being Priscilla. All of this is weirdly coincidental. In fact, it's beyond the realm of coincidence, and that's why I can't get it out of my mind."

"Surely there's an explanation for this, a common denominator that will explain it all," Gail reassured him.

Cody walked to the window and looked at the heavens. The sky had cleared and the stars shone brilliantly. "Yes, I agree. There must be an answer to it all."

"Yes, but where?" Gail asked.

He pointed to the sky, "Out there somewhere, beyond the farthest star."

Although Gail prepared a hearty breakfast for him, after a few bites, Cody just pushed the food around on his plate.

Sympathetically, she said, "Don't force yourself to eat more than you want. You'll just make yourself sick." She took his plate to the sink and brought back more coffee.

Cody took his cup and stood at his favorite window. The sun was rising and with it, optimism seeped into his weary, dejected mind. The sunlight glistened off the newly fallen snow. "Perhaps I've taken all this too seriously. I really don't know if Malia was in her right mind. What could possibly go wrong to make this beautiful day so horrible?"

He sensed Gail approaching behind him. She put her arms around his waist. "Why don't you go on in for your first appointment and reschedule the others. Then, come home for a nice relaxing afternoon like the one we discussed. You could take my Jeep again. The Jeep is fun to drive in the snow. Meanwhile, you should try to take a nap. It's still early, and you won't have to leave for the church for several hours."

Cody stretched out on the bed and closed his eyes, attempting to do breathing exercises to calm himself. After a few minutes, he drifted off into a fitful sleep. He awoke peacefully, but after a moment, a tsunami of existential dread swept over him as he recalled the events of the previous night. Another panic attack hit him like a boulder falling from the sky. His heart became a pounding sledgehammer in his chest. His breathing was swift and shallow and driblets of sweat began to fall onto the sheets. His unbridled mind raced with fear as he dwelt on Malia's dark prophesy.

He called out to Gail, who gave him a tranquilizer and held him in her arms until the drug took effect, and his fear subsided. She then gently coaxed him into the bathroom for a long, hot shower.

After thanking his wife profusely for her support, he dressed and drove to work. He promised to return shortly after his twelve o'clock appointment.

Mrs. Kilibrew showed up at noon, and as Cody had predicted, she needed money.

She shoved a redlined letter across her pastor's desk. "They're gonna shut off my lights and heat if I don't pay up by five o'clock this afternoon. They surely is."

Cody reached in his desk for a pad of vouchers for the electric company. He filled in the required amount, signed and stamped it, and then handed the paper across to the grateful woman.

Mrs. Kilibrew thanked him and stood to leave. She hesitated a moment. "Reverend, excuse me for saying so, but you don't look so good. Are you feeling poorly?"

"Thank you for asking, ma'am, but I didn't sleep well last night. I'll be fine."

"Well, you look after yourself now. I don't want nothing happening to my favorite pastor," Mrs. Kilibrew said.

Cody watched on the CCTV system as the woman exited the building and then began the wait for his one o'clock appointment to show up. He had successfully rescheduled his two o'clock counseling session but couldn't contact Mrs. Jeter who was set to come in at one.

Like many of the neighborhood folk, she periodically let her telephone minutes expire, so he probably had no way to contact her via phone until her next paycheck. He knew where she lived and could go by the house, but had learned early in his ministry that church members didn't always appreciate unannounced visits to their homes. Therefore, he decided to wait until one-thirty and then leave if she hadn't shown up.

He checked the clock again on his desk. One-twenty-five. Time to start packing up to leave for the comfort and safety of home.

His cell phone rang, and he smiled when the caller ID revealed Gail was trying to reach him, probably to remind him it was time to leave the church.

Cheerfully he answered the call. "Hello, sweetheart. I'm on my way."

"Cody, a man with a crowbar is breaking in the front door," Gail cried out in desperation.

Terror hit Cody in his gut like a wrecking ball. "Where's Uther?"

Gail began to sob so deeply he could barely understand what she was saying. "I let him out a few minutes ago to use the bathroom. I locked the door, came back to the bedroom, and heard two loud bangs. I ran to the front door and looked through the peephole. That's when I saw this terrible man with the crowbar. Cody I'm so scared. He had such hatred in his eyes. I ran back to the bedroom and locked the door but I can hear him trying to get in. I called nine-one-one but the line is busy."

Cody asked, "Where's your gun."

"Oh my God! It's under the cushions of the living room sofa."

"Go get it fast!"

"Too late. I just heard a loud crash. It must be the door. He's in the living room now!"

Cody had dashed out the back door of the church and was already in the car. "Listen, baby. I have to put you on hold for a minute to call the police. See if you can slide the dresser in front of the door."

He roared out of the church parking lot and onto the main thoroughfare.

Gail said, "Cody, I love you."

Cody replied, "I love you, too, Gail. In just a few minutes, I'll be there with the police."

Reluctantly, he put her on hold and scanned his directory for Sergeant Nelson's cell phone. Thankfully, the sergeant answered on the first ring.

"Nelson this is Cody. Someone has broken into the house. Gail is home alone."

"I'm on my way," Nelson, shouted. "I'll call in extra units."

Cody hung up and switched back to Gail's line. He heard nothing but silence, followed by a dial tone.

Cody's heart sank, yet he drove on with a firm resolve. He expected another panic attack to strike at any moment, but it never came. Instead, what must have been some basic, primordial survival instinct took over his mind. He knew that if he was to help Gail, he must remain calm and cunning.

With a sudden jolt, he remembered that his car was at the house. Anyone who drove by would assume he was home alone, and that Gail was at work.

He dwelled on how quickly the line had gone dead after he put her on hold. Calling Sergeant Nelson, along with finding the officer's number on his directory, had taken little more than ten seconds. How could the perpetrator break in the room, locate Gail's phone, and turn it off in that short time?

Then, he thought maybe she'd turned it off. She didn't want the intruder to hear him on the phone and learn he was on the way home. Perhaps Gail had powered down the phone to protect him.

He drove recklessly through the icy streets, not bothering to stop at red lights. Because of the snow, few cars were on the road.

Cody's phone rang, and he quickly answered without checking the caller ID. "Gail, is it you?"

Nelson's voice shot back out of his cell phone speaker. "Cody, where are you?"

"I'm almost ready to turn off onto my street, so I'd say I'm a minute away."

"I'm right behind you with four other units. Don't go in until we get there. It's too dangerous."

"Okay, I'll wait."

"We'll be coming in without sirens. Wait for us in your car. God, what a perfect day for a crime. Almost all my officers are working traffic accidents. Still, we have plenty of backup. I broadcast the code for Officer in Trouble."

"Thanks. See you in a minute."

Despite slowing down as he approached his home, Cody slid past his driveway. As he backed up, he saw something that broke his heart. Uther was desperately crawling up the stairs on the side of the building to their garret hideaway. He was down but still moving.

Cody left his car on the street and instinctively ran to the aid of his dog.

Someone had shot Uther twice in the back. He appeared to have no movement in his hindquarters. The devoted canine was pulling himself up the stairway using his front legs only.

Quickly, Cody tried to comfort him and ran the remainder of stairs two at a time. He rushed past the open front door and back to the bedroom calling out for Gail. His soul darkened with despair when he saw that the invader had smashed both the bedroom and bathroom doors.

He found Gail's precious, lifeless body lying by the shower where she must have made a last gasp attempt at defending her life. She lay on her back with lifeless eyes staring vacantly at the ceiling. Desperately, Cody checked for a carotid pulse. He found none, nor any sign of respiration either. Several bullet holes marred her beautiful body. Frantically, he began CPR.

Then from directly behind him a malevolent voice boomed and echoed off the walls of the tiny bathroom. "Hello, Reverend," the man said callously.

Cody snapped his head around to see a vaguely familiar man with what looked like a 9mm gun aimed at his head.

"I'm Elijah Coffin's brother from Chicago. The police don't know me down here. I came to set the ledger straight. You're responsible for the death of Elijah. Now, I'm going to take your life. That's what the Bible says, don't it? 'An eye for an eye and a tooth for a tooth.'"

"But why did you shoot my wife?" Cody said, trying to control his rage. "She's no part of this."

The villain grinned wickedly, "She was an unexpected bonus. We thought you were home alone. It was so pathetic the way she died. She pleaded for her life, and then begged us not to hurt you, to take her life instead of yours. She told us she was pregnant with your child. She got down on her knees and begged for the baby's life. That's why I shot her in the belly first, so she'd know that her unborn child wasn't going to live, either."

They heard heavy, urgent footsteps in the hall. For a brief moment, the gunman turned his weapon onto the bathroom entrance. Cody was still kneeling in front of Gail, and he used the diversion of the footsteps to slip something from his jacket pocket into his hand. He slowly rose to face Gail's murderer.

Suddenly, a huge man who also bore a family resemblance to Elijah Coffin filled the doorway to the bathroom. Frantically, he yelled, "At least five blue lights just turned off the main road. Hurry!"

Coffin's brother shouted, "Get the car going and wait for me in the alley!"

The man turned back to Cody. His eyes looked down the barrel of Cody's small caliber Beretta.

"A minister with a gun? You got to be shittin' me."

Without hesitation, Cody quickly fired five rounds into the man's startled face. As the man fell to the bathroom tile, his gun fired off a random shot on impact. Cody felt excruciating pain in his side. A 9mm bullet had hit him. He slumped down at Gail's feet, his back against the wall.

Cody reached over to clasp Gail's hand. It was already cold. Tears began to fall down his face.

From outside, came the unmistakable sound of gunfire exchange, followed by the rumble of several people running up the apartment stairs.

After a moment, Sergeant Nelson burst into the bathroom, service revolver drawn. Excitedly, he asked. "Just two of them? Did you see any others?"

Cody weakly responded, "I saw only two."

Nelson holstered the gun. Other officers and paramedics crowded the bedroom. He pointed to Elijah Coffin's brother, who lay dead across the bathroom threshold, and said, "A couple of you get this piece of shit out of the way."

The officers moved quickly and soon paramedics were at Cody's side. Another one examined Gail. With a shattered heart, Cody heard the man say, "There's no point working on this one. She has bullet wounds to the abdomen, pubic area, left and right chest and two to the head." The EMT looked at Cody and said, "I'm so sorry, sir. There's no hope for her." Respectfully, he closed Gail's eyes and then covered her with a sheet.

Meanwhile, Nelson examined the murder weapon. "He used hollow-point bullets. She never had a chance."

Hopefully, Cody asked, "And Uther?"

Nelson said, "Sorry, but he used every bit of life left in him trying to get up here to help you. He almost made it, too. We found him on the last landing right outside your door."

Two more paramedics came in to remove Gail's remains. Gently they placed her on a stretcher and began to roll her out. As they passed Cody, he held up his hand indicating he wanted a final moment. They stopped and pulled back the sheet to expose her bullet-marred face.

Despite the oozing wounds, he gently kissed her face and forehead. Finally, he said, "You gave me an incredible life, and I owe you my eternal gratitude. But this is not the final chapter. We will be together again, somewhere beyond the farthest star."

After they wheeled Gail away from the bathroom, the other paramedics had room to stretch Cody out on the floor for a more thorough examination.

Nelson eyed the young minister with admiration. "I'd have given anything to have seen the look on the bastard's face when a clergyman pulled a gun out of his suit. You should have waited for backup, but considering the circumstances, what you did was understandable. If we had been a few minutes earlier, maybe the outcome could have been different. I doubt it though. My guess is that the perpetrator killed her as soon as he had the chance."

In response, Cody let out a protracted groan. "No, he toyed with her. Made her beg for her life."

The chief paramedic delivered his report. "The reverend is fortunate so far. It looks as though the bullet missed any immediately life-threatening areas. However, I'm concerned that his blood pressure is falling. As the bullet exited his body, it may have nicked his posterior vena cava. That's the main vein that returns blood to the heart from the lower body. If that's the case, he could be bleeding internally. We have the blood flow at the entry and exit sites slowed down for now. In any case, he needs to get to the hospital quickly. We'll bring in another stretcher and get him in the ambulance right away."

Cody's mind was racing. He had to get to Malia before he died. She'd said that he must find her before it was finished so that she could guide him; otherwise, he would lose his way. And he knew somehow that he was going to die.

He remembered that the ambulance route to the hospital would likely take them right by the Dettwiller mansion. He had a plan.

Minutes later, he was in the ambulance. A paramedic and Sergeant Nelson rode with him in the back. As the driver pulled out cautiously onto the icy streets, a patrol car from the Southeast Precinct took up a position in front of them while another one brought up the rear.

Cody noticed the car behind the ambulance. He asked Nelson, "Why the escort?"

The sergeant said, "We're not taking any chances on your safe arrival at the hospital. Remember, two thugs already tried to kill you today. We'll stay with you while you're in the hospital and probably long after that. So, get used to us, my friend."

A few minutes later, Cody said to the paramedic, "We'll soon pass Dr. Dettwiller's house. I'm sure his surgeries and office visits were cancelled today because of the snow. Please call his house and see if he'll ride with us to the hospital. His home number is on the cell phone in my jacket."

The paramedic and Nelson exchanged glances. The sergeant said, "You and the doctor must be very good friends."

The paramedic said, "I doubt Dr. Dettwiller would do what you suggest. He's the chief of neurosurgery. I don't think he rides in the back of ambulances."

Impatiently, compellingly, Cody said with authority, "Just make the call."

The man dialed the doctor's number and while it rang, he put the phone on speaker mode.

Dr. Dettwiller answered on the third ring. He began, "Reverend Palmeroy, good to hear from you."

The paramedic said, "Sir, this is actually Andy Kline, EMT. We have the reverend on board our ambulance now and we'll be passing your residence in a few minutes. He has a hollow-point gunshot wound in his left side. This is awkward for me to even suggest, sir, but Reverend Palmeroy asked if you would ride with us to the hospital."

Quickly, the doctor replied, "Of course I will. I'll start gathering my things right now and meet you out front."

The EMT put the phone back in Cody's jacket. He said, "Wow. What a surprise. I was expecting to get cussed out."

Cody looked vacantly at the ceiling of the ambulance. His vision was fuzzy. He felt the warm flow of blood spill into his body cavity. He was on the edge of losing consciousness.

With a jolt of intense energy, Malia's voice crashed into his mind. "I know you're near. Remember, you must get to me before you die. We must do this together if I'm to guide you. Don't grieve for Gail or your unborn child because Infinite Mother has already blessed them with new life. I'll meet you on the staircase."

Malia's telepathic message overwhelmed Cody. How could she possibly know that Gail had died?

He felt the ambulance slow down and crawl to a stop. Cody recognized the driveway in front of the Dettwiller's residence. The EMT and Nelson piled out the back double doors of the vehicle. Dr. and Mrs. Dettwiller stood on the steps close by. As the doctor walked to the rear of the ambulance, Cody activated his plan.

He knew the EMT would take a few seconds to explain his patient's condition out of Cody's earshot. He had to act quickly.

He tore the IV out of his arm and cracked the side door of the ambulance. He knew when he took off the heart monitor leads, an alarm would sound, so he waited to do that chore last. He took off the blood pressure cuff and oxygen saturation monitor on his fingertip.

Immediately, a beeping alarm sounded. He didn't know that the oxygen monitor also had an alarm. Too late now. He saw the EMT walking toward the back doors. Just a few more steps and Cody's plan would fail. He ripped the heart monitor leads away and jumped out the side door.

He felt fainter than he anticipated but managed to make it to the walkway. The site of the bullet entry and his back burned hot as a blacksmith's flue. Blood dripped from his side.

He took large, limping strides toward the house. Behind him, he could hear the footsteps and shouts of his pursuing caretakers get closer with every labored, painful step he took.

He wouldn't make it. Even if the front door was unlocked, he couldn't meet Malia on the stairs for their critical rendezvous.

Then in a flash of awareness, he remembered feeling something quite heavy in the right front pocket of his trousers when he jumped from the ambulance. Now, he recalled that after he shot Gail's murderer in the face he had put the gun in his pants.

When he got to the front door, he spun around and pointed the Beretta at his pursuers even as he lowered his head between his knees to get a little more blood to his brain and prevent fainting. Nelson, Dr. Dettwiller, and the EMT stopped cold in their pursuit. Only ten feet separated them from their gun-wielding patient.

Nelson said, "What the hell are you doing, Cody? You're losing your mind. Put the gun down."

Cody didn't have the strength to answer his friend. Every breath pained him more than the one before. Somewhat surprised, he saw the trail of blood he left along the walkway. The crimson liquid produced an eerily sharp contrast with the newly fallen snow.

In a stooped posture, he reached behind him and opened the front door.

In his best doctor's authoritative voice, Dr. Dettwiller said, "Cody you're delirious. You don't know what you're doing. Put down the gun and let us help you before it's too late."

Cody said, "It's already too late. I'm dying and I know it, but I have to do one more thing."

He took a few steps backward into the house. The others matched his retreat stride for stride but didn't try to close the gap between them.

Cody turned his head and yelled up the staircase, "Malia, I'm here but come quickly. I'm faint."

He turned back toward the group. "Thank you all for trying to help me. And, Nelson, you've been a great friend to me and Gail."

From the top of the steps, a frantic shout from Malia. "I'm coming down. Meet me on the landing."

In total shock, the doctor yelled, "Malia get back in bed. No, no just sit where you are, and I'll carry you back to your room."

Malia took her first steps down the staircase.

Dr. Dettwiller urgently called up to his daughter. "You don't understand, baby. After lying in bed for a year, you'll be dizzy and weak. Your muscles won't be coordinated. Your heart might even fail."

Malia continued her descent, clinging desperately to the banister.

Still pointing the gun, Cody said in painful gasps to the group in front of him. "You think I'm delirious, but I'm not. I ask just one last favor of you. I'm going up the stars. Don't try to follow me."

Dr. Dettwiller shouted, "Okay. Do what you have to do but hurry up. I must get to my daughter."

Cody nodded to the doctor and said, "Go on up."

As Dettwiller ran past him, Cody backed up the few steps to the base of the stairs and then slid his weapon across the marble floor to Sergeant Nelson.

As he started up the staircase, he saw the doctor a few steps ahead of him.

Then, Malia screamed as she tumbled down the stairs.

Cody felt weaker with each step. Nelson and the EMT were gaining on him.

Malia had fallen to the landing and as her father turned her over to administer CPR, one of her hands flung out over the steps where it was visible from below.

If Cody could just stretch himself out enough to touch that hand, he might accomplish what she had wanted.

After a few more steps, he lunged for the hand, but fell at least a foot short. He felt a firm hand clasp his ankle. He turned to see the EMT.

He had failed. Just by a foot or so, but he couldn't reach Malia.

He looked into Nelson's eyes, pleading for empathy. He said to his friend, "Please, help me."

The sergeant hesitated for a moment and then said to the EMT, "Let him go."

The young man didn't relinquish his grip on Cody's ankle. He looked skeptically at Nelson, who repeated his order, this time more firmly. "I said let him go, dammit."

The EMT let go.

Cody felt his chest explode, and his vision dimmed even more. He was dizzy and feeble. For an instant, he forgot what he was supposed to do.

In a final second of clarity, he remembered everything. With all his soul, he took one more step and lunged again for the outstretched hand.

He grasped it and held on tightly.

Before losing consciousness and life itself, he realized this was no ordinary hand he clutched. He held a dead hand.

# Chapter 16

*Beyond the Farthest Star, Something Is Calling*

"Such a thing has happened my friends that, if I tell it, you will
hear a marvel of which no one could have dreamed."
Sophocles, Trachinian Women

"There is a void, outside of existence, which if entered into,
englobes itself and becomes a womb."
William Blake, Jerusalem

"The universe is not only stranger than we imagine; it is stranger
than we can imagine."
Sir Arthur Eddington

After only a few seconds of black void and utter silence, Cody
began to see a scene take shape. The dim depiction developing
beneath him gradually became more focused and bright, as though
auditorium stage lights were slowly rising on the opening scene of a
play.

Cody sensed he had left his dead body and was floating about
twenty feet above it, observing the futile attempts to revive him.
These circumstances didn't surprise him because the scenario was
similar to many accounts given by people who reported details of
near death experiences.

The paramedics pulled him up to the flat landing area of the giant staircase and aggressively administered CPR. Sergeant Nelson sat on the steps nearby with his head in his hands. Several officers from the Southeast Precinct stood quietly in the large foyer downstairs.

Malia's body lay a few feet from Cody's, close to where her fatal fall down the staircase had ended. Dr. Dettwiller and his daughter's day nurse were well underway with resuscitation procedures. Overwhelming despair projected a gray aura around the doctor's face.

Cody sensed the doctor already knew the battle was lost, but he had to try to revive his beloved daughter. Mrs. Dettwiller sat on the stairs going up from the landing to the second floor, sobbing profusely into a white, embroidered handkerchief.

Suddenly, Cody sensed he wasn't alone. Malia floated just a few feet away. She held firmly onto his hand. Her spiritual body appeared much the same as her dead replica on the carpet below, except it was translucent, and the outline of her form glowed blue with shimmering energy. He assumed that he appeared the same to her.

After another moment of witnessing the painful, futile scene unfolding beneath them, she said, "I want to leave now. I can't bear to see these good people so frustrated and sad." Her lips didn't move but the telepathic communication was extremely clear as though she were speaking directly and loudly into his ear.

"I agree," Cody thought and knew that Malia could 'hear' him by understanding his mind.

He asked, "Exactly what should I call you, Malia or Priscilla?"

Surprisingly, she said, "Neither. My name is Eve."

"In the Abrahamic religions that name can mean 'mother of life.'" Cody observed.

"I changed my name when I became a servant of Eve Prime, the creator and sustainer of the multiverse. Sometimes people call her Infinite Mother. All the members of the Sisterhood call themselves Eve. This group of devotees dedicate themselves to service to the Mother."

"Why did you come for me?"

Eve looked anxiously above them. The entrance to a gray, swirling passageway slowly opened. "I'm sorry but time won't allow me to answer your question at the moment. Once the aperture to the tunnel opens, it's best we be on our way. Sometimes it closes unexpectedly, and we could be trapped here as spirits."

With a final glance at the frenetic, depressing scene below, Eve and Cody let themselves respond to the gentle tug of the tunnel until they crossed the threshold and it closed behind them.

Inside the dark passageway, the walls swirled, and a light appeared at the end in such dramatic contrast that it resembled a single star in a black night sky.

Suddenly, the dark walls of the tunnel sprang to life with thousands of vignettes from Cody's life. As he looked toward the end of the round passageway, he saw that these scenes spread out over the entire three-hundred-sixty degrees of its surface and seemed to extend to the very end of the structure.

While they sped along, Cody would slow down occasionally to relive a particularly poignant scene from his life: the joy of a magical Christmas morning, the adoring look on his mother's face as she brought a birthday cake with fourteen candles out of the kitchen and set it before him, the immense satisfaction of helping a stranded family on the interstate.

Frequently, they passed other tunnels that branched off at a right angle. He asked Eve, who still clung tightly to his hand, about these mysterious passageways.

"Those lead to alternative universes depicting your life had you made various other choices, or events had just randomly occurred differently. Here, let me show you something important." They sped up until they reached another artery that moved away from the main tunnel. At the junction, she pointed to a scene from the funeral home where Germ had just informed Cody of the death of the second John Goodman. Cody had dropped a carafe of hot coffee onto the lounge floor. Something had blurred the section next to it and severely distorted the first video down the alternative tunnel.

"Now, this represents a very rare occurrence in the cosmos," Eve explained. "The pictures are out of focus because, just for an instant, you were living in two universes simultaneously."

"But isn't that what happens in alternative universes?" Cody asked "A different version of you follows the path of another life."

"Correct, but under normal circumstances a duplicate self is created to live the alternative life. However, in your case, even if it was just for a second, you were one self who was living in two universes, one in which the younger John Goodman died and another in which he lived. You simultaneously had consciousness of being in these two worlds and your mind couldn't process it. Because of the extreme confusion, you dropped the coffee.

"This is contrary to the laws of the cosmos. Only Infinite Mother can do it. In fact, She lives in all of the universes simultaneously. All of us who are Her servants have been blessed with the ability to live in different universes at will. We choose where we want to be, but we can only be aware of a single place at any one point in time. In that one instance, you were an exception to a universal principle. That's why in the multiverse heaven, they call you magic man.

"Because of your circumstances, I've come to take you before Eve Prime so that she can determine what went wrong. You notice I described her as the creator and sustainer of the multiverse. It is She who must continually seek out tendencies toward mutations and exceptions of natural laws. The cosmos needs constant attention. Where the universes might devolve, she must restore order. I think in your world that you call the tendency toward disorder entropy, according to the Second Law of Thermodynamics."

Confused about the timeline of past events, Cody asked, "Why did you appear to me as Priscilla before I even knew John Goodman?"

"The Infinite Mother foresaw it all. Therefore, she sent me to make contact with you so that when today came, you'd feel comfortable enough to go with me."

She gave Cody a moment to contemplate this and then admonished him, "Don't dwell on time too much as we get into our journey. You'll just become hopelessly confused. Some events are explainable by your logic and concept of time. Nevertheless, you become bewildered because you just don't know the full picture. "For example, why was I dead Priscilla, age sixteen, and then, eight years later became Malia who was also sixteen?

"What happened here is that Malia died in the accident, and Eve Prime immediately sent my spirit to occupy her body. However, you had no way of knowing that. You only knew some of the facts.

"Other apparent problems are much more complicated, but keep in mind that the cosmos is extremely complex. Multiple universes move at different speeds and directions in relation to each other. They even exist in other dimensions. What seems to be a year on earth could be just a minute in another world. You can understand some of this by Einstein's Theory of Relativity.

"Time is something most sentient beings invent to help make sense of their worlds. It doesn't exist by itself. As Eve Prime told her acolytes once while describing eternity, 'For time itself has fled the stage and refuses to return.'

"And now we must be moving on. Infinite Mother awaits us."

Cody looked at the light at the end of the passageway. It appeared much closer now, and they seemed to be moving forward at a greater rate of speed.

Eve informed her charge, "When we pass through the threshold into the heaven of your universe, we won't stop for the Light to greet and consecrate us as others do, for we have to make our way to the portal of the multiverse."

When they emerged from the passageway, they saw below them hundreds of tunnels converging onto a plaza where a figure who emitted a bright blue-white light welcomed new arrivals with opened, outstretched arms. He appeared to be bestowing some kind of blessing on them. As they individually moved on past the Light, groups of heavenly residents, who Cody assumed were deceased friends and relatives, greeted the newcomers enthusiastically. From one group, a small dog rushed forward to meet its former master.

Cody smiled when he saw this scene and wondered if the woman from his Last Days' Diary who'd asked whether she would meet up with her precious canine friend in heaven had experienced a similar joyous reunion.

In the distance, he saw the heavenly city, which bedazzled him with its brilliant light and the overpowering energy of love emanating from within.

Suddenly, they arrived at a large grassy field on a mountaintop. Cody recognized it from a dream he'd had several years before when a massive staircase descended from the stars, and a pack of jackals pursued him from the surrounding darkness.

But today no jackals' wails menaced from the shadows. In fact, no shadows existed anywhere in heaven where a primordial light shined evenly, incessantly.

A massive door with gold hinges stood before them.

Eve explained, "This is the highest point of the heavenly dome that sits atop your universe and the door is the gateway to the multiverse.

"Before we traverse this portal, let me tell you about the wonders you're about to see. Travelers like you are sometimes immobilized by awe when they step through this gateway, so it is best to prepare.

"Your universe is shaped like a sphere and the heavenly city sits atop this in a dome. Likewise, the multiverse is a great sphere and the home of Infinite Mother sits atop it. If we look down from here, we would see billions of galaxies. Our venture to the multiverse heavenly dome is relatively the same, but instead of galaxies, we shall see trillions of other universes. Some of these contain replicas of us as we made different choices, or different events occurred that created our existence in another universe where we live out other scenarios of our lives."

Eve looked at him sympathetically. "I know it's a lot to take in but you'll better understand the experience if you have some knowledge before we go. Are you ready?"

Apprehensively, Cody said, "How could one ever be ready for what you just described?" Pointing to the portal, he asked, "This door is huge. How do we open it?"

Eve said, "Take my hand and let's be on our way."

The pair held hands and turned toward the massive door, which silently swung open for them.

"How did that happen?" Cody asked.

"All you have to do is face the door and let your mind dwell on your intention to pass through and the portal opens," Eve confessed.

They walked through the door onto a large marble platform. A sense of overwhelming awe and wonder washed over Cody like a gigantic wave. No amount of counseling on Eve's part could have ever prepared him for the marvels he beheld. As far as he could see, universes glowed in many different colors. All of them were spherical, some giant, others relatively small. Strings that reminded him of umbilical cords connected some of them to each other.

He forgot that Eve could read his thoughts, so was surprised when she offered, "You're correct. Those smaller orbs surrounding the big ones are baby universes. In time, the cords will disappear, and the baby universe will grow large and start its own family, so to speak."

They laughed at how ridiculous that sounded from the perspective of earth, where their journey began.

Eagerly, she said, "Let me show you my favorite."

Eve pointed to a large universe that looked like a round rainbow. Across its surface, all earthly colors and some new hues that Cody had never seen before glowed in ultra-vibrant intensity. Distinct lines of demarcation separated the various colors.

"It's beautiful," he concurred.

"Now, we must be on our way."

Cody could have marveled at the multiverse a thousand years, but conceded, "I know. The Infinite Mother awaits." He hadn't thought how they would traverse the immense distance to the heavenly dome atop the multiverse.

Suddenly, a majestic staircase materialized in front of them. Cody looked over at Eve, who seemed unimpressed by the marvel that just occurred. She smiled at Cody and asked, "Are you ready to climb?"

He looked skeptically at the stairs that stretched up as far as he could see and presumably far beyond that.

Eve said, "Let's stand on the bottom step together."

Tentatively, he took her hand as they stepped up.

"Now let's imagine we're at the top of the stairs standing before another large portal, a massive stone door with gold hinges just like the one we walked through," she said.

Cody did his best to imagine the scene she'd described. In an instant, they stood at the top of the giant staircase in front of the door to the multiverse dome. Dizzily, Cody gazed down to see the marble platform from which they came, but he couldn't see the bottom of the stairs.

Eve said, "Faith and imagination make this possible. In time, you'll learn this, but for now, you can achieve this only because you're with me. Do you see the importance of having someone to guide you? That's why it was essential that we die together. Without me, you surely would be lost by now."

Cody agreed. "Certainly, I would never have made it up all those stairs."

"Now, let your mind dwell on our intention to pass through this door," Eve instructed.

Almost before she finished her sentence, the door swung open, and they stood before a massive plaza. A square dais lay at its center, and there on a golden throne, sat the mysterious woman, the pregnant apparition from Cody's dreams.

On each corner of the plaza rose an immense pyramid, and on top of each of these structures, a blue flame burned high into the heavens. Multihued trees the likes he'd never seen before lined the perimeter of the space, and Cody saw angels and ordinary-looking people milling about. Some gathered in small groups and pointed at the new arrivals. As they approached the dais, Eve Prime stood to greet them with a smile of approval that made Cody feel cleansed, loved, and affirmed.

She descended the stairs and hugged Eve. "Well done, my faithful servant. Receive my blessing." The deity placed both hands onto Eve's bowed head. Cody sensed that some kind of energy transferred between them. As Eve raised her head, she manifested a glowing smile of gratitude.

Infinite Mother turned to Cody. "Thank you for coming to see us," She smiled. "My blessings are upon you also." Cody bowed his head and felt immense goodness, security, love, joy, and a river of warm, positive emotion flow into his being.

River, he thought. Where is the river?

Reading his question, Eve Prime said, "Of course, you want to see the river." She extended her right arm to the side and said, "Behold."

Cody turned in the direction the deity pointed and saw a river gradually materialize; it flowed through the plaza. At its source grew the immutable, immovable Tree of Life.

Infinite Mother said, "Come and drink of the river."

Reverently, Cody and Eve followed her to the edge of the stream.

In his mind, he heard Eve say, "Drink now."

Cody kneeled down, cupped his hands, and tasted the water. Besides its exceptional clearness, the sacred liquid tasted no different from ordinary water—but he felt a change in his being, a closure, a fulfillment, as though he had been on a long journey and had returned to his home. He felt the water was magical, and that somehow he was transformed for having tasted it.

He heard Eve Prime's voice as though at a great distance. "Arise, child of the Light, and never thirst again."

Cody and Eve followed the deity back to the dais, climbed the steps, and sat at Infinite Mother's feet as she took her throne.

"As my servant Eve explained, a man or woman resides in many universes simultaneously, but can be conscious of living in only one at a time," She declared to Cody. "This law I established for the good of humankind, for your psyche couldn't process the dual experience. It would be like seeing one universe with one eye and another universe with the other. If the situation became prevalent, humanity would quickly descend into madness.

"I see that you're a good man with the purest of motives, and living in two universes and being aware of it wasn't your will or intent. This I knew when I touched your head to give you my blessing. Thus, I attribute your dual experience to some chance anomaly. A ripple in the cosmic ether caused a small tear in the fabric of space-time at the precise moment you heard the news of John Goodman's death. I've gone back and changed the experience for you." She smiled understandingly. "I know you like to think that even the deity can't change the past, but I can and I did.

"Evil forces continually attempt to disrupt the moral and natural laws I provided for the order and well-being of the cosmos. They'd like to see the world plunge into chaos. So when anomalies such as you experienced occur, I must thoroughly investigate the cause to discover if it was rooted in wickedness. Eventually, I will rid the entire cosmos of evil, but that's a battle for another day."

She waved her arm, and suddenly holographic images representing breakdowns of natural law surrounded them. Cody felt revulsion at viewing the images as he would if presented with pictures of grotesque human mutations. Included in the depictions were clocks running backward, a place where rocks were falling up instead of down, and a scene where cause and effect were disharmonious so that an action upon an object would cause an effect on a completely different object. As Eve Prime walked past the images, she corrected each anomaly with a brief touch of her hand. Another picture appeared that was completely out of focus. It showed a natural world with overlays of different realities. When she touched the image, it quickly came into focus on just one possibility. Cody then understood that the universe consisted only of alternate potentials until God Herself perceived it and gave it a specific truth.

Suddenly, Eve Prime let out a brief cry of joy. She declared, "It's time for this new universe I've been nurturing to be born." She turned to Cody with a pleasant smile. "I'm happy for you to witness this. The birth of a new universe is really quite amazing."

Soon the dais filled with attendants from the Sisterhood to help Infinite Mother with the birth. Cody moved to the edge of the platform to stay clear of the many Eves assisting with the nativity ritual. He was thankful that his special Eve who'd escorted him from the earth stayed with him, holding his hand tightly.

Clouds of incense rose from large alabaster urns at the corners of the platform. Two angels brought up water from the river in golden vases.

The ritual itself was in a language Cody didn't understand. However, by his side, Eve kept him advised of the meaning of the ceremony. She said, "This is a prayer of thanksgiving for Eve Prime's ability to create new life. Next, the heavenly hosts shall say, 'Blessed is the womb of Infinite Mother and blessed be the womb that is the new universe.' Then, we will hear the Mother Herself consecrate the new world so that it may prosper with abundant life."

After the sacred rites, Eve Prime allowed her attendants to remove her robe. There she was, Creator of the cosmos, standing naked and uninhibited before her subjects. She had no navel. As Cody watched, astounded, her pregnant belly began to shrink until it was entirely flat. Then, from within her abdomen a single seed of bright white light emerged and hung suspended in the air.

Eve squeezed Cody's hand. She said, "That is the super atom which will explode to form the new universe."

Cody watched in utter awe as the Infinite Mother gathered the pinpoint of light tenderly in her hands and gently blew on it. The super atom flew out into the void between two already existing universes, and in a blinding flash exploded as a new and unique Big Bang.

Joy rippled through a large crowd of angels and other heavenly creatures that had formed around the base of the dais to witness and celebrate the spectacle.

Eve Prime said, "I consecrate this new world. Blessed be the life that will come from it and blessed be all of creation. Let us rejoice."

She beckoned Cody and Eve to her side while attendants poured water from the river over her and then covered her with a new robe.

"Also, I sanctify you, Cody." She stretched out her arms and placed her hands on his bowed head. "From henceforth you have the power to visit other spheres of the cosmos and to live your life in any parallel universes you choose. And I give to you my servant Eve to be your guide."

He stood straight and said, "Thank you, Infinite Mother. I'm not worthy of this."

She said, "You are worthy because I've declared you to be so."

She took Eve's hands into her own. "Come back to visit here, my child. You have been a good and faithful member of the Sisterhood." She paused a moment and added enigmatically, "Blessings upon you and your travels to the new frontier."

After their farewells, an angel escorted Eve and Cody to a threshold at the top of the multiverse's heavenly dome. Showing some discomfort, Eve said, "I've never before seen this portal. Every gateway I've traveled has led downward into the multiverse."

As she spoke, the familiar stone door with golden hinges opened, and she and Cody walked out onto a platform. As before, a majestic staircase materialized before them.

Looking confused, Eve confessed, "I don't know how to visualize our transit on these stairs because I don't know what's at the top. I don't know where we're going."

Even as she spoke, Cody felt a gentle tug and then a strong tow pulling them up the staircase. As they floated along at an ever-increasing speed, Cody looked back at a startling revelation.

The multiverse heavenly dome was now just a speck of light on top of the cosmos. Suddenly, into his field of view appeared the edge of another multiverse with its own dome at its summit. As he and Eve moved ever faster up the staircase, more multiverses came into view. At first, he saw several, then hundreds, thousands, millions, and billions, an uncountable, unimaginable number of multiverses.

As Cody continued to look behind in awe, he didn't notice the new reality they were approaching. The number of myriad multiverses continued to expand until they seemed to coalesce in an opaque kernel or shell. Beside this shell were three others like it, all resting in the palm of Eve's hand.

Suddenly, Cody became aware they were no longer moving on the stairs and that their journey had ended on a beautiful beach at sunset. He looked at Eve and then at his own hand. Their bodies were no longer translucent and shimmering with energy. They were just as normal as the bodies they'd left behind on the Dettwiller's landing, except they were alive.

Someone's voice called from a house along the shore. "Eve, it will be getting dark soon. Time to come inside."

Cody saw the woman standing in front of a house painted like a rainbow.

Eve gently put the four granules of sand she held back with the billions of others on the beach. Cody wondered if all the sand particles contained unfathomable numbers of multiverses like the one from which they had traveled.

Eve called back to the woman, "Coming, Momma." She stood and let her robe fall to the ground revealing her naive nakedness. Cody's eyes were riveted to her midsection. She had no navel.

Despite the fact she referred to the older woman as her mother, Eve was made, not begotten.

She said to him, "Stay here on the beach. A big surprise is coming for you." Then she ran inside the rainbow-colored house.

Cody waited. He looked in both directions. He saw nothing special, just a few beach houses with a sandy road extending behind them and in the far distance a woman taking her dog for a sunset walk along the shore.

Cody sat on the sand and patiently waited. He contemplated his incredible journey. He admired the setting sun and the different colored clouds above the horizon.

After a while, he noticed that the woman and her dog were continuing their walk and had come much closer. The scene saddened him profoundly as he thought of Gail, Uther, and the terrible deaths they'd suffered.

He peered again, and the dog was running down the beach, probably chasing seagulls that were perched on the shore. But he dashed past the frightened birds, who safely took flight over the water. The dog ran on, and Cody thought something about him seemed familiar. When the canine approached to within about a hundred yards, Cody jumped to his feet. "Uther!"

The German shepherd's frantic and happy yelps upon reaching his master removed all doubt concerning his identity. Enthusiastically, Uther jumped up on Cody with his big forepaws, almost knocking him down. Cody knelt to pet the dog, who would tolerate a few quick strokes then dart around in circles of excitement.

Finally, Cody heard the voice of the one he loved calling his name. He turned to look down the beach. Gail was hurrying to meet him. He raced toward her. Uther passed him and led the way to the blissful reunion.

At last, Cody held her in his arms. After they embraced and kissed, neither of them spoke for a while. Words were neither needed nor adequate to convey the power of the ardent love between them.

Finally, she said, "Cody, I missed you so much. But the woman from the rainbow house told me not to give up. She said if I walked the beach every evening at sunset, you would eventually come."

Cody asked, "How long have you been waiting for me?"

"I don't know. A few weeks maybe," Gail replied. "But it feels like an eternity."

Cody gently placed his hand on her stomach. "How's the baby?"

"Perfect." She smiled. "Cody, I'm so excited."

Again, they fell into a long embrace.

Gail looked around them. "It's growing dark. We should be getting home. The kind woman from the rainbow house gave us a nice cottage on the beach."

"Which way?"

She indicated the direction she had been walking. "Just a short way from here."

With Uther jumping excitedly around them, the couple held hands as they made their way along the shore. They passed a deserted public beach with a sandy parking lot, a snow cone stand, and a freshly painted sign Cody hardly noticed.

St. George Island
The Uncommon Florida
Welcome Guests
1953 Summer Season

## ABOUT THE AUTHOR

**Paul Moore** has worked at a funeral home, state prison and urban church. He is a graduate of Rhodes College, Trinity University and Vanderbilt Divinity School. A native of Tennessee, he currently resides with his wife Gayle in Nashville and the Virgin Islands.